For Valour

Also by Douglas Reeman

For Valour

Douglas Reeman

ARROW

Published by Arrow Books in 2001

3 5 7 9 10 8 6 4 2

Copyright © Bolitho Maritime Productions 2001

Douglas Reeman has asserted his right under the
Copyright, Designs and Patents Act, 1988 to be
identified as the author of this work

First published in the United Kingdom in 2000 by William Heinemann

Arrow Books
The Random House Group Limited
20 Vauxhall Bridge Road, London, SW1V 2SA

Random House Australia (Pty) Limited
20 Alfred Street, Milsons Point, Sydney,
New South Wales 2061, Australia

Random House New Zealand Limited
18 Poland Road, Glenfield
Auckland 10, New Zealand

Random House (Pty) Limited
Endulini 5a Jubilee Road, Parktown 2193, South Africa

The Random House Group Limited Reg. No. 954009

www.randomhouse.co.uk

A CIP catalogue record for this book
is available from the British Library

Papers used by Random House
are natural, recyclable products made from wood grown in
sustainable forests. The manufacturing processes conform to
the environmental regulations of the country of origin

ISBN 0 09 928062 0

Typeset by Deltatype Limited, Birkenhead, Merseyside
Printed and bound in Germany by
Elsnerdruck, Berlin

For you, Kim,
my Canadian girl,
with all my love

Contents

Is Anything Impossible?

Anyone who had known the small Essex port of Harwich on England's east coast might remember it as a haven for coasters, and occasional ferries to and from the Continent. Now, after three years of war, it was equally hard to imagine it as anything but the bustling, overcrowded and vital naval base which necessity had made it, where two rivers, Stour and Orwell, embraced, and where swift currents and unhelpful tides could make pilotage and coming alongside a nightmare for the inexperienced or the overconfident.

This bitter December afternoon was much like any other, hard and bright, but without the usual raw wind from the North Sea.

Here there were vessels of every kind, hard-worked escorts, hulls dented and scraped from East Coast convoys, when columns of obedient merchantmen sometimes grid-ironed through another convoy passing on the opposite course, every skipper very aware of the narrowness of the swept channel, and the lurking minefields often on either beam. Under normal conditions it was bad enough, with ships depending on good lookouts and skilled seamanship; in poor weather and under cover of darkness it required nerves of steel. There were minesweepers, many of them fishing craft before the war; some were paddle steamers, which had once carried children and carefree holidaymakers on day trips. Under a coat of grey paint, and armed only with Lewis guns, they had become men-of-war overnight.

And destroyers, perhaps the most versatile of them all. The new, smaller ships of the Hunt Class had been designed as fast escorts, and denied the formidable array of torpedoes which had become part of a destroyer's legend, her life-blood. They looked neat and at odds with the thin-funnelled veterans of the Kaiser's war, the old V & W Class destroyers, outdated in appearance, but without which the war at sea would already have been lost.

Three long years of it. Mounting losses of ships and men and military defeats: Dunkirk and Norway, Greece and Crete, Singapore and Hong Kong, and only the English Channel between *us* and *them*. And yet here, forged out of their own kind of war, seamen could still turn and stare at a newcomer, or at something unusual. The navy, they said, was like a family; it took care of its own. When yet another ship was reported lost or missing on the news bulletins few sailors would comment. They had built a shell around themselves, if only to withstand the glib explanations by 'experts' on the wireless or in the press who spoke of *strategic withdrawals* or *tactical deployments*, rather than use the cold, correct term: retreat.

But it was there, all the same. When one of their ships had returned from patrol to this same harbour, her plating scarred and pitted after an engagement with a German E-Boat or destroyer, and a line of covered corpses laid on her quarterdeck, there had been only a silence which spoke more than words. *The family.*

On this day, though, it was something different.

The destroyer had entered harbour just before sunset the previous evening, and had moored fore-and-aft to allocated buoys. The light had been almost gone by the time the cable had been secured.

In her new dazzle paint she seemed to shine against the backdrop of the Harwich Force. The older hands were familiar with these now famous Tribal Class destroyers; the youngsters often dreamed of the chance of joining one. Or commanding one.

Perhaps the Tribals represented better than most the change from peace to war. A rare example of foresight, they had been laid down and launched as the clouds had gathered over Europe, and were in action within weeks of Chamberlain's grim and inevitable announcement.

Ordinary people had been brought up to accept the Royal Navy as an invincible power, the sure shield; it had become over the years something both familiar and proud. Setbacks, defeats and evacuations had changed all that. Names so well known even to those who never saw the sea were gone like chalk sponged from a blackboard. *Royal Oak, Prince of Wales, Repulse, Barham, Ark Royal.* Gone.

It seemed now that wherever the war at sea was at its toughest the Tribals would be a part of it. Like this one, H.M.S. *Hakka*, her pendant number, *G-44*, freshly painted on her side before she had quit the Tyne, where she had been laid down and had first tasted salt water.

She seemed to tower over the other destroyers around her. In fact she was some fifty feet longer than most of them, and broader in the beam, with a superbly flared forecastle and a raked bow to add to the immediate impression of strength and speed.

Only a more experienced eye would pick out the scars and gashes beneath the dazzle paint. It had happened in the Mediterranean, when *Hakka* had been supporting the Eighth Army as it fell back under the unstoppable weight of Rommel's Afrika Korps. But she had survived, and after some makeshift repairs at Gibraltar she had returned with a convoy to England, back to her birthplace on the Tyne.

A small motor boat surged in a tight arc, the bowman ready to hook on to the accommodation ladder, above which the duty quartermaster and sentry stood watching with interest. The 'bowman' was in fact a girl, a Wren, who executed the task with obvious indifference to her audience. The coxswain, another Wren, waved a gloved hand, and loosened the chinstay keeping her cap from being blown away.

She was used to the stares, the suggestive glances. You had to be, or you went under.

She called, 'One to be signed for! I'll come aboard!'

The boats with their Wren crews were as much a part of the harbour as the sea itself. Carrying mail, passengers, bags of coal, light stores nobody else wanted to deliver, they were everywhere.

The coxswain, her face pink from the bitter air, strode across the quarterdeck, pausing only to toss a salute before she unbuttoned her dripping oilskin and reached inside for the envelope.

She had seen him by the after lobby, above which a pair of four-point-seven guns had been trained abeam, probably for cleaning. There were two officers, and a civilian in a boiler suit who was jabbing at a large notebook. But she knew the one she wanted; she always did. That was something else she had found impossible to explain to her mother and father when she was on leave.

She saluted again. 'Lieutenant-Commander Fairfax, sir?'

Both officers were wearing raincoats, without any markings of rank. *But she knew*, although she did not see the surprise in his eyes. The uncertainty.

'That's me.'

She opened the envelope and took out a smaller one, then offered her little pad and studied him as he signed it.

Young, late twenties; his eyes were grey, what she had seen of them. Boyish even, except for the lines of strain around his mouth, a tenseness which she had come to recognise, especially in destroyers.

Lieutenant-Commander James Fairfax watched her hurry back to the ladder, and wondered briefly what she looked like without the bulging coat and seaboots.

She had called him by rank, and he had almost failed to respond to it. The new half-stripe had been advanced for him, and he was not used to it.

He glanced up at the forward funnel where some painters were examining their workmanship. A new stripe there too, for *Hakka*. He felt the bitterness welling up again, like a pain, a deep hurt. He was being stupid. He had heard himself reason it out, over and over again.

He sensed that the others were looking at him. The scruffy one in the boiler suit was an electrical engineer, who had come down from the Tyne with them. He would be leaving now, his part was done. Back to Newcastle, that place of noise and shipbuilding, and friendly people who always 'shifted up' for a sailor.

He folded the brief signal and put it in his pocket.

He saw the painters lowering themselves to the deck, and said, 'The new captain is joining ship, day after tomorrow.'

Maybe he had still hoped. It had all seemed so definite at the time. The half-stripe, then he had been told to stand by until repairs were completed and new orders made out. He gazed at the

4

ship's name beside the lobby door. *Hakka.* The brass was gleaming despite the damp chill. He had been her first lieutenant for two years. In war that was a long time, a career.

And she was to have been his. He could have had some other command. The navy was always desperate for experienced captains.

He said, 'Tell the cox'n, will you, Pilot. We can discuss it at lunch.'

The electrician grinned. 'Says in th' paper today that Rommel is still fallin' back, from that place, El Alame'n, worn't it?'

Fairfax looked up at the bridge, empty now but for the duty signalman. Where it had all happened. *Zulu*, another Tribal, had bought it that day off Tobruk.

Hakka had slowed down to pick up survivors from another ship which had been torpedoed by a submarine earlier. Maybe it had been wrong. God knew they had been forced to leave enough good men to perish, men they had known. Family . . . *Close the gaps. Don't stop.* The signals never relented.

But they had. And he had gone down to the iron deck by the whaler where some seamen were ready with scrambling nets for those able to pull themselves aboard. The aircraft had come from nowhere. Out of the blue, as they always said. Like a bandsaw, cutting across the side and the bridge, smashing down an Oerlikon gunner even as he had slammed a new magazine into place. The yeoman of signals had been killed instantly on the bridge, his station; he had died without fuss, as he had lived. Others had also died that day, but all Fairfax could remember was the scene on the open bridge when he reached it, the blood, faces once so familiar to him ugly with agony and shock, and somebody screaming like a tortured animal in a trap.

And the skipper. Huddled down in his bridge chair, his eyes filling his face as he clung to life, although the fight was already lost. The man Fairfax had served for two years, from Norway to the Med, standing watch-and-watch, coming to know him and be known with an intimacy few outside the navy could ever understand. Sharing a last pipeful of tobacco, or a quiet run ashore. Talking.

He had clung to Fairfax's jacket, his hand like a bloody claw as he had measured each word.

'I – want – you – to – have *Hakka*, Jamie. She – needs – *you*. . . .'

Then he had died.

Fairfax crushed the signal in his pocket into a tight ball.

'. . . to receive Commander Graham Martineau, Victoria Cross, Royal Navy, in command.'

Some seamen hurried past him, chased along by Pike, the chief boatswain's mate, the Buffer. New faces. Replacements for men killed or badly wounded in the attack, or others who had been sent away to attend advanced courses. *New faces*. The captain would expect every one of them to be carefully listed and appointed to their proper parts of ship. It was a first lieutenant's job.

He touched the ship's name and heard the Wrens' motor boat spluttering away from the side.

Probably everybody in the base, in the whole fleet, knew by now.

Graham Martineau, who had been awarded the Victoria Cross by the King himself, was a true destroyer man if ever there was one. He had placed his own ship between a scattered convoy and a German cruiser. Out-gunned and out-ranged, he had pressed home the attack and had rammed the enemy.

He had lost his ship and to all accounts most of her company, but the enemy had broken off the action before reinforcements could arrive.

Fairfax looked up at the bridge again, hearing the scream of the aircraft, seeing the black shadow rip across the deck. *She needs you*. . . .

He straightened his cap on his unruly hair and sighed.

He thought suddenly of *Hakka*'s motto, *Is anything impossible?* It was as though she had shouted the words aloud.

The portly coxswain was waiting for him with his clipboard. Routine.

So be it. The first lieutenant.

Commander Graham Martineau declined the chair offered by a white-jacketed orderly and walked to one of the tall, narrow windows. There was not much to see, except another wing of the building and a haze of green Suffolk countryside beyond, and the splinter-proof net pasted on the glass in case of an air raid did little to help. A hotel in peacetime, like so many other establishments it had soon settled into its wartime role as a hospital.

After the cold air outside the room, once part of the hotel lobby, seemed almost stuffy and humid; the old-fashioned radiators were too hot to touch. It even smelled like a hospital, something he hated. Everything painted white, magazines left unread by nervous visitors who probably dreaded each confrontation even more than those they had come to see.

He knew the duty staff nurse at the semicircular desk was watching him. She had been pleasant enough, but not effusive. It was a naval hospital now, like all those other places around the country. Holiday camps for car workers in the north and Midlands, turned within days into training establishments and bases, where the White Ensign, a few painted stones, discipline and a portion of imagination completed the transformation.

He saw his reflection in the window, the new greatcoat, the gold lace bright on either shoulder. He wanted to unbutton it, take it off, but the same reserve held him back. He should accept it if he could not fight it. Like the cap beneath his arm with the oak leaves on its peak. *The step up.* It was no longer a possibility, something in the hazy future; it was tomorrow. They had given him a comfortable billet in a small commandeered hotel just outside Ipswich, not much more than twenty miles from Harwich.

His mouth was dry and he wanted to move about, but in this quiet, watchful place it would not help.

Martineau was thirty-three years old and had been in the navy since boyhood. Over twenty years in uniform. It did not seem possible, especially now. Today. As if nothing else had existed before the war or until that day only a few months ago. He tried to relax, muscle by muscle. A lifetime . . .

Most of his naval service had been in destroyers, in one capacity or another, showing the flag in the Far East, South Africa and in the Med. Naval reviews, fleet regattas, and then the Spanish Civil War and its grim aftermath.

If there had been any doubts or uncertainties they had remained dormant. He was doing what he wanted, what was expected of him; nothing else mattered. Must matter.

At the outbreak of war he had been serving in one of the navy's crack destroyer flotillas. Eight ships, ready for anything. When he had last heard, only one of them was still afloat.

Carefully he allowed his mind to explore the outline of his new command. *Hakka*, one of the famous Tribals. No officer could ask for a better ship, a finer recognition, if that was what it was.

Newer destroyers were coming off the stocks every week, but the Tribals were still part of the legend. He swung away from the misty window, angry with himself. Who was he trying to convince?

The nurse put down a telephone. Even they seemed soundless in this place.

'The P.M.O. says he will not be long, sir.'

He nodded. The P.M.O. It must be bad.

He recalled the soldiers he had seen unloading something from their Bedford truck outside. In response to a question, one of them had jerked his head in the direction of the door.

'Where most of 'em step off, poor sods!'

Crude? Brutal? Unfeeling? But true.

Tomorrow, then. They always said, *not to worry. They* would be more nervous about their new lord and master. It would be a piece of cake. . . . Martineau had held two commands. It was simply not true. *For me anyway.*

Somewhere in the building he heard the clang of metal doors, the sudden purr of a lift, the murmur of voices. A new arrival, maybe, or one less fortunate, who had just 'stepped off'. Almost reluctantly he unbuttoned his greatcoat and laid it on the chair, the cap with the bright oak leaves on top. He wanted to yawn, the way men do when they are about to go into action. Not fear: there was never time for that.

He should not have come. Nobody would have blamed him. Not more than they already did.

Footsteps on that polished linoleum floor so beloved by hospitals, then the resonant tones of the P.M.O. and a woman's voice.

He turned towards the corridor and saw her, all in blue, a naval

8

crown in diamonds glittering on one lapel. Alison always looked elegant and attractive no matter what she wore, and despite the war and the rationing. She had laughed at him when he had remarked on it, the laugh which could turn any man's head, and said, '*This* thing? I've had it for years! You never notice!'

He had first met her just as a complacent nation was at last realizing war was inevitable; it had been at Portsmouth, when he had just put up his second stripe. It seemed a hazy dream, like so many he had suffered in hospital after he had been brought back, after losing his ship. Trying to piece the fragments together. Alison's smile at the church, the avenue of drawn swords on their wedding day. Two years ago.

She was looking at him now, and her chin was lifted slightly, her eyes very bright as if she had been crying. She did not smile or offer her hand. In his mind he could see her throwing her arms around him or one of her friends, kicking up one heel as if to seal it. She was twenty-seven years old, and she was a stranger.

The P.M.O., a bluff surgeon commander, shook hands and said, 'Sorry to have kept you hanging about, Graham. Short-staffed.' He peered at his watch, frowning. 'We shall have to operate, I'm afraid. Sooner rather than later.'

He leaned over the desk to speak with the nurse on duty, and Alison said, 'It was good of you to come. I hear you're joining your new ship.'

'Tomorrow.' He glanced at her hand. No ring. 'How is he?'

He. Another stranger. Lieutenant Mike Loring had been first lieutenant in his last ship, the F Class destroyer *Firebrand*. A good officer, and a firm friend, he came from a well-established naval family; one of his ancestors had been at Trafalgar, and his father was an admiral. After that last tour of duty he was to have left *Firebrand* for a command of his own. It had been a straightforward convoy, no better or worse than others they had done together.

Alison had told him when he had left their borrowed flat to return to sea. It could not have come at a worse time, although there was never a suitable time, especially in war. Separation, and eventually divorce.

And now Mike Loring was to have another operation. How

9

many was that? *Firebrand* had already been hit several times, and then one of the enemy's shells had killed or wounded the damage control party he had been leading.

Alison said, 'More splinters. In the spine. He is heavily drugged most of the time.' She sounded as if she was repeating it for her own benefit, as if she could not come to terms with it. She was strong-willed, determined, but this was something she could not control.

Martineau said, 'Are you managing?' He stared at the window again. He could not even call her by name. *What is the matter with me?*

'I shall stay here until I hear something.'

When he was able to face her again he saw her eyes move away from the small crimson ribbon with its miniature cross. It had taken only a split second, but her expression was quite clear. Resentment, anger, because he was alive and the man for whom she had left him, her lover, was fighting for his life. At best Mike would be a survivor, and she would have nothing.

'If there is anything I can do . . .'

The P.M.O. put down a telephone and said abruptly, 'I can give you a few minutes, Graham.'

Martineau turned to follow him but stopped as he heard her say softly, 'Haven't you done enough?'

The room was in semi-darkness, blackout curtains drawn almost to their night position, so that bars of hard sunshine played across the white-painted bed and glittering instruments like searchlights.

Mike Loring was connected by tubes and wires to a side-table, one bare arm lying motionless on a pillow, the skin pockmarked by probes and needles. He still wore a bandage across one eye, but the other moved slowly as if independent from the rest of the body, as if that was already dead.

Martineau made to reach out, but saw the P.M.O. shake his head.

Instead he said, 'Rough, is it?'

'I – I did walk, you know.' Loring closed his eye as if the effort was too much. Then he added, 'Back in that other bloody place. *I did walk.*'

Martineau said, 'I shall keep in touch. . . .'

10

Loring moved his head from side to side. 'You'll be too busy.'

So he knew about *Hakka*, even here. Like this. The family.

Loring persisted, 'Your new Number One, what's he like?'

'Not met him yet.'

'Give him hell, eh?' He turned his head again as someone laughed, outside or in a corridor. Just a laugh. Something to take for granted.

When Martineau looked again he was shocked to see a tear running down his cheek. Reminded of some precious moment, or person? Of Alison, his friend's wife. His lover.

Sunlight flashed on the P.M.O.'s wristwatch. It was time.

Martineau said, 'I have to go, Mike.'

The drug was taking charge again. His voice was dull, slurred. But he said, 'Sorry about the mess, Skipper.'

The surgeon commander opened the door; a nurse and two orderlies were waiting to enter.

'We'll do what we can, Graham.' His mind was already moving on. Martineau had seen him looking at the crimson ribbon also. *All right for some*. But he was one of those who had to pick up the human pieces and try to mend them. Afterwards.

The duty nurse was still at the desk. She said brightly, 'One of our people will give you a lift, sir.' She could not sustain it. 'Mrs Martineau left earlier.'

As soon as I was out of the way. So she did blame him. Did the rest count for nothing?

'She left you this, sir.'

Martineau picked up his cap and took the small buff envelope. There was no letter, only the wedding ring. Alison's timing had always been impeccable.

So why could he not accept it? Every day somebody was going through it, on the wireless and the interminable news bulletins. *The Secretary of the Admiralty regrets to announce the loss of H.M.S. so-and-so, next of kin have been informed*. All those telegrams, *father . . . husband . . . son*. Or that well-meaning letter from a 'friend'. *I thought it only right that you should know about your wife carrying on while you're away. . . .* And so on.

The nurse studied him. She knew what he had done, that he had rammed an enemy cruiser with his own ship, even how old he was;

11

it had been in all the papers. And she had seen the medal ribbon for herself. This was a real hero. A lively, alert face, she thought, not silly and boasting like some they got in here. Very dark hair, and she had seen the flecks of grey at the temples when he had tugged on his cap. And there was sadness, and she sensed it had nothing to do with the scene she had witnessed earlier. A lot of men, his men, had died that day.

She had said as much to one of the sick berth petty officers. He had retorted, 'Well, he had a choice, Sister, those poor buggers didn't!'

Outside in the biting air Martineau saw the car which was to take him to Ipswich. Tomorrow there would be no comparisons, no contests. It was a new beginning. It had to be.

He glanced back at the lines of faceless windows and thought of the man he had wanted to hate.

Sorry about the mess, Skipper.

It had saved him.

The train was so overloaded that it sounded as if it could barely drag itself along the track. And it was packed with humanity, a few patches of khaki or air force blue, but overwhelmingly navy.

Extra carriages had been added along the way, most without corridors, so that in each compartment there were men who were wishing they had not drunk an extra pint of beer before climbing aboard, or praying for the next stop, when there would be a concerted rush to the station's meagre facilities. The truly desperate were not so particular.

The initial disturbance, good-natured or otherwise, had given way to the usual dull acceptance of men returning from leave. Leave at the end of a training course or following promotion, local leave for the lucky ones, compassionate leave for others who now had little to say and sat mostly in silence, even looking forward to going back to routine and the disciplined life they had always been ready to curse. Men whose families had been killed or injured in air raids, men who, in many cases, had only been able to visit an empty space, or the charred wreckage where they had once lived, loved, and hoped.

And there were still a few for whom it was all part of a continuing adventure. Ordinary Seaman Ian Wishart sat jammed between two other sailors, one in the corner seat asleep with his head lolling against the window, on his other side a fat three-badged stoker jerking back and forth, playing cards with some friends sitting opposite. It was a non-smoking compartment and the air was solid with fumes, both pipe and cigarette, and there was a strong smell of rum; Wishart had seen a large bottle being passed around the card players, growing emptier by the mile. Wishart had been in the Royal Navy for only a few months, and until yesterday he had been under training at the shore establishment H.M.S. *St Vincent* on the Gosport side of Portsmouth Harbour. Everything at the double, everything strictly pusser. He had noticed the uniforms of the men in the compartment: real sailors, some of them going to the same destination, maybe the same ship. Real sailors, in their skin-tight tailored jumpers with low fronts and collars scrubbed so hard that the cloth had faded as pale as Cambridge blue. Bell-bottomed trousers, far wider than those issued at stores, and caps worn flat-a-back. Wishart thought of his own cap, the bow tied correctly above his left ear. These sailors, 'Jolly Jacks', one of his old instructors had scornfully described them, had hand-made bows flapping rakishly above one eye. At *St Vincent* you would be crucified for that.

It had not been easy, but Wishart was as quick to learn as he was to observe, and this was what he had wanted. Like many of the boys in his class at school, he had been dreading that the war might end before he could join up.

He had got used to the rough, often crude humour from other recruits no older than himself, had learned to put up with the jibes at what they called his posh accent. He had been attending a local grammar school when his papers had at last been accepted, but the way some of his companions pulled his leg about it anyone would have thought he had been at Eton or Harrow.

But it was behind him now. The square-bashing, the intricacies of gun drill with some elderly six-inch pieces from the Great War, the seamanship and the boatwork, bends and hitches, taking a ship's wheel, albeit a working model, for the first time.

He looked around the compartment again. And he was listed as a potential candidate for a commission, Hostilities Only of course. That was for ever, as far as he could see.

His senior instructor, an old Chief Petty Officer brought back from retirement, had explained the importance of the rigorous training.

'Wherever you go, my son, no matter what ship you land yourself in, you will be grateful to this place.' He had offered a rare grin. 'It is, I agree, a fucking awful place to be in at the time!'

Wishart smiled. He had even blushed about that.

The train gave a great lurch and two small cases fell from the luggage rack overhead.

Someone shouted, 'Bloody cow! One more jerk like that an' I'll have to piss out 'er the winder!'

The fat stoker grunted, 'You'll follow it if you does!'

Wishart picked up one of the cases and tried to stand up, but the man next to him was suddenly awake, and said, 'That's mine!' He shook his head as if to clear it. 'Give it to me.' He looked at Wishart for the first time, that single glance taking in the new uniform and dark collar, and the youthful face above it.

He said, 'Sorry,' and folded his hands across the little case, closing his eyes again.

Wishart studied him, still startled by the edge in his voice. He recalled seeing him being stopped by the naval patrol at the ticket barrier, where the redcaps and R.A.F. provost allegedly hunted for deserters and enemy agents. He had heard one disgruntled seaman say, 'Couldn't catch a bloody cold, that lot!'

An interesting face, hawkish, it might be described in the *Rover* or the *Hotspur*, Wishart's two favourite magazines. Intelligent, too. A slight accent, a Londoner perhaps. He could even smile at his own speculation. Before joining *St Vincent*, he had never been further than Brighton for family holidays.

The other man said suddenly, 'What ship?'

Wishart thought of all the posters and warnings about careless talk, and the cartoon of Hitler and Goering kneeling under a table where a loud-mouthed sailor was spilling secrets of the next convoy to his tarty girlfriend. But he answered readily, 'H.M.S. *Hakka*.' He saw the eyes open again. 'A Tribal Class. I was told that –'

The man dug him with his elbow. 'Me too. Name's Bob Forward. Very apt.' He did not explain. 'Leading Seaman.' Then he looked briefly at the broken threads on his sleeve, which Wishart had already noticed. '*Ex*-leading seaman.'

Wishart nodded, and tried to contain the rumbling of his stomach. Forward studied him.

'Not eaten lately?' He unclipped the case and took out a bar of chocolate. 'Here, have a bit of nutty.'

Wishart took it gratefully and did not see Forward gripping the lid of the case, nor that he was staring at the bundle of letters and papers which had slid to one side of it. The photograph was looking directly at him, and even in the poor light he could see her smile, provoking, mocking. The compartment was quiet, and for an instant he thought they were all watching him. But he was mistaken, as if he had been temporarily rendered deaf. *God help me!*

Like the moment, the second she had realized that he knew. That it was over. Mercifully that same deafness had acted like a shock-absorber, otherwise . . .

And she had still been staring at him. Despite the terrible wounds, the blood.

He said in the same abrupt tone, 'I'm in Nine Mess. Suit you?'

'I expect I shall be detailed . . .'

Forward looked at his hands. As if expecting them to be shaking, or that he would still see the blood. Like the moment when the naval patrol had stopped him. Afterwards he had almost laughed aloud. How could they know anything? How could anybody?

He said, 'I'll fix it, OK?'

Wishart nodded. He was no longer just a recruit.

Graham Martineau stooped almost to the sill of the window to look at a rectangle of sky above the opposite rooftop. It was cloudless, what he could see of it, another fine, crisp day, although the street below was still in darkness. He moved back to the table, hearing the floor creak underfoot. The owners of the hotel, whoever they were, must have been delighted to hand it over to the navy for the duration. Even the sparse items of furniture seemed to lean towards you as you passed.

He glanced at the half-empty cup of coffee and decided against it. He could not recall when he had last eaten a proper meal. He had risen even earlier than usual, his mind clearing reluctantly while he sorted through what he had to do. The uniform laid out across two chairs: his other self. His defence. Notes and intelligence folder arranged and packed, like the rest of his kit. Ready to go.

He had gone down to breakfast and had found one other officer at a table, the *Daily Mirror* propped up in front of his plate. The headlines were glaring: MONTY ADVANCING. AFRIKA KORPS ON THE RUN. Was it really possible? After so many reverses, it was unwise to believe in anything.

He had had too many gins the night before, hoping for one good night's sleep, to prepare himself. It should have worked; there had been only a few drunks in the street, and then the voice of authority, moving them on. Not like London . . . sirens, the drone of aircraft, the sickening vibration of falling bombs. It never failed to surprise, even to move him, that civilians managed to put up with it, going about their work, trying to lead normal lives in a world which was threatening to destroy them. He had seen the great gaps where houses had stood, the walled-up shops, the air raid shelters, men and women sleeping as best they could, curled up on the platforms of some miserable Underground station. At sea it was different. Or so they all believed.

The dream had come then. More intense than last time, vivid and stark, with faces he could recognize. And *Firebrand*'s bows rising up in front of him like a ram, the vague outline of the cruiser reaching out in both directions like some jagged grey cliff. In the dream there were always guns firing, soundless and terrible. Sometimes he tried to see it as it had been, how his poor, reeling ship must have looked to the enemy in those last insane minutes. The German captain had attempted to avoid the collision, probably astonished that his blanket of heavy shells had not smashed the destroyer into oblivion even before she had worked her way into range. He could not imagine how *Firebrand* had appeared to the handful of merchant vessels as they struggled to disperse and take advantage of his desperate gesture.

They had fired all their remaining torpedoes, otherwise . . . That

16

one word. *Otherwise*. In his heart he knew it would have made no difference.

At one moment the ship had been out of command when a shell had exploded on the port wing of the bridge, killing most of the men in the wheelhouse, and then an unknown voice had called up the pipe, 'Steady as she goes, sir!' Then, seconds before the surging, nauseating impact and the thunder of tearing steel, he had heard a terrifying scream. Like the ship herself. A last defiance.

The rest was blurred. Icy water. Voices calling out and then fading. And then boats, hands hauling him to safety. As they had done themselves so many times.

Hospital, a different routine, and an undemonstrative, reserved sympathy. They would all have cracked otherwise.

The madness did not stop there. He had not even realized he had been wounded. He had seen it again this morning when he had crossed the room to find his shirt. The rickety wardrobe had curtsied towards him, its door swinging open. In the mirror the scar looked absolutely straight, from his right shoulder to his left hip, a splinter which would have ended his life then and there had it struck him an inch more either way.

Alison had not even asked about the wound. Nor had she come to see him in hospital. He thought it was just as well.

He buttoned the reefer jacket and stared at his reflection. Thirty-three, but he looked older. Mature, Alison had once said. He forced a smile. Bloody bushed, more likely.

He glanced at his watch; it had somehow survived the one-sided battle and the destruction of his command. It was about the only thing which had.

It was time. The commodore at Harwich was sending a car for him, but, thank God, they were leaving him alone to make the first, vital step. Not like it had been in London, the Ministry of Information people, the hand-picked journalists and war correspondents . . .

He found he was clenching his fists. *Seeing what a hero looked like*. He calmed himself with an effort, patted his pockets. All new uniforms: like someone else's. He had already heard somebody take his cases downstairs. The car was waiting.

The ship was waiting. A new life. He felt the fresh shirt scrape the scar, like a reminder. *A new life for me, anyway.*

A last, slow look around the room. How many like him had waited and fretted here? He thought of the hospital, of Alison, and of the man who had been his friend, and an inner voice seemed to plead, *stay away from it, leave it behind – others will look to you now.*

He walked out of the room without another glance.

Down the stairs, hearing the buzz of voices from the dining room; more people up and about now. As they would have been since the first pipe aboard *Hakka. What will he be like? Will he be as good as the old skipper?*

He stared at the Wren chatting with the porter at the desk. Martineau was tall, but she was almost his equal. She was wearing driving gloves, and swung round as he approached.

She reached out for his briefcase. It had been a present from his mother and was real leather; he had wondered how she had managed it amid the austerity of war.

'I'll take it, sir.' She let her arm drop. 'Leading Wren Tattersall, Commodore's driver.'

He felt the cold air on his skin, heard the porter call after him, 'Good luck, sir!'

She held the door for him and he slid into the seat, the smell of damp leather somehow refreshing after the seediness of the room.

'I'll take you to Parkestone Quay, sir. They're expecting you.' She let in the clutch expertly and the big Humber glided away from the hotel.

The waiting was over, and there were many who would envy him this day.

For something to say, or perhaps to compose himself, he remarked, 'Tattersall? I had a signalman of that name in my last ship.'

Just the merest blink of the eyes meeting his in the driving mirror.

'Yes, sir, my brother. He was killed that day.'

Martineau said nothing. It was always happening in the navy; it would happen again. But somehow he knew the Wren had asked for this duty on this particular morning. To see for herself. To know why.

He leaned back in the seat, the contact broken, and watched the passing scene.

He thought how pleased the surgeon had been who had dealt with the wound.

A very nice job if I say so myself, old chap!

Maybe he was finally coming to terms with it.

He turned suddenly, taken off guard by a poignant little vignette on this ordinary stretch of road which led to the sea. Because it was so unexpected it seemed a more brutal intrusion than the mindless onslaught of torpedo or bomb.

A postgirl standing by a garden gate, obviously worried or embarrassed. A young woman in an apron with a dog staring up at her. A few passers-by, unsure what to do. The young woman was holding a telegram. *The* telegram.

The Wren's eyes met his in the mirror.

'Nearly there, sir. Another ten minutes.' Then she returned her attention to the road again, and said, 'It'll take time, won't it.'

She had spoken for all of them.

2

Letting Go

Chief Petty Officer William Spicer rocked back slightly on his heels, the top of his cap almost brushing some deckhead pipes in the quartermaster's lobby. As *Hakka*'s coxswain he was well aware of today's importance, and half his mind was keeping tabs on the destroyer's harbour routine. He was an impressive figure by any standards, massively built, with heavy red features which seemed to defy sun and storm alike. His uniform was a perfect fit, the lapel badges of crossed torpedoes and ship's wheel shining in the reflected light, leaving no one in doubt as to his status. To many the coxswain was the most important man in any destroyer; to most, he *was* the ship. Responsible to the first lieutenant for the daily routine, and matters of discipline, destroyers carrying no master-at-arms as did larger ships, he could also recommend any rating he thought fit for promotion or some better station on board. He took the wheel when the ship was entering or leaving harbour, and was answerable only to the captain at action stations or when manoeuvring at speed, when experience was often the margin between success and a court-martial. Spicer had been in *Hakka* since she had first commissioned, and none knew the ship better.

He watched the first lieutenant's glance moving over the last list of names, their messes, duties and parts of ship, noticing the shadows beneath his eyes. Right up to the last he had expected to be given this command, but the new painted line around the funnel had made it very clear. *Hakka* was to be the half-leader in a new flotilla or group, with a full-blown commander on the bridge. He kept his face immobile as Fairfax looked up at him. One with a Victoria Cross at that.

Fairfax said, 'Seems fine, Swain. Two men adrift, though?'

Spicer grunted. 'The police have been on about Able Seaman Downey. Detained in hospital. A punch-up in some pub, I gather, sir. Awaiting escort.' He paused, seeing his words fit into the pattern. Poor old Jimmy the One was feeling it. A right good piss-up in the wardroom last night, according to George Tonkyn, the chief steward. To welcome a new signals officer who was required for flotilla duties, they said, but more likely to help Jimmy-the-One get over his disappointment.

He added, 'Ordinary Seaman Abbott is still adrift, sir. Done a runner, I reckon.'

The quartermaster who had been standing just outside the door, very aware of the two men who controlled his daily life, switched on the tannoy and moistened his silver call on his tongue before sending the shrill call around the ship.

'*Stand easy!*'

Fairfax said, 'I'll get on to the Commodore's office about that.'

Spicer smiled gently. 'All done, sir. Abbott'll be no loss to anyone!'

Fairfax walked out into the hard light as working parties broke off and scampered below for a mug of tea or a quick cigarette.

The ship looked good. People like Spicer ensured that it stayed that way.

He saw two officers on a nearby destroyer watching *Hakka* through binoculars. A new captain always excited comment. He bit his lip. Especially if it was somebody else's.

He had already been aft to the captain's quarters, which were spacious compared with most destroyers. He had expected another grim reminder of the man who had lived there when he was spared from the small sleeping cabin on the bridge, but it was as if he had never been. Fresh paint, a different rug by the desk, no photographs. No memories.

A seaman was walking towards him, pointing out something on the X and Y gun mountings, and his companion was shading his eyes to follow the gesture. The seaman was Forward, broken from leading hand for becoming involved in a brawl in Malta. The case

21

could be reviewed soon; he would tell the coxswain to look into it. Forward had been a good leading hand, a skilled torpedoman, too valuable to waste in a ship like *Hakka*. There were some twenty new names and faces to be accounted for, to measure, to trust or otherwise. Like her officers, *Hakka* carried them all. *All two hundred of us.*

Spicer folded his lists with elaborate care. 'Soon, then, sir?'

Fairfax nodded. 'Any minute, I should think.'

'The yeoman has got it in hand, sir.'

They both glanced up at the bridge; one of the signalmen would be stationed there to watch for any approaching boat.

But Fairfax was thinking of the new yeoman of signals, a chief petty officer like the coxswain, and with about the same amount of service. He had volunteered for *Hakka*, although on the face of it he had a soft number as the Commodore's own yeoman, a barrack-stanchion, the lower deck called them.

During his morning inspection Fairfax had seen him staring at the sprawling naval training establishment H.M.S. *Ganges* at Shotley Point, watching the first cutters heading out for boat-pulling drill, or to study the warships their young crews would one day be joining. You could almost feel their eagerness.

Fairfax wondered how long that eagerness would last once they saw their first disaster at sea. Like the youngster Forward was showing around. He had even managed to wangle him into his own mess, so the coxswain had obviously approved.

Spicer cocked his head as the tannoy squealed again, 'Out pipes, hands carry on with your work!'

He knew about the new yeoman, whose name was Onslow, but it was something private. You never abused privilege by discussing a messmate, even with a reasonably decent officer like Fairfax.

Onslow had had a young son at *Ganges*, no more than a boy.

It had been nobody's fault, but then it never was in the Andrew. He must think about it every time he saw the great mast which dominated the training establishment; it was a local landmark. All the boys were expected to climb it, just as men had once done when it had been stepped in a ship of the line. The boy had fallen, bounced from the safety net, and broken his neck.

Macnair, the yeoman of signals who had been killed during the air attack, had been a man full of yarns and experience almost worshipped by his young signalmen, his 'bunting tossers', unless they fell short of his high standards. Onslow knew his job backwards, would need to, being on the commodore's staff. But it was hard to see him settling into the boisterous bonhomie of the Chief and petty officers' mess.

He saw the first lieutenant staring towards the shore, to Parkestone Quay, the small boats milling about, the patrol vessel *Grebe* going astern, preparing to leave harbour, hands fallen in on quarterdeck and forecastle. She was commanded by a lieutenant. Making another comparison, maybe?

The officer of the day was consulting his watch. Soon time to pipe *Up Spirits*, when the air would be thick with the heady aroma of rum. The ship's company was a young one for the most part, only half of them old enough to draw a tot, and a tot was currency on the lower deck. To pay for dhobying, and again to bribe the boiler room staff into allowing the clean clothing to be hung there to dry. For favours asked, for favours granted. A way of saying 'thank you'.

Fairfax rubbed his eyes and regretted the amount of gin he had consumed. For the new signals officer, they said. One fragment remained, along with the headache. When asked about the Captain, the signals lieutenant had said, 'The V.C. didn't do *him* much good. I heard his wife walked out on him for his Number One!'

Someone else had called, 'Better watch your step, Jamie!'

A ship without a captain. A captain without a ship.

The pipe again. '*Up Spirits!*' With the usual muttered rejoinder from the older hands, 'And stand fast, the Holy Ghost!'

The telephone buzzed by the lobby door and the quartermaster called, 'Yeoman of signals, sir!'

Fairfax took the handset. 'First lieutenant, Yeo.'

He would get used to the voice in time, but in his mind he could still see Macnair. Calm, unruffled, utterly dependable.

'Commodore's launch shoving off from the quay, sir. No broad-pendant hoisted.'

'Thank you, Yeo. Good work.' There was no response.

Spicer said, 'What about the rum, sir?'

23

'Carry on. No ceremonial, Swain. Man the side and inform the wardroom. I'll tell the O.O.D. myself, right?'

Spicer's eyes glinted beneath the peak of his cap. 'Right, sir!'

Fairfax walked unhurriedly to the accommodation ladder. He saw two seamen on their knees scrubbing a grating. Their brushes moved in unison, but both were watching the oncoming launch.

Spicer hid a smile. Who would be a bloody officer?

As the thought crossed his mind, he called out, 'Forward, over here, my son.' He studied him thoughtfully. 'I've listed you as quartermaster.' Then, 'Everything settled at home? I was sorry about your father.'

Forward said, 'A heart attack.' Then he nodded deliberately. 'Q.M. will suit me fine, Cox'n. Might pick up my hook again a bit faster, eh?'

Spicer shrugged. 'We'll see. Keep your nose clean an' stay out of trouble.' He turned to his young companion. 'Wishart. You're assisting the navigator's yeoman. Report to him after you've had your grub, got it?' He strode away, the ship's routine unrolling before him like a carpet.

They make a funny pair, he thought. I'll have to watch Forward. A bloody good hand in a tight corner. But all the same . . .

He saw the big launch swing round in a welter of spray, the bowman standing very erect as if at a peacetime review.

'Attention on the upper deck! All hands face aft!'

He heard the squeak of fenders and drew his heels together as the cap with the bright oak leaves appeared over the top of the ladder.

'Pipe!'

The calls squealed. Fairfax stepped forward and saluted.

'Welcome aboard, sir.'

The captain's quarters aboard *Hakka* seemed luxurious after all the other destroyers in which Martineau had served or had visited during his career, and consisted of a day cabin containing a study and dining space and a sleeping cabin and bathroom. Also, unlike the others, his new quarters were situated in the after superstructure, next to the sickbay and somewhere beneath X Gun position. In destroyers like *Firebrand* the officers' cabins and wardroom

24

were built right aft, between decks, and in heavy weather it was not unknown for them to be marooned in their quarters, unable to make their way forward to the bridge without the very real risk of being washed overboard. In such cases the captain and whoever was on watch at the time had to manage on their own.

Martineau heard Tonkyn, the chief steward, murmuring something to one of the messmen in the sleeping cabin. He had met Tonkyn during and then again after his tour of the ship. He shook his head. *Was that only today?*

Tonkyn was one of those indispensable characters you could not imagine doing anything else. Tall and slightly stooped, with a permanently melancholy expression, he was probably the oldest man in the company, and had retired from the navy a year before the war and opened a small boarding-house in Devon. Now it seemed he had never been away.

Martineau walked across the cabin and looked at the ship's crest on the bulkhead, an exotic phoenix emerging from flames with Chinese characters in the background. And below, *Hakka*'s motto, *Is anything impossible?*

The last captain's personal effects had long since been removed, and there was nothing here to give any clue. *The man who never was.* Even the Commodore had referred to him only as 'your predecessor'. The navy's way: no comparisons, no looking back. But he had seen it in their faces today as he had been introduced to the officers. Their lives might depend on him. It was only to be expected.

It was a mixed wardroom, half of whom were reservists, hostilities only; even the gunnery officer, Lieutenant Driscoll, was R.N.V.R. But people no longer made the old *Really Not Very Reliable* joke about them. The volunteers had become the professionals.

Lieutenant Kidd, the navigating officer, was another reservist but of a different breed. A merchant navy officer in peacetime, he now wore the interwoven gold lace of the Royal Naval Reserve. He was a bear of a man with a shaggy beard and a powerful voice to match it. The engineer officer, the Chief, was Lieutenant (E) Trevor Morgan, from Cardiff. Like so many ship's engineers he was softly spoken, in spite of his daily confrontation with the din of machinery. Down there in engine and boiler rooms lip reading was not just a skill, it was a necessity. Merely talking to Morgan was enough. You could feel the man's pride, his eagerness to describe or explain any aspect of his separate world. With forty-four thousand shaft-horsepower under his gloved hands, it was just as well.

Two sub-lieutenants and one midshipman, the latter, surprisingly, a regular, and the new signals lieutenant named Arliss completed the wardroom, except for Mr Arthur Malt, the Gunner (T), a square, unsmiling warrant officer who had come up the hard way from being the lowest of the low, a boy seaman.

They were still waiting for a doctor. The previous one had quit the ship when she had returned to the Tyne for repairs.

Tonkyn stood in the doorway. 'Anything else, sir? A drink, maybe?'

'No. I'll wait for the first lieutenant.'

Tonkyn adjusted an overhead air valve and said, 'That should do it.' He peered around, his eyes lingering on the desk beneath the gleaming crest. 'Bit stuffy in here.'

Tonkyn would have known his predecessor better than anyone. Except, perhaps, for the first lieutenant.

Martineau heard the door close and sat down abruptly in the desk chair. Where they had gone over the signals, and the relevant ship's books, before he had been taken to meet the officers.

He dragged open a drawer: it was empty but for a slim volume of Shakespeare's sonnets. It had been new, some of the pages still uncut. A gift, then? In it he had found a photograph. He took out the book and opened it again. The photo was of a girl, professionally taken in some studio, although it was neither inscribed nor dated.

She had long hair which hung down across bare shoulders. Calm, level eyes, unsmiling, as if she had just said something.

He had mentioned the book to Fairfax after he had discovered it pressed between two official volumes.

'He wasn't married, sir. Like me, he thought it was too dicey in wartime, being separated for so long. . . .' He had attempted to cover his embarassment. 'I – I'm sorry, sir. I only meant . . .' It had made it worse. So they knew about Alison. Probably the whole ship by now. Good or bad, what did you expect in destroyers?

He studied the picture again and wondered who she was. The ship was quivering around and beneath him. Machinery, perhaps one of the Chief's generators.

He thought of the unknown people who were now under his command. Some writing last-minute letters home. *Yes, the new skipper came aboard today.* But nothing that might irritate the censor.

He heard footsteps outside and replaced the book in the drawer.

Fairfax came into the cabin and glanced around, as if making sure there were no loose ends, and that nothing had been overlooked.

'Drink, Number One?'

He saw the momentary hesitation, as if he were suspecting some sort of test. Then he grinned.

'Horse's Neck, if that's all right, sir. I'll ring for the steward.'

'No.' Martineau unbuttoned his jacket and threw it on to a chair. 'Allow me.' He could feel the other man watching him, probably wondering how they were going to get along. He said over his shoulder, 'You should have a command of your own, you know.'

He put the glasses down side by side. 'You've earned it.'

Fairfax bit his lip and said, 'Never given it much thought, sir.'

Martineau smiled. 'I did, all the time, when I was a first lieutenant.' He raised his glass. 'Selfishly, I'm glad you stayed with the ship. To us, then.' He thought of the photograph again. Perhaps Fairfax had known her. 'Unless there is a last-minute change of orders we will leave harbour at noon tomorrow. Are you all buttoned up?'

Fairfax nodded, his eyes distant, as if he were seeing through each bulkhead and into every department.

'Yes, sir. Those two ratings are still adrift, and no news at all about Ordinary Seaman Abbott. He was fairly new, so I'm not that well clued-up as to his background.'

'That I can understand.' Sailing at noon. He had seen it in their faces when he had told them in the wardroom. Liverpool, Western Approaches. To join the new group. The Atlantic.

Hakka had seen most of her service in the Mediterranean, a war

27

of survival protecting and supplying the embattled army in North Africa. Six of the Tribals had gone down there alone, to gun, torpedo, mine. Others had ended their days elsewhere, and one, the *Punjabi*, had been sunk in a collision with the battleship *King George V*, the flagship of the Home Fleet. *Hakka* was a lucky ship, they said. Until that day when she had been raked by an undetected aircraft while men were watching their own kind being picked up, rescued from an earlier attack. It was human enough. And it only needed a few seconds to die.

A lot of the old hands were realistic about it. *You don't ask when, but how. So you can be ready. . . .*

But *Hakka*'s captain should have known better, and men had died because of that lapse, act of humanity or not.

There were more voices and Fairfax half-rose to his feet as one of the stewards opened the other door a few inches. Beyond him Fairfax saw the pointed face of Rooke, the Petty Officer Telegraphist.

The P.O. said, 'Sorry to trouble you, sir.' He looked at the new captain, in his shirtsleeves, the jacket with its crimson ribbon tossed over a chair. 'Just been sent over by the S.D.O., sir. Thought I should bring it meself.'

'Thank you.' Martineau took the folded signal and read Rooke's round handwriting beneath a desk light.

Rooke was backing away, the steward frowning with disapproval. Fairfax asked quietly, 'Bad news, sir?'

Martineau looked at him, surprised that he could share it. With anyone.

'Lieutenant Mike Loring died in hospital. This afternoon.' So he had lost after all. *We all did.*

'I'm sorry, sir. I read about him, of course . . .'

Martineau's shadow moved over him as he walked to the drinks cabinet. He would write to Alison. In the same breath, he knew he would not.

So often, over and over again, he had tried to relive the last hours before he had flung his ship against a vastly superior force. It was all destroyer men knew. *Seek out and destroy the enemy.* Seal your mind against everything else. Once an objective was

28

realized there was no room for choice. Or had something else decided him on that terrible day?

Fairfax was staring at the captain's table. He had eaten several meals there. Now it looked stark, alien.

When they had nursed the ship back to Gibraltar and then brought her all the way home to the Tyne, he had been ready, tested and prepared. Now, as he watched Martineau, and in some small way had shared the anguish with him, he knew in his heart that he was not ready for command. And he was shocked by his discovery.

He turned, afraid for a moment that he had said it aloud. But the Captain was looking past him, as if remembering something.

'She was a *fine ship*, Number One. You could not ask for better.'

Then he walked into the adjoining cabin and closed the door.

Fairfax picked up his cap and left the Captain's quarters.

Even though darkness had fallen over the crowded anchorage he could recognize the navigating officer's familiar outline. They fell into step, their feet avoiding ringbolts and other hazards without conscious effort.

Kidd asked, 'How was it, Jamie?'

Fairfax heard one of the local boats chugging abeam, liberty-men going ashore to forget their troubles if only for an hour or two. He was almost surprised by his own answer.

'He'll do me, Roger.' He touched the ice-cold guardrail. 'Just what she needs!'

Lieutenant Roger Kidd climbed on to the gratings in the forepart of *Hakka*'s open bridge and peered over the glass screen. Behind his broad back and below his feet the bridge was going through the usual orderly preparations for leaving harbour. He had been up here since the pipe, 'Special sea dutymen to your stations!' Slow and methodical, leaving nothing to chance. He felt the keen breeze through his beard and patted his pockets, as usual. Several pencils, an extra notebook for unofficial calculations; he had already checked the chart table.

It was cold up here, but nobody would dream of wearing a duffle coat on a day like this one. He was even wearing a collar and tie. All eyes would be watching *Hakka* today. The Commodore, Captain (D), everybody. He glanced at his watch and wondered what clown had decided to get under way at noon. He had a large appetite, and his well-worn seagoing reefer confirmed it. It was much tighter than he had recalled it in the Med. The refit and repair work, and all those runs ashore. A little too much of everything.

The new yeoman of signals was watching some passing supply vessel through his big telescope. The ship had come alive again, and here on her bridge were the experts. Below him in the wheelhouse, Spicer the coxswain would have been at his station from the first pipe too. A big man, with hands like hams, and yet he seemed to handle the wheel delicately, as if to detect every reaction before it happened. His quartermasters manning the telegraphs, boatswain's mates at the ranks of voicepipes, and deep down in his world of machinery and heat the Chief would be waiting.

Kidd had been at sea almost all his life, beginning as a cadet and working his way up the ladder, step by step, ship by ship. His last ship, the *Port Stanley* of the Roberts Line, had worked out of Liverpool; it would be strange going back there in a crack destroyer. He had been first officer in the *Port Stanley*, and a naval reservist, as required by the company's owners. They had carried general cargo and a few passengers, and it had always been interesting. Suez, Port Said, the West African ports, or across to Montreal and New Orleans. Hard work, the captain had never been known to turn his back on a few extra pennies, and often enjoyable too; a few of the women passengers had found his rough humour irresistible.

Six months after Kidd had changed uniforms, the *Port Stanley* had been torpedoed in mid-Atlantic. She had been carrying ammunition and there were no survivors. He was still unable to accept that he would never see the old ship again.

A boatswain's mate said, 'Over there, lad!'

Kidd climbed down and faced him. The new assistant navigator's yeoman was slightly built and shivering in his Number Threes, and he looked nervous, unsure of the muttering voicepipes

30

and the occasional shouted orders from the forecastle where the hands were removing unwanted wires.

Kidd asked, 'Know what to do, Whitehart?'

The youth nodded, and said, '*Wishart*, sir. To . . . to assist here and on the plot.' As if he had rehearsed it.

Kidd hid a grin. As green as grass. But willing enough, and he had come with a good report.

'Where are you from, er, Wishart?'

'*St Vincent*, sir.'

Kidd sighed. 'No, your home, lad.'

'Surbiton, sir.' Almost a defiance there, and Kidd guessed he had been ribbed about it many times.

'Well, your place for both action and defence stations is here or on the plot. Next, to make sure that when you bring me something hot to drink, you don't make marks on the chart, right?'

'Yes, sir.'

Kidd knew that Wishart's part of ship was the quarterdeck, where Malt, the Gunner (T), ruled. Malt was known to hate and despise would-be officer candidates, perhaps goaded by the constant thought that they would outrank him once they had gained that little wavy stripe.

Somebody murmured, 'Cap'n's comin' up, sir.'

Kidd had never gone out of his way to seek popularity. He had seen too many others fall apart when it came to the test. But here in *Hakka* they seemed to like him, and, more importantly, they trusted him.

He turned, saluting as the Captain walked through the gate and on to the gratings.

'Good day for it, Pilot.'

Kidd saw one of the subbies, Humphrey Cavaye, edging round so that the Captain might notice him. *Conceited little prat.* Maybe old Malt had a point after all.

Martineau felt the stares, the curiosity. He glanced at the tall chair which was bolted to the deck on the port side of the bridge. His place, when he chose. Where his predecessor had been cut down by cannon shells.

Fairfax had come to report to him just minutes ago. The ship was ready to proceed. Was he feeling it today? The first lieutenant checking everything for the last time before sailing. The slip-rope had been rigged through the ring of the forward buoy, the cable unshackled and rejoined to its anchor, the stern rope ready for letting go. He looked briefly at the compass and beyond it to the land, and the other ships.

He had done it so many times. In harbours he could scarcely remember, in others he would never forget.

He looked over the screen, the pattern already in position. Fairfax down there with a burly leading seaman, the captain of the forecastle, and girded with a self-made belt of holsters, the tools of his trade. Hammer, marline spike, and a wicked-looking knife. Like the rest of the forecastle party he wore thick leather gloves. The slip-rope was not rope but wire, like all the other warps and springs, and one broken strand could carve a man's hand to the bone when it was hauled through the fairleads with the weight of all his mates on the end of it.

He made to look at his watch, but instead readjusted the heavy binoculars around his neck. It was time.

Right forward by the bull ring a young signalman stood smartly at the jackstaff, ready to haul down the flag the instant the ship parted from the buoy. He could see the Wren's eyes in the driving mirror. Hear her voice. *My brother. He was killed that day*. That day . . .

He looked into the wind, and saw an Oerlikon gunner turn to watch. The quay, the lines of moored vessels, the run of the tide.

He lowered his head slightly to the bell-mouthed voicepipe.

'Bridge.'

'Wheelhouse, sir. Coxswain on the wheel.'

Martineau looked towards the bows again. The buoy had been hauled so tightly beneath the flared stem that it was barely visible. Fairfax was right there, beside the young signalman.

The yeoman's voice now, the clatter of a lamp. *'Proceed when ready*, sir.'

Martineau nodded. *'Affirmative.'* To the voicepipe he said, 'Stand by.'

The response was instant, as if the Chief had been crouching over his controls like an Olympic sprinter.

He felt the slow tremble moving through the bridge structure, heard the creak of steel, the rattle of a pencil falling from the ready-use chart table, saw an angry gesture from the bearded navigator.

Down, and through the Channel, 'E-Boat Alley' as the press had christened it. The sailors referred to it as Shit Street. Where you could often see the occupied coast, and they could see you. Dive-bombers, mines, and certainly E-Boats. Lying in that unfamiliar bunk he had heard the M.T.B.s returning to base in Felixstowe across the estuary. Maybe they had been on a successful sweep along the enemy coast. The Glory Boys, they were called.

He rested one hand on the chair and felt it shivering. Alive.

'Let go aft.'

He heard the order repeated, the vague scrape from the quarterdeck, and saw a small cluster of houses beyond the water begin to swing as if they and not *Hakka* were moving.

'All clear aft, sir!'

She was swinging too fast. But he waited, measuring time and distance in his mind.

'Let go forrard! Slow ahead together!'

Then, 'Slip!'

He saw the buoy lean away, the wire, snaking inboard, writhing into a tangle until seamen ran to control it.

He stooped over the compass and peered through the bearing prism.

Spicer's voice again. 'Both engines slow ahead, sir. Wheel amidships.'

'All clear forrard, sir!'

Martineau watched the nearest buoy. 'Starboard ten!' He waited, seeing a fast-moving launch tearing from bow to bow. 'Midships. *Steady.*'

He made himself walk to the opposite side, and saw *Hakka*'s starboard watch smartly fallen in for leaving harbour. *First part, forrard. Second part, aft*, as the tannoy directed. He wanted to lick his lips. They were like sand. *How long ago was that?*

He returned to the chair, and rested his hand on its back again. As if he was sharing it.

He saluted the flotilla leader as they passed abeam, while calls shrilled in mutual respect.

Kidd said, 'Coming on now, sir.'

He swung the compass repeater prism from one bearing to the next. Landguard Point, with one of the M.T.B.s returning to her base, her side splintered by gunfire. The Glory Boys did not have it all their own way.

He heard Spicer call, 'Steady, sir. Course one-seven-zero.'

Then Kidd again. Angry. 'Signal that bloody boat to stand off!'

Martineau raised his glasses and saw the cause of the navigator's wrath. One of the *Ganges*'s cutters, the oars momentarily stilled, was drifting crabwise towards *Hakka*'s port bow.

There was room enough. Some of the boys were waving, cheering, their voices lost in the whirr of fans and the murmur of machinery.

He heard himself say, 'Give them a wave, eh? They'll know soon enough.'

He saw the yeoman staring at him and was glad he had said it. Gratitude.

'Half ahead both engines.'

He saw the waves parting and rolling away from the raked stem as she gathered speed.

The yeoman glanced astern at the cutter, the oars rising and falling like wings once more.

Martineau turned away. *Letting go*, perhaps.

Fairfax was here now, his eyes everywhere.

'You can fall out the hands now, Number One. Port watch to defence stations.' He glanced abeam, but the land was already blurred. Or was it? 'I never thought I'd say it, but it's good to be back at sea.'

Fairfax studied his profile. Strong, calm, and yet, just then, he sensed a flicker of something like pain.

He saw the new rating, Wishart, turn and give a small smile as the voicepipe reported, 'Cox'n relieved, sir. Able Seaman Forward on the wheel. Course one-seven-zero, one-one-zero revolutions!'

Martineau climbed into the chair and half-listened to the various reports and acknowledgements around him.

She was his ship now. All else was left astern.

3

Welcome Back

James Fairfax turned away from the voicepipes and reported, 'Ship at action stations, sir.'

Martineau eased himself forward in the tall chair, glad that he had taken the time to go down to his sea cabin and put on a thick sweater and duffle coat. The North Sea in winter was no place for a rig-of-the-day mentality.

'Very well.' Fairfax had sounded terse, thinking, perhaps, that he might have been sitting in this chair, or expecting some criticism of the ship's company's performance when they had first exercised action stations on leaving Harwich. Or now, when it might be in earnest.

Fairfax had, after all, virtually trained and welded the *Hakka*'s people into a working machine. And they reacted well.

It was still hard to believe how smooth leaving harbour had been. It was a busy place in every way, with many local craft on the move, and moored warships swinging to their buoys as an extra hazard. And yet it had gone without a hitch, as if the ship herself had been responding to his intermittent flow of helm and speed orders. He had never visited Harwich before in command of his own ship, and he doubted if the burly coxswain had had much experience of the place either. Following the marks and the buoys, taking a quick fix every so often with the gyro repeater to check some obvious landmark, St Nicholas Church, with its distinctive stone buttresses, and Landguard Point itself where they had made a wide sweep into open water. He had been momentarily surprised at the way she had handled, and had said as much to the navigating officer without realizing he had spoken aloud.

The bearded lieutenant had grinned. 'Like a London taxi, sir!'

Later he had seen Kidd watching a small formation of merchant ships being herded into line by some fussy armed trawlers in readiness for a northbound convoy. Most R.N.R. people were like that when they saw defenceless ships in convoy. The targets. The victims. Part of themselves.

He was glad of Kidd's company. He was good at his job, and had that independent attitude which even the Royal Navy could not dampen.

They had passed the Cork light vessel, and some of her crew had appeared on deck to wave as they had ploughed past, although they must see hundreds of ships every day. It had moved him in some way, like the sight of the young woman in the apron, holding the telegram.

Theirs was a lonely job all the same; they were sitting ducks. He recalled the East Dudgeon light vessel being bombed and her boats machine-gunned by Stukas in the early days of the war. But such incidents were rare, German senior officers having soon realized that the light vessels and buoyage systems were as useful to their own captains as to their enemy.

Martineau took his pipe from his duffle coat pocket and put it between his teeth. It had been a very expensive pipe, a Dunhill no less, and a present when he had left his first command to take over *Firebrand*. The stem was still discoloured by salt water. Like his watch, it was one of few survivors.

He thought of the other reminder. Their orders were to rendezvous with another destroyer off the Nore. The *Falkland*, which had been undergoing the indignities of a refit at Chatham after a clash with E-Boats, was a typical pre-war ship of her class, with little variation in size or design. But as she had headed out from the grey mass of land, her light blinking diamond-bright in greeting, Martineau had felt it again like a cold hand. She could have been *Firebrand*.

He asked, 'Satisfied with the allocation of new hands, Number One?'

'I think so, sir.' Again that hesitation. 'A few are pretty green.'

36

Or was it the unexpected change in the orders? The patrol vessel *Grebe*, which had left Harwich earlier, had suffered delays on passage to Portsmouth. Martineau recalled seeing her going astern from her moorings on the day he had arrived to assume command of *Hakka*.

She was to join them for what Kidd called the diciest part of the passage, through the Dover Strait itself. Aircraft, E-Boats, plus the awesome hazard of the big guns which the Germans had mounted on tracks near Cap Gris Nez. Mostly they fired blind, their high-trajectory shots intended for any fast-moving convoy, if there was such a thing, or the town of Dover itself, only twenty-two miles away.

It was already darker, with plenty of cloud about, although there would be a moon. He had heard Fairfax discussing *Grebe* with the pilot. Now listed as a corvette, although the navy quietly resented the change of classification, *Grebe* was typical of the small vessels which had been built in the Thirties and designed for escort and anti-submarine duties. Armed with only one four-inch gun and a few automatic weapons, and carrying a small company of sixty, they were considered perfect for a first command. *Grebe*'s commanding officer was a lieutenant, and would be fuming over the delay.

Fairfax could have had her for himself. No fleet destroyer like *Hakka*, with her powerful armament of eight four-point-sevens in twin mounts, her torpedo tubes and sophisticated radar. But his own.

Kidd said, 'North Foreland lighthouse abeam to starboard, eight miles, sir.'

Martineau looked at the radar repeater below his chair, and listened to the regular ping of the Asdic signals. Feeling her way. Like the men at their various stations around the ship, at the guns and depth charges, damage control and ammunition parties. And up here in the bridge, the nerve centre. The stammer of morse from the radio room, the occasional reports and requests from the ranks of voicepipes. All very aware of the land closing in, like the neck of a bag.

All those names from the past, Ramsgate, Hastings, Eastbourne, when the sun had always shone, or so it seemed now.

He straightened his back as a motor gunboat surged past, the throaty growl clearly audible above the whirr of fans and the noises of sea and metal. There were two M.G.B.s, for their size the most heavily armed vessels afloat, just in case there were E-Boats about. The Glory Boys would be back to Harwich and the pub when this boring escort job was over.

He smiled. It was strange to think that the first destroyers, the old turtlebacks, were not much bigger. Working with the Grand Fleet or taking part in daring raids and attacks on enemy shipping, they were a nightmare in bad weather. His father had commanded one, and had often told him about the appalling conditions in what he had called 'those little terrors'. So foul that their lordships used to pay him two shillings a day hard-lying money. But always he had spoken with a kind of affection, as well as pride. Martineau glanced at the radar repeater again, seeing the gleaming blips of the other destroyer astern and the two M.G.B.s. What would his father have made of all this?

His mother had stayed on in the same house on the edge of the New Forest after the Commander, as he was known locally, had died there between the wars. He had never fully recovered from losing an arm in an explosion at Odessa, possibly sabotage, when he had been evacuating White Russians fleeing the Revolution. That, and his rejection by the one life he had known and loved, had finished him.

Now his mother was alone, but she remained very active with her work in the Women's Voluntary Service, her First Aid classes, and looking after evacuee children who had been moved away from inner London and the bombing.

Nothing had ever been said, but she had not got along with Alison, or maybe it had been the other way around. *And I was never there. There was always the ship.*

'Radar – Bridge!'

Fairfax moved like a cat. 'Bridge.'

'Ship at one-nine-zero, sir!'

'That will be *Grebe*, sir.'

Somebody said, 'We hope!'

Another murmured, 'And about bloody time.'

Martineau glanced at the sky. Not much longer. Through the Strait and into more open water.

'Inform *Falkland* – they probably know anyway.' He raised his voice. 'Make a signal to the leading M.G.B., Yeoman. Bearing and distance. *Investigate.*'

He heard the clatter of the signal lamp, and what seemed, almost immediately, the mounting roar of engines from the nearest motor gunboat.

A boatswain's mate said, 'Bloody show-off!'

'No more signals until we're in company, Number One. You know the drill. The last thing we need right now is a Brock's Benefit!'

He felt his teeth grate on the empty pipe as the words came back at him; it was exactly what Mike Loring had said when they had jumped two German destroyers off the Norwegian coast. And even then he and Alison must have been lovers.

Somebody handed him a mug of tea and he realized how cold his fingers had become.

'*Grebe* can take station astern of *Falkland*. It'll be as black as a boot soon.' He raised his glasses and watched the other ship's silhouette lengthening against the murky backdrop.

A green light appeared across the starboard bow, *blink*, *blink*, *blink*. On the chart it stated that there was a bell too, but he could not hear it above the noise. A wreck buoy; there were dozens in this area, maybe hundreds. Sometimes you could even see the dead ship in the shallows when the sun was out. Perhaps one you had known.

He put the mug on a tray as someone else brushed past the chair.

Fairfax said, 'I'd better go aft, sir. It's just that I thought . . .'

Martineau was watching him when suddenly he saw his eyes light up as if someone had shone a torch in his face. He did not feel himself move. *'Full ahead both engines! Starboard ten! Midships! Steady!'* Seconds. It felt an eternity. Then came the explosion, hard and solid, more like a blow than a sound, as if the ship had rammed the submerged wreck.

'Both engines full ahead, sir! Steady on one-nine-eight!' The coxswain sounded very alert.

Grebe had hit a mine. A drifter; it could be nothing else out here.

They were reaching her now, and Martineau could hear the gunnery control rattling off instructions to *Hakka*'s four mountings. But the radar remained silent. A mine. One chance in ten thousand. But all he could hear was his own voice. *It would have been us.*

The bridge was suddenly swept with light as the stricken ship exploded in a ball of flame just forward of her bridge. Ammunition, fuel, it was impossible to know, but you could taste it from here.

Martineau put the pipe in his pocket and gripped it hard.

'Signal the senior gunboat to stand by and assist.' He imagined he could feel the heat as more flames and sparks burst into the air. 'If the German gunners don't see that they must be blind!'

Fairfax was staring at him. 'We could stand off and lower a boat, sir.'

'Is that how it happened the last time?'

He saw Fairfax recoil as if he had struck him.

To Kidd he said, 'Resume course and speed. Yeoman, make to *Falkland, remain on station.*'

Fairfax was still there, staring at the other ship, now down by the bows. Martineau added quietly, 'And I suggest you do the same, Number One.'

He watched Fairfax walk to the ladder, framed against the fires and drifting smoke. A ship dying, her people too. *I know what he thought. What he thinks.* He strode to the chart table and pulled the canvas cover over his head, his world confined to the small light and Kidd's neat calculations.

He wrote slowly on a signal pad and then stood up again, grateful for the cold air.

'Tell W/T to code this up and send it off.' He did not turn as another explosion sighed against the hull, and the orange glow was extinguished. They could think what they liked. '*After* we're through the Strait, right?'

Kidd nodded, and watched him climb into the chair again.

It never left you. It was always there, you expected it and

40

insisted that you were prepared. What to say and do, how you would appear to those who depended on you.

Not fear, it was more like anger. He had heard Fairfax's suggestion and the Captain's response. And he knew Fairfax well enough by now to understand how he was feeling about it.

He thrust his head beneath the chart table screen and peered at his notes. And the Captain was right. That was almost the worst part. You could not win a war with gestures, no matter what the reason. Humanity, saving people like yourself, was well down the list.

Their orders were to reach Plymouth without delay. Then on to Liverpool, unless some brasshat had now decided on something different. It was a long time since he had been to Liverpool, but he could probably tell his yeoman every chart he would need.

The Captain had been right about the other thing, too. They had been caught napping, despite the nearness of the enemy, and men had died on this very bridge because of it. Just below bridge level, an Oerlikon gunner had been trying to fit a new magazine to his weapon, simply because his loading number had run to the opposite side to watch the rescue attempt. The careless never lived for long.

He looked over at the figure in the tall chair. To him the ship came first. And he was a man who knew danger and death at first hand. A hero.

It was his decision. And for that Kidd was thankful.

Directly below the destroyer's open bridge the wheelhouse seemed crowded and confined. With shutters locked into position and deadlights lowered, the motion felt more pronounced with no natural horizon to compensate for it. Small lights shone like markers on the essential machinery, the telegraphs on either side of the helm, a quartermaster standing loosely at each with the revolution counter in easy reach, voicepipes, manned by boatswain's mates and messengers, and in the forepart, like the hub of the whole place, was the wheel, a solitary bell-mouthed voicepipe, the old-type magnetic compass, and the ticking tape of the gyro repeater.

The coxswain was a big man anyway, but on his grating, his

hands on the polished spokes, his eyes glinting slightly in the reflected glare, he was a giant.

To one side, partly separated by steel plating and a long blackout curtain, was a plot table. On it was the chart in use, and beneath it another small light moved in time with the ship's progress, so that by glancing through a magnified spy-hole in the deckhead the navigator or officer of the watch could check the position, and the presence of navigational hazards which might pass undetected by the radar's invisible eye and remain unseen by even the most vigilant lookout.

At the rear of the bridge structure was another, larger space, and a more sophisticated plot table as well as the Asdic hut and W/T office.

Hakka's only midshipman, Alan Seton, stood at the plot, his eyes slitted with concentration while he readjusted the chart. This was his first active service appointment and he was very aware of it. To serve in one of the famous Tribals was not just a privilege, it offered a chance of advancement or promotion which might be denied to others less fortunate on routine convoy work.

Seton was also aware of the more obvious mistakes made by others, which could still endanger his own progress.

His promotion to sub-lieutenant was now in sight. He would leave this ship and probably go on to something entirely different. He would miss *Hakka*, but his father's words were ever-present in his mind. 'You're in the service for a career, not an episode!' Seton smiled. *Never mind the war.*

He glanced at the new rating by his side. Ordinary Seaman Wishart, straight out of training and looked it. Seemed pleasant enough, and did not ask too many pointless questions. They said he was a candidate for a temporary commission. He sighed. His father wouldn't approve of that, either.

Wishart was watching him as well, but was careful not to show it. It was stuffy in the sealed wheelhouse, but he was still ice-cold, and could scarcely stop himself from shivering. It had all happened so quickly. The quiet concentration of the men around him, the only movement the coxswain's big hands, this way and that, the only sound the gentle tick of the gyro repeater as he corrected the trim of the ship's head. The others lounging at the

42

telegraphs, his new friend Forward giving him a nod, as if the midshipman was invisible.

Then the sudden clamour of engines, the wheel going over, a terrible convulsion as if they had been torpedoed, or how he imagined it would be. One messenger had shouted something about another ship blowing up, and he had seen Seton make some pencilled markings on the chart, eyes wide, no longer so self-possessed.

A boatswain's mate had said, 'We're leavin' the poor sods to die! She's th' *Grebe* – I've got an oppo in her!'

Spicer's eyes had barely moved. '*Had* an oppo, more likely! Hold your noise!'

Wishart watched the plot indicator moving imperceptibly beneath the chart. The Dover Strait. Even on this chart it looked narrow. He twisted round and tried to see the gyro repeater. They had altered course again. He was terrified of being sick, of showing it in front of the others. He glanced at the midshipman, so like one of the heroes in the books he had in his room at home, even the white patches on his collar, the confidence. *How would I ever . . . ?*

They all jumped as the tannoy squeaked into life. Here, and throughout the ship.

'This is the Captain speaking.'

Wishart could picture him, as he had seen him on the upper bridge, and on the Gaumont British News at a local cinema, receiving his V.C. from the King.

'We shall be entering the area for the Channel guns shortly. They may or may not open fire. We shall take avoiding action if they do.'

The speaker went dead.

Seton said casually, 'Probably won't happen.'

Standing by the port engine room telegraph, Forward grimaced. How would he know? He tried to remember what he had heard about the guns. When you saw their flashes it took a full forty seconds for the shells to climb and come pitching down on you. Not like the Med, where even the bloody tanks would take a pot-shot if you moved too close inshore.

He thought of his return to the ship from leave. Compassionate leave, because of his father. It had been a long way from Newcastle to Battersea in London, with a strange, light-headed feeling after the confines and comradeship of a destroyer.

His father had worked on the railway, most of them did who lived around Clapham Junction, the huge shunting and marshalling yard, so vital now in wartime. Forward supposed there was a sort of camaraderie there, too. Long hours, taking cover every so often when the sirens wailed their warning, and never knowing if their houses would still be standing after every shift.

Coming back this last time had been bad. He saw the youngster Wishart watching the midshipman. Poor little sod, he'd soon learn. Unless he became one of them. . . . The kindness had been the worst part. Tots of rum, sippers, gulpers, as much as he could carry. What would they have said? His father had died even as he had walked along that familiar street which led down to the Thames. They had never been close, and he had been sorry because of that. Angered too, that nobody had cared to tell him about it earlier.

So he had gone to see Grace. To share it, without telling anybody. He had grown up with her, and they had kept in touch even after he had joined the navy. Always good company, stunning to look at, but that was as far as it went. Or so he had believed.

He should have left after the funeral, gone straight back to the Tyne and the ship. He glanced at the coxswain by the wheel. Spicer had been good about it too, and had said that Jimmy the One was interested in seeing him rated leading hand again.

Grace had moved from her old place, and had left her job at the Arding and Hobbs store at the Junction. But he had found her eventually.

He clenched his fist around the telegraph lever until his fingers throbbed.

It couldn't be. Not like that. A bloody tom, a common prostitute, doing it for anybody who could pay for it. And she had laughed at him.

The coxswain leaned over the spokes and snapped, 'Here we go!'

44

How could he know? Something over the voicepipe he was not meant to hear? Training? The old Jack's instinct?

They did not have to wait long.

'Full ahead both engines! *Port twenty!*'

The bells clanged and hands darted out for support as the helm went over and the high, raked bows began to swing.

'Midships! Steady! Steer two-two-zero!'

Wishart seized the table and tried to prevent the parallel rulers and the freshly sharpened pencils from skidding over the edge.

It seemed an age before the shells exploded. Near or far, it was impossible to tell. It was only afterwards that they heard the actual fall of each one, like tearing canvas, ripped apart by a giant.

Someone gasped, 'Missed, you bastards!'

'Starboard twenty. Ease to ten. *Steady.*'

Another explosion, a different bearing, or so it felt.

There were two more shots, and another voice ordered a reduction of speed and a fresh course to steer. The navigating officer.

Wishart straightened his back and contained the vomit in his throat. He had been under fire. He repeated it in his mind. *Under fire.*

He could feel it around him. These same men. His new companions.

A boatswain's mate was saying, 'Should 'ave worn yer brown trousers, Swain!'

And the massive Spicer's retort, 'Too late for *you*, by the smell of it!'

Midshipman Seton said, 'There, that wasn't so bad, was it?' He picked up a pencil. 'I'll show you how to lay off a course and allow for variations.' But the pencil did not move, and he said in a different voice, 'I'll do it later.'

Wishart nodded and rearranged the instruments, his breathing slowly returning to normal, or so he hoped.

He saw Forward give him a casual thumbs-up and wanted to say something to the midshipman which might be of help.

But he had never seen naked terror before, and he decided against it. Instead, he looked at the others. *We did it. Together.*

His old instructor at *St Vincent*, who had once made him blush, would have been proud of him.

Lieutenant Eric Driscoll, *Hakka*'s gunnery officer, stood straight-backed on the newly scrubbed grating in the forepart of the bridge, one hand resting lightly on the binoculars slung around his neck. He did not even deign to hold on to anything as the ship swayed steeply in the offshore swell.

Everything moving on time. Just as he liked it. They had already slowed down to drop the motor boat in the water to dash ahead of the ship with the two buoy jumpers in their massive life jackets. An unenviable job, he thought, for anyone with imagination. He had heard of cases where a commanding officer had approached a mooring buoy too fast and had ridden right over it, the two seamen bobbing up gasping for breath, if they were lucky. And of a destroyer which had mistakenly gone astern with such force that the picking-up wire had snapped and had all but decapitated the first lieutenant.

He looked at the Captain as he bent over the gyro to check a bearing again. The coast of Devon had greeted them at first light. A far cry from Tobruk or Alexandria. He gave a tight smile. Or Harwich either, for that matter.

Driscoll was twenty-four years old, and prior to the war he had been training to be a surveyor and working in the business of selling houses to dull, suburban people. All his spare time he had spent sailing in small boats, eventually becoming a weekend volunteer in the R.N.V.R. He had a good singing voice and had belonged to a local Gilbert and Sullivan society. It had been like being someone else, a different person altogether.

He had soon discovered the doubts and the suspicions of the regular navy, especially when he had chosen the gunnery branch for his proper place in the war.

But even the hardened cynics amongst the training staff at the gunnery school at Whale Island had been made to eat their words.

On this cold day, with his cap tilted over his eyes against the harsh glare from the anchorage, he not only looked the perfect naval officer, he knew he was as good as any strait-laced regular.

'Hands fall in for entering harbour, Guns.' Even the Captain's casual acceptance made Driscoll very aware of how far he had come.

He had been in *Hakka* for eighteen months, and had witnessed some of worst of the fighting along the North African coast. Dazed and exhausted soldiers, demoralized by retreats and losses, but he had seen that same army draw breath and prepare to make a last-ditch stand under their new and little-known general. In the desert Rommel had been God, and even the Eighth Army, the Desert Rats, had admired him. They had picked up some music in the W/T office, a sultry-voiced singer, and 'Lili Marlene' had become a part of every man's desert war. Monty intended to change all that. And if you could believe the newspapers he was doing it, all the way back from El Alamein.

He thought of the blind bombardment in the Dover Strait, the aftermath of shocked surprise in some of the men in his division. He glanced over at the Captain again. Another fifteen minutes with the unfortunate *Grebe* and those great guns might not have been so inaccurate.

He saw the navigating officer with his familiar notebook, his forehead set in a frown as he made some last calculation. Tide, current, wind, speed and distance. Driscoll was officer of the watch, but from now on it was the Captain's head on the block.

Martineau was well aware of the lieutenant's interest. He looked over the screen and saw the forecastle party fallen in as before, with Fairfax right in the bows by the bull ring, and perhaps the same signalman with the Jack folded and ready to hoist. A lot of ships around, some moving but mostly moored or farther out at anchor, destroyers and some weather-worn corvettes from Western Approaches, supply vessels and two lordly cruisers. He lifted his glasses. Plymouth had been badly bombed, like Portsmouth, and the scars were visible from here.

He bent forward again. 'Port ten.' He barely heard the acknowledgement. 'Ease to five.' He felt the glare in his eyes; the sheltered water was like burnished pewter. 'Midships. Steady.' He saw the motor boat making a tiny wash as it moved away from the indicated buoy, the two seamen crouching there, one ready to take

47

the wire and secure it, the other to stop him from going into the drink.

Hakka's bows must look like a giant axe to them.

'Dead slow.'

Fairfax was right in the eyes of the ship now, gesturing to the buoy jumpers, his leading hand ready with a heaving line, and another in case he missed. Fairfax pointed with his arm but did not look up at the bridge.

Closer, closer, the shadow of the bows reaching out towards the two watching seamen. The buoy would already be hidden from the coxswain at his clearview screen. He could almost feel him holding his breath.

'Stop engines! Slow astern starboard!' He saw the heaving line hurtle over the side and pictured the buoy jumpers hauling down the wire, hooking on to the encrusted ring.

'Stop starboard.' A signal from Fairfax, men scampering to lower the cable and shackle.

'Both engines stopped, sir. Wheel amidships.'

And there was the Jack, breaking to the cold breeze as if it had always been there.

One of the cruisers had swung to her cable, and Kidd was the first to see the destroyer lying beyond her.

'*Zouave*, sir. Starboard bow.'

Martineau smiled. 'Thanks, Pilot. Not long now.' He did not raise his glasses. They were powerful, and so were those on the other destroyer's bridge.

Zouave, their sister ship, with barely a month between them. If you served in any Tribal you could find your way around any of them blindfolded.

'Ship secured, sir!'

He heard the motor boat bring the two seamen around to the ship's side. There would be a tot of rum for each of them, unofficially.

He heard the clatter of the signal lamp's shutter, and waited.

But *Zouave* was different in one respect. She wore a broad black band on her funnel. The leader.

Onslow called, 'From *Zouave*, sir. *Welcome back. Captain repair on board.*'

'Finished with engines. Well done, Swain.' He clipped the voicepipe shut. 'Motor boat in ten minutes, Guns.'

Then he did turn and look across at the other destroyer. He had not wasted much time.

4

And Goodbye

Commander Graham Martineau folded the papers he had been
studying and looked around the room. The officers' club had seen
better days, he thought, and even the large paintings of sea battles
long past could not disguise the shabbiness, the tiredness of war.
In one room he had seen great cracks down the wall, evidence of
one of the air raids which Plymouth had endured.

An elderly servant in a white jacket was at his table again.

"'Nother gin, sir?"

He looked at the empty glass. He could not remember how
many he had consumed since his visit to the *Zouave*, and Captain
'Lucky' Bradshaw.

'Why not?'

Bradshaw was a bit of a legend in destroyers. During the
evacuation of Crete he had made several attempts to get alongside
bomb-blasted jetties, lifting off exhausted soldiers with every gun
firing at the unhindered German aircraft. On another occasion his
ship had been straddled by a stick of bombs which had put the
steering out of action. The ship had been badly holed and many
would have abandoned her. Not Bradshaw. He had conned her
with the emergency steering aft, and had somehow managed to
shoot down one of the dive-bombers.

Martineau had served in the same flotilla as him, a year or so
before the war, and like most of them he had been astonished
when Bradshaw had been pensioned off by yet another Admiralty
axe. It was said at the time that he had been too outspoken about

something. Being recalled had seemed like a miracle to him. *As it would have been to my father.* Older, larger than life maybe, but still the same 'Lucky' Bradshaw.

The new flotilla was one of several still in the planning stage, a force which could be used for either special escort duty or for more aggressive operations against enemy shipping. There were eight destroyers in the group, or would be as soon as they had all been mustered at Liverpool, three Tribals, two J Class ships, and two of the powerful K Class like Mountbatten's ill-fated *Kelly*. And one other, the *Harlech*, already a veteran of the North Atlantic.

Bradshaw had boomed, 'I'm damn glad it's you in *Hakka*. You're what she needs.' His eyes had moved to the ribbon on Martineau's jacket. 'A destroyer is for hitting the enemy, not sodding along with some eight-knot collection of rust-buckets!'

Martineau glanced across the long room. One officer was asleep in a chair, and two others were engrossed in earnest conversation, the waiter lining up the drinks with tired regularity.

It was not much of a place, but it was somewhere to get away from the people you served with, and a change from the din of a Barbican pub or dragging out the time in somebody's house.

They would be having a wardroom party in *Hakka*. Fairfax had asked him if he would care to join his officers, and some of those from other ships. Bradshaw had suggested much the same aboard the leader, but had seemed relieved when he declined. Maybe he had his feet under the table locally, as Jack would put it, but Martineau suspected it was just another symptom of the uneasiness people so often showed in his presence. As if the V.C. made him different in some way, as if the medal itself overshadowed the reason it had been given. Bradshaw had put his finger on it. *A damned hard thing to win, but a bloody sight harder to wear!*

Absurd, and yet it was always there.

He tried to clear his mind, to think of the next move. Liverpool, then the Western Ocean, the killing ground. Every day convoys fought their way across it. Many were indeed old, worn out, the rust-buckets Bradshaw had called them, but without their precious cargoes the war would have ended long ago. Torpedoed, bombed and shelled, the seabed was littered with them. And yet the survivors, men like Kidd, went back to sea again and again.

And if it was true that Britain and her remaining allies had at last made a stand and were fighting back successfully, the next year would see cargoes even more precious, and ships big and fast enough to carry them. Men, with all the weapons and equipment they would need for what had once been considered a propagandist's dream. Invasion.

He sipped the gin; it could have been anything. The sleeping officer had vanished, spirited away. The other two were preparing to pay up and leave. So, back to the ship. They had probably been talking about the *Grebe*, and their captain's inhumanity. *My ship, and I am a stranger.*

From the opposite end of the room the servant sighed and looked at the clock. Not much longer. The sirens would probably sound, although the raids were not so savage any more, not surprising with all the extra anti-aircraft batteries and the flak from the harbour. He peered beneath the counter of his bar, seeing the bottle of gin disguised in a carrier bag, and the steel helmet he kept for emergencies. The gin was a perk, and why not? They made the bloody stuff just down the road.

He heard the door rattle and the hall porter speaking with somebody. *Not another one. At this hour.*

But it was a woman this time. A Wren officer, her raincoat collar turned up, her shoulders dappled with heavy drops.

The porter said helpfully, 'The Tribal that came in today, Ted. *Hakka* or some such name, eh?'

The servant looked at the girl, for that was all she was. Pretty too, he thought, somebody's bit of stuff, most likely.

'*Hakka*, you say, miss? We're not supposed to know them things.'

She swung round as Martineau got to his feet, unable to conceal her surprise, a sudden anxiety.

Martineau said, 'I'm *Hakka*'s commanding officer.' He held out his hand, aware of the others staring at them, and the expression on the girl's face. 'Here, sit down for a bit. Is something wrong? How can I help?' The words flooded out and he cursed the amount of gin he had swallowed. But it was not that. His mind had never been steadier. Aware.

She sat down abruptly and said, 'I'm making a fool of myself.' She shook her head and he saw her hair catch the harsh light above the table as it curled beneath her neat tricorn hat.

In the photograph the hair had been long and had looked much darker. It was chestnut, the colour of autumn. And her voice, very low and barely under control, unexpected. North American.

The waiter put down another gin but she said, 'No. I'm all right. Really. I have to go. There's a car waiting. I – just thought –'

He said quietly, 'You thought I was somebody else.'

She nodded, and some rain fell from her hat and marked her face like tears.

'I've been away – quite a long time – I've just come back from a course. I heard *Hakka* was in Plymouth.' She clenched one fist on the table. 'He's dead, isn't he? I should have known. I'd written, you see.' She looked up sharply, the eyes very direct. 'But just now when I came in, you *knew* me.'

He said, 'There was a photograph. It was in a book of sonnets – I found it when I assumed command last week.' Absurd. How could it be only a week?

'No letters?'

'I'm afraid not.'

She looked at the gin and then picked it up. 'I should have known. But I've been so busy.' She was miles away now. Seeking explanations, asking questions, trying to accept something. The man she had cared about enough to correspond with, and to give a photograph of herself.

Then she smiled; it only made her look more despairing.

'Sorry, sir. I'll leave now.'

She began to rise but he took her wrist.

He said, 'I'm Graham Martineau, by the way.'

Like everyone else's, her eyes moved to the ribbon. 'I should have realized, but I was too full of my own troubles.' She half turned as voices filtered from the entrance. 'My name's Roche. Second Officer.' She looked at his hand on her rain-spotted sleeve. 'I'm in Operations.' She pulled her arm away as the porter appeared in the doorway. 'It's the car.'

He said, 'The photograph?'

Her eyes were distant again. 'Oh, that. Had it done a long time ago, when I was at U of T.' She seemed to realize what she had said, and added, 'University of Toronto. A hundred years ago!'

She moved away, and said, 'I hope everything goes well for you this time.' She shook her head again. 'That's not how I meant it. Sorry.'

He said, 'And I wish you better luck, too. I mean it.'

She gave him that direct look, and then, like the girl in the photograph, she reached out impetuously and touched the crimson ribbon.

'For both of us.'

He said, 'I must be going, too.' He saw her turn as he signalled to the waiter and picked up his cap and raincoat.

She said, 'I can't offer you a lift, I'm afraid.'

They stood together outside the club. It was pitch dark, and still raining. A solitary searchlight beam played back and forth across the clouds, and true to form the air raid sirens began to wail.

He saw the car. Like the one in which he had been driven to Harwich, the engine throbbing impatiently.

The girl in the photograph. And Fairfax had known nothing about her. He had too open a face to conceal a lie. And she was going.

He said, 'If we meet again . . .'

She might have smiled. 'Better leave it right there, *sir.*'

He opened the car door for her, felt her brush against him as she climbed into the rear seat.

She wound down the window and said, 'Goodbye. And thanks for being so nice about it.' She said something to the driver and the car jerked into gear. She called, 'Anna. The name's Anna, by the way.' The car's dark shape merged with the night and he was alone once more.

When she had recovered from her obvious distress at the death of someone who must have been more than just a friend, although he had been careful to conceal it from his subordinates, then she might share it with her comrades.

But somehow he knew she would not.

The name's Anna, by the way.

It was little enough. But to Graham Martineau, it was like a lifeline.

The Turk's Head pub was packed and the air thick with unmoving smoke. Bob Forward found a corner and took a swallow of beer. He had stopped at several pubs on this run ashore, moving on whenever he had spotted someone he knew. He peered around the bar. Sailors for the most part, trying to drink as much as they could before they returned to their ships. In another corner there was a group of red-faced chiefs, probably 'stanchions' from the barracks at Devonport nearby. They never went to sea, living happily on bribes obtained from those willing or desperate enough to pay to avoid an uncomfortable draft-chit, or to wangle more leave ashore than they were entitled. He smiled. It was the world he knew and understood.

There were a few soldiers too, in their scruffy battledress, and two or three W.A.A.F.s in air force blue from one of the airstrips around Plymouth, outnumbered and yet strangely safe in this all-male bedlam. The landlord shouted something, shrugged when unable to make himself heard, and held up a much-handled board with *Air Raid Warning* painted on it. It was greeted by laughter and jeers by those still steady enough on their feet to notice it.

A blackout curtain billowed inward and another sailor pushed through the street door.

It was the youngster, Wishart. More at sea than ever in a dump like this. After several attempts to reach the bar he called, 'Could I have a beer, please?'

The perspiring barman regarded him grimly. ''Ow much? 'Alf a pint or 'alf a gallon?'

A big three-badgeman beside Forward shouted, 'You old enough to drink, sonny? What will your mother say?' That brought more laughter.

Forward nudged the big seaman with his elbow. 'What does your arse do for laughs, matey?' He shoved past him. 'Two pints, chum.' He nodded to the three-badgeman. '*There* now. Nice and easy.'

Wishart took the glass in both hands. 'Thanks. I'll buy the next round.'

Next round, Forward thought. If he got this one down he would probably have to be carried back to the liberty boat.

But in some strange way he was pleased that he had stopped the jokes at Wishart's expense. More so because the big three-badgeman had been ready for a punch-up. Asking for it. But when their eyes had locked, he had backed off. They usually did.

Wishart was watching him gravely. 'Cheers, then.'

Forward nodded. Likely the first pub he'd ever been in. He thought of the street in Battersea. It was funny. The kid was from another world, and yet . . . Wishart wiped some froth from his mouth and said doubtfully, 'Maybe cider would be better.'

Forward signalled to the barman. 'Not here it wouldn't. Burn the lining out of your guts!' He put the glass down on a shelf already dripping with spilled beer. 'All ready for the next bit of sea duty, then?'

Wishart smiled. 'I – I think so, Bob. I was a bit scared at the time.' He seemed to consider it. 'Very scared.'

'You were fine. Just do your job and keep with your mates. The Skipper can worry about the rest of it.'

Wishart tried another sip. 'Poor Mister Seton took it badly.'

Forward shrugged. 'Nearly shit himself, more likely!'

Wishart looked away, feeling his cheeks flaming. It was always the same. Some of them did it deliberately to embarrass him, like the big sailor who had moved away up the bar after Forward's quiet words. He had not met anyone like him before. Tough, confident, and somehow dangerous.

He ventured, 'I heard that you're getting your hook back soon.'

Forward glanced at the clock. 'Jimmy the One seems to think so.' He smiled, and was momentarily a different person. 'Don't worry, Ian, I'll not let it go to my head!'

Then he froze, the noise, the laughter and the smoke blurred into one. And yet his voice was quite calm when he spoke, so calm that it almost unnerved him.

'Here, chum, what have you done with the paper?'

The man, one of the soldiers, pushed it towards him between two tight groups of drinkers.

Not much in the papers these days. Four pages for the most part and that was it. *The war, you know.*

It was a London edition. Yesterday's. A photograph of two Spitfires doing something spectacular, and one of Montgomery addressing his troops somewhere. It was such a small piece, and yet it filled the paper, screamed at him, like she had that night.

Following the murder of the prostitute Grace Marlow at Chelsea as reported in Friday's edition, police are now following new leads which they hope will identify her killer. Witnesses have come forward, said a police spokesman, and an arrest is anticipated.

It was impossible, of course. And tomorrow it would be forgotten. Thousands were being killed every day. Why should they waste their time on her? He almost spoke her name. *Grace.*

'Are you all right, Bob?'

He looked at his slightly built, fair-haired companion. Chalk and cheese, as his awful granny would have put it.

'Sure thing. The bloody beer, I 'spect.' He punched his arm. 'Let's catch the boat. We can share a tot.' He winked, although his mind was still reeling. 'A proper drink, eh?'

Wishart was not sure what had happened, or how he had helped in some way.

He smiled into the steady rain and tilted his cap over one eye. The unknown sailor was right about one thing.

What *would* his mother have said?

Lieutenant Driscoll lightly touched the peak of his cap and reported, 'That's the last of our visitors, Number One.'

Together he and Fairfax stood by the companion ladder and watched the motor boat's frothing wake until it was lost in the darkness. Fairfax said wearily, 'Good party, I thought.'

'Big mess bills after that lot!'

Fairfax walked between the ranks of depth charges. A good party, but, as usual when old ships got together, it had gone on too long. Noisy, too, and as the gunnery officer had so dourly remarked, with a lot of booze to be paid for. Perhaps he should have asked some women, nurses or a few Wrens, but there had not really been enough time. He stared into the rain. That had not been the reason and he should admit it. He had just wanted to blot it all out. The stark memory of the stricken *Grebe*, men floundering in

57

the blazing fuel, a soundless picture of destruction. A drifting mine. Of all the bloody luck. It happened. . . . But it was not that. The voice again. *Admit it*. It had been the unspoken reprimand when the Captain had reminded him of their first duty, and of what had happened the other time they had tried to perform a simple act of humanity.

It was all the more painful because he had always been able to share his thoughts, even his doubts, with his previous captain. Martineau was reachable in matters of ship's routine, or the advancement or otherwise of individuals, but there was always the shutter, like that moment on the bridge, after which he became remote.

The ship seemed strangely quiet now. The libertymen were all offshore, a few barely able to pass Driscoll's eagle eye as they lurched aboard from the busy M.F.V.s that ferried seagoing personnel around the harbour. No defaulters, and even at the party there had been only a few breakages when two of the guests had decided to become fighting bulls, using chairs for horns. His opposite number in *Zouave* had arrived late, but had been the last to leave. Fairfax tried to clear his head. *Zouave*'s Number One had gone to collect a parcel from the naval club. While they had been privately discussing their respective captains he had mentioned seeing Martineau at the club, with a Wren officer. It was not disloyalty; first lieutenants looked upon such a trust as self-preservation.

But the Wren, who was she? Martineau's wife had walked out on him. It was rarely that simple. Suppose Martineau's behaviour with another woman had prompted it?

He had asked his opposite number what the Wren had looked like.

He had replied thickly, 'Didn't see her face. Young, though.' He had regarded his empty glass sadly. 'But still, you don't look at the mantelpiece when you poke the fire, do you?'

But all in all, it had been a good party.

Now they could go back to war.

Second Officer Anna Roche sat on the edge of the iron bedstead and studied the neat array of kit laid out and waiting for tomorrow.

She had closed the adjoining door but could still hear the monotonous drip of the tap there. This was a temporary place, where nobody stopped long enough to get it fixed. She glanced around the room. It had been a hostel for serious anglers before the war, and there had still been a few stuffed and mounted fish in glass cases when she had first been billeted here, most of them since shattered during an air raid. Someone had told her that most of the prized trophies had proved to be made of plaster.

Tomorrow, then. Transport to the station, travel warrant and ration card, something to read on the train. She grimaced. *Trains.* She shivered and buttoned the thick pyjama jacket up to her throat; it was ugly but practical. If you had to run to the deep shelter in the night, you could not afford to be fussy.

She looked at the uniform on the chair, her best, with the two blue stripes and CANADA stitched on each shoulder. It still made people stare and ask her questions, which she found amusing considering the whole of England seemed to be full of foreign uniforms. It had taken a lot of getting used to. She smiled wryly. Even for a girl who thought she knew it all.

She loosened her hair and flicked it over her collar, remembering how he had looked at it, then she stood up and walked to the wall mirror. Even that was cracked. She had grown up after crossing the Pond, or thought she had. But it was still there. The hurt, the disbelief, and something utterly alien. Shame.

Suppose he had still been in the ship, and that he had been there in the naval club when she had barged in. Looking for what? Revenge, reconciliation? She touched her breast, and felt the sudden urgency in her heart. Over. It was over. He was dead. Missing him, blaming him, hating him, it was pointless now.

It would be Christmas soon. In Toronto the decorations would be up, peace or war. Friends calling, but fewer now with many of the men overseas and in uniform of one kind or another. Even her kid brother Tim was over here somewhere. Turned down for the navy, he was in an infantry regiment and the last she had heard he was under training, and probably fretting at being away from the action.

What would Liverpool be like? Some of the others tried to make light of it; some had called it a dump. *Best seen over the stern of a fast-moving ship!*

She thought of the course she had just attended, at an anti-submarine establishment called H.M.S. *Osprey*, stuck out like a miniature Gibraltar on Portland Bill.

Now it was time for the real thing. The Battle of the Atlantic was vital, and deadly for those who fought it. She would be part of a team, under a senior officer who had apparently given the go-ahead for her appointment. She was twenty-four years old. Ancient, compared to the last intake of Wrens she had seen.

She heard a door slam, feet on the stairway. Second Officer Naomi Fitzherbert had been down to the basement, where a bath had been installed in the middle of nowhere. They were about the same age, but that was as far as it went. Naomi was of 'a good family', as they called it over here, and her father was a lord, with little money apparently, but a lord nonetheless.

She was the sort of girl with whom Anna would never have believed she could share a room, let alone actually become fond of. She could be outrageously rude, offhand even with certain senior officers who might have imagined a chance for themselves. She would miss her more than anyone.

The door banged open and her room-mate strode barefooted across the cracked linoleum floor.

'Would you bloody well credit it! The hot water's *off* again! They couldn't organize a bottle-party in a brewery, this bloody bunch!' She paused, the towel barely covering her full breasts. 'You'll be well out of it!'

She often walked about their quarters in this fashion, and Anna had once believed she might be *one of those*, like a girl they had whispered about at her school, and another with less concern at university.

She looked now at Anna's kit and said, 'I hope it suits you, girl,' then sat heavily on the opposite bed and searched in her bag before pulling out a pack of duty-frees.

They watched the smoke twisting into the bedside lamp.

Then Naomi asked, 'How was it?'

She was on her feet, her fingers entwined as she moved about the room.

'I should have known. I wrote to him. He would have written back. Said *something*.' She faced her friend, her eyes desperate again. 'If I hadn't been in such a rush, getting back from Portland . . .'

She sat down beside her and felt the arm around her shoulders. 'I heard about *Hakka* coming in. It was all a bit hush-hush. Otherwise . . .'

Naomi shrugged and inhaled, and it brought on a fit of coughing. 'You'd have gone to the club anyway, if I know you, girl.'

Anna nodded, unable to find the words. Naomi was the only one who had known the whole story; she was like a rock when it came to secrets. Now the whole base probably knew, if anyone cared that much any more.

Liverpool would be a new beginning.

'What's he like?' She stared at her. '*Him*. The V.C.'

She thought about it, the stares, the old man in the white coat, the hall porter with the knowing smile.

'He was nice. I would have been annoyed, if I'd been him.'

Her friend grinned. 'You kill me, you really do sometimes! You're a very attractive girl, and there'll always be men trying to impress you, touch you up – you've met a few of them!' It was not working. Maybe she could no longer shock her, shake her out of it long enough to seize another chance.

Anna said softly, 'When I realized who he was, I was surprised. I think that's what I felt. He guessed what had happened, and he was trying to help.' Deep in her own thoughts, she did not notice her friend's sudden sadness. She was going. In the navy you had to expect it. *You shouldn't have joined if you can't take a joke.*

But Naomi would miss her more than she cared to admit. She would go back to being the *Hon Fitz* as she was called, but not to her face.

Anna was still thinking of their brief exchange, her own astonishment when she had found herself touching the medal ribbon. And the photograph; what had he done with it?

She said, 'Anyway, he was really nice about it. I think he's had a bad time.' Then she looked up. 'Don't worry, I won't make the same mistake twice! I'm not *that* stupid!'

They both stared at the shuttered window as the siren wailed again. The All Clear.

Naomi exclaimed, 'Well, that's a bloody change!' She watched Anna climb into bed, and sighed a little, wistfully.

Never say goodbye.

Martineau rolled over in the bunk, entangled in a blanket, fighting to come out of the dream. He was sweating and his heart was pounding like a drum, and his legs were over the side of the bunk feeling for his shoes before he realized that there had been no alarm. The bunkside telephone was buzzing in its leather case, as if an insect was trapped there.

He had to clear his throat. 'Captain.'

Fairfax. Who else had he expected? He peered at the nearest scuttles, but the deadlights were still screwed in place; the ship was motionless. Nothing had changed.

Fairfax said, 'I'm sorry to disturb you, sir. The guardboat is coming over with some despatches.'

Martineau lifted his wrist and peered at his watch. Six-thirty; the hands had been called an hour ago. And he had heard nothing. Felt nothing.

He thought he heard Fairfax's breathing, and said, 'You did the right thing. Call me when they've dropped them.' He lay back on the bunk and listened to feet thudding along the deck. *Hakka* had come to life again, like all the others around them. He heard the clatter of crockery. A steward would be coming in with his coffee at any second.

He felt his heartbeat returning to normal, remembering the dream. Always the ship charging into oblivion, and a last cry choked out of him by the icy water.

Then he was on his feet and striding through to the other cabin as if he had known the ship for months.

He switched on the light over the desk and pulled out the book of sonnets, which had obviously never been read. For a long moment he held the photograph in the yellow glare, turning it carefully to catch the detail, to hear her voice. Anna. Anna Roche, who had once been at the *U of T*. He smiled, as if she had said something.

He replaced the photograph and wondered what story lay behind her eyes. He would probably never see her again, and even if he did . . .

The door opened and Tonkyn padded into the cabin.

'I thought we should have some breakfast today, sir. I am doing some scrambled eggs an' a friend got me some bacon from the barracks. They lives real well over there, sir.'

Martineau stood up, feeling the ship move very slightly for the first time. He could not recall having a proper meal since he had first stepped aboard. And, until the dream, it had been the best sleep he could remember.

He was suddenly very hungry.

'I'd like that. Very much.'

Tonkyn's melancholy expression did not change, but he seemed satisfied.

He could hear the guardboat coughing alongside, the quartermaster and bowman exchanging greetings or insults.

He looked at the closed book. He was ready.

5

'You're Not God!'

Lieutenant Roger Kidd straightened his back at the chart table and allowed himself a moment of private satisfaction. He should have known, they all should. Nothing in this man's navy ever went according to plan. He had been enjoying a quiet breakfast in the wardroom when Fairfax had marched in after being with the Captain.

The leisurely departure from Plymouth in company with the leader and two other destroyers was off. The guardboat and the despatches had changed all that. Instead, *Hakka* was under immediate orders for sea. The Chief had charged off to his engine room, muttering something about thoughtless idiots who had no idea about the needs of a ship and her machinery, and for a few moments more, until the pipe *'Special sea dutymen to your stations!'* there had been pandemonium. He gripped a rail as the ship tilted over steeply, spray pattering across the glass screens and stinging his face. *They should have known.* And now the weather was getting lively, too.

He glanced at the others on the bridge. Lieutenant Giles Arliss was the O.O.W., supported by the haughty sub-lieutenant, Humphrey Cavaye. Kidd hid a smile. The blind leading the blind. Arliss had made no secret of the fact that he resented standing a watch. He had been appointed for flotilla signals duties. And in any case . . .

That was as far as he had got. Fairfax had sounded unusually angry.

'We have *not* joined the flotilla yet, in case you hadn't noticed! And in this ship we don't carry passengers!'

But Kidd had to admit they had all done well. It was two hours since they had cleared Plymouth Sound, and with the *Jester* following astern had butted out into grey and worsening weather, which was nothing new in these parts.

Jester was also part of the new flotilla, one of the J Class destroyers. She made a fine sight with her single raked funnel, and her bow slicing through the offshore swell like the thoroughbred she was.

The bridge chair was unoccupied. The Captain had gone down to the chart room to study the next chart for himself. The task they had been allotted was an important one, an emergency. Listening to Martineau's calm voice, Kidd had been able to see it all, perhaps more clearly than any of the others.

An eastbound convoy had been attacked twice by U-Boats; that was nothing unusual. But one of the ships was a giant tanker, fully loaded with fuel, and on the final approach via the south of Ireland she had been singled out for attack by a long-range bomber. The tanker had been damaged and her steering put out of action, but her cargo was apparently intact. The convoy had included a rescue tug, but she was obviously no match for such an unmanageable charge. It was always the hairy part, with the end of yet another hazardous convoy almost in sight, and warships were no different. Many were sunk when their crews believed the worst was almost over, and they were returning to base and home. A momentary lack of vigilance could bring disaster. *Like right here on this bridge.*

At Falmouth lay the one hope, the huge salvage tug *Goliath*, the only vessel near enough with the capability and the experience to do it. Kidd did not need to consult his soiled chart again: Falmouth was somewhere up there, beyond the starboard bow. Thirty miles since they had put to sea, and two hours. Not bad at all.

A boatswain's mate coughed significantly and Kidd turned as the Captain's head and shoulders appeared through the gate.

Martineau climbed on to the gratings, and studied the other destroyer.

'Taking it well, Pilot. But we'll have to reduce revs once we've got *Goliath* in company.' He was thinking aloud. 'The tanker will be drifting in this little lot. The south-westerly wind is strengthening, and that other tug will be hard put to keep her under command.' He looked up as spray drifted over the bridge.

Like someone measuring an enemy's strength, Kidd thought. Looking for a trick.

'She'll clear the Scillies with any luck. Swansea Bay is the best bet. There's more shelter there and they're used to handling lame ducks.' He smiled briefly. 'Should be, after three years of it.'

He put one hand on the chair as the deck lifted and then dipped again.

'If the weather worsens the job will get harder.' He shrugged. 'But of course if it was a perfect day, the enemy would arrive in force. The sea may be an ally this time.'

Sub-Lieutenant Cavaye said, 'Time to alter course, sir.' But not for Arliss's benefit, Kidd thought. It was merely to show the Captain that he was on the ball.

He realized that Martineau was watching him, his eyes very clear. Like the sea itself.

'What d'you know about *Goliath*, Pilot?'

So casually asked, but Kidd was a seaman to his fingertips.

'She can manage fifteen knots with a following wind and all the stops pulled, sir.' He tilted his head as more spray bounced off his cap. 'But in this I'd give her ten.'

Martineau nodded, and felt in the pocket of his duffle coat. 'It will be dark early. Very early. We must make contact before that. Otherwise it will be too late.'

Kidd waited. No *ifs* or *buts*. Or *they should have thought of this earlier*. There was nobody else.

'St Anthony Beacon at two-nine-zero, sir!'

Fairfax had appeared on the bridge, his tanned face reddened by the wind.

He said, 'You did it again, Pilot! I thought we were lost!'

Martineau had heard them talking, friends, long before he had stepped aboard. He steadied his binoculars and waited for the bows to climb again, wondering how the new hands were managing in their as yet unfamiliar quarters. *Like mine.*

He stiffened and said, 'And there she is, gentlemen!'

66

He ignored the clatter of the signal lamp, the bright winking eye of the great tug's acknowledgement. Huge indeed, one of the largest ocean-going tugs in service, and always in demand. In tonnage she was not much less than *Hakka*, but she seemed to stand out of the leaping waves like a rock.

He tugged his cap more firmly over his hair and stood on the top grating so that the *Goliath*'s master would be sure to see him, and would know who was making the signal.

He called, 'Ready, Bunts?'

'Aye, sir.' But it was Onslow, the chief yeoman, as he had somehow known it would be, even though the ship was at defence stations.

'To *Goliath* from *Hakka*. *Time is the enemy. At thirteen knots we will do it.*' He knew that Kidd was beside him, watching for an irate signal, or an outright refusal. There was none. '*Follow father.*' He raised one arm towards the massive tug and said, almost to himself, 'Lucky thirteen. This time.'

Fairfax and the bearded navigator both heard it. Neither understood.

Onslow called, 'From *Goliath*, sir. *Remember what happened to David!*'

Martineau heard the sudden laughter, even from those who had not comprehended the signal.

'Take station ahead, Pilot. Then alter course as plotted.' He peered aft as a downdraft brought the acrid tang of smoke from the big forward funnel. '*Jester*'s skipper has his orders, he can take over the sweep astern.'

Arliss sounded surprised. 'U-Boats, sir?'

But Martineau was bending over the chart again.

Kidd brushed past him and murmured, 'What d'you expect? This is Western Approaches, remember?'

With one elbow wedged against the table to lessen the violent motion, Martineau checked the pencilled calculations and compared them with his own. There was always hope, but there was a lot of that scattered across the bottom of the Atlantic. A valuable cargo of fuel; for Spitfires or tanks, it was not their concern. Every drop was vital. But all he could think of were the men who would be out there now, with nothing to cling to but the hope of rescue. *Like me. And the thirteen who were with me that day.*

It was barely possible to believe that just a few hours ago he had been looking at the photograph, and contemplating breakfast. A better dream, but a dream nonetheless. . . .

He shook himself angrily. Even if they made a perfect rendezvous, there would be next to no time to grapple with the helpless tanker and get some way on her.

Kidd had merely confirmed what he already knew about the area. The tide would be bad enough, but if the wind rose any more *Goliath*'s master would never dare to risk his ship in a senseless collision.

He made up his mind and pushed himself away from the chart table, and covered it with its waterproof hood.

'We could try something which will give us a bit more time.' He had their attention, the wind and the tumbling grey waves momentarily forgotten. 'We have the speed, the agility.' He knew Fairfax understood that it was for him alone. 'It's a risk, of course.'

Fairfax said without hesitation, 'A boarding party, sir? Be ready for *Goliath*'s first attempt.' Surprisingly, he smiled. 'I'd ask for volunteers.' He seemed to take Martineau's silence for doubt, and added firmly, 'I can do it!'

Martineau touched his sleeve. Lightly, the way the girl had touched the ribbon.

'I'd not ask anyone else.'

Martineau crossed the bridge, the steep motion testing his stomach like a taunt.

'I shall want signals made to *Jester* and separately to *Goliath*.' Onslow was busy with his pad. 'Admiralty, sir?'

Martineau faced him and smiled. 'Not at this stage, I think.'

Kidd said in a fierce whisper, 'What the hell are you thinking about, Jamie? You know the bloody risks in that sort of caper!'

But Fairfax was watching the Captain, recalling how the strain had dropped away after he had made his decision. Young again, like the man who had married an unfaithful wife. In wartime, what did that mean? Or was it the one he had been with at the officers' club?

He turned, startled out of his thoughts, as the Captain said, 'Twelve men should do it. Don't expect too much help from the tanker's crew. They've been through enough already.'

There it was again. Sharing it, or blaming himself for something.

The hand on his sleeve once more. 'No heroics, Number One.'

Fairfax looked at the sea. He had never been afraid, or so he had told himself often enough. It was all part of it. Destroyers, the madness and the exhilaration when it was at its worst.

But this was different. He said, 'Right, sir.' It was too late anyway.

Fairfax gripped the handrail of the bridge ladder and waited for the deck to surge up beneath him. Down here, below the bridge and forward funnel every sound seemed louder, more violent, the sea closer to the deck itself.

The party of volunteers was wedged together as if for comfort, maybe wondering what insane impulse had made them come forward. In the navy they always said that a volunteer was someone who had misunderstood the question in the first place, or a bloody fool. The old hands said, never volunteer for any damned thing. But they did.

He looked up as another signal flashed from the flag deck. He turned and stared steadily at the crippled tanker. For hours, or so it felt, they had watched it loom out of the drifting spray which occasionally floated above it like smoke. Now the tanker filled their horizon, huge, low in the water, and motionless. Or so it appeared.

Fairfax had gone through the last approach, step by step. The other tug was still hooked on, but acted as little more than a sea-anchor. At least they were clear of the Scillies with their treacherous rocks, the deathbed of many ships from as far back as the first sailing traders. But the whole area was pockmarked with isolated shoals and unexpected shallows, enough to break the back of any ship. Kidd had described it without dramatics. You respected it, or you paid for it.

Fairfax heard Arthur Malt the Gunner (T) offering advice to the assembled men.

'One and for the King an' one for yerself. No time for soddin' about. Remember that, Wishart, if you want to better yourself!'

Fairfax glanced at the young seaman. He was not required on the bridge to help the navigator. The ship was at defence stations, half the company standing to, the others ready to use muscle and blood when it was needed if the first attempt failed.

Malt was reliable but unimaginative. Even in his shining oilskin he was completely square, his cap jammed flat on his head like a lid, as if to contain the temper that was his weakness, especially with new hands like Wishart. Mothers' boys, he called them.

Ossie Pike, *Hakka*'s chief boatswain's mate and her most experienced seaman, edged closer and growled, 'I 'ope they're not all dead over there!' The Buffer, as he was always known aboard ship, had wanted to go across when the time came. Fairfax had said, 'Suppose something happened to me? Who would run the ship then?' It had seemed to quieten him for the moment.

Perhaps he should have declined Wishart's eagerness to volunteer. The boy was untried, inexperienced. But this called for the nimble-footed and the quick-witted. The master mariners would have to wait.

He steadied himself as the ship turned more steeply, the sea spurting over the deck by the whaler's davits, looking at the big Carley float which would carry them to the tanker once the Skipper had worked round to offer a lee and to use the wind as an ally. *No heroics*. Just a brief moment, and the rift had gone. They trusted each other. They needed each other.

He cleared his throat. 'Once in the float, secure the lifelines provided. We'll use the paddles, but we'll be depending mostly on the drift.'

He peered across one stooping figure and saw the tanker again, a good cable away, although from here it looked right alongside. Water pouring off the low superstructure in rivers, small breakers sweeping across the broad, red-leaded deck as if she was already going down. All that bloody fuel. How did men sail with lethal cargoes like that, time and time again?

Hakka was altering course once more, making it seem as if the tanker had suddenly gathered way. A tiny figure stood up on her

70

deck and waved jerkily, before ducking again as the sea boiled towards him.

It was little enough, but somebody gave a wild cheer. It was all they needed.

Fairfax jabbed the petty officer's arm. It felt like a piece of timber.

'Right, Buffer, man the tackles. Here we go!'

He tightened the strap of the Schermuly line-throwing pistol to make sure that the rocket was secured and glanced at the two men with the case containing the line. Like a piece of thread against this sea and wind. But it had been done in worse.

One of the men nodded to him. It was Forward. The wheelhouse was fully manned, and he had volunteered with a wry grin. 'Might help with my promotion, sir!'

The youth Wishart was with him. An unlikely pair, but it seemed to work.

He thought of the other destroyer, churning back and forth, sweeping for any possible U-Boat, although it was unlikely around here these days. Air cover, and the range of the new escort carriers had driven the wolf packs into deeper waters. But you could never be certain.

He tucked the towel more securely inside his upturned collar. He need not have bothered; it was already sodden. He could feel the St Christopher against his skin, the one she had given him after the party when they had sailed off to the Med. A pretty, laughing face, but he could not recall her name.

'Right, lads! Two at a time when I give the signal!'

He saw the line-handling party ready, their oilskins like wet coal in the dim light. Ossie Pike watching the blocks and the tackles, the way each man stood, how he was balanced.

Some wag called out, 'Must be cushy enough if Jimmy the One is goin'!'

That brought more laughs, and a lump to Fairfax's throat. In minutes they could all be drowned, or sucked into *Hakka*'s churning screws. It had happened.

Wishart watched the big Carley float being swayed up and over the side. They said it would hold thirty men in an emergency. At least it was something to cling on to if the ship was going down. Against the dark waves it looked like a tiny dinghy.

He heard Forward say, 'Once you're in, just hold on. Don't try to do anything! Got it?'

He nodded, his mouth too stiff with cold to form a reply. The Gunner (T) had been goading him again, backed up as usual by Morris, the leading hand of the quarterdeck, Malt's division. Morris was sweating on his next move up, to join a petty officer's course at Portsmouth. Without Malt's backing he stood little chance, and he knew it.

It was always the same. How he talked. How he looked. Even the wristwatch his parents had given him when he had joined up. *Real sailors don't wear pansy little watches now, do they?* Malt was good at it. Relished it.

When he had heard the clamour for volunteers he had not hesitated. He had not thought of danger or death. It was blind, resentful anger. And now he was here.

Eventually he managed to speak.

'Have you done this before, Bob?'

Forward came out of his thoughts and stared at him. Seeing the harm that old prat Malt had done, recognizing the fear.

''Course. Dozens of times. Piece of cake!' He spat over the side as salt squirted into his face. 'Stick with me.' He turned away to watch the first lieutenant, and to hide his surprise. It had worked. Like that day when the Channel guns had begun to fire, and the snotty had almost thrown up.

The Carley float was edging down, and down, until it was bouncing heavily on the broken water surging back from the stem.

Fairfax waited, counting seconds, watching the float rearing about like a mad thing. He could sense rather than hear the changing note of *Hakka*'s engines, her flared side heeling to another turn of the wheel. He wanted to lean out and look up at the bridge, but he knew his resolve would shatter like glass if he did.

He could see them anyway, big Bill Spicer on the wheel, his face a mask of concentration, his attention confined to the voicepipe and the ticking gyro tape. The Chief down among his racing machinery, yelling soundlessly to his crew, the fans and shafts joining in like an orchestra gone berserk.

72

Kidd with his chart and his notes, soundings, tides and currents. *The enemy below.* And the Captain, who carried them all.

'Ready, sir!'

Fairfax felt the deck tilting again. It looked as if he could reach down and touch the sea.

He heard himself yell, *'Now!'* And then he was falling, reddened faces peering after him, the breath suddenly knocked out of his lungs as he hit the curved side of the float. Half-blinded by the spray, once with his head completely submerged, then his fingers fastened on one of the Buffer's lines and locked on to it like claws. The float was rising again, trying to dislodge him, the ship leaning right over him, with just enough speed to hold the tow alongside.

'Next!' Anonymous figures sprawled beside him, one even managing to yell an obscenity before the fight for survival took charge.

And suddenly they were all there. Packed together, numbed fingers fastening their safety lines, eyes blind with spray, peering around seeking a friend or anything familiar, for that extra strength.

Fairfax jerked a paddle out of its fastening and shouted, 'Together, lads!'

The float had been cast off from the destroyer's side but was still attached by another line, which was being paid out rapidly even as he watched.

He tried to peer ahead, to estimate their progress, or if they were moving at all. His breath was rasping, and the paddle weighed a ton. If he looked back he knew that *Hakka* would be out of sight, no matter how far they had come. The raft was rearing up and down, jerking at the remaining line as if to tear itself free and hurl its occupants to the sea.

Someone cried, *'Hold on, Tom! Keep going!'*

Tom? Which one was that? But his brain refused to respond any more.

He thought of the photograph which had been found in the Skipper's quarters, recalling a sense of hurt and exclusion because he had not known who she was.

73

He could not manage more than a few strokes. He raised his head, gulping air, and there right above him was the tanker.

There were faces, too. Not many, but someone was lowering a ladder despite the deluge of sea and spray.

He heard himself shouting, *'Up you go! Chop-bloody-chop!'*

Figures scrambled past him, someone even croaking an apology as he trod on Fairfax's hand.

Then, staggering like drunks from a dockside bar, they dragged themselves across the unfamiliar deck with its alien fittings. The float had already drifted away, or was being hauled back to the ship.

A voice shouted, 'This way!'

Fairfax ducked beneath some glistening superstructure and made sure that his whole party was present, and felt his jaw crack into a grin. *No heroics.*

'They did it!' Kidd could not contain his excitement and relief. 'Old Jamie's got his lads aboard!'

'Let me see.' Martineau brushed past him, shielding his glasses from the pellets of spray while he waited for the bridge to level itself. He saw the Carley float swaying across the water, the towline rising and tightening like cheese-wire as the Buffer's party heaved on their tackles.

He managed to train his glasses on the tanker, and thought he saw some of Fairfax's men pulling themselves around the bridge. Several times during the attempt they had lost sight of the float in the deep troughs, as if it had been swallowed up completely.

He wiped the gyro repeater with his sleeve. 'Bring her round, Pilot. We'll keep up to wind'rd while we can.' He ignored the terse helm orders, the sudden increase of revolutions, and studied the ill-assorted collection of vessels all drawn together like the lines on Kidd's chart. The tanker, with the small tug still attempting to hold her head on to the sea and wind. And the one rust-streaked corvette which must have been with the convoy when it first set out, as she had doubtless done countless times before. And the massive salvage tug *Goliath*. The contrast was at its greatest there, he thought. The little corvette, one of hundreds built for the Atlantic war and rolling off the stocks every day, was pitching like a toy boat. Lively ships at the best of times, this one was living up to their claim that they could roll on wet grass; he could see down her solitary funnel one moment, and the length of her bilge keel the next. By comparison *Goliath* remained like a reef, the sea surging around her and spray streaming from her derricks and upperworks like powdered snow.

There was not much the corvette could do now. Her depth charge racks were empty, evidence of the convoy's earlier encounters with the enemy. She would be short of fuel, too. But her commanding officer had signalled his determination to remain in company. *To watch my betters at work.*

Martineau recalled something he had heard the King say at the Palace, about heroism and its just reward.

All these men were heroes. Someone should tell them.

'Steady on zero-two-zero, sir.' Kidd lowered his glasses. '*Jester* is taking up position to the west of us. If there's anyone nasty hanging about it's likely they'll come from that bearing.'

Lieutenant Arliss said, 'Asdic reports back-echoes and interference to the north-east.' It sounded like a question.

Kidd said, 'Isolated shallows. No real danger until the Seven Stones, but we should be well clear by then.'

Martineau eased himself into the chair. The light was holding, and even the sea seemed a little easier. *Goliath* would begin to close with the tanker, and Fairfax would be ready to make fast the tow if they managed to get a line across. Always tricky: it was sensible to have several ready to shoot in case of accidents.

He said, 'I think we should rustle up something hot to drink,' and Kidd gestured to a messenger.

'Jump about, Tinker!'

He could sense the figures around him relaxing slightly. He gripped the pipe in his pocket again. There was water even in there. *Why can't I let things run on their own?* They were doing all they could. And they might easily have lost Fairfax and his volunteers.

Maybe I was ashore too long. Maybe I lost it, back there in Firebrand.

There was a dull bang and he saw a puff of smoke from beneath *Goliath*'s bridge.

There was a chorus of groans and a few jeers as the first line fell short. *Goliath* was edging round, her bulky shape shortening, her low stern almost lost in a welter of foam from her big screws. The two hulls were overlapping, an illusion perhaps, but time was running out.

Bang.

'I think so!' Kidd was standing on his toes to watch. *'Got it!'*

Martineau wiped his glasses and tried again. *Goliath* was moving across the tanker's outline, cutting it in half like a giant gate, but not before he had seen the scurrying figures on the red-leaded plating, and a line rearing over the side like a serpent before being manhandled through a winch. The heavier towing wire would follow immediately. Without Fairfax's party it was unlikely they could have managed it.

Somebody cried out, 'Bloody hell! Man overboard!'

Martineau caught the briefest glimpse of a tiny figure flinging out his arms, perhaps trying to regain his balance, before vanishing over the tanker's side.

Kidd said softly, 'Poor bastard!'

Cavaye's voice intruded. *'Jester* reports a contact at two-eight-zero. *Investigating.'*

'Very well. Retain contact with *Jester.'* He turned away, sickened that he could close his mind to what he had just witnessed. *Jester* had reported a find on her Asdic. A submarine, a submerged wreck, a back-echo from some freak formation on the seabed. *No chances.* It seemed very unlikely that a U-Boat had been standing off all this time, when a fanned salvo of torpedoes would have despatched the tanker without difficulty. There had only been the corvette, and she was toothless as far as U-Boats were concerned. A straggler, then?

Arliss called, 'Tow's secured, sir. *Goliath* is getting under way.'

It might be too much. The tow could easily part under the strain. The sky was darker, and he had scarcely noticed it. They would have to stand by all night.

'From *Jester,* sir. Still in faint contact.'

Kidd said, 'Shall I signal the corvette to close with *Goliath,* sir?'

Martineau stared at him. 'So that we can join *Jester* and do a box search?'

Kidd looked at the sky. 'Might save time, sir.'

'No.' He heard the sound of a shot, probably another line being fired. It did not seem important, or real. 'Those shallows, Pilot. Show me again.'

He leaned over the chart table, watching Kidd's brass dividers trace the area to the north-east of their position.

He could sense Kidd watching him, feel his heavy breathing through his duffle coat. Was not this the very mistake they had always been taught to recognize and avoid? He felt unable to move, unwilling to believe it.

Then he said, 'Then *that's* the route he'll use.' He pushed the dividers down on the chart. 'And I nearly missed it.'

And still he felt nothing, neither emotion nor doubt.

He said, 'Close up depth charge crews, and pipe Action Stations.' He caught his sleeve. 'No alarms, Pilot. No noise. Just have it piped around the ship.'

Kidd was staring at him, hanging on to every word, although he probably thought his captain had cracked at last.

'Sir?'

He straightened his back. 'Then we will begin the attack.'

It was only a few seconds before anyone moved, but it felt like an eternity. Martineau climbed into his chair, his mind only half aware of the sudden stammer of voicepipes, the terse acknowledgements from the bridge team.

Suppose I am wrong?

'Ship at action stations, sir.' Even Kidd's voice sounded different. Or was it that he had become so used to Fairfax?

'Tell Asdic to belay transmissions.' He sat forward in the chair and studied the flickering phosphorescence on the radar repeater. 'Tell Lovatt to take nothing for granted.' He thought he heard Kidd's intake of breath. Surprised that they would be without their Asdic sweep, or that he had managed to remember the senior operator's name. It was always like that. It started on the bridge, with the team, then it felt its way out through voicepipes and along wires to every section of the ship, eventually to all the various departments. The cooks and stewards, the supply assistants and stokers, the sickbay, and the nerve centre, the transmitting station and fire control systems. He was astonished that he could smile. And finally, to the faces across the table as requestmen or defaulters.

He gripped the arm of the chair, feeling the engines pulsing through it. And he had been determined not to allow himself to get so close to a command again. Different faces, dialects from Glasgow to Penzance, all held together by a ship, and by their trust.

How must it have been for those other men when they had heard his last command? *Stand by to ram!*

He said, 'Get me the gunnery officer.' He did not recognize his own voice.

Driscoll sounded clipped and formal, as usual. It was easy to picture him at his fire control position, headphones over his cap, and probably wearing the white silk scarf Martineau had heard about.

Driscoll listened without interruption, then he said, 'Starshell, sir. Another if necessary. I've told B Gun. Then, rapid fire.'

No questions. No doubts. It was better to be a Driscoll in this sort of warfare, he thought.

Kidd said, '*Jester*'s just dropped a couple of depth charges, sir.'

The explosions had been muffled by the fans and the creak of metal.

'Depth?'

'Thirty fathoms, sir. For a while yet.'

Martineau nodded. Like a complex puzzle. A falling tide and a treacherous current, but the wind dropping as if to compensate. No word from *Goliath*, so the tow was holding. They would be on their way.

Unless. Suppose *Jester* had found a firm contact? A U-Boat which was even now making a final strike at the tanker.

It was taking too long. 'Check, Pilot?'

'Five miles, sir.'

He pressed his spine against the unyielding chair and tried to clear his thoughts. Too long . . . too long. He had fallen into the oldest trap of all, and had left the door wide open. *Jester* too far away to offer assistance, the corvette unable to attack.

It was like hearing Alison, that first evening when he had taken a few days' leave.

'The ship! The ship! Is that all you can think about, Graham? They can manage without you, you're not God!' And much more. Maybe that was when it had all started to fall apart.

He did not look at his watch. There was no point.

'Course to steer to rejoin *Goliath*, Pilot?'

Maybe that was why Lucky Bradshaw had sent *Hakka*. To test him out, so as not to damage his own reputation by leaving it until he had joined the new group.

'Radar – Bridge!'

He bent over the tube. 'Bridge.'

It was Lovatt, concerned but definite. 'Strong echo, sir, dead ahead of us, zero-three-zero.'

Martineau peered at the repeater, holding his breath in case he missed something.

There it was, like a tiny winking eye.

Lovatt was saying, 'About eight thousand yards, sir.'

Martineau heard the click of metal and knew that Driscoll was already setting his sights on the estimated bearing. He crouched over the compass.

'Starboard ten ... Ease to five ... Midships ... Steady.' He heard Spicer's acknowledgement as he added, 'Steer zero-three-zero.'

He stared at the repeater. A lot of interference, and for a moment he could not see the elusive blip on the small screen. Maybe the U-Boat was fitted with a radar reflector and had already seen through their silent approach. He wanted to clear his throat. It was bone dry. *Maybe there was no submarine at all.*

Then he saw the blip again, clear and bright, as the interference pulled away like weed. Too small for anything else. And on the surface, trimmed down to offer the smallest contact.

Any second now and the U-Boat commander would realize what was happening. He might turn away and run for it on the surface; he might even risk diving in these dangerous waters. Either way they would lose him.

'Steady as you go, Cox'n!' Unconsciously, he had dropped his voice, but Spicer heard him well enough.

Without taking his eyes from the radar repeater he reached out for the red handset.

'Chief? This is the Captain. When I ring for it, give me everything.'

He could picture Trevor Morgan down there in his white boiler suit, listening intently, his eyes alive in the reflected lights and dials. Like Malt, the Gunner (T), he had risen from the lower deck, to become a senior engineer in one of the navy's finest ships. He was owed an explanation.

'Sub on the surface, Chief.'

He heard Lovatt report, 'Target's altering course, sir!'

Martineau slammed down the handset and called, 'Full ahead both engines! Fire, starshell!'

Not an echo any longer. A target.

He felt the bridge jerk violently as one of the guns recoiled and the crash of the shot ripped into the darkness.

The second gun in that mounting would be ready and waiting.

Martineau lifted his glasses, then winced as the starshell exploded against the low clouds and lit up the sea like some eerie glacier landscape. The waves, their crests unbroken now, looked solid, like molten glass, and the glare held the scene until it seared his vision.

And there, no more than a darker shadow against the vivid backdrop, lay the submarine.

'Open fire!'

'Port ten! Midships! Steady!' *Hakka* turned only slightly, but the after guns were able to open fire immediately.

'Straddle, sir!'

Martineau lowered his glasses; he did not need them now. *'Steady*, Cox'n. *Easy.'*

Kidd turned to stare at him, his face quite clear in the hard light. It was as if the Captain was speaking to the ship.

The U-Boat was diving, the sinister shape lengthening as she continued to turn away.

Martineau clenched his fist. There were still the stern tubes.

'Stand by, depth charges!'

He watched the distance falling away, the submarine's deck alive with foam as she vented her tanks for a crash dive. Two shells burst almost alongside. In that sealed hull they would sound like hammers from hell.

'Tell Asdic to begin a sweep, Pilot!'

He strode to the opposite side. The submarine had disappeared. They would be down there trying to plug leaks, restore order, and all the while they would be hearing *Hakka*'s screws roaring towards them, *like an express train*, one submariner had described it.

'*Continuous echo! Fire!*'

Hakka surged into the returning darkness, dropping her charges and firing two more as she passed over the U-Boat's estimated position.

'Hard a-port!' He recrossed the bridge and looked at the gyro. 'We'll make another sweep.'

But it was not necessary. It was more of a feeling than a sound, with the sea suddenly boiling and flinging up a great column of water like something solid which would never disperse. Perhaps the U-Boat had been carrying mines.

Asdic again, quiet, very contained. 'No further echoes, sir. Sounds of hull breaking up.'

Kidd shouted, 'We did it, by God!' He almost clapped Martineau on the shoulder but restrained himself. 'You knew, sir! I'll never know how, *but you knew!*'

The column of water had subsided, and the sea's face was unbroken once more.

Martineau climbed into his chair. 'Course and speed, Pilot. Pass the word, *well done.*'

He watched the huge bow waves dying away as *Hakka* reduced speed and pointed her raked stem towards the other ships.

Men had just died. Choking, crushed, obliterated. Men who would have shown no mercy if their cards had been played in the right order.

Aloud he said, 'He was a brave man.'

Kidd shook his head. He had been in the war from the beginning, but like most sailors he had never seen a U-Boat before, had known only the shadow, and the sudden roar of a torpedo in the middle of a convoy. Something to fear. And out of that fear had grown the hate and the skill to hit back, and destroy the enemy.

81

It made Martineau's quiet tribute to the German all the more moving.

6

High Standards

The journey to Liverpool took far longer than she had expected, and it was almost a day and a half after leaving Plymouth before the train shuddered to a final halt. There had been one delay after another; they had been kept waiting in a siding while more important traffic went thundering past, and somewhere else a goods wagon had become derailed in a tunnel. That took even more time to put right.

The train had been packed for the last leg of the journey, but she had managed to get a window seat and was able to find some pretence of seclusion, interrupted only by an earnest young artillery captain who had just got married and wanted to show her photographs of the event.

Much to her surprise her progress had been monitored, and she was astonished to find a car waiting for her, with a tough-looking Royal Marine driver who obviously knew the city well.

Anna Roche had heard a lot about the headquarters of Western Approaches Command, but nonetheless it was not what she had expected. Derby House, in the city itself, had been taken over shortly after the outbreak of war, and following a lengthy conversion into a bomb- and gas proof citadel had proved its worth many times over. The choice had been due to the foresight of Winston Churchill himself, when he had been First Lord of the Admiralty, and one of only a few who had recognized the true menace of an all-out battle for supremacy waged on the Atlantic lifelines.

She glanced at the passing scene, blacked-out windows and throngs of servicemen, most of them sailors. The driver kept up a steady patter about the places she should know. Gladstone Dock, *where our lads tie up*. The signals station. The cathedral. It was so dark that she could have been anywhere.

And she felt like death.

A hot bath, even the one they had shared at Plymouth, a clean shirt, time to gather her thoughts. It was not to be.

The driver opened the door for her. 'I'll keep an eye on your gear, miss, er, ma'am. They'll be waitin' for you, I expect.'

Security checks, a murmured telephone call. She was to go straight to one of the offices. Even this part of the citadel must be underground; the air felt tired, lifeless. She thought of the other places she had been stationed after her application had been accepted for Operations. Larne in Northern Ireland, Portland Bill; even poor, battered old Plymouth with its air raids was preferable to this.

There were a lot of Wrens in Western Approaches Command, and it was her decision. She made another effort, and rapped on the door.

'Come!' A woman's voice. Anna took a deep breath and pushed it open.

The only occupant was sitting at a desk on the far side of the room beneath a huge map of the British Isles. The desk was quite empty, and the Wren officer who occupied it, her fingers interlaced, gave the impression that she had been sitting here just waiting for this first encounter. She did not rise, nor did she smile.

'Take a pew,' she said. 'We don't stand on ceremony here.'

Anna sat on a hard-backed chair, which also looked as if it had been prepared for her. Like being at school, she thought.

She studied the other woman as she opened the envelope which had travelled all the way from Plymouth. She could have been any age, in her thirties or possibly older. Everything about her was severe, as if she had done all she could to dampen any familiarity at the outset. The hair was pulled so tightly to the nape of her neck that it looked as if it might be painful, and her features, which were certainly striking, even attractive if they had been given the chance, seemed detached, aloof.

The two and a half blue stripes on her sleeves showed her to be a first officer, and her name was Crawford. Naomi Fitzherbert had heard of her, but then she knew just about everybody. *All for the service, my girl, and no time for anyone who thinks differently. A battle-axe on the outside, but a bit of a love when she feels like it.*

That part was harder to believe.

'I've seen your dossier, of course. You come to us highly recommended. But . . .' The *but* hung in the air as she turned over the letter. 'A Canadian, too.' A pause. 'We have a lot of your countrymen in and out of here.' She looked up suddenly, her eyes very still. 'I'll take you into the main Operations Room shortly. After that, the Boss will want to see you. Commodore Raikes has very high standards, so be warned.' She picked up her hat. 'Come with me.'

Anna Roche stood up and followed her to the outer door. They knew enough about her to send a car to collect her, and the R.T.O. would have explained about the delays on the line. But so far nobody had thought it necessary to offer her a cup of tea, or show her a place where she could make herself presentable.

Surprisingly, it calmed her. She had met with this kind of thing before.

If they can be tough, so can I!

First Officer Crawford walked with her down a long, narrow tunnel, confining and painted white, and lighted at intervals by shatterproof lamps. Her voice echoed around them.

'Western Approaches is a vast concern now, with repair facilities large and small to keep the ships at sea. Londonderry, Greenock, Belfast, even St John's in Newfoundland. And it's all beginning to work. When I came here, we were losing an average of four hundred thousand tons of shipping a month. Crippling. Not enough escorts, no long-range air cover, and the enemy building more submarines than we could hope to destroy.'

They strode past a man sitting in a small telephone box, who was writing something on a signal pad. He did not look up. Anna could hear the other woman's heels clicking in the stark tunnel, and quickened her pace to keep up.

'But it's changing now.' She opened another door. 'And we are in the centre of it. The hub!'

Anna glanced at her. No boast. It was pride, personal. *As if I don't exist.*

She walked through and stopped by a safety rail. The Operations Room seemed to engulf her.

The walls were giant charts, each one covered with coloured markers and numbers. Long ladders glided soundlessly back and forth, as Wrens added fresh information, and removed others.

Crawford said, 'Everyone is represented here.' She gestured to one of the big tables which faced the main wall. 'R.A.F. Coastal Command, the signal traffic officer – you'll be helping her, by the way. The one with the beard is the submarine tracking officer, and the chap next to him is the Met expert. *He* thinks so, anyway.'

Anna glanced at her pale profile, but there was no hint of humour.

'See that convoy they've just moved? From Canada, coming here ... Thursday, all being well. That one further over is on passage to Gibraltar. You can see the disposition of the escort group clearly from here.'

She frowned as a burst of clapping erupted from the lower floor. A seaman messenger, hurrying past with a tray of signals, said breathlessly, 'Got a U-Boat! It's just been confirmed!'

Like the marine driver, as proud as if he had been there himself.

Somebody was moving another marker, and a voice said, 'That was *Hakka*'s kill. Confirmed. Bloody good show!' There was utter silence again.

'We'd better move along.' Crawford looked at her searchingly. 'What is it?'

'It's all right. I saw *Hakka* in Plymouth just after I'd returned there from Portland.' But all she could see was the concern in his eyes when he had offered to help her at the naval club. And he had been out there. It looked like the Scilly Isles on the giant chart.

Hakka's kill.

Crawford was saying, 'She'll be here in Liverpool in a day or so.' She waited, as if testing something.

'Is it always like this?'

'Hmm. Usually. And now we've got a new C-in-C, Admiral Sir Max Horton, took over last month. He's a real ball of fire.' She hesitated, and then added quietly, 'Commodore Raikes admires

86

him very much.' They paused by yet another door and faced one another. 'I thought you should know.'

So Naomi, the Hon Fitz, was right about that too.

She smiled. 'I'm ready.'

The hot bath could wait.

Commander Graham Martineau stepped over the coaming of a watertight door and paused to accustom himself to the stillness. He looked down at his damply crumpled duffle coat, stained from various encounters on *Hakka*'s bridge, and came to terms with it. This was the first time he had left that bridge since the ship had departed so hurriedly from Plymouth, and he was feeling it, even though he had spent far more time at sea on almost every other occasion. Maybe he was still deluding himself and he was not ready; maybe his enforced stay ashore had left him lacking something he had previously taken for granted.

He pushed open the door and was taken off guard by the white, shining interior of the ship's sickbay. With the deadlights lifted from the scuttles it seemed almost blinding, especially after their arrival in Liverpool in the grey half-light of morning.

After the strain of the last few miles, nursing the damaged tanker into safer waters and the swept approaches to Swansea Bay, their entry here had been unnerving. It seemed that every person on the base had turned out to greet them and give them a cheer as they had manoeuvred carefully towards Gladstone Dock. At one point there had been crowds of Wrens, hundreds of them, joining in the welcome, and even the normally imperturbable coxswain had exclaimed, 'All that crumpet! Turned out just for us!'

And now the ship was still. Alongside. He peered through the nearest scuttle and saw a giant gantry, its huge crane towering above the masts, moving soundlessly on invisible rails, as if *Hakka* was still under way.

The sickbay was situated in the after superstructure, almost next door to his own pristine and empty quarters, and the bunk he had hardly used since taking command. But now there would be formalities to undergo. Captain (D) to be entertained, reports to be made, signals to be authorized. And there were other matters, no less important. The rest could wait.

The inner door opened, gleaming in the deckhead lights like polished marble.

The sick berth attendant, Petty Officer Pryor, known in his own mess as 'Plonker' Pryor, was good at his job, and Fairfax had spoken highly of him. The last doctor had applied for a transfer after the savage air attack and it had, surprisingly, been granted. A new doctor would be appointed very soon, although Martineau suspected that if Pryor was like most of his breed he would deeply resent it.

He was watching him now, obviously surprised by a visit from his commanding officer but doing his best to conceal it.

'How's the patient?'

Pryor gave up trying to hide his astonishment. 'Doing well, sir. A couple of stitches here.' He touched his own skull with one fat finger. 'A few grazes.' He nodded. 'He was lucky, that one.'

Martineau walked into the other part of the sick quarters. White-painted, folding cots, racks of bottles and jars which were still rattling despite the ship being alongside, disturbed by some piece of Morgan's machinery buried deep in the hull.

Ordinary Seaman Wishart, one of the first lieutenant's volunteers, was indeed lucky to be alive. He had lost his balance when he had tried to secure a line as the tug *Goliath* was about to take the tanker in tow. Fairfax had told him that the tanker's crew had been close to exhaustion from their long ordeal after being left by the convoy, and Wishart had been helping one of them when he had gone over the side, hitting his head in the process.

Martineau moved to the one occupied cot and stared down at the face on the pillow. It was very pale, the bandages making it look even younger, defenceless.

Fairfax had been hard put to describe what had happened next. The seaman named Forward had dived over the side without hesitation. He had been wearing a pusser's life jacket, but it would not have saved him in that sea.

'I saw him reach Wishart and take hold of him. The current was running fast – they didn't stand a chance.' He had stared at his own hands as if he had somehow expected to see the Schermuly line-shooting pistol still there. It was the only chance, and he had fired the whole line. Somehow they had managed to haul both of

88

them aboard the tanker, and the vessel's master had produced a bottle of Scotch to help revive them.

Martineau recalled the surprise and the genuine pleasure when he had told Fairfax that he would be putting him up for a decoration, Forward too.

'You did well, Number One! You all did!'

He realized that the youth had opened his eyes and was gazing up at him.

'Just wanted to make certain you're not still full of sea water. We'll get something done about the injuries.'

He saw Wishart's hand move out to touch his sleeve, then it stopped, as if he suddenly realized what he was doing, and where he was.

'I – I want to stay, sir. I'll be all right now.'

Martineau glanced at the S.B.A.

'What do you think?'

Pryor pouted sternly. '*If* the new doctor comes aboard soon, sir, he could deal with it right here, on board.'

Martineau looked at the pale face again, seeing the sudden relief. So it was that important to him to remain in *Hakka*. It had certainly not been an easy start for him. *For any of us.*

He nodded, and felt the deck sway up towards him. Too long ashore.

'Very well.' He picked up his cap from the blanket although he did not remember removing it. 'Where did you learn to swim, Wishart?' He saw the youth's eyes focus on his cap, the fine new oak leaves around its peak. Seeing himself, perhaps?

Wishart's eyes were drooping, but he could still smile. 'The baths, sir, at Surbiton.'

He walked to the door. *And we got a U-Boat.* But at this small moment in time, that seemed almost incidental.

Plonker Pryor readjusted the blanket and exclaimed, 'Well, *really!*'

But he was pleased all the same. In spite of the new doctor.

Tonkyn, the chief steward, watched his captain as he knotted his tie and then stretched his arms.

'A shower and a change of clothes works wonders, sir.' He

89

added as an afterthought, 'I was told you sent for Forward, sir.' Quietly disapproving that a commanding officer should have a mere rating visit him in his quarters.

'Send him in.' Martineau smiled. 'And some more of that coffee, if it's going. I feel better already.'

He glanced at the desk in the adjoining cabin. Signals, some dealt with, or for information only, not much mail; it would eventually catch up with them. One he recognized as a bill from Gieves, and he thought of the young seaman in the sickbay, staring at his new cap. But nothing else. What had he expected? A letter from Alison? It would have to be faced. She wanted a divorce and she would have it. Her father would see to that.

There was a tap at the door, Forward waiting to see him. He was smartly turned out in uniform, a far cry from the half-drowned creature they had dragged from the sea. Dark, hawkish features. Watchful, someone who never took things at face value.

'I just wanted to tell you, Forward. I am submitting your name for some kind of recognition. That was a brave, some people might say crazy thing you did, but you saved his life. I've just spoken to young Wishart myself.'

Forward showed a glimmer of surprise, but contained it. 'I'll bet that pleased him, sir. He wants to be an officer one day.'

Martineau rubbed his eyes. The hot shower was not enough after all.

'The way this war is going, it might be sooner than he thinks. And you can get your hook stitched up again. It will be in orders, but I thought you should know anyway.'

Forward stared at him. 'Thank you, sir. It'll stay there, this time.'

Tonkyn padded in, and Forward left the cabin.

Tonkyn did not properly understand his new captain, not yet. It might take longer with this one, he thought as he expertly refilled the cup. Most captains would have made a bee-line for the senior officer's ship, to grab all the glory, and would certainly not bother about one young seaman who had almost got himself drowned, and another who'd dipped his hook after a fight ashore. Everybody had looked up to and admired the previous commanding officer. Tonkyn had always had a good memory; you needed it in his work with so many light-fingered skates about. But, offhand, he could not recall the other captain doing anything for anybody. He gave a mournful smile. Except for himself.

He looked at the small pile of papers on the Captain's desk. Another big difference. The previous skipper always had a pile of letters waiting every time they came into harbour. Women, mostly; some used to put perfume on them. For all he had cared. He usually chucked them away.

He moved soundlessly around the cabin, and snatched up a telephone as it broke the stillness.

Martineau took it from him and said, 'Derby House. *Today.*' He half listened to the O.O.D.'s explanation, then replied, 'Arrange it, please.'

He looked at the coffee, thinking of the tanker they had helped to save. She would be unloaded by now, her precious cargo pumped ashore. Like her officers and crew, except for three who had died in the bombing attack, she would have a brief respite. Then off again, another convoy, and more U-Boats. And in Germany certain families would be getting those same telegrams, or whatever they sent over there. The bare, brutal facts. What would they think if they saw the real war at sea, the confirmation of *Hakka*'s kill? A few pieces of flotsam, a lot of fuel, and some oilskin coveralls, the kind watchkeepers wore in U-Boats, their only protection when cruising on the surface. Except that these coveralls had pieces of their owners still inside when *Hakka* had gone looking for evidence, the necessary confirmation required by their lordships.

He stood up, angry with himself.

'Good coffee.'

He strode from the cabin. The Captain again.

It was her third day at Liverpool when she was told that the Boss wanted her. It had all been such a rush since she had arrived at Derby House that looking back it was hard to separate the sequence of events, the names, and the faces.

Her first meeting with Commodore Dudley Raikes was something she would not forget. He was, she supposed, most people's idea of the typical naval officer, but she had been more aware of his energy than anything else, as if he could barely contain it, and she had yet to see him sitting down. He had been in a great hurry that day, and any idea she might have had that it was to impress or intimidate her was soon dispelled. He was, apparently, always like that. She had followed him around the various departments and had seen the reactions of those he spoke to; interrogated might be a better description. He always seemed to start off with *Where is . . . ?* or *Why is . . . ?* and *Why the bloody hell not?*

He was treated with great respect, even fear, and she guessed it was to prevent any kind of overconfidence or lack of vigilance.

He obviously took personal fitness very seriously, and, in his perfectly tailored uniform with its single broad ring, he looked the part. Lean and hard, as if all unnecessary surplus had been honed out of him. It had made her even more conscious of her own travel-worn appearance.

First Officer Crawford had tried to smooth the way for her, saying what an asset she would be for visiting Canadian commanders.

He had retorted sharply, 'I need a good and efficient staff, not hostesses!'

Despite all that, she had managed to settle in. Her room-mate was the signal traffic officer, a second officer like herself, named Caryl, who had been with Western Approaches for ten months. *It feels more like ten years!* She was a pretty, long-legged girl of about Anna's age, with very fair skin and short, bouncy curls, which she confided she had modelled on the style introduced by Ingrid Bergman in her first starring role.

Of Raikes she had said, 'Believe me, Anna, his bite *is* worse than his bark!'

She was good at her job. You went under very soon here if you weren't.

Commodore Special Support Groups was an imposing title, and she imagined Raikes was not the sort of officer who would tolerate any slackness from a subordinate which might endanger his own position. You had only to study the giant wall charts to grasp the enormity of the command. Convoys coming and going, escorts being ordered immediately back to sea when at any other time they would be allowed a breathing space for men and ships alike.

You had to concentrate on your own duties, and not be diverted by the harrowing signals, ships lost or sinking, help desperately needed, when there was little enough to offer. As Raikes had explained in his curt manner, 'With Nelson it was always a lack of frigates. With us, it's a lack of destroyers, ships fast and well-armed enough to go after the buggers! For months and months the cast-iron rule was, the speed of the convoy is the speed of the slowest ship in it. Rather like some of the brains in government, eh?' He had hurried on, pausing to stab his finger on a signal pad. 'Who did *this*? Find out and *see me*!' A man who took care over his appearance, who never looked as if he had just been called from his bed. Even his hair, which was completely grey, was neither long nor short, as if it never needed to be cut.

She had been there this morning when *Hakka* had come in, and once again had felt the excitement and pride all around her. Hundreds of Wrens, seamen and dockyard workers cheering their hearts out. It was difficult not to feel emotional about it, and she had found herself waving her hat with all the rest.

And so strange to see *Hakka* after all this time. A ship she had never laid eyes on, but one which had almost broken her heart.

Hakka was to be a part of one of the new support groups. Eventually these ships would go elsewhere, but the Atlantic was the key, perhaps to the whole future of the war.

She stopped outside the office and adjusted her hat. *I'm ready for you this time.*

'Here you are.' Raikes gestured to a chair. 'I'm just about finished with Nobby.'

Nobby was a paymaster-lieutenant who acted as the Commodore's secretary, obviously a demanding job. But she was still taken aback by Raikes's appearance. His cap was on his briefcase and his jacket slung on the back of a chair. Like another person. She glanced at the big desk, and the shelves that lined one wall. There were no photographs; like the room, there was no sense of permanence.

Raikes watched his secretary clipping some signals together. 'I've heard good things about you.' He looked at her directly. He had a clean-cut face, with lines at the corners of his mouth, caused either by strain or by some past humour, both of which he kept well under control.

He took the papers from the other man and stared at them. His eyes were pale, tawny. Like a tiger, she thought.

He said, 'Set it up, Nobby. I'll sign it.' He shook his head. '*No*, you do it, those fools won't know the difference!'

He turned to her again.

'We've got yet another fact-finding mission up from London. As if I don't have enough bumf to wade through.' He was watching her, so still that it was quite out of character. 'Your German and French are good, I'm told?' He did not wait for an answer. 'What we need, or will before much longer.' He reached out suddenly and adjusted a paperweight on the desk. There were, she noticed, no ashtrays. No weaknesses.

He came to a decision.

'The Atlantic war is in hand. Many of the past mistakes have been ironed out. At a cost. There was a strong belief at Admiralty that escort and support groups were interchangeable. They are not. The corvettes and sloops which make up the majority of escorts are too slow to catch a U-Boat once it is surfaced. And too slow to be moved with haste when a particular convoy is in danger of attack by wolf packs, as Dönitz calls them. Destroyers are kept hanging about with convoys crawling along at ten knots or less. This is where our new support groups will come into the picture. There is the Gap, that stretch of ocean which is at present beyond the reach of air cover. New bases and long-range bombers will settle that.'

Anna tried to relax, but it was impossible. In a few terse sentences this remote man had brought the panorama of sea warfare to life. Not mere flags and counters on a chart but ships, and submarines, hunters and hunted. And men.

'There are big plans in the offing.' He was moving again, his shadow leaning across the bare walls like a spectre. 'We shall be needing the most valuable cargo of all if we are to hold any hope of hitting back.' He gazed at her. 'Invading!'

'Troopships, sir?'

He nodded. 'Fast and safe. Where groups like ours will be of paramount importance.'

94

She wanted to push some hair from her forehead but she was afraid to break the spell. How different it sounded from the world she had abandoned when she left Canada to join the W.R.N.S. *Poor little Britain. Starved out and grateful for the food parcels and warm clothing.* Survival had been in doubt. Invasion had never been contemplated.

'I want you on my team.' His hand rose as if to deal with any protest or gratitude. 'It will be hard work, and I know I'm not easy to serve. If you can't keep up, you'll go back to general service, no shame in that.'

The door opened slightly. It was Nobby returning, and she realized she had not even noticed him leave the room.

'Yes?'

'The Admiral, sir. You told me to inform you . . .'

'Later!' He waited for the door to close and asked casually, 'Not engaged to be married, or anything? I'd surely have heard.'

'No, sir.'

'I see. Surprised.' He walked past her and adjusted some books. Somehow she had known that he was not going to touch her, not like one of the staff officers at Larne, who always leaned on your shoulder when he was *trying to help*, or made a handshake last just a little longer than necessary.

She said, 'I'd like to do it. Very much.'

He dragged his jacket from the chair and slipped into it without effort.

He said, 'Crawfie will fill you in. She's pretty genned up on the group.'

Anna licked her lips. *Crawfie.* She had learned a lot in a few minutes.

She heard herself say, 'I watched *Hakka* coming in this morning, sir.'

'Yes. I saw you down there, bright and early. I think that decided me. The team. It's vital.'

He picked up his cap and regarded it impassively. Commodore was a temporary appointment. If he was forced to step down, the same cap would serve him as a captain again. But a step up the ladder would be flag rank.

He said, '*Hakka*'s skipper is coming here shortly. Care to meet him?'

She looked at her hands. 'Later, perhaps, sir.'

'Quite. A bit of a goer to all accounts. He would be, of course, to ram a bloody German cruiser! You'll meet all of them before long.'

She had been unprepared for it, and had told herself she would never make a fool of herself again. Not for any man.

But the man she had just heard described was a stranger. Not the one who had shown such concern for her at the club in Plymouth.

Raikes snatched up a telephone after a single ring and snapped, 'What are you doing about it?' He waited, his eyes on the clock. 'Then *do it*!' He replaced it. 'Another mental pygmy!'

She heard voices and saw him indicate the other door. She went to it, and heard him say, 'I shall now speak to God!'

She walked through an outer office and did not see the Wren writer look up from her typewriter, assessing her. *The new one.*

She would write to her mother about it. Ask about Tim, too.

She stepped into another narrow tunnel and came face to face with him.

He stared at her and then a smile lit the austere features.

'Of all people! Here!'

She said quickly, 'It was supposed to be secret. I couldn't explain.' She saw the shadows around his eyes. 'We heard about the U-Boat. Watched you come in.'

He hesitated, and the eyes were troubled, uncertain. 'I thought . . . So many people. I'm not used to it.'

Doors were opening and slamming and she heard the urgent clatter of typewriters and teleprinters. Putting on a show for the Admiral, God, as Raikes had described him.

She thought of the moment when she had touched the crimson ribbon, and found herself hoping he would remember it too. It was stupid, and she had been warned. . . . Another door slammed. That would be the loyal Nobby fleeing before the great man entered.

He said, 'I'm glad you were there. Perhaps we might meet, have a drink . . .' His voice faltered. 'But I'm hardly in a position to . . .'

That look again, as she put her hand on his arm and said, 'I'd like that. Very much.' What she had said to Raikes. She smiled, unable to stop it.

They stood aside and a seaman carrying a tray of cups and plates pressed past them, his lips pursed in a silent whistle. The smallest glance. *All right for some*, it said.

He had removed his cap. Like the one Raikes had been examining. Not the naval commander, the hero, the *bit of a goer*. Suddenly he seemed much younger, as if the strain were momentarily at bay.

He said, 'I'd better go in. I'll call you.'

He paused, expecting her to make an excuse. When she had smiled at him just now, she had been the student in the photograph again.

She said something and walked away into the tunnel. He went up to the door which had been indicated at the security gate and raised his hand to knock, but something made him look back, and he saw that she was doing the same.

She was no longer smiling, but had extended her hand as if to offer it. Then she turned and was swallowed up by the tunnel.

Nothing lasted for long in wartime.

But he thought of the youth who had been snatched from the sea, his only anxiety that he might be moved away from the ship, and of the tough seaman who had just been reinstated to leading hand, who had gone to the youngster's aid without a second thought. And Fairfax, who had risked everything in his attempt to board the helpless tanker. To prove something to himself, *or to me*? Or to the previous captain who had been killed on that same bridge. A man who had somehow betrayed him, and the girl named Anna.

He pushed open the door. *It lasted*, given a chance.

97

7

A Special Day

Fairfax stepped into the Captain's day cabin, his eyes moving quickly around as if he still expected to see it changed, before settling on Martineau at the desk.

'I came as quickly as I could, sir.'

Beyond the door the tannoy squeaked into life yet again.

'Hands to tea, shift into night clothing. Libertymen fall in!'

It was four in the afternoon, but outside it was as black as a boot.

Martineau gestured to a chair.

'Everything all right?'

'Not many volunteers for a run ashore, sir. The glass is falling again. Bitter.'

Martineau thought of his day. Meeting people, explaining, deciding. Was it only this morning when they had entered port to the cheers of hundreds of men and women?

He decided not to delay matters.

'You spoke earlier about a Christmas party, Number One? And some leave for those still outstanding?'

Fairfax nodded. He did not need to be told; it was in the air, like the frost.

Martineau said, 'It's off, I'm afraid. Orders have been brought forward. We are required to leave in two days' time, in company with *Jester*, *Java* and *Kinsale*. You can look at the details later. I just wanted you to know that I'm as surprised as you are.' He smiled suddenly. 'Not much of a Christmas, though!' He thought of the one man who stood out in his mind. The Commodore, Dudley Raikes, who let nothing slip past him. Where many senior officers he had known would have accepted first impressions, Raikes left nothing open to chance. Even a casual conversation was more like a cross-examination than something to pass the time.

Raikes had been very aware of the risks.

'It will be something of an experiment, the success of which will carry more weight with Admiralty than a ton of written proposals. Four destroyers will meet and replace the other escorts for the last leg of the passage. St John's to Liverpool. Stopping for nothing.'

Martineau said, 'We're to escort several thousand troops, Canadians for the most part.' He saw the words hit their mark, Fairfax thinking of the hundred and one items a first lieutenant would have to deal with. He had met the other destroyer captains; one he already knew, the others would come to terms with it, the new faces, the unexpected change of orders. As Roger Kidd, *Hakka*'s bearded navigator, had remarked, nothing ever went according to plan.

Fairfax's open features did not conceal his surprise, even a touch of resentment.

Martineau said it for him. 'Captain (D) is remaining here with the other ships in case of contrary reports on enemy movements.' Lucky Bradshaw would at least have his Christmas in harbour. He thought of Raikes again, his contained and undramatic enthusiasm for the new support groups. He had leaned forward to brush a speck of something from his impeccable jacket as he had continued, 'These fast troop movements will be the springboard for invasion. Just think of it! Last year it was gloom and disaster everywhere. Singapore and Hong Kong snatched from us, ships and men lost when sensible planning might have prevented much of it. And now we're on the turn. North Africa, the Atlantic – where next? I was saying as much to a new member of my staff, Second Officer Roche. Bright girl – I believe you know her?'

So casually said. But there was nothing aimless about Raikes.

Martineau had replied, 'We did meet briefly.' He had seen the quick scrutiny, the apparent satisfaction. But it would not end there.

Raikes had parted with, 'Good show about that U-Boat. I'm glad you're with the group.'

Fairfax said ruefully, 'The new doc has come aboard, sir. I've got *him* settled in, at least.'

Martineau gestured to the cabinet.

'A gin, I think.'

He could almost feel Fairfax watching him as he opened the cabinet and took out the glasses, carefully arranged some time earlier by the sad-faced Tonkyn.

They drank in silence, the shipboard noises subdued, muffled.

The weather reports were not good. He would speak to the ship's company and explain the importance of this unexpected mission. Not planned especially to ruin their Christmas in harbour, when the whole of Liverpool would be trying to celebrate after three years of war. And not because their skipper had a thirst for glory, no matter what. His grip tightened on the glass. *If only they knew.*

He thought of the girl who had touched the crimson ribbon, and had looked at him as if she expected to see something different because of it. And what of Alison? How would she be passing her Christmas? He could almost hear her laugh.

Fairfax stood up. 'If you'll excuse me, sir. I have to check the men under punishment.' He forced a grin. 'Three.'

As he turned to leave Martineau asked, 'Can we get a shore telephone line?'

'Being half-leader hath its privileges, sir. I'll tell the O.O.D.'

Alone in his cabin again Martineau stared at the neat file of orders, his mind already probing at the speed and size of the ship and her cargo. *Ocean Monarch*, twenty thousand tons at least, a familiar name in the now unreal days of peace. Kidd would probably know her, as he had the giant tug *Goliath*. Fast, stopping for nothing, and the escorts would be expected to place themselves between the big passenger liner and any torpedo, should a U-Boat manage to break through the screen.

Zigzagging when necessary, the ships would also be in danger of collision. It was foremost in everyone's thoughts since the light cruiser *Curaçao* had been rammed and cut in half by the liner *Queen Mary* just two months back off Bloody Foreland while attempting a similar fast passage.

What must they have thought in those final seconds when the great bows had reared over them before smashing them into the depths?

He was in the quartermaster's lobby without really noticing he had left the cabin. Apart from one shaded light by the temporary telephone, and the dim blue police lamp outside by the brow, it was in darkness. He saw someone cover the red glow of a cigarette, and another figure move outside on to the open deck.

It seemed to take an eternity to get through. Clicks and bursts of static, hardly surprising when he considered all the electronic equipment he had seen there that afternoon.

A voice said sharply, 'Operations?' A woman, probably the senior Wren he recalled shaking hands with.

It was. 'This is First Officer Crawford, and I am afraid you cannot speak with any of my staff. In fact it is irregular . . .' She hesitated. 'Who is that, by the way?'

'Commander Martineau. I was hoping to speak with Second Officer Roche.'

'I'm afraid that's impossible. And in any case . . .'

He said, 'I told her I was going to call. I shall not be able to now.'

For a moment he thought she had hung up.

Then she said, 'I shall tell her you called, Commander Martineau.'

He replaced the handset. At Derby House they would know all about the change of orders. Security would take care of everything else.

Perhaps Anna had told them she did not wish to speak to him. It might even damage her relationship with the Commodore.

And what, after all, had he expected? That she would drop everything just to be with him, to listen to his problems, all on the strength of a surprise encounter? She had been hurt enough. She probably realized it now.

He saw that Fairfax was in the lobby.

101

'Surgeon Lieutenant Morrison is waiting to see you, sir.' He hesitated. 'I can put him off until tomorrow.'

'No. I'll see him now.' He had even forgotten the new doctor's name.

Fairfax was still there.

'I'm a good listener, sir, if it helps.'

Martineau touched his arm. 'Thanks. I'll remember that.' Fairfax would probably go aft and tell the others that their *iron captain* was cracking up, bomb-happy. At the same instant he somehow knew he would not.

It was little enough, but at that moment it was all he had.

Lieutenant Roger Kidd walked uncertainly into the bar and looked around with surprise. He had not even noticed the name of this small hotel when he had climbed out of the taxi. After the noise and bustle of Liverpool, the place seemed an unexpected haven. He should have known. All sailors knew. *You never go back.* Ship or place, it would never be as you remembered.

He was not even sure why he had gone to the old hotel where, in those almost forgotten days, you went to meet old friends from other ships when you were in port. Noise, laughter, swapping yarns, exaggerating or complaining about some ship's master or bullyboy mate, but deep down always grateful to have a job. One you thought you would never change.

The old hotel had been burned out; only the tall, Victorian shell was still standing, the blackened windows like dead eyes. Just another casualty of Liverpool's bombing, but to Kidd it had been like a bridge which had been destroyed. He had seen dozens of ships sunk, and had visited towns and cities battered by the strife of war. It troubled him that he should be so moved by it.

He could not recall what he had said to the taxi driver, only that the man had not tried to cheat him. He must have guessed he was not just another stranger, a sailor on a few hours' leave.

Like a different country. Birkenhead, across the water from the great sprawling city, the posh side, as they always called it in those days. Where officers of the merchant service bought houses for their eventual retirement from the sea, with still plenty to remind them of it.

The bar was empty, but there was a lively fire burning in the grate, a rare treat in wartime.

A small, wizened waiter appeared beside him as soon as he sat in one of the worn leather chairs.

'We'll be closing soon, sir.'

Kidd sighed. 'Anything to eat?'

The waiter shook his head sadly. 'The dining room's being fixed up for Christmas.'

Kidd heard the hammering for the first time.

'Well, what about a drink?'

The waiter glanced at the interwoven gold lace on Kidd's sleeve.

'You'll be off the convoys then?' Kidd said nothing. 'I'll see what I can do.'

Kidd considered it. A double Scotch would be just right, but ask for one and they'd probably call the police thinking you were a German spy who didn't know about the terrible shortage of whisky. Except for senior officers, of course.

He looked around the deserted bar. It would fill up at night, he thought, but he would be back aboard *Hakka* before then. There was another flap on; he could feel it. The Skipper had been with the top brass all day. Must be something. He stared at the lace on his sleeve, wondering what had moved the old waiter to change his mind.

That was another thing. He had read somewhere that more experienced R.N.R. officers were to be offered promotion, commands of their own. Not a Tribal maybe, but your own ship. He turned it over in his mind again. Why should it disturb him?

Had he still been in the merchant service, even with the old Roberts Line, he would have been looking for promotion. Had things not changed, he might have been a chief officer or first mate anyway.

He thought of the song the sailors sang to air their feelings.

> If it wasn't for the war,
> We'd be where we were before,
> Churchill, you bastard!

They had songs for just about everything.

But promotion now? Another half-stripe, maybe. He pictured the ship as he had seen her that morning, surrounded by other grey or dazzle-painted hulls, and yet so completely different. The same age as Captain (D)'s *Zouave*, a twin right down to the bunkside switches that cut your fingers, or the bridge ladder that tried to snare your sleeve in the middle of a storm.

And yet so different. But it took a sailor to appreciate that.

Number One could have gone, but he wanted *Hakka*. The kid, Wishart, who had nearly been drowned and could have easily been moved, had apparently pleaded with the Skipper to stay aboard. Trevor Morgan, the Chief, was like that too; God alone knew what Driscoll the gunnery officer thought about it. But even he was good at his job.

He thought about Martineau, and the uncanny instinct which was more than training and the bloody side of war he had endured. Like the drifting mine, and the U-Boat which he had somehow known was there. Enough to risk the tanker, and his own ship on the strength of it.

'I remember you liked a Scotch.'

He half lurched from the chair at the sound of a woman's voice, then stared at her hand pressing on his shoulder as she said, 'No. Sit down. Enjoy your drink.'

He sat, still staring at her. It was impossible, like time stopping. Even the hammering had ceased.

'Evie! I had no idea –'

She sat down opposite him, smiling at his confusion. Small, dark, and very attractive, exactly as he had remembered her, and yet changed in some way in the two years since they had last met. Assured, more mature. Perhaps that was it.

Evelyn Maddocks had begun her career as a nurse in Manchester, but had chosen instead the uncertain life of a stewardess with the old Roberts Line in Liverpool. That had been in the *Eritrea*, one of their passenger and cargo ships on the New York and South America run.

Kidd had always done what he could to make her happy aboard, and when he had left the ship to begin his naval reserve training he had realized that his true feelings went far deeper than that. But she had married the ship's purser, Chris Maddocks.

He asked awkwardly, 'What are you doing here?'

'I could ask the same of you.' She was studying his face, feature by feature. 'I own the place.'

It was always said that pursers owned most of the hotels in various seaports, using their ill-gotten gains from their years in service. Cruel, but supposedly true.

He said, 'Did Chris quit the sea?' He had been a good bit older than her. A lot older.

She dropped her eyes. 'He stayed on for one more trip. The *Eritrea*, same old ship.' She touched her breast as if to adjust a brooch and shrugged. 'I wanted to write to you. But I didn't know, you see. It would have been stupid, unfair.'

He gripped the arm of the chair. 'Malta convoy. Last year. I read about it. But I'd seen you and knew you were ashore. I never thought Chris would sign on again.' He reached out, but withdrew his hand, his mind blurred with events.

She said quietly, 'Where did you just come from, Roger?'

'The old Grand. I didn't know about that, either.'

She nodded slowly, then held out the glass. 'Drink this. To me, if you like.'

He tried to swallow it but almost choked. 'You've knocked me for six, Evie! You look marvellous!'

'Considering.'

'*Not* considering.'

She said, 'You're based here, I suppose? I know you can't answer, but secrets don't last long in this neck of the woods.'

'A destroyer, *Hakka*. I'm the navigator.'

She studied him as he raised his glass again, and did not miss the deep crow's-feet around the eyes, all the signs of strain. Big and clumsy, but she had seen his hands sketching the ships and buildings in ports he had visited. He had been a popular young officer aboard that old ship, especially with the passengers.

She came to a decision.

'Are you ashore for any length of time?'

He shook his head, suddenly ashamed of the grubby cuffs of his shirt, and his untidy beard.

'I think we're off again soon.'

She said, 'Have lunch with me. Now. We can talk. Have some wine.'

'What will people say, Evie?'

'Do you care?' She tossed her head, and even that was painful. She was that same girl again. 'Well, I don't!'

Then she stood up, suddenly and lightly.

'Say yes. It was no accident that brought you, so why not? We can talk about those times, about Chris too if you like. I miss him very much.' She saw him glance at the clock. 'And don't worry, I'll see you get back on time. Running a hotel has some perks!'

It was settled.

She led the way through to a small, private dining room. The table was already laid for two, and a bottle of wine stood in a silver cooler, clearly engraved with the old Roberts Line flag.

'Sit here.' She brushed past him, and paused. 'Is it bad, Roger? What it's done to you?'

He took her hand and pressed it to his mouth.

'Not any more.'

Everything else seemed very far away.

First Officer Deborah Crawford, *Crawfie* to a very few, clenched her jaws to stifle a yawn, and did not raise her eyes to the wall clock, although she guessed it must be nearly midnight. Another day. And tomorrow was Christmas Eve. There was not much sign of festivity in this office, not even a bunch of holly, although in the bustling main operations room she had seen some paper decorations amongst the maps and statistics, and a balloon with Hitler's face painted on it.

She looked over at the Commodore, who was speaking on one of the telephones, his voice crisp but unnaturally patient. It was a tone she had noticed that he adopted when he was talking to a subordinate he considered stupid.

A long day, and it had not been helped by a visit from Captain George 'Lucky' Bradshaw. She had not met him more than a few times, but disliked what she had seen. Full of booming good nature and bonhomie, Christmas spirit too. You could smell it across the room.

He had a great grin, as if his teeth were too large for his mouth, which reminded her of the big false teeth her father had made out of orange peel to amuse her when she was a child.

The Commodore had taken the wind out of his sails by telling him that the remainder of the group would be sent on combined exercises immediately after Christmas, and when they knew that the big troopship was within reach of full air and sea protection.

Bradshaw had snorted, 'Whose idea was this? My officers are already fully experienced in these matters!'

Raikes had replied mildly, 'The Admiral's. He *was* Flag Officer Submarines before he took over Western Approaches, remember? A pretty good submariner himself, to all accounts. So he's sending a submarine of his own choice to test your people. He does not take kindly to arguments.'

The grin had vanished.

Raikes slammed down the telephone.

'Call Security. Check if she's reported in.'

'I just called, sir. A few minutes ago.'

'Then do it again!'

She picked up the handset. He was worse than usual. Funny that she could never imagine working with or for anyone else. Life would be dull by comparison. Like this place, never still, or completely silent. All the doors were open to the harsh lights, as if he could not bear to be caged in. Other people took the war one step at a time, reverses one day, a triumph on another. Not the Commodore. To him the war was constant, personal.

She said, 'Duty officer says not yet, sir.'

'I want to know the instant she arrives.'

She watched him as he picked up the telephone again. This was another side, when she thought she knew them all. Hard, ruthless, dedicated. She recalled the telephone call she had taken two days ago, from *Hakka*'s captain. The quiet hero. She wondered what she had expected. Someone like Bradshaw? *God help us.*

Martineau had probably thought she was lying, but Second Officer Roche had been away from Liverpool with some files from Raikes for the Air Officer Commanding. She was due back now. She would be tired out. Like that first time.

The bell rattled again, and she saw Raikes cover his own telephone with his hand while he waited.

She said quietly, 'Duty officer, sir. She's just arrived. Car broke down.'

He removed his hand and snapped, 'I don't give a damn! *Do it*, and call me tomorrow!' He turned away and she saw him buttoning the top of his jacket.

She said, 'I can do it, sir. It *is* part of my job.'

'And *this* is my department! Ships, aircraft and men working like a machine. One faulty part, one weakness, and the whole structure is endangered!'

She said wearily, 'I know.'

Raikes walked past her and stared through the adjoining offices, the typewriters covered and silent.

He said, 'She has the makings of a good addition to the staff. The next months will be vital. I cannot afford to risk disruption caused by personal misfortunes.' He swung round on her suddenly, reading her thoughts. 'And not merely because it would reflect on *me*, be certain of that!'

She heard his secretary coughing loudly; it was the signal.

Afterwards, although she had no idea how long it was, she thought it had been like a badly rehearsed drama. Raikes very calm, so calm that it was unnatural. And herself, not knowing what to do with her hands, and the loyal Nobby hovering clumsily in the other doorway.

Only the girl seemed composed, her chestnut hair shining in the hard light, her eyes steady as she looked at them, first at Raikes and then at Crawford.

Raikes said, 'You'd better sit down,' and seemed, uncharacteristically, to falter. 'Anna, isn't it? I'm afraid I've got some bad news for you.'

She remained standing, shoulders braced, dark eyes unwavering.

Raikes continued in the same flat tone, 'I made a signal to the R.A.F. H.Q., but you'd already left, so you see . . .'

'It's my brother, isn't it?'

'I'm afraid so. His unit was moved to Cornwall. They were on some kind of exercise. There was a minefield . . .'

She clenched her fists and stared at the floor. 'Oh, my God, poor Tim!' She wanted to cry, to scream, anything, but nothing would come. Except the picture of his face when she had last seen him. When he had volunteered for the army, because the R.C.N. would not accept him. He had wanted to go, and she knew it was because of her, because she was leaving for England in her new uniform.

She knew that the other woman was standing close behind her. Expecting her to faint. To break down.

She heard herself ask, 'Do you know if he suffered?'

'It was instantaneous. There were three of them, all from the same unit.'

She thought of her parents, and her sister, who had married a Yank and moved to Boston where he worked.

Raikes said, 'Your family will have been informed by now. I heard because the local naval station is commanded by someone I know quite well.'

'Thank you.'

Because of me. And to die for nothing. In an accident. *For nothing.*

She clenched her fists again and felt the nails breaking the skin.

Raikes was saying, 'You will be excused duties until we can decide . . .' The far door opened and a petty officer with a telegraphist's insignia on his sleeve stopped abruptly as he sensed what he had interrupted. 'I said I was not to be disturbed!'

The telegraphist stammered, 'Sorry, sir.' But he was staring at Anna. 'It was the signal you were expecting, y' see, sir, an' I didn't think.' He began to back away, but Raikes snapped his fingers.

'As you *are* here!'

Like someone grasping at a lifeline; like those men she had heard about . . .

'Signal from *Hakka*, sir. *Have assumed position George Zebra.*'

Raikes took the clipboard and looked at it. So brief. But it told him everything.

He looked around, taken off guard as the girl said quietly, '*Hakka*?'

First Officer Crawford touched her arm. 'Her captain called you to explain. But you'd gone by then.' She found she did not care

109

about the Commodore's views on it; he probably knew in any case. Another revelation.

Anna looked at her hands and said, 'I'd like to see the big chart in Operations . . .' But instead, she sat down and cried.

Raikes made up his mind. 'I have to go to the Met Office, find out what's happening out there. Take this officer to her quarters.' He seemed to hesitate. 'There's some fine malt whisky in my office. Get it, Nobby.' He looked at the head bowed in grief, the older woman holding her like a protective lioness. 'Tomorrow's Christmas Eve.'

Nobby corrected gently, 'Today, sir.'

He knew he would never be able to see his superior in quite the same light again.

The motion was sickening.

Graham Martineau felt his stomach muscles tighten yet again as the ship beneath him seemed to pause, the bridge shaking to the vibration of the shafts, before sliding over into another trough.

The Atlantic. Not at its worst, but bad enough by any standards.

Conditions had deteriorated almost as soon as *Hakka* and her three consorts had cleared Liverpool, with the seas mounting and a wind across the quarter which made even the simplest task a test of endurance.

He felt the arm of the chair pressing into his ribs, then the steel back nudging him sharply. It was something you accepted in destroyers, but you never got used to it. The towel around his neck was sodden, and when he eased his body forward to peer at the radar repeater he could feel the rawness against his skin.

There would be quite a few of *Hakka*'s company suffering from seasickness, not that they would get much sympathy. As a young cadet aboard a training cruiser Martineau himself had known the first pangs of it, even though the sea had been relatively calm at the time.

Nelson was seasick whenever he went to sea, and still got the job done! So bloody well get on with it!

Dark shapes moved around the open bridge, and he heard the occasional mutter of voicepipes.

Driscoll had just taken over, and said in his clipped tones, 'Port Watch at defence stations, sir!'

Hakka was working watch-and-watch. Four hours on, four off. It was unlikely that the men who had just clambered to their positions throughout the ship had been able to dry or rest themselves during their time below.

The forenoon watch, again. Eight in the morning, but visibility was virtually unchanged: shades of grey, with glassy black walls to betray the next trough. *Jester* was abeam somewhere, the others following astern. But for the murky blips on the radar repeater they could have been quite alone on this vast desert of an ocean.

People ashore could never visualize its power, its brutal majesty, and the smallness of a ship as it challenged wind and weather. On the chart, a pin's head represented the maximum distance that any lookout could cover.

He looked at the repeater again. The unseen eye, without doubt the greatest step forward, the margin perhaps between survival and defeat, that sailors had ever known.

He thought of Lovatt, the senior radar operator, now an acting petty officer, who should be off watch, trying to find something warm to eat or drink, or to wear. But radar was a world of its own, and Lovatt knew the importance of the day, probably better than anyone. He was a slightly built, serious-faced man, who looked more like the schoolmaster he had been than a veteran of the Mediterranean and the Atlantic. You never even questioned it any more, although there had been plenty of regulars who had sniffed at the idea in the early days of war.

No more. Errand boys, bakers, shop assistants and postmen, they had all had to change with the rising demands of war.

He recalled the signal he had sent, massaging his eyes, and trying to clear his thoughts. *George Zebra*. Brevity of every signal was essential. But the Atlantic seemed to be theirs. No convoys, no stragglers, and no U-Boats. Yet.

He heard another fanny of cocoa coming into the bridge. Pusser's ki, they called it, so thick with hand-sliced cocoa and condensed milk that you could stand a spoon upright in it. It lined your ribs, the old hands insisted. Today it would be laced with rum.

111

He listened to the regular throb of engines. In these four weather-tossed destroyers the most important men were the chief engineer and the cook, in atrocious conditions like these.

But it *was* brighter. He groped for his binoculars, and saw faces turn to look at him. Faces which had been dark, featureless blobs before.

Then he saw *Jester*, on the starboard beam, heeling over to the ridge of water which had just passed under *Hakka*'s keel before rolling away into the unbroken curtain of spray. He could even make out the tiny patch of colour which was her tattered seagoing ensign.

He thought of Liverpool. They would somehow find time to celebrate, even with somebody like Raikes in control.

What would she be doing?

He slid from the rigid chair, and saw Fairfax and Ossie Pike, the chief boatswain's mate, their streaming faces only inches apart but shouting at one another as they peered up at the foremast, as if concerned about some intricate piece of weaponry. He felt his mouth crack. Which perhaps it was, in its own special way. It was a huge wreath, almost as large as a Carley float, which they had constructed out of wire and hand-painted leaves, as well as some real holly which somebody had found on that last run ashore. None of it would survive very long unless the wind eased, or they could turn into it again.

'Ki, sir?'

That was Sub-Lieutenant John Barlow, who shared this watch with Driscoll. *Hakka* was his first ship. Before joining the navy he had been a schoolboy.

He saw Kidd appear from the chart space, and recalled the officers' conference he had convened before leaving harbour. He had noticed a difference then in the bluff and usually outspoken navigator, and on the bridge as well. Not subdued, but introspective; maybe he was considering the A.F.O. which had mentioned the possible advancement of R.N.R. officers with his qualifications. He had noticed that Kidd had also somehow found time to trim his beard.

The new doctor had visited the bridge. Once. The passage from aft had been hazardous, with lifelines to prevent the unwary from

112

being swept overboard by the heavy quarter sea. Not so young as most ships' doctors, or *medical students dressed up as officers*, as Martineau had heard voiced often enough, he was a quietly spoken, withdrawn man, who had been serving aboard a fast fleet minelayer until he had requested a transfer.

Of the minelayer he had said only, 'All the hands were too fit to need a doctor. In that job, if things go wrong, a chaplain is far more use!' It would be interesting to see how Plonker Pryor got on with him.

He levelled his glasses again. How frail the other destroyer looked against the heaving grey backdrop.

He moved to the rear of the bridge and looked aft. Oilskinned figures were moving warily about the glistening deck, checking the boats, making sure they were snug against their davits, securing wires, dodging each torrent of spray.

At their stations, the gun crews took what cover they could behind the shields, but he saw a lot of faces defying the wind and spray and peering up at the bridge. The yeoman of signals, Onslow, was here as well, watching Pike's men to make sure that the great wreath did not foul the halyards or interfere with aerials or gunnery controls. And like the others, remembering, thinking of this day.

He could taste the rum in the cocoa now. Like that which had been forced between his teeth when he and a handful of others had been dragged from the sea. These men didn't ask for much for what they did, and what they saw. Like that curt signal, *George Zebra*. They had steamed another three hundred miles or so since then, to a pencilled cross on the chart somewhere to the south-west of Iceland. It meant nothing to most of them.

He reached out and felt Kidd put the speaker in his hand. *He would know.* He stared down at the crouching figures who had suddenly appeared as if to a pipe.

'This is the Captain.' He waited for the next crest to break over the side and surge past the torpedo tubes. In all his service it had never happened before, and yet he knew it had never mattered more. In peacetime, at sea or in port, the senior officers would wait on tables to serve their ratings, and afterwards everyone could play silly buggers to his heart's content.

There would be solemn prayers, and all the usual hymns. That was then.

He saw Fairfax and Midshipman Seton; even the boy Wishart who had been saved by the first lieutenant's and Forward's immediate action, was watching, his head still wrapped in a bandage.

There were other faces too, from another ship, men who had trusted him without question. *Firebrand*'s people.

He said, 'Christmas Day, lads. All I can offer you is a tot of rum and a soggy sandwich.' He looked at the sea, and sensed that Kidd had moved closer.

'What we are doing here is important, especially to those loved ones we are all thinking of today.' He could not go on. 'Hoist away, Number One!'

There were cheers as the makeshift wreath was hauled smartly to the masthead. There would be cheers too from *Jester* as she thrust into another barrier of bursting spray.

Kidd said, 'That was great, sir.'

Driscoll frowned. He did not understand what he had heard and witnessed. It did not go by the book.

Neither did he understand the man himself. An officer with a fine record, a coveted V.C. to prove it, and command of this first-class destroyer. With luck he should be promoted to full captain, further if the war went on much longer. He had no need to prove anything to these men.

Only Kidd really understood, because until a few days ago he had felt much the same as the Captain. Completely alone.

'Radar – Bridge!'

'*Bridge!*'

'Convoy and escort at three-one-zero. Range one-double-oh!'

Martineau said, 'Alter course, Pilot.'

Kidd strode to the voicepipes. 'Right on time, sir!'

Martineau smiled. *Just in time* would be closer to it.

8

No Better, No Worse

'New course to steer is one-two-zero degrees, sir.'

Fairfax lowered his binoculars and watched his breath fanning out like steam. It was bitterly cold; he could almost feel ice rime on the screen and bridge fittings. But the motion was easier, a deep, unbroken swell, without the savage rolls and plunges, and even the galley had managed to return to some sort of routine, producing tinned, square-shaped sausages and powdered potato. Bangers and mash, with a bit of imagination. And it was hot, too.

Fairfax watched as Martineau consulted the gyro repeater and walked a few paces to ease his legs.

It was strange to take orders from the ship you were escorting. But there were no chances with this one. The *Ocean Monarch* was a giant when set against her four lithe escorts, twenty-six thousand tons, with every foot packed with troops. There were apparently six thousand soldiers and their equipment inside that proud hull. Sardines. He had heard Kidd telling Midshipman Seton that *Ocean Monarch* had set several records as a passenger liner on the New Zealand and South African routes before the war. He could well believe it. Even the drab grey paint could not disguise her elegant lines and spacious superstructure. She had naval signalmen and a few gun crews aboard, but speed was her greatest defence, as well as a destroyer on either bow and another on each quarter, ready to respond to any signal, no matter what.

No one watching her could forget the tragedy only two months ago, when the *Queen Mary* had rammed and sunk her cruiser escort. The *Queen*, as Kidd had called her, was twice the size of this beauty, over eighty thousand tons. Nobody knew the full story; perhaps it would never be explained. Maybe the cruiser *Curaçao* had zigged when she should have zagged after the emergency report of a U-Boat. The liner had orders not to stop for anything, and both ships were making full speed at the time of the collision. Stories had filtered through of horrified soldiers aboard the *Queen* – she was said to have been carrying ten thousand of them, the largest number of people ever contained in a single ship – of how they had thrown rafts and lifebuoys, anything that would float as the great ship had surged over the broken *Curaçao*. Some soldiers had claimed they heard and felt nothing, only a slight tremor.

Fairfax wiped his face and turned to watch the liner, her huge stem smashing through the water with something like contempt.

Three hundred and thirty-eight men had perished that day. Less than a hundred of her company had been picked up. Fewer still would ever get over it.

He glanced at Martineau. How did he manage to keep going? He had scarcely left this bridge for more than minutes. *If I crashed down now I'd never wake up.* It was the routine that took it out of you. No alterations of course unless so ordered. Everything worked out to allow for any possibility. And no signals, only in those first minutes when the original escorts had handed over their massive charge.

There had been a few hasty Christmas greetings, and even the flashing signal lamps had seemed dangerous. The usual witty one from their senior officer: *We shall leave the easy part for the amateurs!* Someone had signalled, *Good luck!* Only to be answered curtly, *Actually, we rely on skill!*

Like hurried handshakes, people meeting in a busy street, not in this vast, hostile ocean.

Two more days. He peered at the sky, but there was nothing to see but solid cloud. And no horizon. Just a grey wilderness, and five ships.

Martineau said, 'Weather will be our best ally, Number One.'

Fairfax smiled. He was getting used to the uncanny way the Captain seemed to read his mind.

116

'It was like that on the Arctic runs – you had the choice. In good weather you had to follow the ice edge, up around Jan Mayen and Bear Island. It was quite a haul, with long-range bombers, surface units, all eager to have a bash at you. In the winter the ice closed in and the weather got worse.' His teeth bared in a grin on the stem of his unlit pipe. 'But at least it kept Jerry from bothering you too much.'

Fairfax saw him clench the gloved fingers of his other hand. Was that how it had been? The German cruiser, breaking the pattern to go after some helpless merchant ships?

One ship alone between the cruiser's captain and his prey. He glanced up at the masthead, where their wreath had finally been ripped to pieces by the wind. But not before the soldiers aboard *Ocean Monarch* had seen it. All Canadians, it said in orders. He was glad they had made the gesture.

Martineau said quietly, 'The cruiser was the *Lübeck*.'

Fairfax nodded, but said nothing, afraid to break the spell. Everybody knew about the *Lübeck*. It had made all the headlines, as had the earlier act of courage when *Glowworm* had rammed the cruiser *Hipper*, giving them back their pride after so many defeats. But *Glowworm*'s skipper, who had been awarded one of the war's first Victoria Crosses, had not lived to share it.

Lübeck was renowned for her gunnery; Fairfax had even been aboard her at one of the peacetime Spithead Reviews. Nine five-point-nines against Martineau's four smaller guns, all of which had been knocked out when he had charged to the attack.

Martineau raised his binoculars to study the liner, but somehow Fairfax knew he was not seeing it.

'I was at H.Q. before we left Liverpool. Derby House. Makes *Hakka* seem like yachting. Wouldn't do for me.' Then he turned and looked at him directly. Like that moment on this same bridge when *Grebe* had been mined. 'The Commodore showed me some R.A.F. reports. *Lübeck* was in Norway, Trondheim, for a while, undergoing repairs.' He removed the pipe from his mouth and studied it. 'She's not there any more.'

Fairfax said, 'Perhaps there was nothing more they could do, sir.'

'They *did it*, all right. She's probably at sea at this very moment.'

He thrust the pipe into his pocket and added abruptly, 'It's hard to take, for me, that is. All those men.'

'Preparative, sir. Alteration of course!'

Fairfax turned. 'Stand by. Warn the wheelhouse and fetch Pilot. He's in the chart room.'

He noted the diamond-bright eye winking from the high-sided liner, the acknowledgements from the escorts. He could almost see the chart in his mind, and imagined the one at Derby House. And that had been in Martineau's thoughts ever since. At the officers' conference, after he had come offshore for the last time. When he had tried to telephone somebody. And when he had spoken to *Hakka*'s people on Christmas morning.

All those men. It was like stumbling on someone's secret. Or guilt.

'Course to steer is zero-seven-zero.'

Fairfax moved to the voicepipes even as Kidd clambered up from the chart room.

Martineau said, 'No. I'll take her, Jamie.' Then he smiled a little. 'You *are* a good listener.'

'Port ten.' He glanced quickly at the ticking gyro, and then across the salt-patterned screen as the great ship began to turn. 'Increase to fifteen.' His mind barely recorded the quartermaster's voice but he saw Forward's face, when he had told him about his rerating as leading hand and of the recommendation for a medal for his part aboard the tanker, and saving Wishart's life.

'Midships.' He felt the compass quivering under his hands, the whole ship responding. 'Steady!'

'Steady, sir. Zero-seven-five.'

'Steer zero-seven-zero.' He straightened his back and stared at the liner. As before, as if they had never shifted.

East-north-east. He said, 'Go round the short-range weapons, Number One.'

He tugged down the peak of his cap to stare at the clouds. Something made Fairfax hesitate at the bridge gate. 'Can't rely on air cover this time, or anything else, for that matter.' He stared at

118

the deep swell, a garland of gulls riding over it, like a wreath, he thought. 'There's only us. Tell them that, will you?'

He climbed back into his chair. The waiting was almost done.

As in other destroyers, the ratings' messdecks were situated in the forepart of the hull, and to any landsman or casual visitor they would appear exactly the same, with no thought for comfort or privacy.

Number Nine Mess was no exception, a long scrubbed table clipped to the deck, with a bench seat along the inboard side. Opposite, and curved to fit the great flare of the hull, were lockers which also acted as seats, and as bunks for off-watch hands who were lucky to find enough space to lie down. Hammocks were not slung at sea. They impeded movement, and would prevent men escaping by way of the solitary deckhead hatch if the worst happened.

At the head of the table was the mess cupboard, where all the 'traps' were stored in racks. Plates, cups, knives and forks, and a roll of oilcloth to use as a tablecloth when the occupants were having a meal.

But exactly the same? That was a joke to the men who lived here. They yarned and argued, wrote letters and compared photographs of families and girlfriends, and woe betide anyone who disgraced the mess by untidiness or offensive behaviour.

Three other messes shared this space in *Hakka*'s forecastle, but you would scarcely have known it. The identity of each one was completely different.

Ian Wishart, the young seaman, sat at one end of the table, resting his chin in the palm of his hand while he wrote a letter to his parents. It was hard to describe this place, and how he lived and worked with these characters who were lounging around him. Some were dozing, and one two-badge seaman was squinting with concentration while he darned a sock, indifferent to the occasional lurch of the hull, the boom of the sea as it thundered along the side.

He gingerly touched the bandage on his forehead. Even that had given him something. The others had offered him sippers of rum; one had washed out his overalls for him. Perhaps he would never be completely accepted in their world of coarse, often brutal humour and toughness, but he knew he would miss them, if and when he was sent to the officers' training establishment.

He sat recalling the rescue, how he had felt Forward holding him above the waves, the line, fired out of nowhere, being fastened around his shoulders.

Nobody here had made a big thing of it. He smiled to himself. Almost as if he had become the mess mascot.

But to describe it to his mother and father in Surbiton?

His father was assistant manager at the local bank where he had worked all his life, since he had been discharged from the army at the end of the first war. A quiet man, firm but always reasonable. *Not the sort who would ever manage his own branch*, he had overheard his grandmother say. And he never spoke about the war, although he had served in Flanders with the county regiment. Once a year, that was all. He would put on his dark overcoat with its poppy and his medals and he would join some of the others at the war memorial. Local again. It had always touched Wishart. Creepy in a way: on the stroke of eleven all the traffic would stop, bus and tram drivers step down and stand in silence. Most of them wore their medals too. One year Wishart had discovered his mother crying. She had lost two brothers on the Somme.

The clock chimed, somebody might even sound the Last Post, and then life would restart. As his father had remarked softly, 'For the lucky ones.'

He stared up at the circular hatch. Forward had told him when he had joined the mess, 'When the alarm goes, you drop everything and fly!'

The first time it had happened, it had been an exercise when they had left harbour. Some of the old hands were quite plump, and awkward, or so he had thought. But when the alarm had shattered the silence he had found himself almost the last one to reach the ladder. He had learned a lot since then.

They were working watch-and-watch, so that the next would be the First Dog at four o'clock. Only two hours this time, then back here for something to eat. He would be on the bridge, helping the navigating officer. *Sharpening the pencils.* A rather fierce-looking individual, he had once thought, but Kidd was never too busy to explain some aspect of the charts, or the corrections required almost daily to navigational statistics.

Midshipman Scton was all right, but he rarely shared his thoughts. He looked so good in his uniform with its white patches . . . a regular officer, too. What more could anyone want?

He had confided as much to Bob Forward, who had merely grinned and said, 'Scared of his own shadow, that one!'

'Then why. . . ?'

Forward had frowned. ''Cause his dad's an admiral. It's what *he* wants, see?'

It was strange that Forward never wrote to his girlfriend, although he had seen him looking at her photograph a couple of times. But he could not ask him. It might spoil things. Maybe later on . . .

The tannoy crackled. 'All the Port Watch. Port Watch to defence stations!'

Some men reached for their oilskins, or paused to fold a letter or hang a pair of dhobied seaboot stockings on a warm pipe to dry out.

Wishart climbed up to the outer darkness, his feet no longer missing a rung, and without the first panic when he had thought he had lost his way. He would finish it when the watch stood down. *Dear Mother and Father, This is a fast escort job.* He shook his head. The censor would have something to say about that.

In the wheelhouse, it was as if they had never left the place. Leading Seaman Bob Forward took over the helm and repeated the course and revolutions to the chief quartermaster who was stepping down. He then called the forebridge and reported his presence to the O.O.W. Snotty Driscoll again, with his affected drawl and constant moaning about something or other.

Forward nodded to the two telegraphsmen and a boatswain's mate and smiled at Wishart, who was collecting some papers for the navigating officer. He had seen him writing his letter; he seemed to write one every day.

He thought of the one his own mother had sent him, because someone at the railway's head office had at last decided to write an obituary for his father.

He watched the gyro repeater, the tape ticking this way and that.

He would have to be bloody careful. A few degrees off course and that bloody great liner pounding along just abeam of them would be joining them in the messdeck.

But he should have known. Guessed. Something . . . Like that time in the pub, when he had taken the pongo's newspaper. It was right there in the paper his mother had sent him.

Yesterday, police reported that they had released the man suspected of being connected with the murder of Grace Marlow at her address in Chelsea.

He gripped the spokes more tightly. At least they had not openly called her a tom in that report. It would die down after this. And anyway, there was nothing to connect him with it.

The voicepipe snapped, 'Quartermaster! Watch your steering.'

'Aye, sir.' Bloody little prat.

He wondered who the man was, if he had been one of her regulars.

Why should he care? Anybody else, and . . .

Lieutenant Kidd strode through the wheelhouse and paused at the plot table.

'Got 'em?'

Wishart nodded. 'All but the last one, sir.'

He stood aside as Kidd hurried on. Curt. Angry about something. It was not like him.

Kidd slammed into the chart room and laid out the papers. The motion seemed worse in here, with all the usual smells, oil, damp, sweat.

Another full day and then the cavalry should be with them for the final approach. It would be a miracle if they saw another ship, let alone the Brylcreem Boys of the R.A.F.

He pressed both hands on the table and stared at them. Something would happen soon, or not at all. There had been only one U-Boat report from the Admiralty. Probably one had surfaced to send a signal to its own high command. No submarine could hope to keep pace with this group, not even surfaced. The final approach to the north-west coast of Ireland would be the most likely place.

He clenched his fists. It was no good. He kept thinking of it, or her, the way she had looked at him when he had kissed her hand in that quiet room. She had asked almost abruptly, 'How long do you have?'

He had tried to brush it aside. It was bad luck to talk about sailing times. Like walking to the end of a pier.

But she had insisted, 'You might never have come here. I might never have seen you again.' She had gripped his hand between hers and pressed it to her breast. 'You know that, Roger. It was meant.'

He had stood up slowly, holding her gently at first as if he had been afraid of breaking something. That he had misunderstood.

'You want me, don't you?' She had been unable to sustain it and had pressed her face into his chest. He had forgotten how slight she was. Until then. 'Then let's not waste it. Do it!'

The rest had been like a wild dream. He did not even recall how they had reached the other room, or what it had looked like.

It had been with him ever since, like guilt, like ecstasy. That final moment when she had lain there, looking up at him, her body twisting from side to side.

'It's been so long. Don't stop. No matter what I say, what I do!'

She had cried out when he had entered her, but afterwards there had been only peace. Like nothing he had ever known.

She had called for a car from somewhere while he had struggled into his uniform again. She had even wrapped a bottle of wine in a towel for him, the one which had been waiting in the cooler with the company crest. Like the meal, untouched.

It was all he could think of. The future, something they had sworn never to do. In this regiment, the future was the length of the next watch, maybe less. It had been so easily said, then. Not any more.

And he still didn't know the name of the little hotel, the one old Chris the purser had bought for her before he had gone back to sea for the last voyage; and it had been the last for many on that terrible Malta convoy.

He sighed and opened his much-thumbed notebook. *Don't make a bigger fool of yourself. This is your world.*

He half listened to the muted ping of the Asdic, the occasional stammer of static from the W/T office beneath his feet. *My world.* And if he survived, what would there be when it was all over?

He picked up a pencil and looked at its point. He would have to apologize to Wishart for biting his head off just now.

And would she still feel the same when she had had time to think about it?

He thought of her hand at the hotel window when the hire car had pulled away. Just the hand, small and pale; she had not even had time to get dressed. She might regret the sudden impulse, the need which they had both recognized.

He leaned over the chart once more. *It's up to me then, isn't it?*

The stark clamour of alarm bells shattered the stillness, froze the mind like a seizure.

'Action stations! Action stations!'

Like most of them, Kidd had heard it a thousand times. But as he snatched up his binoculars and took a quick look around the compartment, he was conscious of something new. It was fear.

'Ship at action stations, sir.' Fairfax peered around the open bridge, identifying each figure more by stance and position than visual recognition.

Martineau was standing on the starboard side gratings, his glasses trained on the massive grey outline on the quarter.

He said, '*Jester* got a radar contact. About eleven miles, up to the nor'-east. Pretty good in this weather.'

Fairfax joined him, and heard Kidd dragging the hood over the bridge chart table. Martineau sounded calm, he thought, almost unconcerned.

'Sub on the surface. Big one, I'd say. Trying to work round our line of advance.'

A boatswain's mate looked up from a voicepipe. 'Lost contact, sir.'

'Dived.'

Fairfax glanced at the luminous gyro. The course had hardly changed.

The first definite contact. Maybe the U-Boat commander had surfaced to take advantage of the extra speed, or to send off a signal to his base. Or perhaps it was mere coincidence.

Martineau moved his glasses slowly. 'Tell the yeoman to make sure his men keep their eyes open for *all* signals. Anything.'

124

'*Jester* requests permission to intercept, sir!'

Martineau shook his head. '*Denied*. At that range they'd lose it anyway, and *Ocean Monarch*'s starboard bow would be wide open.'

'Alter course, sir! Steer zero-one-zero.'

'Port ten.' Martineau saw the pale grey shape start to turn, only the height of her bow wave betraying her power and speed.

'Midships. Steady. Steer zero-one-zero.' He scarcely heard the coxswain's replies. Spicer was on the wheel. He needed no second order.

Jester's skipper was probably cursing him, but it was too great a risk. Unless the U-Boat had surfaced again, the chance of getting an Asdic contact was minimal at that range.

He heard the click of metal from B Gun mounting forward of the bridge. He could imagine the language down there. Probably itching to loose off a few shells, if only to break the discomfort and boredom of playing at sheepdog.

He thought of the soldiers over that black strip of water, half a cable away. How did they feel now, he wondered. Days of altering course, eating and sleeping as best they could, not even understanding what was happening. Knowing only that they were the prime target, and had been all the way from Newfoundland.

Martineau could remember a convoy on that same route, U-Boats surfacing at night to overtake the slow-moving merchant-men, creating havoc as they chose. Only a handful of ships had reached England.

He took a quick bearing on the *Ocean Monarch*. As before. And she was making a good twenty knots without even trying.

He had snatched a few minutes to go down to his sea cabin, his ears pricked the whole time for a call or some unforeseen emergency.

Even so, he had paused long enough to pull open a drawer and remove the book, and had seen her face looking up at him. As she had done at the officers' club and at Derby House when they had almost collided in the bomb-proof corridor.

He used to have a picture of Alison in a silver frame. He could remember when she had visited the ship, and had laughed about it. *Still got that old thing?*

He tensed; that must have been when she had first met Mike Loring.

They had got on well from the beginning. Loring was always good company, interesting, witty. . . . Strange that when he recalled the last time he had seen him in hospital, a man already dead but refusing to accept it, he could feel no anger or bitterness.

He moved to the opposite side, past duffle coats and figures in oilskins, people he had come to know by sight and by name. Something he had wanted to avoid, although he had known from the start that it would be impossible. Like the Wren who had driven him to Parkestone Quay to join the ship. This ship. *He was my brother. He was killed that day.*

Jester's U-Boat . . . there might be others. One would be enough. *And if a torpedo heads for* Ocean Monarch *we must stop it.*

He was killed that day.

Kidd said, 'My God, there's a star!'

Martineau gripped his steel chair and swung round to search the full-bellied clouds, just in time to see it. One tiny star. Like those you saw when you were watchkeeping on some far-off sea. In peacetime . . .

Kidd had gone back to his chart again. He would know better than most. The forecasts were never very reliable. In mid-Atlantic it did not matter so much. But by dawn, the sky could be clear. And the planes would be ready. Theirs, ours, it was still a gamble.

He caught the scent of peppermint and guessed it was the young, baby-faced signalman named Slade. He had seen Onslow the chief yeoman watching him on occasion, perhaps seeing the son who had died at *Ganges*.

He ran his hand along the steel plating, feeling the cold through his glove. No better, no worse than any ship's company. Not here from choice, or even out of ambition, but held together by something stronger than any of them would admit.

He felt the steel shudder as *Hakka*'s raked stem ploughed into another trough, heard the rattle of bridge fittings as she rose above it. *Our ship.*

He gazed at the sky once more, but the star had gone, and nodded, as if someone had spoken.

And we are ready.

She awoke in an instant, aware of the hand cold and hard on her shoulder, gripping it, touching the skin, as if to restrain her.

She twisted round, the blanket caught in her legs, ready to scream, to . . .

'Easy, girl. You must have been having a bad dream.'

Anna was suddenly conscious of the shaded flashlight, the glint of buttons, the slow release of the hand.

She had been in a deep sleep, the first since she had heard about her brother. She reached out, fumbling for the bedside lamp, aware of her heart pounding in her breast against the pillow.

It was First Officer Crawford, whose hand had frozen a scream as the memory had flooded back.

'There's a flap on.' Crawford raised one hand. 'Easy does it. You are excused duties. But I thought I should come myself.'

Anna was fully awake now, and her throat felt raw. Some of that malt whisky the Commodore had prescribed, and she was not used to it. She winced. Or ever would be.

She sat up and put her feet on the floor, pulling her pyjamas across her body.

'Tell me.'

Crawford studied her impassively. 'In this work we know too much, hear too much. We must never forget all those out there who are depending on our absolute reliability.' She waved her hand vaguely, as if to encompass the whole of the Western Ocean. 'Dedication.'

She walked to the blackout shutter across the window and adjusted it, although it did not need it. She said, 'When I was at college I took up fencing. It taught me a lot about other people's reactions, strengths or otherwise. That's how it is up here. Hate and revenge are no longer enough. Perhaps they never were. The enemy gets a new weapon, then we have to discover countermeasures. It never stops, and the men who are doing the fighting need all the help they can get, everything we can give them.'

'I won't crack up, if that's what you mean.'

Crawfie looked at her and smiled. Anna had not realized before what fine eyes she had. Like someone else looking out.

'I know that. I just wanted you to know what it demands. I wanted it all, just like most girls. My brother was lost in *Repulse*, and the man I hoped to marry was shot down during the Crete fiasco. Now, all I want to do is *win*.'

Anna started to get dressed. The bedside clock said four in the morning.

'Take your time. Always look your best. Set an example.' She took out a cigarette case and lit one.

She said, 'You've got a nice body. Don't waste it.'

Anna peered at herself in the mirror. Cracked, like the one at Plymouth. *The war, you know*. They always used it as an excuse in England.

She said, 'Thanks for what you did. I won't forget.'

Crawfie shrugged. 'You'll get letters from home soon. Then you'll have to go through it all over again.' She turned her head, listening to the jangle of bells in the street, police, fire, ambulance; it could be all three in Liverpool.

'The Boss would get you sent back to Canada.' She watched her reflection in the glass. 'No half-measures with our commodore.'

Anna turned and faced her. 'I want to be part of this. It's what I've been trained for, what I can do.'

The other woman nodded, and then looked round for an ashtray.

'So be it. Join me down at Operations.' She saw the sudden understanding and was moved by it, and a little surprised at herself. After Crete . . .

'It will be today. Or not at all. That's why it's so important.'

The door closed and Anna stared at the other bed, where her friend with the Ingrid Bergman hairstyle slept. She had been sent to the anti-submarine exercise area, and would be back tomorrow. She looked at her reflection again, into her own eyes. She had to get herself through it. It was something that was happening every day, every hour: letter, telegram or word of mouth from 'people who knew people', like Commodore Raikes.

Nothing could bring Tim back. Crawfie was right about the letters. She could imagine what it would do to her mother, and her father too. And she had not told them anything about Paul's death aboard *Hakka*. It had been through her father that they had been

128

introduced, when Paul had been on some exchange visit with the R.C.N.

Paul. She thought of the hand on her shoulder, and the dream. She reached for her hat. *This is all I want now. All I need.* She looked at herself again, and tried to ignore the lie.

9

Win One ... Lose One

First light, always the most testing time in any Atlantic convoy. And worst of all was the knowledge that it was almost over, with thoughts of a safe harbour, doing ordinary things, pushing your nerves back from the edge, within reach.

Tempers flared because of an unnecessary sound; there was resentment at any seemingly superfluous order.

Martineau could feel it all around him, below the bridge, throughout his command. In the engine and boiler rooms, where the mind could play tricks at the slightest change of note in the racing shafts. The curved hull, picturing the torpedo transforming that whole section into hell. In the sickbay and emergency first aid stations, the damage control parties, crouching, staring at nothing, drained by the cold and the lack of something hot to drink when they most needed it. And up at the gun positions, the short-range Oerlikon and pom-poms as well as the main armament, the crews rubbed their salt-reddened eyes and waited.

Martineau looked at the sky directly ahead of the ship. The heavy clouds had gone and the light was hard and bright, like molten pewter. There was no sun, only a glare from horizon to horizon.

A pencil clattered from the chart space, and Findlay the leading signalman turned, his face contorted with anger. And he was an old hand, experienced. Kidd was wiping his binoculars; he had forgotten how many times. He wanted to stretch, to yawn out loud, but knew it was dangerous. Men yawned when they were apprehensive. Afraid. He tried to push it aside, but recalled what she had said to him. *Is it bad, Roger? What it's done to you?*

He had never allowed himself to consider it before. You put up with it. You survived. You drank too much afterwards. *Afterwards.*

Perhaps that was it. He had not weighed the chances, because there was no one in his life to worry about. To love.

He thought of Fairfax, down there in the T/S, the ship's nerve centre which could, if necessary, control the guns and torpedoes and just about everything else. Fairfax was a good friend and an experienced officer. He would be ready to take over command if the bridge was destroyed. He could remember how they had discussed the advantages and the folly of becoming involved with someone, let alone getting married. *We all agreed.* He glanced at Martineau by the gyro compass. Like his predecessor. *Too chancy in wartime.* Kidd had heard rumours about him since he had died here, and he had seen the hurt on Fairfax's open features.

He looked at the Captain again. His wife had left him. He stifled the yawn angrily. Better to end it before it got serious.

He turned away. It already *was* serious.

'Radar – Bridge!'

What everyone expected, but it was still a shock.

'Bridge. Captain speaking.'

'Aircraft. Bearing three-two-zero. Range two-double-oh. Closing.' The voice was very calm and unhurried, as if addressing a mathematics class.

'Start tracking.' Martineau raised his glasses and adjusted them with care. The glare was almost painful. Twenty thousand yards: ten miles. Before radar it would have been far beyond the limits of a man's eyesight.

Hakka was on the port bow of the formation. The aircraft had probably circled round to make a careful approach.

He heard the rattle of orders, and saw the muzzles of the guns below the bridge swing to port, lifting in unison as if to sniff at the danger. Maybe it was Coastal Command. In his heart he knew otherwise. Four destroyers, with the great liner steering between them, even bigger now in the metallic glare. The U-Boat, and now an aircraft, when there was little time or space left to make a wide alteration of course.

'Signal the group to keep close station *at all times*.' Unnecessary, when they were all professionals? He bit on the stem of his pipe. *No chances*.

'All guns follow Director.' That was Driscoll. He sounded wide awake.

'Aircraft! Red four-five! Angle of sight three-oh! Closing!'

Martineau held his breath and steadied his glasses while he waited for the ship to lift over a long, unbroken roller.

Then he saw it, and held it in the lenses as the ranges and bearings chattered all around him. A big aircraft. One of their long-range Focke-Wulf reconnaissance bombers which had proved so effective in locating and shadowing convoys while they wirelessed information for the U-Boat packs. Usually they kept out of range, and flew around a convoy until support arrived. This crew had probably enjoyed a hot breakfast in France while *Hakka* had been reeling about trying to keep station on her charge. He watched the glistening shape shorten suddenly, and heard the nearest bridge lookout call, 'Approach angle zero!'

Kidd said, 'What the hell does he hope to do?'

The gunnery speaker intoned, 'A, B, X, Y, *load*, *load*, *load*!'

Martineau stared over the screen and aft along the deserted deck. Only the slender muzzles of the anti-aircraft weapons moved, and further still he saw the other guns of the main armament following their instructions. The Tribals were different from other destroyers in that they had mounted extra guns at the expense of one set of torpedo tubes. Martineau had not seen the sense of it when he had first studied the details of this class of ship. But like others in the 'trade', he had too often watched torpedoes being used on their own ships to prevent their capture after they had been rendered useless in an attack.

Once, he had picked up survivors of such a destroyer off the Norwegian coast. The other ship's captain had been one of them. Martineau had seen his face when he had ordered the torpedo to be fired. It could have been his own.

'Still closing, sir!'

Martineau said, 'Signal *Ocean Monarch*. *I am taking station*

132

ahead of you.' He ignored the clatter of the light and added, 'Warn the Chief. Full ahead, then tell *Kinsale* to assume our station immediately.' He looked around, picturing the four destroyers and their arc of fire. *Ocean Monarch* could supply some flak, but not enough.

He felt the bridge jerk violently as the revolutions mounted, with the sea boiling away astern in a dirty yellow furrow.

He looked again. The aircraft had turned very slightly, and he could see the light glinting on its perspex and fittings.

Too big. It was not built for this sort of thing.

The pilot would know. *As I did.* No alternative. Hit the target. Others will finish the job.

He gripped the back of his chair; it was shaking.

'Open fire!'

'Barrage! Commence, commence, commence!'

The four-point-seven guns recoiled immediately, the smoke swept away even as the next shells were slammed into their breeches.

And it was still coming. Martineau wanted to wipe his glasses but dared not lower them. The four shining arcs of the bomber's props; it had turned very slightly. He saw smoke spurting past it, then long snaking lines of bright green tracer. Other shells too, bursting like stars, drawing together, closer and closer, but the bomber seemed unstoppable. It was planing down in a steep descent, the bay doors open, a machine-gun firing from somewhere, its tracer apparently unaimed.

'Got the bastard!'

Martineau saw pieces of the aircraft peel back from the nose, fragments spinning away as more shells bracketed and held on to the range and bearing. He saw the bombs falling like chips of ice while the Focke-Wulf continued its approach, heard the scream of engines, and imagined he could feel the great shadow as it tore over the ship, pursued by cannon shell with even the pom-poms joining in.

Then came the explosion, muffled and solid, like a depth charge exploding prematurely.

He gripped the screen and shouted, 'Did they hit her?'

133

But the bomber had already ploughed into the sea, a mile clear of *Java*'s starboard quarter. Kidd said thickly, 'It's *Kinsale*, sir!'

Martineau stared as the destroyer began to heel over, smoke and flames suddenly erupting from her deck, when seconds earlier she had been speeding to take her position on *Ocean Monarch*'s port bow. Where *Hakka* had been before the German pilot had made his suicidal attack.

Suicide? Or were more aircraft already heading to this position?

'Resume station, Pilot.' He raised his glasses and watched the *Ocean Monarch*'s huge bow wave surge away from the stem, washing against and over the listing hull of the *Kinsale*. He moved the glasses again and saw a mass of khaki figures crowding the liner's guardrails, some turning to look up at the boat deck as a solitary figure in kilt and bonnet started to play the bagpipes. It was something they had seen every day, even in foul weather: the lone piper, the soldiers waving, the sailors making jokes about it.

Leading Signalman Findlay, who came from Edinburgh, said quietly, 'A lament. And rightly so.' Then, surprisingly, he saluted.

Midshipman Seton gasped, 'My God, that was terrible!'

Kidd seized his arm and held out his own binoculars. 'Take a good look, *Mister* Seton, and don't forget it. They're not just people back there! They're me and you, see?'

When he looked back once more, Martineau saw nothing to mark what had happened. No smoke, no wreckage, although at this speed there would have been little enough. A destroyer, newer and slightly smaller than *Hakka*, had vanished. How many of her one hundred and eighty men had lived long enough to see their only hope holding formation at full speed? The bombs had been meant for the liner; one hit would not have crippled her, but it might have slowed her down, or left her drifting helplessly like the big tanker, until the wolves had come for her. But one bomb was more than enough for *Kinsale*. Moving and turning at speed to obey the last order, she must have been torn apart by the explosion. Ready-use ammunition, fuel, a magazine, it could have been anything.

They could not stop to search for survivors; it would put them all at risk. It was not a matter of conscience or even duty, it was a total responsibility.

Tell them that.

And the German pilot would never know how close he had been to achieving the impossible with such a large aircraft. He had probably been dead before he had smashed into the sea.

Martineau said, 'My compliments to the first lieutenant. Tell him to stand down action stations, but to keep the hands at quarters. Have the galley send some tea and sandwiches around the ship.' He heard a boatswain's mate passing his orders, probably wondering how anybody could so callously discuss routine when some of their own had just died.

He climbed on to his chair and stared at the bright expanse of water across the port bow where he had first seen the bomber. By so doing he could exclude *Jester*, and the great bulk of the *Ocean Monarch*. It was like having the sea to yourself. Empty. Clean. He felt for the pipe in his pocket but his fingers scraped on the broken pieces. Clean? It would never be that.

An hour later more aircraft were reported, but they soon proved to be friendly, a giant Sunderland and two Catalinas of Coastal Command.

The soldiers lining the *Ocean Monarch*'s rails waved and cheered, the sound blurred by the roar of fans. On *Hakka*'s deck there was only silence.

Fairfax arrived on the bridge and stared up as one of the awkward-looking flying boats roared over the ships.

'We felt it down there, sir. Thought they'd hit the trooper.' He watched Martineau. 'I've learned a lot since . . . well, ever since you took command.'

Martineau dragged his thoughts back into order.

'Don't worry, Jamie, you'll get a ship of your own. You can do it, all right.' He touched his arm and saw the baby-faced signalman Slade pause in folding a flag. 'One thing never changes. It's still a lot easier to do a risky job yourself than to order someone else to do it.'

He thought of *Kinsale*'s commanding officer: the same year at Dartmouth, the same flotilla when the Germans had marched into Poland. He had even got married around the same time as well.

At noon they sighted Malin Head, the most northerly point on the rugged Irish coast. A blur in a bank of haze, it might have been anywhere. More aircraft and two destroyers accompanied them as they headed into the North Channel, and then south into the Irish Sea, and the Mersey.

Martineau stood on the gratings and watched the towering grey hull slide past, tugs and pilot boat fussing around as if theirs was the only part which really counted. Outgoing corvettes and a fleet minesweeper were hooting wildly, and signals flashed back and forth as if it were a regatta.

Set against the loss of one destroyer, it was worth it. It had to be.

Onslow was standing beside him. 'Signal, sir.'

'Read it, Yeo.' He raised his glasses again. How many times, he wondered. How many more?

Onslow said, 'From *Ocean Monarch* to *Hakka*.' He hesitated. '*God bless you*, sir. Ends.'

Martineau raised his hand to the great ship. It *had* to be worth it.

He said, 'Take her in, Number One.' He could not face him. 'Put one of the subbies on the fo'c's'le for a change. Do him good.'

'Hands fall in for entering harbour! All men out of the rig of the day off the upper deck!'

Fairfax smiled and touched the salt-smeared glass. 'We did it!'

Kidd wanted to share it. But all he could think of was the lone piper, and the ship which had died in *Hakka*'s place.

Commodore Dudley Raikes sat with his buttocks perched on the edge of his desk, arms folded as he watched Martineau read the signal he had just taken from his file.

'The Admiral is extremely pleased, Graham, and so are their lordships. It proves a point in our favour, and that can't be bad, eh?'

Martineau looked at him, aware of the stillness in the room. Raikes seemed very relaxed, the broad gold band on his sleeve shining in the overhead lights, never a neat hair out of place.

He said, 'But we lost *Kinsale*, sir.'

The slightest frown. Raikes said, 'But you saved six thousand young soldiers. That's worth remembering!'

Martineau had only just found time to snatch a hot shower and put on a clean shirt after he had received instructions to report here. His entire body ached from strain and lack of sleep, although he knew he would be on the move again as soon as he returned to the ship.

They would get over it. They always had. There was no other way.

Raikes said, 'Good news for your first lieutenant.' He snapped his fingers. 'What's his name again? Fairfax?' He nodded. 'That's the chap.'

Martineau doubted if Raikes ever forgot anyone's name. Especially one in his own command.

'His D.S.C. has been confirmed. The Admiral will make the presentation here, rather than have your Number One gallivanting off to London. Sounds like a useful man. Can't have too many of those. He should have got it earlier, after the North African affair, when he had to take over command. I believe *you* had a hand in it?' He made a gesture. 'Don't want to know! Best not to!'

He was not jovial, but as close to it as he would ever be. He stared hard at the wall, as if he could see through and beyond it to one of his huge maps. 'The threat's still there, of course. The enemy is building more U-Boats than we can sink, and too many of our destroyers are tied up for other emergencies. *Tirpitz* is still a major problem. While she lies in that damned Norwegian fjord she is a constant menace. The Home Fleet has to keep half of our battle fleet rusting at their buoys at Scapa Flow just on the off chance that she might break out into the Atlantic and decimate the convoys. Her sister ship *Bismarck* did it, and it took half the Home Fleet to catch her and finish the job.' He looked away, as if remembering something, or somebody. 'But not before she had sunk *Hood*.'

Martineau eased his back. The scar was hurting him, maybe because of that steel chair on *Hakka*'s bridge.

He looked up, suddenly alert as Raikes said, 'There was something else I wanted to ask you. A favour, actually.'

Here it comes. He glanced at a calendar. In three days' time it would be another year. How was that possible?

Raikes said, 'I would like you to hold a reception in *Hakka*. The public relations gnomes have been snapping at my heels. It would

137

be a good scheme to let them know about your chap's gong.' He frowned again, his eyes almost disappearing. 'Your rating is getting something too. Nice touch. Levels it out a bit.' The mood passed just as quickly. 'I'll bring some of my people, the Chief of Staff is very keen. I'm not too sure about the Admiral. Very much his own man.'

So it had all been arranged, as soon as it was reported that *Hakka* had returned in one piece. Martineau felt his taut muscles relaxing, giving way. Perhaps it was a good idea. It would at least make *Hakka*'s company feel they were not left out. Raikes's term, 'levels it out a bit', added to the sense of unreality.

Raikes seemed to have taken his silence for opposition.

'And don't worry about the mess bills, Graham. We can help share the load, this time!' Then he said briskly, 'Time to go. I'll get Nobby. The Admiral asked to see you as soon as you were alongside.'

He paused at the door. 'Won't be a second. One thing, though. My new staff officer – Anna Roche, remember? She won't be coming. Her brother was killed a few days back. Bloody accident in Cornwall. You know what the army's like.'

The door slammed shut.

Martineau moved to the desk and back. It was out of character for Raikes to show such consideration, openly at least. Was it that he wanted her at the press affair, needed her for his own presentation, *part of the team*? Or was it important for her, something which might otherwise fire into a threat to her future?

He had not known she had a brother, but they had only exchanged a few words, in the club, beside a car, and in this same bombproof headquarters.

He remembered the mass of cheering khaki figures on *Ocean Monarch*'s decks. Canadians, like her.

He picked up his cap and saw the card wedged inside it, where he had written her telephone number, all those sea miles ago. He would call her, say something. Maybe write a short letter. He heard doors slamming, the jangle of telephones. It would only make it worse.

The other door opened and there she was, a signal pad in one hand. She stared at him as if uncertain. In a moment she would make an excuse and leave.

She said, 'I knew you were in . . . we've all been watching things. So glad you got back safely.'

He saw the strain, the shadows beneath her eyes. A strand of her hair had come unfastened and fallen across her cheek.

He walked over to her and took her hands in his, and the signal pad fell to the floor. She looked at the hands on hers and then at his face, as if she were unable to move.

He said, 'I heard about your brother just now.' He felt her hands begin to pull away but held them more firmly. 'I wanted to tell you. Tell you myself. How sorry I am. For you.' The words came out as if someone else was forming them; he was conscious only of the need to make her understand. 'Maybe . . . one day . . . you'll want someone to talk with, to share it.' He thought of Fairfax. *I'm a good listener.*

She withdrew her hands very gently and stooped to recover the pad. Without looking at him, she said, 'He told you about the press people?'

'Yes.'

She stood up and faced him again, a small pulse jumping in her throat as she pushed the loose hair from her cheek.

'Aboard *Hakka*?' As if she were testing herself.

'I'd see that nobody bothered you.'

She regarded him gravely, the same eyes as in the photograph. 'I know you would. I've never been on board *Hakka* before.'

The main door opened and Raikes said, 'Oh, there you are. Ready, Graham.' Even the use of his first name sounded unreal.

But she seemed not to notice. She smiled suddenly and said, 'Yes, I'd love to come to your ship,' and he saw her eyes rest briefly on the crimson ribbon with its miniature cross, as if remembering.

Raikes said impatiently, 'That's settled, thank God!'

But for reasons of his own, he was pleased.

Fairfax paused at the top of the ladder to get his bearings, surprised that the destroyer's upper bridge could seem so alien in the darkness. A place he knew so well in all conditions, and yet he felt like a stranger.

No familiar figures in their shapeless duffle coats or oilskins, no murmur of machinery, or ping of the Asdic, or the tap and clatter of a hundred other devices. The flag locker was covered, the slim-barrelled Oerlikons on either side of the bridge pointed blindly at the dark sky, the signal lamps were shuttered and silent.

He turned and reached down to take her hand.

'We made it!'

He put his hand under her arm and guided her past the usual traps and hazards, watched her climb on to one of the gratings and saw her silhouetted against the uncertain sky. There was a bit of a moon about, showing itself occasionally through the long, ragged layers of cloud. Without her tricorn hat, and wrapped in a borrowed duffle coat, she was a girl again. He smiled. A girl you would want to know.

She said, 'I thought it would be like this. No comfort. No shelter.'

Her hand touched the tall chair and she said, 'The Captain's chair.'

Fairfax waited, thinking of the din they had left below in the wardroom. The people from the press bureau had not been much trouble. *The importance of convoys, the courage of the merchant seamen who depended on naval protection.* He had seen the chief interrogator pressing questions on the Captain, but he had not been able to hear. Martineau had seemed relieved at the interruption when he had told him that Second Officer Roche wanted to visit the bridge. He had said, 'Look after her, Jamie.' Their eyes had met, and he had added apologetically, 'I'd show you myself, but . . .'

She put her hand on the chair.

'Is this where it happened?'

It took Fairfax by surprise.

'The previous captain? Well, yes, as a matter of fact.' He tried to push it aside. 'The Skipper always sits there. Sees everything, and it's too uncomfortable to sleep on.'

'Did you get along with him all right – Paul Bickford, I mean?'

Fairfax walked to the sealed chart table and leaned on it. 'I'm not sure I know how to answer that. He was killed in action, right here. And several others bought it that day.'

She tried to control her breathing. She knew the custom, had heard of it many times. Never mention the man's name after he's gone. *Bought it.*

So why can't I lay the ghost? The man I loved, thought I loved. Who used me, lied to me.

'You see, I met him in Canada some years ago. I wrote to him. And then when I came over in the Wrens, he got in touch.'

Fairfax said, after a moment, 'I didn't know. Honestly.'

He had been very pleasant to her since she had come aboard, and she could see why people liked him; anyone would. Even on their way up to the bridge, guiding her around some hidden obstacle, she had felt the pressure of the hand holding hers, had sensed his interest. An easy one to want to know better. And he did not know about Paul . . .

She had been on a course at Portsmouth when he had telephoned her. He had two days' leave, but had a meeting to attend in Southampton. He had asked her to join him at a house there; she was not to worry, there would be others around. Friends . . .

The friends had soon made themselves scarce and he had entertained her both with pleasure and with charm. His ship, his new command, would be leaving soon. It might be some while before they met again. But it could not, must not end there.

She walked to the side and pressed her body against the unyielding steel. And the worst of it was that she knew she had wanted him. But not like that. Like the nightmares, the degradation, the shame. Blood on the bed, and Paul exclaiming, 'How was I to know? Anyway, you wanted it, and so did I!'

Despite that, she had written to him. So why had she gone to see him again when she had heard that *Hakka* was in port?

Fairfax said suddenly, 'He was a very private person, except where the ship was concerned.' He shrugged. 'There were women, I believe. I'm sorry if you've been hurt.'

Hurt? She took a deep breath. *He raped me. I must have been so dumb, so naive, I asked for it.*

Somewhere a watertight door creaked open and they heard music, a woman singing.

Fairfax said, 'W/T pick up the best programmes. That's German. They always seem to get the good songs!'

They both laughed, and she said, 'I'm so glad about your medal, Jamie. You must be really thrilled.'

'I have my skipper to thank for that.' He smiled. 'A good bloke, but I think you know that.'

'We'd better go down.'

She did not resist as he took her in his arms and kissed her. 'Thanks for coming. Made it special, for all of us.' He hesitated. 'You know what I mean.'

She tugged the handkerchief out of his jacket pocket and dabbed his mouth with it, to give herself time.

'Lipstick. Don't want them to get the wrong idea!'

Fairfax gripped her wrist. 'So I've had too many drinks. But it's not every day you get a gong, or get kissed by a lovely girl. So – so maybe I'm allowed to speak out of turn.'

She waited, knowing that it was important to him.

'The Skipper's had a bad time, in more ways than one. I watch him relive it every day, see him trying to come to terms with it.'

She put her hand on his.

'Go on. Don't stop now. Please.'

'His wife cheated on him. He must have known about it when he gave the order to ram that bloody cruiser, when so many of his people were lost. He cares, you see. But I think he cares too much.'

He guided her to the ladder. A boat was chugging abeam, drunken voices raised in song.

'How I was a goddamned fool,
in th' Port o' Liverpool.
On th' first night when I came home from sea . . .'

Somebody's libertymen returning. Mercifully not *Hakka*'s.

Fairfax saw the quartermaster and gangway sentry stiffen as they approached, cigarettes skilfully cupped and hidden in their palms.

But all he could think of was his own irresponsibility. Right at the time, maybe, but looking back it seemed disloyal and pathetic. She might go straight to her boss, the Commodore, and complain about his behaviour.

The tall figure of Tonkyn, the chief steward, leaned out of the darkness.

'The party's spread itself, sir. Gents of the press down in the wardroom,' he made a quick gesture like someone downing a glass, 'an' some of the others have gone ashore.' He turned, ghostlike in his white jacket. 'The Captain asked if you would join him in his quarters.' He melted away just as quietly.

Fairfax said, 'A real character, that one.' A memory flashed through his mind: Tonkyn destroying letters which Bickford had thrown out unopened.

He took her arm. 'Ready?' and she smiled at him.

'Yes. I'm learning a lot tonight.'

It was a small gathering in Martineau's spacious day cabin. Raikes was there, and the faithful Nobby, First Officer Crawford, and the Admiral's Chief of Staff, an urbane captain named Tennant.

Martineau took her borrowed coat and tossed it to a steward. 'You're cold.' Then, 'Look after you, did he?'

She pushed her hair from her forehead. 'I don't know how you stand it up there, day in, day out.'

The door of the heads banged open and Captain 'Lucky' Bradshaw stepped into the cabin. He had obviously been having a good time, and one of his fly buttons was unfastened.

But he was cheerful enough, and showed his huge teeth in a grin when he saw Anna Roche.

'Well, what d'you think of destroyers?'

'The ladders are a bit steep, sir.'

His grin widened. 'Pity it wasn't broad daylight.' He gazed deliberately at her legs. 'The lads would have loved that!'

Crawfie scowled.

Martineau glanced at her hands; there was always some grease on the bridge.

'Go through there. You can wash your hands in peace.'

There was more laughter behind him, and under the cover of it he said, 'Glad you came,' and paused, looking at her directly. 'Anna. More than I've a right to say.'

Tonkyn was here, a tray with one glass on it. *A real character, that one....* She saw the scar on his hand, which she had not noticed before. She knew he had been wounded in that one-sided battle. But that had been different, as if it had happened to someone else. A stranger. This was real.

She took the glass from him and said softly, 'I think you have every right.'

Lucky Bradshaw announced loudly, 'Well, I must be off, gentlemen!'

Martineau said, 'I'll see him over the side.'

Outside on the cold deck Bradshaw said, 'Good show, Graham! I wanted to cheer with all the rest when I saw that bloody great trooper coming in. You really tricked those bastards that time!' He became serious. 'Pity about that westbound convoy, of course. Ran smack into the U-Boats which were being homed on to you. Bloody shambles, but there you are, win one, lose one, eh?'

He straightened his back and marched towards the gangway.

Martineau stood by the guardrail and stared along the length of his command.

It never leaves you.

When he reached the cabin the others were preparing to leave.

Raikes was obviously pleased, and so was Captain Tennant, the Chief of Staff; that would mean a good report from the Admiral.

'Better say our farewells to the press people, I suppose?' Raikes did not sound very enthusiastic, but the others nodded.

She hung back and waited for Martineau.

She said, 'I wanted to tell you myself. About the westbound convoy.'

She had seen it in his face when he had returned to the cabin. Exactly as Fairfax had described. *He cares too much.*

Surprisingly, he smiled at her.

'We make a good pair.'

Raikes called, 'Come on, Anna – we'll visit the Ops Room, show them we're on the ball, right?' Yes, he was in a good mood.

She said quietly, 'Call me.'

144

Then she reached up and touched the crimson ribbon.
It was enough.

10

Hit and Run

Commander Graham Martineau leaned on one hand and peered at himself in the small mirror, the hot water helping to take the rawness out of shaving. All those hours, days, on the open bridge made him wonder why he bothered. Perhaps he should grow a beard like Kidd and some of the others in the ship.

He touched his skin and winced, his hand tightening on the metal wash basin as the ship dipped suddenly into a trough.

In his mind he could see it clearly. Like a giant chart, or a gull's eye view.

They had been ordered to sea on New Year's Day. He had heard one of the leading hands say, 'Somebody sure loves us at the Admiralty, I don't bloody think!'

Further north this time, to rendezvous with an important convoy on passage to Iceland, mostly American ships, loaded with aircraft parts and army personnel for the growing garrison there. An attack by U-Boats had been forecast, signals had been intercepted. A job for the support group, then. The weather had been better than usual in the great expanse of sea between the Hebrides and Iceland, but bitterly cold, with off-watch hands kept busy clearing the decks and weapons of ice.

They had two destroyers in company, *Inuit*, another Tribal, and *Harlech*, one of the older ships built in the early Thirties, similar to those which had taken part in the first battle of Narvik, when Warburton-Lee, the Captain (D), had won his V.C. And had paid for it with his life. Older in appearance and performance than

Hakka and her sister ship, *Harlech* had been a true Atlantic veteran long before she had joined the group, with two U-Boats to her credit.

There had been an attempted attack, but the torpedoes must have been fired at extreme range, or the U-Boats' commander may have been discouraged by the size of the escort. So they were ordered back to base. It was a strange feeling to have this great, pitiless ocean quite empty but for their two companions. No ancient merchantmen trying to keep the pace, no ship falling slowly out of line, another victim. Nothing.

They had seen no land at all, although they had had a murky radar image of the nearest Faroe Islands when they had made their rendezvous.

Going home, or as close to home as it could be. A time for vigilance.

He dabbed his face with a towel and studied himself critically as he might a requestman or a defaulter at the table down aft.

He thought of Iceland, what he might have done if he had been able to get ashore. He had called there in the past . . . his mind shied away from it. A Danish possession which had been liberated, or invaded by the allies, occupied, the Icelanders termed it; it depended on your point of view. The stark fact was that Iceland boasted a fine new airfield, constructed by a German company just before the war. Very suitable for long-range bombers, which would now become a vital key in the Atlantic war. As Commodore Raikes had put it, 'They didn't build the thing to carry boxes of codfish to the Scottish markets!'

But there were shops a-plenty, and with British and American servicemen almost outnumbering the inhabitants they were doing well. And there was no blackout.

He listened to somebody shouting, then ignored it.

The restaurant had been small and very crowded; anybody out of uniform would have looked like an intruder. And yet, surprisingly, they had been able to talk, interrupted from time to time by overworked waitresses, and by two young subbies having an argument over the bill.

He had found himself talking about things he never discussed.

147

About his parents, his late father, the Commander, the house by the New Forest, naval life before the war, even the ship.

Once she had reached across the minute table and touched his hand, and asked, 'What about this?'

He had attempted to pull his hand away but she had insisted. 'The scar. I saw it when I came aboard *Hakka*. All those people getting high on your gin, not really caring, not giving a damn about the men they supposedly write about.' He had felt her eyes on him, and had wanted to seize the hand that held him. 'Don't be ashamed of it. You should be proud.'

He had looked up at her face then, as she had said, 'I am.' There had been tears in her eyes. For him, for herself, for her brother. He was still not certain.

He had even told her about Alison, that a divorce would be the outcome.

She had said, 'You keep it all there, in the background, don't you? As if it was somehow your fault.'

The restaurant manager had come to the table. 'Sorry to interrupt.' His glance had fallen on Martineau's sleeve and he had added hastily, '*sir.* But if you've finished, I've several customers waiting for a table.'

He had been angry, but she had laughed. The first time he had heard her really laugh, and several people had turned to look and grin, as if sharing it.

Outside in the cold air he had said, 'Hardly the Savoy, was it?'

She had watched him in the darkness. She would have known then that *Hakka* was being ordered to sea. *I wanted to tell you myself.*

But she had said, 'I've never been to the Savoy, or likely to!'

Then she had stooped and murmured, 'Damn! My best stockings!'

He had heard that you could buy all the stockings you wanted in the shops in Reykjavik.

The small speaker crackled. 'Captain on the bridge, please!'

He snatched up his jacket and cap and hurried to the door. As he knocked down the clip on the steel he saw the scar on the back of his hand.

Maybe it was all my fault . . .

148

She was a bright, intelligent girl, and would probably be moved on somewhere else. The navy was like that.

It might be better for both of them if that happened.

He climbed out and up, the freezing air on his freshly shaved skin making him wince.

A quick look around, faces, positions, the metallic edge of the horizon. *Inuit* on the port quarter, and the sturdy *Harlech* to starboard, her narrow hull like polished glass in the hard glare.

Kidd said, '*Inuit*'s got a contact, sir. One-seven-zero, moving right. Requests instructions.'

Martineau climbed on to the forward gratings and was rubbing the ice rime from the gyro compass repeater before he realized that he had forgotten both his gloves and his bridge coat.

They had done it often enough, and rehearsed it so many times. But always with those helpless ships to consider first, to protect no matter what, or who, paid the price.

This was different.

Kidd said, 'Asdic team closed up, sir, first lieutenant's with them.'

He imagined them throughout the ship. A combined effort. By the book. *Maybe.*

He said, 'Open R/T contact. Start the attack!'

Then Fairfax's voice, equally calm. 'Got it, sir. Same bearing, still moving right.'

Martineau bent over, feeling the spray sting his face. 'What's it look like, Number One?'

'Submarine, sir. Can't be anything else.'

Martineau said, 'Tell the Chief.'

'Done, sir.' That was Kidd.

'Good lad.' He bent over the gyro again and did not see the bearded navigator grin.

He had to shut out everything else, concentrate on the speed, the change of bearing. It could have been a waterlogged wreck, drifting and dead. Fairfax knew otherwise.

The U-Boat had probably detected their presence. *You must assume that.* All those other times, with slow, overworked escorts which could barely keep pace with a submerged submarine, let alone one on the surface. An escort could get only so near before contact was lost. Charges would be dropped, but it took an age for that same escort to turn around to try and recover the scent with her Asdic. That's when you lost it. And the enemy was using a new device to create a false echo when the hunt got too near, something to throw the Asdic operators off while the sub changed course and probably depth. Good Asdic operators were able to detect even that, so something new would soon be on the market.

'Signal *Inuit*. Affirmative.' He did not even look up as the yeoman's lamp shuttered off the brief order.

Someone said, 'Watch 'er go!'

Inuit made an impressive sight as her bow wave suddenly rose higher, spray drifting over her forward guns as she altered course very slightly to starboard.

Kidd said, 'Black flag's hoisted. She's going in.'

Faster and faster, until Fairfax called, 'Still moving right. Increasing speed.'

'Signal *Harlech*, *Stand by to engage*. Tell Guns to open fire immediately if the sub breaks surface.' It had happened, and a U-Boat had still got away, because gun crews had been caught napping.

Inuit had turned again, almost on to her original course. Martineau saw the charges splash from her stern, while the others were fired from either beam. They would have lost contact by now. With luck they were right over the bloody thing. He felt the explosions, crashing against the lower hull before flinging up great columns of water, higher and higher so that they seemed to hang there, frozen, before cascading down again as *Inuit*'s helm went hard over and she started to turn as she reloaded her throwers. Martineau could imagine what it felt like to the Chief and his stokers. How must it be in the cramped confines of a submarine?

'Target's turning away.'

Harlech's chance now. He saw the smoke thickening from her twin funnels; probably due for a boiler clean. She deserved it.

He raised his glasses. And so like *Firebrand*. He found he was able to make a comparison. How long had it been?

The U-Boat was heading away, but even in this light there was no time for her commander to surface and use his maximum speed to try and escape.

From one corner of his eye he saw *Harlech* thrusting past, the black flag streaming out like a sheet of metal.

It was like hearing someone speak. *The U-Boat was heading away.*

He called, 'Hard a-port! Full ahead together!'

He felt the immediate response, the groan of bridge plating as the rudder went over. You could never catch Bill Spicer out with an emergency order.

He heard the Oerlikon gunner below the bridge swearing, his boots skidding from the mounting as the hull swayed over until *Hakka*'s reflection was visible on the sea alongside.

'Midships! Starboard twenty! Ease to five!'

He tensed, his skin ice-cold against his sodden shirt, and yet the lookout's voice was almost laconic.

'Torpedoes running to starboard, sir!'

'Lost contact, sir.' Gibbons, one of their best Asdic operators.

Martineau said, 'Resume course and speed.' He should have known. Heading away. To use the stern tubes. He should have known . . .

Kidd said, 'Nice one, sir!' The grin was there again. '*Harlech*'s still on to him!'

Martineau moved to the opposite side, watching the other destroyer. He could imagine the bell sounding at the depth charge positions as her Asdic pinged a continuous echo.

More explosions, the columns of jagged water crumbling in a sudden gust of wind.

'Nothing, sir!'

'Bloody hell!'

Driscoll's voice broke the spell.

'Action starboard! *U-Boat surfacing!*'

'Steer two-one-zero.' Martineau raised his glasses, a seaman ducking down to clear his field of vision.

It was not something you saw every day. Dark grey, covered with slime. On its way back to Germany, perhaps after a long and fruitful patrol.

In a moment she would be completely surfaced, and men would emerge, to surrender, and to receive treatment they so often denied to others.

And the bows were still turning. He snapped, 'We're going in! Tell Barlow, *full pattern!*' What a job for a subbie not long out of school.

The submarine seemed to lie like a breakwater at a forty-five-degree angle from the bow.

This time he did hear the bell ring, and saw the starboard charge fly into the air, while the stern charges rumbled from their rack.

'Open fire!'

Only the forward guns could be trained to bear, and backed up by two Oerlikons they smashed shot after shot into the motionless hull.

Martineau swallowed hard as the first charges exploded. The U-Boat was *not* motionless. She was still edging round when the charges burst alongside to add their din to the crash of exploding shells. Half a minute more and either *Hakka* or *Inuit* would have been in their sights. At this range they could not have missed.

'Half ahead together!' He looked again, and the sea was empty. Now came the oil; he could even smell it, rising to join the slow whirlpool of gutted fish and seaweed.

Bubbles too, huge and obscene, joining the dance with the dead fish.

Martineau looked at the colourless sky and took a deep breath. How much better to die up here than to face an end like that.

A kill, then. Their lordships would call it a probable.

He leaned over the screen and watched *Hakka*'s bow wave pushing the flotsam aside. The victor.

This time.

Men were cheering, and he saw two of the signalmen shaking hands with excitement.

He said, 'Make to *Harlech*, *Yours, I believe?*'

Fairfax called, 'No contact, sir.'

Martineau saw Kidd lift the hood from his chart. He would be thinking the same. The sea was very deep hereabouts; the U-Boat would not even have reached the bottom yet. Some might still be alive. He thought of the drifting lifeboats he had seen, their crews shrivelled and eyeless. But somebody must always have been the last to die, perhaps still clinging to hope.

'Resume formation. But pass the word, no slacking!'

But they were still cheering.

Suddenly he was shaking and could not control it.

Kidd brought a duffle coat and held it while he pushed his arms into it. Even that was hard to do. Shivering all over, the soaked shirt dragging at the scar on his back like a wire.

Someone murmured, 'The Skipper must be half-frozen!'

Another said, 'Got us out of that little lot, though, didn't he?'

Don't be ashamed of it. You should be proud.

She would know that *Hakka* was on her way back, just as she had known when she was leaving. It must be so much harder when you had to stay silent about it.

Kidd was saying, 'I can take over, sir, if you want to slip down to your sea cabin.'

Martineau looked at him. 'I know you can, Pilot. But I'm fine now.'

He doesn't believe me. Nor does he realize that if I went below now, I'd never have the strength to come back again.

Perhaps it was best to be like Lucky Bradshaw, *Bash on regardless*, as he was known by his officers. Don't question it. Just do it.

He glanced around the bridge as things returned slowly to normal. A fanny of pusser's ki would be up soon, a new course would be laid off. And tomorrow, the Mersey again.

He thought of her up here with Fairfax during the reception, as Raikes had called it. What had she discovered? What might it have brought back?

Someone put a mug of cocoa in his hands; it was Tonkyn. He very rarely visited the bridge; even seeing him without his white jacket was vaguely unreal.

Tonkyn almost winked. 'Drop of good stuff in the cocoa, sir. Set you up like new.' He peered around the bridge, pale eyes watering in the cold air. 'Well, that's one less of 'em, sir. We showed 'em!' And gave the nearest he could manage to a smile.

Martineau sipped the drink and watched the horizon tipping from side to side as if to dislodge the three ships. He could taste the rum in the thick mixture, could feel it burning through him.

Lucky Bradshaw was wrong. Tonkyn's quiet, *'We showed 'em!'* said it all.

Anna Roche sat at the small, rickety table and watched her room-mate putting the finishing touches to her make-up with more care than usual. A rare evening off, a run ashore, as it was termed in the navy even if you were a thousand miles from the sea. Outside the building she could hear the occasional rumble of heavy trucks, or the snarl of a motor cycle. She looked at her locker beside the bed, and thought of the letters she had received from home. Mostly about Tim, as if they still expected to hear it had been a mistake. That somehow he had survived.

She had written to her parents, and had tried to share it. Deep down, although she could not explain it, she felt that her mother, at least, thought her daughter should be at home, where she was needed.

She was almost glad there was another late briefing at the Support Group's offices tonight. Better to be a part of that than to reproach herself.

Her friend Caryl turned away from the mirror and said, 'Well, what do you think?'

She was wearing her best doeskin uniform, and had somehow found time to arrange her rebellious Bergman curls. She was a pretty girl, who never seemed to worry unduly about anything.

Anna said, 'Special, is he?'

'Sort of. The best yet. But I'll not do anything stupid.' She had an infectious giggle. 'Not right away.' She looked over at some stockings which were hanging on a makeshift line to dry. 'He has a friend – he's often on the America run. He brings stockings back with him every time – his rabbits, he calls them.'

She pulled up her pleated skirt. 'See for yourself. You know what they say: a woman's legs are her best friends.' The giggle again. 'But even the best of friends must part! Not yet, though.'

She rummaged through her shoulder bag. 'Could you lend me a quid, Anna, 'til my ship comes in?'

Anna laughed. She would turn any man's head. You would never think she was one of the Commodore's most efficient staff officers.

'I think I can manage that.'

Caryl walked past her, suddenly serious. '*Hakka*'s coming in tomorrow, or so Ops reports. You *will* see him, won't you?'

She paused and put one hand on Anna's shoulder. 'He seems like a nice bloke. Been through the mill more than most, by the sound of it.'

'He's easy to talk to.'

'You nut! You really kill me! *Easy to talk to*! I saw it in your eyes when you got back from your run ashore together. So he's married, or was. As any first lieutenant will tell you, you've got to think of Number One!'

She laughed again, but the hand did not leave Anna's shoulder. 'I think he'd be good for you. *To* you.'

Anna knelt down to drag her bag from under the bed. 'All right, Auntie Caryl. I'll think about it.'

She straightened her back, her hand still on the bag. Then she turned her head and looked at her friend. She too was quite motionless, lips slightly parted, as if she were listening to something.

'What was it? I thought I heard . . .'

Caryl stared at her, eyes wide, as if she could not move.

Then she said, 'Flak. Heavy stuff. Not from around here, though.'

She held out her arms, her voice drowned completely by the terrible scream, louder and louder until it blotted out everything else, even the power or the will to think.

The first explosion was muffled, jarring the room, and the house where they all lived a stone's throw from the H.Q. buildings, and for a second Anna believed that it was past. The second bomb seemed to explode right underneath, lifting the floor, cutting off lights as walls collapsed, and more debris was hurled in confusion.

She tried to move, but she was pinned down, covered, choking, her lungs unable to respond. She thought she heard a scream and knew it was her own, and felt stark terror as the overwhelming pressure increased.

Then she sensed a small movement, slow at first, until a hand touched her face and tried to brush away the grit and plaster.

She could hear nothing; the blast had done that. As if the whole world had stopped. Just that small, warm hand, patting her gently, never moving away. She wanted to cry, to call out, but nothing

155

came. She was not alone, and she needed Caryl to know what it meant.

But when she tried to kiss the hand the pain came, and then there was even deeper darkness.

Lieutenant Roger Kidd stared at his greatcoat and cap, which she had hung by the door, and had to tell himself he was not dreaming. Like that first moment when she had come down the stairs, one hand on the banister, and had stopped and looked down, as if she had known he was there.

He had held her for a long time; all the rest was a confused background. People calling out greetings or making their departures, the clatter of glasses from the bar, the smell of something from the hotel kitchen, which he had not yet seen.

He had said, 'You knew I'd come, Evie. After what we said.'

She had leaned back in his arms to study his face, like that last time.

'I hoped. I prayed you would.'

As if to some signal they had moved to the parlour, his arm around her small waist, her hand clinging to his as if she was afraid he might let go.

'How long?' Just two words. How much they meant in wartime.

'Tonight. Maybe longer. Some things need doing.'

He recalled the last-minute signals when they had begun their final approach. *To take different berths as instructed.* There had been a raid, not like the earlier ones Liverpool had suffered, but a hit-and-run attack. Some fleet oilers had been in port, and one of them had been hit; you could smell the stench and see the hovering black cloud long before they had begun their approach.

It had taken every fire-tender and hundreds of servicemen and civilians to bring the fire under control. Had it spread many other ships would have been set alight, or sunk.

Theirs was a sombre arrival this time, no cheers, no celebrations. The successful action against the U-Boat, another kill for the group, seemed like part of something else.

'Tonight.' She had been smiling. 'And there'll be others. So many you'll regret you ever found me again!'

He thought of Fairfax, still aboard *Hakka*, in charge while the

Skipper was ashore. And Martineau's face when Jamie had told him about the raid, and that some bombs had straddled the living quarters at H.Q.

They had tied up alongside a light cruiser, and Fairfax had gone aboard to enquire about a shore telephone. The cruiser had one installed, like most of the larger visitors to Liverpool.

Fairfax had told him the rest. How the Skipper had used the telephone and then called for the motor boat. He had not even stopped long enough to change out of his scuffed, seagoing clothing.

'Make your report, Number One. Tell the commodore or any-one else who's got nothing better to do than ask questions that I'm at the hospital.'

Nothing else, but there did not need to be. Fairfax had already told Kidd that he had shown the girl named Anna Roche around the bridge. Their world.

Evie had come back into the room and was studying him.

'I'm still pinching myself, just to be sure it's true. You're real.' She half listened as someone dropped a glass. 'Not too busy on Mondays. All their cash has run out by now!'

They sat together, almost like strangers.

He said, 'There was another raid. We heard about it when we came in.'

'Not as bad as some, over that side, at least.'

'I was worried all the same. Thinking about you, Evie. About us.' She opened her mouth to speak but he said with sudden intensity, 'I knew I was in love with you, Evie, despite dear old Chris, God rest his soul. But today was the first time I saw what love could do, an' that's a fact.'

A bell tinkled and she stood up.

'I'm wanted. The laundry, I expect.' She gestured to the sideboard. 'Help yourself. I won't be long.' She touched his face very gently. 'Then we can have that meal I promised you.'

She moved to the door, but would not look at him. 'But it might have to wait a while longer.'

The surgeon commander, not the most patient of men at any time, regarded his unexpected visitor impassively.

He said bluntly, 'My petty officer told me of your arrival. You are not related to the injured Wren officer, I take it?'

Injured. Just that word alone, when he had arrived here unannounced. Even as he had been looking for directions, the right door, someone to ask, he had seen two S.B.A.s putting clothing in a rubber bag. Clothing? Hardly that. Rags, soaked in blood, the twin blue stripes on the jacket sleeves hitting him like a fist.

Injured.

'Not related. I know her. She is Canadian. Her young brother was killed recently.' It was like watching the fall of shot. You could never be certain.

The surgeon said, 'Well, then . . .' His eyes rested briefly on the gold lace on Martineau's jacket; one piece had been torn loose, and there were stains in a dozen places. He must have come straight from his ship. Some of his own fatigue eased, and he said, 'You must be *Hakka*'s captain.' And when Martineau nodded, 'Good. Good show!'

'Is it bad?'

The surgeon pursed his lips. 'Could have been much worse. Three were killed in the same attack.' He marked off the points on his fingers. 'Shock, concussion, some bad bruising, but not too severe when you consider that half the building fell on her.' He saw his petty officer S.B.A. trying to catch his attention and decided to ignore him. Others would be waiting; they were always waiting. Men from the ships, survivors picked up in convoy only to be torpedoed again before reaching safety. Burned, broken, limbless. And the rest. The skivers, men trying to work their ticket and fake a case for discharge. Plus the usual procession of fools who took the risk of having a good time with the Maggie Mays of this port, and caught the boat up as a reward.

Just this once, they could all wait.

He said, 'She's in a darkened room, with her eyes covered. The blast was severe, although of course she won't remember it.' Then, abruptly, 'Can't allow you very long with her. She's sedated. No more shocks at this stage, right?'

They eyed each other, the same rank, and so utterly different.

The room was small, square, and soulless.

A nurse was sitting beside the bed, reading a book with the aid of a very dim lamp.

The surgeon said sharply, 'That won't do your vision any good.'

She closed the book, stood up, and left the room without a word. Martineau guessed it was some kind of signal.

Anna lay on her back, her hair tied with a piece of bandage, her eyes covered with a sort of mask. A sheet was pulled up to her chin, and her shoulders were bare ... like the photograph.

The surgeon said, 'A visitor, Anna.'

Martineau saw her head turn very slightly, one hand lifting towards him as she said, 'Graham? It's you. . . . You came.'

The surgeon took her other hand and felt the pulse.

'No excitement. That's an order.' He glanced at Martineau. 'Ring the bell if you need me.'

Martineau sat on the nurse's chair and took her hand.

'Yes. It's me. I came as soon as I heard.' As she moved again he saw the bruising on her body. 'It's going to be all right.' He turned over the gashed hand in his. A near thing.

'I didn't want you to see me like this.' She touched the mask, but let her hand fall again. 'I saw the flash. White ... a white flash. I always thought they were scarlet or orange ... like fireworks.'

He saw a pulse jerk in her throat.

'My friend Caryl stayed with me all the time. Otherwise ...' He saw that she was growing weaker, but when he gently withdrew his hand she clung to it with unexpected strength.

'No, don't go! You came. You knew.' She reached up and felt his jacket, the lapel, until she had found the medal ribbon. 'You came. I can smell the ship. The sea. Straight from the ship.'

He said, 'You'll be getting some leave.' He felt the fingers curling in his grasp, as if afraid of something. 'It's the navy's way. You could go to Hampshire. My mother would love to take care of you. I'll call her.' He closed both his hands around hers. 'Please say you will. I might even be able to get down there myself for a day or two. It would do you good.'

The door opened soundlessly and the nurse was back.

'Time, sir.' She observed him without curiosity; she had seen it all.

159

'Thank you.' Then he bent and kissed the girl's cheek. She did not move or speak, probably gone into another deep sleep.

Outside he found the surgeon commander.

'Thanks. That was good of you.'

'I'd appreciate it if you'd ring first next time. We might have to move her.'

Martineau paused in the lobby. 'I'd like to thank the other Wren officer, if that's possible.'

'She was killed. Outright, or almost. They were together when the rescue team reached them.'

Outside in the jostling street, past saluting sailors he did not even see, Martineau walked, quite alone with his thoughts.

In destroyers you soon learned the hard way not to trust in miracles. But, in his heart, he knew he had just seen one happen.

11

Trust

It was one of those rare occasions when a ship of war was quiet and without movement. Saturday in port, and, with everyone but the duty part of the watch gone ashore as libertymen, almost deserted.

In Number Nine Mess, Leading Torpedoman Bob Forward sat at the table, and, after a quick look around at the other messes, took out the small leather box and opened it.

It was like something you read about, or saw on the newsreels, he thought. Men you were used to seeing in scruffy overalls or seagoing kit, or at most in their Number Threes for entering or leaving harbour, all decked out in their best uniforms, gold badges, properly creased trousers, tiddly bows, the lot. *Just for the three of us.* Lieutenant-Commander Fairfax, a chief petty officer from another ship he did not know. He grinned awkwardly. *And me.*

He stared at the bright new Conspicuous Gallantry Medal. His head ached from the rum he had been offered after the ceremony, his shoulders from the slaps and thumps he had received from men he scarcely knew.

How his mum would have loved it. He sighed. His dad, too, if he had lived to see it.

And the Admiral, the great man himself, the one they always spoke of with awe. Searching, keen eyes as his aide read the citation, a handshake and a smile. 'Well done, Forward. Proud of you.' Not one of those soft, wet handshakes either, but he had heard that the C-in-C played a lot of golf between his stints of duty.

But for Fairfax he would never have got the medal. It was hard to remember in some ways. The ship under air attack off the North African coast or wherever it was. Fire breaking out near some wounded sailors, even closer to a pile of ready-use ammunition. He had put out the fire, and had manned the abandoned Oerlikon gun himself, even though he was a torpedoman.

Anger, defiance, the madness of a fight, it had been a little of everything. He grinned. In a funny way it had lost him his leading-rate; he had confronted the one who had deserted his station when the fire had broken out, a fire which might have cost them the ship. They had met ashore, and he had half-killed the other man. It had been worth losing his hook just to do it. His attempt to rescue young Wishart after he had taken a dive from the tanker had brought it all back, and a medal to boot.

They always said that the previous skipper would have put him up for a gong. How little they knew.

Not like the new skipper. He had to admit that, although he disliked officers for the most part. Martineau had seemed genuinely pleased. 'Glad for you, and glad for the ship too!'

Forward was not used to it. He pulled out his ditty-box and regarded it thoughtfully. Most regular sailors had them, made with their own hands, and the more little drawers and secret compart-ments the better.

He unlocked it and took out another package, which again he opened with great care.

It was a watch, complete with expanding strap, and his initials stamped on it. He could see Wishart's face when he had received it, eager, pleased, anxious. That had really knocked him for six. Nobody ever gave him anything like that. He had been confused, embarrassed that he could not cope with it.

'What's this, then? Think I can't afford one of my own?'

Wishart had said quietly, 'My parents wanted you to have it. It's not new, but it's a Hamilton, a good one. My dad knows about watches. You can't get decent ones over the counter in wartime.'

He shook his head. Another world. If only the kid realized. It

162

was to be hoped it didn't all rub off when he got that first wavy stripe on his sleeve.

Wishart's father was a bank manager or something. Nice house, he imagined, probably a car as well. The only cars in Forward's street belonged to a bookmaker and a grocer who was in the nick for black-marketing rationed goods.

I don't know how I ever got mixed up with his sort in the first place.

And when he became one of the pigs down aft, he might become another snooty Cavaye, or Driscoll, who was all mouth and trousers at the best of times.

But he was a good kid. Took all the knocks from his messmates about his posh accent, and his good manners even when eating the stodge slopped out from *Hakka*'s galley.

He placed the medal inside the ditty-box and was about to close it when he saw her photograph. It still turned his guts over, remembering how she had once been, and all his secret hopes.

He locked the box, angry with himself, and knowing why. Because he felt no guilt? She was gone, that was it; somebody else, not Grace.

He heard voices from the upper messdeck, water sloshing as some of the duty watch took a moment to dhoby their underwear before the ship became too crowded again.

Deliberately he unbuttoned his left cuff and fastened the watch into place, then held it to his ear. A good sound, like the clocks all going at once in the old shop off Lavender Hill near his home.

He saw Wishart at the foot of the ladder and winked.

'How about this, Wings? Thought I should give it an airing, but if that old fart Mister bloody Malt says anything I'll probably dip my hook again!' He added casually, 'Might want to pick your brains later on when I write a note to your people to thank them. But now, what about a run ashore?'

He looked away. It had been worth it just to see the kid's face.

Commodore Dudley Raikes marched into his office and handed his cap to a steward.

'Went off very well, I thought. It'll give those press wallahs something to write about.'

He glanced at the clock.

'Bit early for me, gentlemen, but if you'd care for a gin, please carry on.'

Captain Lucky Bradshaw said, 'It's *exactly* the right time for me, sir.' He gestured to the steward. 'Large pinkers, right?'

Martineau walked to the solitary window and stared along the road. From here he could see the fallen bricks and smashed rooftops. There had been fire, too, caused by a gas leak, they had told him. And she had been pinned under it. It was incredible that the rescue workers had got to her in time.

He said, 'The same, please.'

Now that it was over he needed to be alone for a while, or as alone as it was possible to be. The handshakes, the excitement, the unusual turnout and ceremony were rare these days. Fairfax had seemed overwhelmed by it.

Raikes was saying, 'As you know, although it is supposed to be a secret, another support group is due to join us shortly. At present they are enjoying the full attention of my umpires at Larne. For tactical training exercises.' He gave a wintry smile. 'I gather you do not always approve of such methods, Captain Bradshaw?'

'You have to trust your instinct. Get the enemy's measure. That's my view, sir.' He reached out for the tray as the steward reappeared. Martineau had noticed the formality between them, dislike perhaps. He knew that Bradshaw had once been Raikes's superior, until Lucky's downfall under the Admiralty axe.

Raikes said, 'The pace is mounting. It will, I promise you, get hotter. Russia, like it or not, is a valuable ally, but under great pressure all along the eastern front. Should Russia collapse, all of the enemy's hitting power will be directed at *us*, in the Mediterranean where we are at last making encouraging progress, and in the Atlantic, where we are still losing more ships than we can spare.'

Martineau said, 'Russian convoys again, sir.'

Raikes stared at him. 'Exactly. Every kind of supply you can think of. From tanks and first-line aircraft right down to food, medical supplies, even the boots to march in.'

Bradshaw grunted, 'They'd not help us if the role was reversed.'

Raikes said calmly, 'Perhaps. But whatever we may think, it is a time for all-out effort. The Admiral has stated, and I agree, that we can no longer tolerate half-measures. We need destroyers, and we will get them.' The brief smile again. 'Eventually. Until then, every commanding officer must keep his ship ready to respond to any emergency. If a ship is in need of a boiler clean, or repainting, let it wait if the other need is greater. If he drives his command until a shaft seizes up, let him carry on with the remaining one.' He looked directly at Martineau. '*Hakka* is to be fitted with Bofors guns – the multiple pom-poms have proved unreliable. It would normally take the dockyard six weeks to make the change. It will be done in two.'

Bradshaw said uneasily, 'But can we be certain, sir?'

Raikes glanced once more at the clock. 'I have explained to our engineering people that if it is not so, some of them will be replaced by those who *can* do it. The prospect of some sea-time for a change is often a great incentive!'

He turned sharply. 'Yes?'

It was a Wren officer, with one stripe on her uniform jacket. She stared around, almost terrified, before stammering, 'Sorry, sir, wrong door!'

Raikes folded his arms. 'Takes time, I suppose.'

Martineau said, 'The big German ships, *Tirpitz* and *Scharnhorst* . . . they may try more attacks when we increase these Arctic convoys.' He could hear his own voice, level, unemotional. But all he could think of was that bitter sea, the cold grinding away a man's strength, his will to survive.

Raikes replied, 'They will continue to tie up all our capital ships in that area. Like a common mine, they are a menace merely by being there. Hitler will not risk *Tirpitz*, I think. Not after *Bismarck*. But *Scharnhorst* and some of their cruisers, that's something else, as we have already seen to our cost.'

The other door opened gently. It was Nobby, Raikes's secretary. Martineau noticed that he had gained a half-stripe between his other two.

He said, 'Congratulations.'

Nobby regarded him gravely.

'We try, sir.' Then, to Bradshaw, 'The Admiral will see you now, sir.'

The door closed and Raikes said, 'The Admiral will love that, stinking of gin at this hour!'

Martineau relaxed slightly. He was beginning to understand the Commodore. He after all had encouraged Lucky to have a drink, or two.

'Wanted to have a word anyway, Graham, before I visit the Plot Room.' He moved some papers on his desk. 'You know all about Anna Roche, of course. I understand you saw her at the hospital?' He held up one neat hand. 'Not probing. But they're shifting her to one of our hospitals in Manchester. Not all that far away.'

'She's not being transferred, sir?'

'Not at this stage. She's good. A quick thinker, but I expect you know that.'

Martineau waited. He had called the hospital again but had been unable to speak to her. The voice on the telephone had been curt. 'She has to rest. She has been through rather a lot.' He had thought of the two S.B.A.s with the torn and bloodied uniform which he had believed was hers. They had probably broken the news to her about the friend who had died beside her.

'When do you think *Hakka*'s new guns will be fitted, sir?'

Raikes was not surprised by the change of tack. If anything, he was expecting it.

'Just as soon as we know about the next operation. I shall inform you.' He waited until Martineau had almost reached the door, and then asked, 'What do you really think about the Russian convoys?'

His timing was perfect, exact, like the man.

'In my view, the Germans will not risk their big ships on the summer convoys. With the ice edge so far north they'd be too far from base if they were called to action.' It was like hearing his father all over again, the old destroyer hand. *You can't just sit and wait for them to come out when they want to. Give them the bait, and go in after the buggers!* 'The ice edge is low now, sir, south of Bear Island. While winter holds, it's our best chance, I think.'

He turned and stared at the window again, but saw nothing.
What are you saying?

Raikes rubbed his chin. 'It is true that most of our convoys to Russia have been attacked and crippled by U-Boats and bombers.

Sinkings by surface craft have been few, three to be precise, over the past two years.' His eyes gleamed in the hard light. 'This may be the chance to spring the trap.' He reached out and shook Martineau's hand. 'Good. Good. We'll see you Captain (D) yet!'

Martineau left the office and walked along the corridor. *Hakka* was at a state of readiness again, fuelled, ammunitioned and stored. They would be off again soon; Raikes could not have made it much plainer. The Support Group was ready, another on its way. Raikes was doing well, and it was obvious that Lucky Bradshaw hated him for it.

'Commander Martineau?' It was First Officer Crawford. She stood half in and half out of her office, and another Wren officer was sitting by the desk, talking on a telephone and making notes at the same time.

He smiled. 'They're keeping you busy, I see.'

She said, 'I was glad to see your first lieutenant get his decoration from the Admiral. We were all very proud.'

He waited. There it was again. Pride. Then he said directly, 'Is she going to be all right?'

She studied him gravely. 'They think so.' She hesitated, then took his arm. 'It's wrong to get so fond of people, that's what they keep telling us, but I do. I care for both of you.' She thrust out a piece of signal pad. 'This is the hospital. Give her my love, will you?' Then she turned and hurried back into her room.

I care for both of you. Not an easy thing for her to say.

Nor could she have known just how much it meant.

Fairfax and Kidd sat in *Hakka*'s wardroom, sipping their drinks and half listening to the bored voice of a B.B.C. news announcer as they waited for Tonkyn to serve supper, for that was all it was with most of the ship's company ashore.

'So we're off again soon, Jamie?' Kidd wondered what he would think if he told him about Evie.

'Looks like it. The whole group this time. The Old Man has been at H.Q. for most of the day.'

Kidd almost smiled. *The Old Man.* He knew that Martineau was thirty-three years old, a year younger than himself. The navy's way.

The emotionless voice broke into his thoughts.

'*The Secretary of the Admiralty regrets to announce the loss of H.M.S.* Linnet *on active service. Next of kin have been informed.*'

Not where, or how. Was that all it took? Like a pencilled cross on a chart, soon forgotten. He clenched his fist around his glass. He should be used to it by now.

Fairfax said, 'Sloop. She was out in the Med for a time. Put in more sea miles than many newer ships.'

Kidd eyed him warmly. Fairfax never seemed to change; promotion, and now the little blue and white ribbon of the D.S.C., he was still the same.

Fairfax put down his glass with deliberation.

'I know I mentioned it before, Pilot – that A.F.O. about possible promotion and command openings for R.N.R. types with your "qualifications".' He smiled. 'Well, that's how their lordships describe them!' Then he was serious again. 'What about it? You could do it standing on your head.'

'I'm not so sure about that.'

'Oh, come off it. I've been with you up on that bloody bridge, remember?'

Kidd said, 'After the war, always assuming we win it, and we're still in one piece, what sort of life will the sea have to offer me? I had it rammed down my throat often enough what happened after the last lot. Greedy owners cutting down on crews, officers selling their souls just to get a berth. It will be worse this time.' He shook his head. 'I'm not sure I could take it, starting all over again. And promotion?' He waved one hand and slopped gin over his sleeve. 'This lady'll suit me.' He made up his mind. 'And besides, I'm going to get married.'

Fairfax jumped to his feet and reached down to hug him.

'You crafty, secretive old bugger! You're a lucky chap! Not sure about her, though!'

Kidd grinned self-consciously, glad that he had told him. 'It'll be you next, you'll see.'

Then he said, 'So I don't want to change things just now.' He gazed at the ship's crest above the empty fireplace. 'She owns a small hotel over the water, in Birkenhead.' He regarded his friend steadily. 'I love her. Very much.'

Fairfax had never seen him in so serious a mood before. He

thought of Martineau striding ashore without even changing into his proper rig. Once, he might have pitied both of them. Now all he felt was envy.

Martineau ran up the last few steps of the light cruiser's accommodation ladder and touched his cap in a brief salute to the quarterdeck.

She was only a small cruiser, not unlike the one rammed and sunk by the *Queen Mary*, but after *Hakka* she seemed like a battleship.

They were all present. Quartermaster and boatswain's mate, Royal Marine bugler, midshipman of the watch and various other figures, all of whom reminded him of that other navy, in peacetime, before the brutal ugliness of war. Perhaps that was the navy's secret strength. Able to hold on to something, tradition, ceremonial, routine; he could not imagine it otherwise.

He was met by a lieutenant, who said, 'The Captain is expecting you, sir.' He lowered his voice. 'But he asked me to show you to his lobby first. There is a shore telephone call for you.'

Martineau followed the midshipman, his mouth suddenly dry. It was probably someone from Derby House, but he knew it was not.

'In here, sir.' He did not see the midshipman's eyes as he stood back from a door. He was seeing someone else entirely: the destroyer ace, the man who had won the V.C. after ramming a German cruiser. A man who feared nothing.

He picked up the telephone. She must have heard the sound, and said, 'It's you, Graham.' So close that she could have been in the next cabin, or beside him.

'Are you all right, Anna? Tell me.'

'Yes. I can't talk about it, we might get cut off. But you know what's happening, Crawfie told you. She's quite a dear, just like Naomi said. I didn't really believe her.'

'I tried to call you again. I wanted to hear you, talk to you.'

'I know ... they told me. It was a lovely thing to do.' Her Canadian accent was even softer on the telephone. 'I was a bit out of it. I'd just heard about poor Caryl ... I still can't believe it.'

He heard the catch in her voice and sensed the urgency.

He said, 'You'll be hearing from my mother. I called her. She'd love to put you up.'

There was a long pause, then he heard her exclaim, 'She doesn't even know me!'

Maybe *put you up* was only a British expression. He said, 'I must see you again, soon. So much to talk about, so much to share.'

She said, 'In the hospital room.' Her voice broke. She tried again. 'You kissed me. I didn't want you to go.'

'I didn't want to leave.'

She gasped, as if moving to a different position. 'Ouch! That hurts!' Her voice was suddenly stronger. 'I didn't want you to see me like that. I couldn't even see you.'

'How are your eyes, Anna?'

A longer pause. She was tired, or drugged, perhaps, for the journey to Manchester. Not all that far away, Raikes had said. It was if you were heading up into the ice, to the unseen enemy.

'They're fine. Really. You mustn't worry about me. Take care of *yourself*. Will you do that? For me?'

He gripped the telephone harder to steady himself. *How can I tell her? I am afraid. I am afraid.*

She said intensely, 'You will be careful. Promise me, Graham. I want to see you again ... so much. You probably think I'm just another nut!' She laughed, and turned away in a fit of coughing. There was another voice in the background. Authority.

He said, 'I think you are a wonderful girl, and a very brave one too.'

A metallic voice intoned, 'This line is needed, please finish your call.'

She said quietly, 'Be very careful. You see, I think I'm in love with you.'

The line went dead, and no amount of clicking would shift it.

Somebody must have helped her to hold on to the line until she knew he was aboard. Crawfie? Or the paymaster two-and-a-half called Nobby?

In her work at Operations she would have known about the Russian convoy proposals, just as she would be aware of the enormity of the risk. Choosing the right measures, the best times

170

of the year, discussions, signals, counter-proposals, with the Admiralty always in the background to stir things up. She had been going on duty that night when the bombs had buried her alive.

Her voice was with him again, as if she had just spoken aloud. *You see, I think I'm in love with you.*

And now they were off once more, and she knew where he was going, and, more to the point, what it was costing him.

A steward had materialized out of the shadows. 'The Captain is through here, sir.'

She might already be regretting what she had said. But just to see her, to hold her, was like a dream in itself.

The cruiser's captain had several other guests, none of whom he knew except by sight. He was able to join in, even to answer questions about the Norwegian campaign, but it was like being an onlooker, someone else playing a part.

She had never spoken of *Hakka*'s previous captain, the one who had wronged her, maybe more than she knew or would admit.

It did not matter. *You see, I think I'm in love with you.* That was the only thing that did.

It was bitterly cold that night in Liverpool, and some two hundred miles to the south it was not much different. London was settling down, bracing itself for another night of air raids: the river, dockland, which had been flattened in places by the first attacks, or further south, the factories, the warehouses, and the railways.

The air raid sirens had already been sounded; that meant nothing any more. The attack might take the form of high-level bombing, massive incendiary raids to light the way, or a sneak hit-and-run assault on individual targets. The enemy airfields were, after all, only twenty miles or so across the English Channel.

But at Lavender Hill police station it had all the makings of a normal night: blackout shutters in place, the white-painted sandbags piled around the entrance and yard, a fire in the grate, a cat curled up on the station officer's rug enjoying the heat.

The night duty relief had already been paraded, given their instructions and gone out to their various beats. They were a mixed bunch because of the war and the suspension of police recruitment, old hands and special constables, and a sprinkling of War Reserve men. Enough, but only just.

With his back to the fire and leaning on one elbow, the station sergeant, who would have been retired but for the war, was going through the daily Occurence Book, a fresh mug of tea within easy reach. The cells were almost empty: two army deserters awaiting military escort, a drunk who had been found smashed in a shop doorway sleeping off his booze-up, and a vagrant who needed a bed for the night. The station sergeant could remember when that same man had been an earnest young tailor, a cutter in the factory near Clapham Junction. Then one evening he had gone home to his little house in Clapham as usual. There had been no house. No wife, no kids, just a bomb crater. His real life had ended then and there.

In the Job, as the cops called it, homelessness was nothing new, and in wartime it could only get a bloody sight worse.

But in Battersea it was all quiet. So far.

The constable on reserve duty passed through to poke the fire but paused, blinking in the hard gaslight as the station sergeant said, 'Give them stray dogs something to eat, will you, Tom? They'll be collected tomorrow, poor little sods.'

He picked up his pen. 'Now then, about that accident down at Arding and Hobbs. Could you get me the book . . .'

He swung round, irritated, as the blackout curtain moved aside and a P.C. in a cape peered in at them.

The station sergeant said, 'Bloody raining again, is it?' A glance at the old clock. 'What are you doing back, Mason? You only just went out.'

The policeman's mouth split into a great grin. 'I've got Jack the Ripper with me, Skipper. Says 'e wants to see you – *especially* you!' It seemed to amuse him, and the other constable moved closer to share it.

The station sergeant was not amused. It would be a long enough night without this.

Jack the Ripper was the nickname given by the local officers to a man called Roy Harper. A mechanic by trade in a small way, he had, like many others, fallen on unexpectedly prosperous times working in one of the countless factories, some no more than huts, which had blossomed everywhere to help the war effort. And to make far more money than any poor serviceman who would eventually be called to use the product.

Harper chose night work, which was even better paid, but unknown to most people he would often take an hour or so off to visit a prostitute. On one such night not long ago he had been found covered in blood, running from the scene of a savage murder. The station sergeant had seen some of the photographs, and with over thirty years in the Job, he had still been sickened.

The case had gone through magistrate's court, with Harper protesting his innocence, although circumstantial evidence had been found at the girl's Chelsea apartment to connect him with the killing.

Harper hardly fitted the part, and without more solid evidence the case had been thrown out without going before a judge. Harper had since become something of a local celebrity, and made a point of visiting the station whenever he could, to offer his 'advice'. To the other cops, Jack the Ripper was a joke. To the station sergeant he was not.

He snapped, 'Bring him in! Three minutes, then kick his arse out of it, right?'

But when Harper ducked around the dusty curtain he knew something had changed. He was different. No insults, no swagger. If anything, he appeared to be suffering from shock.

The station sergeant took no chances.

'Make it short, Harper, I'm busy. There's a war on, or haven't you heard?'

Harper took out a newspaper and spread it on the desk with care. The other policemen moved closer to watch. It was a south London paper, by the look of it a few days old.

There was a photograph of a sailor. From the white ribbon on his uniform, it had probably been cut from a wedding group some time ago.

The headline shouted, COURAGE UNDER FIRE. LOCAL MAN A HERO.

Harper was staring at them, his mouth trembling with what might have been fear.

'I kept telling them, didn't I? Nobody would believe me, *then*!'

He held up the newspaper and shook it. 'D'you think I could forget, *ever*? This was the face I saw that night, the man running away from her flat!'

The station sergeant kept his voice low. 'Ring around the pubs, Tom. See if you can raise the D.D.I.'

The officer, unwilling to miss anything, said, 'The pubs'll be closed by now, Skipper.'

The station sergeant did not take his eyes from the man on the other side of his desk.

'Pubs are never closed to the C.I.D. I'd have thought you would have known that by now.'

Carefully, almost gently, he took the newspaper, and murmured, 'Well, well, there's a turn-up for the book.'

Harper was backing away, eyes wild.

'Told you! *Told you*!'

'Let him go. We know where to find him.' He looked down at the cat by the fire. 'They'd better not cock it up this time!'

It was not such a bad night after all.

It was cold on *Hakka*'s upper bridge on the day of departure, but not unbearably so, and the rain had finally stopped.

This was the first time they had sailed as one complete group, with *Zouave*, the leader, followed closely by *Inuit*, *Java* and *Jester*, heading down through the anchorage, hands smartly fallen in forward and aft, the air cringing to the shrill of calls, and the occasional lordly blare of a bugle from one of the larger onlookers. They would make a fine sight for those watching from the shore and aboard the many merchant vessels.

Hakka would follow with *Kangaroo*, and *Harlech*, now affectionately known as 'the Old-Timer' by the more modern and rakish members of the group.

Martineau stood on the forward gratings and waited. In this berth there would be few of the staff from Derby House who would see them leave, he thought. He noticed that the officers and key ratings on the bridge had discarded their duffle coats and oilskins, and he was glad he had decided to leave his own heavy coat in the sea cabin.

He studied the other destroyers as they followed *Zouave* past two giant tankers. In each ship, every man from the leading supply assistant, or Jack Dusty, up to the skipper on the bridge this morning would be going over everything, in case he had forgotten some item which was his personal responsibility.

He looked down at the forecastle again. Fairfax was in the eyes of the ship, the same signalman beside him ready to haul down the Jack, until the next time. On bad days Liverpool could look bleak enough, but it was Monte Carlo compared with Scapa Flow.

He saw Fairfax's leading hand gesturing with a gloved fist. No mistakes, especially when casting off from a cruiser. *Hakka* had singled up all her lines, reduced now to head and stern rope, and one spring. He had heard the young navigator's yeoman, Wishart, asking someone why they were still called ropes, when they were in fact thick, dangerous wires. Nobody had answered.

Wishart was here now, chinstay tugged under chin to anchor his cap in the cold wind. It was probably the only one he had after his confrontation with death in the sea. He had been incredibly lucky that day, which now seemed like a year ago. He was waiting with Midshipman Seton for the navigator's instructions. Seton looked very pale and was biting his lower lip, troubled about something. His father, the Admiral, maybe? Or the next step in his career? Working so closely with Kidd, he would learn more about navigation and pilotage, and even ship-handling, than he ever would on the bridge of a cruiser or battleship, where he would have had to wait in line.

He saw some seamen running along the cruiser's immaculate deck, chased by a fierce-looking petty officer. When *Hakka* took the strain on that head-spring, woe betide anybody who moved too slowly to wedge a rope fender or two between the hulls to prevent damage to paintwork or worse. He leaned out and stared aft. He could see Malt's square shape by the guardrails, his own party of seamen loosening the wires around the bollards. The Gunner (T) was a good man when it came to creating order from the twisting chaos of incoming wires and springs. Martineau moved back again. A captain must never be prejudiced.

He put one hand in his reefer pocket and was taken by surprise. It had happened this morning just after Colours, when they all knew that the order to move was not going to be rescinded.

It was a pipe, a good make too. Fairfax had offered it almost shyly.

'I saw you'd lost yours, sir. I was given this a year or so ago.' He had grinned. 'Couldn't carry it off somehow. A quick drag on a hand-rolled Ticklers is about my mark.'

People might be surprised how close those links were. Fairfax had seemed embarrassed, even a little apprehensive that he had stepped out of line, a diffidence strangely at odds with the man who had taken command of *Hakka* under fire when his captain had been killed, and who had volunteered to board the drifting tanker when it was known that U-Boats were nearby and they might all have died for it. And he had still been quick enough to use his wits and save the lives of two of his boarding party.

He had added, 'I did try it a couple of times, but it's clean now, sir.'

Martineau had seen Onslow the yeoman of signals turn as they had laughed together, and he had answered, 'If that's the worst thing we ever share then I'll not complain!'

He dabbed the lenses of his binoculars and examined them without noticing he was doing it.

He had telephoned the hospital again and had managed to speak to some junior doctor. Anna had left and would be in Manchester by now, although her heart would still be here, with the ships and the battle she had so wanted to be part of.

He had also called his mother in Hampshire.

'Of course, Graham, I'd be delighted to have her here! But I can't stop now. I've got to rush off and . . .'

His mother kept very busy, with the W.V.S. and several charities as well as helping to organize outings and entertainment for older people who had been evacuated from London. Most of them seemed a lot younger than she was. And she always said, 'I've just got to rush off and . . .' especially when she did not want to make a decision on the spot. She probably thought he was about to make a fool of himself. He had known very early in the marriage that she had never really accepted or liked Alison.

'Signal, sir. *Proceed when ready*!'

'Acknowledge.' He walked to the forepart of the bridge again and saw Fairfax look up at him and raise his hand. To the voicepipe he said, 'Stand by, Swain!'

'Aye, sir.'

He looked at the masthead pendant, gauging the wind. The cruiser was moored fore-and-aft. She was like Gibraltar; you could not gauge the current from her.

'Let go aft!'

He heard the order repeated, the immediate scrape of wire over the iron deck, someone falling and being roundly cursed by Leading Seaman Morris, who would know by now that his request for a petty officer's course had been rejected.

'All clear aft, sir!'

This was the moment. 'Slow ahead port.'

He felt the vibration through his shoes, the distant thrash of one screw. Dead slow, but enough to carry her forward.

He ignored the bustling figures hauling the fat rope fenders along the narrowing gap of water as the spring lifted slowly to become bar-taut.

'Let go forrard.'

He saw the forecastle party dashing towards the bridge, hauling the rebellious wire with them.

'All gone forrard, sir!'

Just the spring now. He glanced aft and saw the stern slowly angling clear from the other ship. Wider and wider, almost forty-five degrees. He raised his hand and heard the last wire screeching through the bull ring in the eyes of the ship.

The Jack had vanished; the hands were already falling in again, distance hiding the patches and darns on their working Number Threes.

'Stop port.' They were clear.

He waited, counting seconds as a fresh-water lighter with a bad list chugged dangerously close astern. There was nothing he could do.

He saw the cruiser's captain watching him from his lower bridge, oak-leaved peak shining in the grey light.

'Slow ahead together. Port ten.' He studied another harbour craft and nodded, as if the burly coxswain could see him. 'Increase to fifteen!'

'Fifteen of port wheel on, sir!'

He saw *Kangaroo*'s raked stem coming around the cruiser's quarter, heard the shrill of calls, the salute answered by a bugle. Probably the same Royal Marine who had been on watch when he had gone aboard to speak to her on the shore line.

'Midships. *Steady.*'

Big Bill Spicer knew what to do; unnecessary helm orders only confused things when leaving harbour. Trust reached in both directions. Martineau looked down at some seamen running aft with spare wires to be stowed away. Did they know him enough yet to trust him? Did they have cause to? He touched the new pipe in his pocket. And back there in that vast Operations Room, where the battle was really fought, *Hakka* and her consorts would already be only a coloured marker, or an arrow.

Somebody said, 'Here comes *Harlech*. God, she's smoking a lot today!' and he heard another laugh.

'I said she should try to give it up!'

He must never give up, not for a second. He would crack wide open, and their trust would have been a lie.

'Fall out forrard, fall out aft! Starboard watch to defence stations!' The tannoy gave them no peace. 'Hands will exercise action stations in thirty minutes!'

The forecastle was empty, as was the Gunner (T)'s domain aft. A few of the off-duty hands still lingered at the guardrails, some with their special friends, their wingers, others quite alone, watching the land opening out to release them. Wondering perhaps, when, or if, they would see it again.

Martineau took out the pipe, and waited while Kidd took a fix on the old monument ashore, probably as much to occupy himself as to help Seton and train young Wishart.

'Starboard watch at defence stations, sir.'

'Very well.'

Sub-Lieutenant Cavaye had come to the bridge. He had proved himself a very competent officer. Martineau watched a starboard hand buoy sliding abeam. It was a pity he was so unlikeable.

He raised his glasses again and *Harlech*'s upper bridge leaped into focus; he could even recognize her captain's wind-reddened features. *Old-Timer.* He would be proud of that.

178

He saw the smoke, remembering the sky which had greeted their return here. The street, where one brave girl had died, and another had survived. And had saved him.

He could almost hear her laugh.

12

The Suicide Run

Scapa Flow, the main fleet anchorage in two world wars, was the Support Group's next breathing space before final orders were received. *Scapa*: even the word was enough to set the sailors' teeth on edge. A grey, cheerless place in the midst of the Orkney Islands, and protected by nets and booms, with gates to allow only authorized vessels to pass in and out.

Fairfax walked along the iron deck, and paused to listen as Ossie Pike, the chief boatswain's mate, gave instructions to a stand-by whaler's crew.

'If you fall in this lot,' he gestured around the Flow with his hand, 'you don't drown, you dies of poisoning, see? So watch yer step!'

Fairfax felt Midshipman Seton behind him, so close that he could hear his teeth chattering. He would have to get used to it. The stores people had done well, and there was plenty of warm, protective clothing on board. If the latest buzz was true, they were going to need it.

He looked at the swirling current alongside, dark, like the place and its reputation. The war had been only a few weeks old when a U-Boat commanded by the ace Günther Prien had made a mockery of the Flow's impressive defences. Submerged, he had waited and watched until the boom-gate had opened in Kirk Sound to allow a ship to enter, and had simply followed her through. It was not certain which target he had been hoping for, but the *Royal Oak* was the first big ship he had discovered. It had been night, and many of her people were in their hammocks when Prien had fired his torpedoes. Most of the first salvo had gone astray, so he had calmly reloaded and fired again. The great battleship so often shown at the beginning of cinema newsreels, her *R.O.* painted on a forward gun turret, turned turtle and sank. They said you could still smell the oil seeping from her.

Scapa's defences had been strengthened since Prien's daring attack, although most sailors classed it as another stable-door blunder. Now only the oil and a green wreck buoy marked the place, reminders of a great ship and her company, over eight hundred of whom still lay with her.

But there was humour too, as might be expected with the navy. Like the story of a sailor who had been caught trying to have his way with one of the many Orkland sheep, and had protested his innocence to his commanding officer by claiming that he had thought the sheep was a Wren in a duffle coat.

Atlantic escorts came and left as swiftly as possible; bigger ships swung around their anchor cables, and prayed that their German opposite numbers would leave their Norwegian hideouts, if only to end the boredom of waiting.

Fairfax had been doing Rounds with Pike, the Buffer, the previous evening after they had finally anchored and secured the ship. Outside the chief and petty officers' mess Pike had grinned and said, "Ere, sir, listen to this. The old Scapa 'and!'

It had been 'Knocker' White, the Chief Stoker, a man rarely seen about the upper deck, but who obviously had a very fine singing voice. Urged on by tipsy cheers from his messmates, he had been finishing what was apparently a song written just for Scapa.

> 'No bloody sport, no bloody games,
> No bloody fun, no bloody dames,
> Won't even give their bloody names,
> Here in bloody Scapa.
>
> Best bloody place is bloody bed,
> With bloody ice on bloody head,
> You might as well be bloody dead,
> Here in bloody Scapa.'

They had continued with their Rounds without disturbing the mess.

Pike saw Fairfax now and grinned.

'Just givin' these jolly jacks a few hints, sir.'

They all laughed, as if it was a great joke.

Midshipman Alan Seton gripped the guardrail below the whaler's davit and gritted his jaws together so tightly that the pain seemed to steady him.

He had seen how easily Fairfax got along with the ratings, without ever seeming to lose his authority. One of the seamen joining in the banter had been on the first lieutenant's report as a defaulter just before leaving Liverpool, and Fairfax had come down on him heavily. *A bottle*, they called it. If you got caught you took what was coming. No grudges. And Fairfax was always so confident.

He had heard his own father say it often enough. 'Never try to be popular. They think it's weakness – wet, if you like! They'll end up having you for breakfast, mark my words!'

It always came back to *him*.

He looked away, sweat like ice rime under his cap. It was coming again. He gripped the guardrail even more tightly. *Please, God, no.*

He tried to think of anything which would hold it at bay. Even of his father, the Rear-Admiral, who never seemed to be satisfied. Seton had two older brothers in the service, both lieutenants, one in the Med when he had last heard, the other on a long navigational course.

Making something of themselves.

He had never understood why his father was the way he was. His mother rarely commented on it, or merely said, 'He's only thinking of you, dear!'

It had all begun when he had told them that he did not want to follow family tradition and enter Dartmouth. Now, he could scarcely believe he had had the courage at that early age to say it.

And everybody else seemed to be better than he was. Under training, even aboard the old cruiser where he had done his first sea time, and where he had been prepared to come to terms with it, something had gone wrong. The instructors had offered little sympathy. *'We all went through it – what's so special about-you?'* was the main argument. And of course his father always got to hear about it.

He was not good at team sports, and disliked those who were. Only when he had joined *Hakka*, his first operational ship, had he found a glimmer of hope. The tail-end of the North African operation, when the captain and several others had been killed, had left him shaken but more confident than he could ever remember. Then the slow passage back to the Tyne where this ship had been built. He felt his shirt sticking to his skin. Impossible in this wet, cold air. But it was.

Newcastle ... a different world. He had met a subbie from another destroyer undergoing a refit, whom he had known briefly at Dartmouth although he had been in a senior class.

It had been like meeting an old friend. They had met several times, and then his friend had told him that his ship was leaving. They would have a party.

Seton did not drink, not to that extent. He could remember very little of the party, except that their number had thinned out until only his friend and two girls were left. He could not even recall the house, or to whom it had belonged.

He only remembered the girl. Short blonde hair, and a wide, sensuous mouth. She had done everything, had laughed at his clumsy inexperience. He had become a different person again when she had roused him to a state of excitement he had never known before.

The next day before joining his ship his friend had dismissed it airily, the man of the world. 'Don't get so serious about everything, Alan! A quick shag – she expected it, you didn't. Perfect combination!'

He should have known. Guessed. They had seen enough of those terrible films which showed what disease could do to a man so infected. At first he had refused to believe it.

Soreness, discomfort; you could expect that when you were in and out of the same blanket, on and off watch, trying to learn from your superiors. He heard Fairfax laugh again. *Like now.*

183

And that night when they had gone through the Channel and had seen *Grebe* explode, men on fire in the sea.

They had imagined that he was seasick, or so scared that he had wanted to throw up.

Damn them. Damn them all!

It was not going away. It was worse. He screwed up his face. *Worse than when?*

'We'll check the motor boat. It's coming back now.' Fairfax looked at him. 'All right, Mid? Coming down with something? Why not have a chat with the new doc, he'd welcome some business.' He turned aside as the Buffer called out to him.

Seton said, 'No, sir. It's nothing. Something I ate.' He was not even sure if he had spoken aloud, but the first lieutenant was on the other side anyway, watching the motor boat as it spluttered towards the boom.

'Excuse me, sir?'

He turned and saw Wishart hovering beneath the whaler. The boy who wanted to be a naval officer, who had no background, no tradition. An ordinary, middle-class boy, probably with parents who were proud of him.

He asked, 'What is it?'

Wishart frowned. 'When you lay off a course, sir, and you allow for the current, I'm not sure how you should make a fix.' He half-smiled. 'It got me a bit tied up, sir.'

Seton nodded, his mouth like parchment.

'Chart room. I'll show you. Pilot been on to you, has he?'

Wishart followed him, glad that he had plucked up courage to ask. He watched Seton striding ahead, so smart in his uniform with its white collar patches. He would be leaving for his sub-lieutenant's course soon. He sighed. He would have no trouble. An admiral's son; it would be taken for granted.

'Wait there.' Seton did not look at him. 'I'll get my notebook.'

Wishart waited, but all he could hear through the watertight door was Seton retching, almost sobbing, as if he were in pain.

Leading Seaman Morris, a heaving line coiled over one

shoulder, paused to say, 'Crawlin' round the officers' bums again, are you? You'll get no change out of that!'

Bob Forward appeared from around the forward funnel. 'That's right, Hookey. Didn't do you much good, did it?' He rocked gently on his feet, balanced as if for an attack. 'I could have told you. Thick as two planks, you must be!'

Wishart could only watch, unable to move. He had seen his friend like this before, with the big three-badgeman in that pub when he had made some sneering remark about him. As if it was always there, waiting to come out. And it was happening again.

The other leading hand said angrily, 'Can't you even take a joke in this ship?'

Forward smiled, but his eyes remained hard, steady. 'You're the only joke around here, *matey*!'

The door swung outwards and Midshipman Seton said, 'Come on, then.'

Forward watched them going to the bridge ladder. Something funny was going on there. Seton looked like death. As if he'd lost a quid and found sixpence.

He smiled and held up his wrist to examine the new watch. Then he turned and shaded his eyes to peer up at the bridge, the *clack-clack-clack* of the signal lamp. *Trouble*.

He covered the watch with his cuff again. It was to be hoped that it was waterproof.

Fairfax looked swiftly around the wardroom and saw Tonkyn give a curt nod.

'All present, sir.'

Martineau said, 'Please be seated if you can find a pew.'

He had never seen the wardroom so crowded, except for a party. Officers, chief and petty officers, every head of department large or small, their faces set in varied expressions as they waited for him to speak. Behind the pantry hatch he could hear the occasional stealthy clink of glasses, the stewards making the most of their privileged positions while they pretended not to listen.

Not that it could make much difference, not any more. With the other commanding officers of the group, he had listened to Lucky Bradshaw as he had put them all in the picture.

The next convoy to Russia was on. Some of the ships were already gathered in Iceland. Words like *essential*, *vital*, *strategic necessity*, seemed somehow at odds with the personal opinion Bradshaw had expressed to Commodore Raikes.

He looked around at their faces, Kidd with his notepad, Driscoll, keen-eyed, probably thinking of his guns and what would be expected of them. Trevor Morgan, the Chief: a different set of calculations. Miles steamed, fuel, wear and tear of everyday machinery, condensers, fans, everything. And Lieutenant Giles Arliss, the signals expert. He would be more than busy when the group was called to join the fight.

And fight there would be. He said, 'We shall leave Scapa in three days, so this is the last chance I shall get to talk to you all together. You will all be far too busy later on, Number One will see to that!'

It brought some grins, as he knew it would.

'It's a convoy to Russia.' They knew, of course, but he let it sink in. No doubts. They would all have their own ideas about the Arctic convoys. The Russians were bearing the brunt of the fighting until the Allies could put their feet on European soil again. It was so easy to explain, to justify, but there had been so many disasters. Only last year a convoy had been wrongly ordered to scatter. The merchantmen had been massacred.

He said, 'At this time of the year, daylight is reduced to a couple of hours or so each day. The rest is almost perpetual darkness. In its favour, it makes it harder for shore-based aircraft to locate and attack a convoy, likewise enemy submarines. The Russians are in desperate need of war supplies. We must deliver them. Those of you who have not served in those waters before will have heard all the horror stories. Those who have will know that most of them are true.'

More grins, and he saw Pike, the Buffer, nudge his friend Crabb, the torpedo gunner's mate.

'Our job is what it says. We support the escort commander whenever we can. Anti-submarine work, driving off surface craft, and covering the larger ships in convoy, if so requested.' He looked slowly around the wardroom, faces he had thought he would never come to know, had perhaps even dreaded it. 'Go to your departments and tell each man why this is important. You can blame their lordships, you can lay the blame at *my* door if you like, but tell them.' It was like hearing someone else. 'Like most of you, I've seen too many men, and women, killed for no good reason. Let us not forget them.'

He saw the new doctor, Surgeon Lieutenant Morrison, fingers interlaced in his lap, the scarlet cloth between his stripes like blood in the deckhead lighting. How did he feel about it, he wondered. After a big fleet minelayer with all the comforts of home despite the lethal cargo between decks, to be tossed into Arctic convoys. One would be enough.

The sailors had a word for that, too. The Suicide Run, they called it.

He gestured to Kidd. 'Pilot here will brief you on the possible route we shall be taking, ice and the enemy permitting. The rest you will be told closer to the time.'

The pantry hatch opened half an inch, and he added drily, 'After that, some refreshments will be available.' He smiled at Fairfax. 'At the wardroom's expense, of course.'

A gale of laughter echoed through the wardroom flat, and to the icy deck beyond.

They got to their feet as he picked up his cap from the table, and Bill Spicer, the coxswain, easily dwarfing everyone else, said, '*Hakka* won't let you down, sir.'

Martineau turned and looked at him, seeing some of those other dead faces as if they too were loath to go, to leave him in peace.

'I never doubted it, Swain!' He paused. 'And thank you. All of you.'

He heard the din as the door closed behind him, rank and status momentarily put to one side.

But all he could think of was The Suicide Run. What was being asked of men like those he had just left in the wardroom.

Three days later, as promised, the seven destroyers, with Captain Lucky Bradshaw's *Zouave* in the lead, passed through the boom-gate and headed out to sea in the middle of a blizzard.

An old sailor working on the boom-gate vessel watched them leave. He had spent a lot of time at Scapa in the Great War, and yet he could still feel the sense of pride when he saw destroyers on the move, showing off their paces and their perfect lines. But the weather soon hid them from view, so he was not certain how many there were.

But, on their job, it was better not to count them, he thought.

In Liverpool, and in the underground Operations at the Admiralty in London, the arrows appeared as if by magic.

And at the hospital in Manchester the girl Anna stood by a window, wrapped in a dressing gown while she watched and felt the window quivering in its frame, rain lashing at the glass.

But all she could see was that tall steel chair on an unprotected bridge, somewhere at sea at this moment. And the man who had been killed there. And the one who had taken his place.

She stared up and down the corridor, feeling trapped. *I'm useless here. I must get back. Then he'll know.*

But the wind and the rain had got louder. As if it had already been decided.

The second day out of Scapa Flow, and the weather had worsened from the start of the morning watch. Heavy seas driven by a biting north-easterly wind made every movement about the decks dangerous. Somehow the seven destroyers managed to keep some sort of formation, although but for the hazy radar pictures they could have been completely alone. Wrapped in their newly issued protective clothing, the watchkeepers and gun crews hung on to their positions while the hull lifted, rolled and then dived again, waves rising above the lee side to sweep along the deck like a tiderace. The heavy clothing was a reminder, too, that if a man was swept overboard it would certainly drag him down instantly. The *Java* had already reported a man lost in this fashion; it was useless to speculate about it. His cries would not be heard, and there was no chance of lowering a boat in these seas.

On the upper bridge Martineau sat wedged into the tall chair, the thrusting pressure of its metal arms against his ribs one moment, then falling away, while the shadowy figures held on for dear life, too battered even to curse their discomfort.

Men off watch were flung about on their messdecks, bruised and sore from encounters with guns or other immovable fittings, and unable to sleep because of the noise and the violent motion.

It was almost noon when daylight showed itself, if you could call it that. If anything, it was worse than the ignorance of darkness. The waves seemed bigger, not grey but green, rising up along the flared forecastle deck and smashing into the bridge structure like a solid mass. The gun crews below the bridge trained their weapons into the wind, and clung behind the shield for some protection, like seals marooned on a rock.

Martineau had studied the details of the convoy. Twelve ships in all. It did not seem very many to warrant the size of the escort and the back-up provided by the destroyers. There was even a small escort carrier listed. Unheard of a year or so ago, nobody had given them much of a chance. Built on the hulls of merchant ships and awkward to handle in any sort of bad weather, they were not much to look at, 'flat-tops' as their American builders termed them.

But within a year they had done the impossible, and had bridged the infamous Gap in mid-Atlantic which had until then been beyond the reach of shore-based aircraft. The Gap, where the sea-bed was strewn with the wrecks of precious merchant ships and their desperately needed cargoes, was the hunting ground of the U-Boats, where they could pursue their quarry on the surface with no chance of being attacked from the air.

The escort carriers carried the familiar Swordfish torpedo bombers, the Stringbags as they were affectionately known by the men who flew them, and some Seafires, the naval version of the legendary Spitfire. Not more than twenty aircraft altogether. But enough: the margin between survival and wholesale slaughter had been found.

Martineau remembered when convoys in these uncertain waters had been forced to rely on fighter catapult ships, converted merchant vessels with a fighter plane perched on a shaky-looking catapult. He had never met one of the pilots, but would have liked to. What kind of man would volunteer for such dangerous work? On the approach of enemy aircraft the fighter would be launched, fired from its catapult. There had been several reports of successes; no German bomber pilot would be expecting to be confronted by an eight-gun fighter hundreds of miles from nowhere. And afterwards? The fighter would be forced to ditch, its pilot baling out at the last minute, in the hope that one of the other ships might see him hit the water. A boat would be lowered, but it all took time. A man could freeze to death within minutes if his luck was against him.

At least the escort carriers had a deck to land on. Even that was probably hairy enough until you got used to it.

Martineau had studied the names of the ships in convoy. Most of them were large, and would be packed to the deck beams with brand-new weapons, tanks, aircraft, trucks. Three of the ships were American, two Canadian. The others were British. Not a fast convoy, but not a snail's pace either.

Below in the wheelhouse the motion seemed even worse. Faint grey light filtered through the clearview screen, but there was still no horizon to prepare them for the next roll or plunge.

Forward was the quartermaster, his eyes very steady while he watched the ticking gyro repeater, his legs slightly bent to lessen the shock of every unexpected movement. As if he was riding the ship, taming her. One of the bridge messengers had been sent away after retching over and over again, until he had had to run for the ladder. But he had left it too late, and the stench soon put two more men out of action.

Forward could put up with the weather, if it was going to keep the krauts grounded or in harbour. Not like the Med and the fight to force convoys through to beleaguered Malta. Bright, clear sky: you could see them coming for miles, the brown patches of flak seemingly useless as they flew on, their bombs ready to go.

'Port fifteen!'

Forward turned the wheel deftly. That was the Skipper's voice.

'Fifteen of port wheel on, sir.'

There was another voice up there now, the bearded navigating officer. He had heard someone say that the lieutenant had found himself a nice piece of crackling back in Liverpool, or somewhere close by. Lucky bloke.

'Steady.'

'Steady, sir. Three-two-zero.'

He eased the spokes back half a turn and murmured, *no, you don't, my girl.*

The Captain again. 'Good. Steady on three-two-zero.'

There were not many skippers who would think to thank a helmsman for doing a good job. They would expect it.

Someone had appeared with a mop and bucket, making a big job of it, while another messenger began to swallow hard, and retch.

He saw Wishart by the other door, his face screwed in concentration, two steaming mugs in either hand. It was always funny to watch, he thought. One leg raised as if to begin a dance or jig, but the deck suddenly tilting away, leaving Wishart swaying over again, but the mugs still intact.

'Good lad. Shove mine down there, eh?'

Wishart handed out the other mugs and then clung to a handrail, his face wet with spray or sweat.

Forward grinned and then swung the wheel again as the gyro tape ticked over the line.

Wishart watched and wondered if he would have the confidence to take the wheel. He had done it on the trainer at *St Vincent*. But you couldn't ram anything with a classroom.

Forward asked between his teeth, 'Where the hell are we, Wings?'

Wishart forgot his nausea. Forward's question made him feel less of a passenger, as he had heard Kidd describe somebody. *An officer, too!*

'The Faroes are to the west of us. About where we got to last time.'

Forward stared at the compass and said, 'We were on the other side of 'em then. That's how I like it. Between us an' the bloody German airfields in Norway.'

The door banged open and the coxswain strode into the wheelhouse, his eyes moving automatically to gyro, revolution counter, even the bulkhead clock.

He said, 'I'm taking over, Forward, so jump about, will you!'

Forward repeated the given course to steer. You couldn't even take offence at the coxswain's blunt manner. A true professional, and pusser to the soles of his boots. He noticed that he had somehow found the time and the place to have a shave, and had cut himself on the chin.

He asked, 'Flap on, Swain?'

Spicer was leaning forward towards the voicepipe's bell mouth. 'Cox'n on the wheel, sir. Course three-two-zero.'

Martineau must have said something. Spicer gave a grim smile. 'Thought you might, sir!'

He glanced at Forward. 'Bloody *Java* lost a screw, would you believe? Guess who's got to stand by!' He forgot Forward and the others and said, 'Half ahead together, sir. Both telegraphs repeated half ahead. One-one-zero revolutions.'

The deck reeled over and Forward said, 'Sod it!'

Wishart could not resist it. 'You shouldn't have joined if . . .'

Forward pushed him to one side. 'Cheeky little bugger!'

Wishart grinned and then became serious. 'What does it mean?'

Forward looked at the spray bursting over the squeaking clearview screens.

'Means the group will be two short. Cap'n (D)'s not going to like *that*.'

On the upper bridge, Kidd had just made much the same remark.

Martineau levelled his glasses and watched the other destroyer turning slowly towards him, her slender hull heeling over as the sea explored her weakness. Anybody could lose a screw under bad conditions. But *Java*'s commanding officer should have been doubly careful. If he was found to be at fault it could be serious for him. If the enemy found them, it would be that for both of them.

He said, 'They'll send assistance from Iceland. That will still give us the chance to catch up with the group.'

He never gives up, Kidd thought. He saw the light blinking from the other destroyer.

Onslow said, 'From *Java*, sir. *Nice to have you around.*'

Like Spicer, the yeoman did not need to be called. He knew.

Martineau looked at the other ships; they had almost disappeared in the murky haze of spray. Glad to be on their way. Nobody in his right mind wanted to become a sitting duck.

He said, 'Make to *Java*. *Don't lose the other one or I'll scream!*'

One of the lookouts laughed, but did not lower his binoculars.

Martineau said, 'Tell the first lieutenant –'

'I'm here, sir.'

'Good show. Could have done without this. But it might have been us.'

Fairfax's mind was already busy. It could end up as a towing job. *That's all we need.*

The darkness closed in again, and the strain of keeping station on the other ship became more intense. Not so close that they might collide, but not so far that they could not respond if *Java*'s other shaft seized up and left her a drifting hulk.

During the dog watches, when the motion had eased slightly and the cook had decided to serve some hot food, the radar reported an aircraft on a converging course, and just as quickly lost contact. A reconnaissance bomber looking for the convoy or its escorts, or perhaps it was only a coincidence.

Martineau knew from bitter experience that in these waters there was little chance of that.

Lieutenant Giles Arliss closed the chart room door behind him and faced the group by the table. Despite the piped heating the confined place was clammy, the sides and deckhead dripping with moisture.

Martineau and Fairfax, with Kidd bending across the table, looked up as he said, 'Signal, sir. From Admiralty. Most urgent.' He had a calm, level voice, as if it was not really his concern, which had been his whole attitude since he had joined *Hakka* as signals officer for special flotilla duties.

Martineau took the pad, dismissing his other thoughts, forming a mental image.

'R.A.F. Air Reconnaissance have reported that three German destroyers have left Trondheim. Believed to be *Hans Lüdermann* class.'

He looked at Arliss's blank features. 'Is this *all*? Don't they know when? For God's sake, man, they could be on the moon for all we know.'

Arliss said, 'Bad visibility, sir. Patrols were curtailed until –'

Kidd said angrily, 'Till we see the buggers coming hell for leather after us!'

Fairfax was thinking on a different plane. 'They're big, five five-inch guns. Eight torpedo tubes. Thirty-six knots. Nasty.'

193

Martineau stared down at the chart, Kidd's neat calculations. If it wasn't for the other destroyer crawling along at about eight knots, all she could manage with one prop without asking for further damage, it would not have mattered. The convoy was on the move, escorts in position, the little carrier *Dancer* well able to give extra cover if enemy bombers arrived. But surface vessels, that was something else. Fairfax had described them perfectly. About the same age as *Hakka*, and well armed.

He said, 'We have to assume that the enemy, Group North in particular, knows all about the convoy. They will have agents in Iceland, and there have been several cases of Icelandic trawlers supplying stores and information to U-Boats cruising offshore.' He smiled at their strained faces. 'It was Nelson who said that war makes strange bedfellows, I believe.'

A hatch slid aside and Petty Officer Telegraphist Rooke peered through, his breath hanging in the air like steam. He spoke to the signals officer, but his pointed, terrier face was looking at Martineau.

'Another one, sir. From Admiralty, concerning Captain (D)'s instruction. *Disregard. Rejoin Group forthwith.*'

Fairfax looked dismayed.

'Leave *Java*, sir?'

Kidd said, 'She wouldn't stand a chance!'

Martineau rubbed his salt-inflamed chin. Kidd was right. Three big destroyers? One would be more than enough for *Java*.

He pictured *Java*'s commanding officer. Lieutenant-Commander Hayworth, nicknamed 'Rita' by his men, was a keen, intelligent skipper. He did not know him well, but well enough; they had, after all, sunk a U-Boat together, while Fairfax and his crazy volunteers had been securing the big tanker.

Bradshaw must have gone over his head, direct to Admiralty where every move concerning the convoy would be under close scrutiny, as it would be in Western Approaches Command.

Over my head. His excuse would be that he could not break radio silence to speak ship-to-ship. No one would expect it. He saw his own hand on the chart, the deep scar which she had noticed, and was surprised that it was not bunched into a fist with anger.

He said, 'I will not leave *Java*. I shall tell her as much. Hayworth should know.'

Fairfax said abruptly, 'Could I say something, sir?' He looked at the others. 'Alone?'

Martineau felt his mouth crack into a smile. 'Spit it out, Number One. They have the right, too.'

'If we meet up with the destroyers, and there's a strong chance they'll be well away by now, maybe to escort one of their larger units . . .'

Martineau could feel his reluctance, and prompted gently, 'We might lose the day, and still not be able to save *Java*, is that it?'

It was the urbane signals officer who said it first.

'You'd be held to blame, sir.'

Kidd turned on him.

'Leave 'em, then? Is that what you're saying? By God, I'm glad you're not my C.O.!'

Driscoll's pacing on the deck above had stopped. As if the whole ship was trying to listen.

Martineau shook his head. 'This is what I intend. Stay with *Java* as ordered, until I know she's within safe reach of assistance. If we are attacked, then we'll turn and fight. Together we might at least divide their fire.' He felt the ship sway beneath him, more evenly this time. If the R.A.F. had been able to do a recce over Trondheim, then the Luftwaffe would be out and about, too. He looked at the scar again, and repeated, 'I will not leave *Java*.'

He looked at them. Crumpled and stained, skin raw from watchkeeping up there above their heads, but they were grinning at one another as if they had just been told of some great victory.

He thought of the high-sided waves, green and overwhelming, like that day when *Firebrand* had gone down. *Because of me.*

Then he pictured his father as he had last seen him, and as he had always remembered him.

Of command, he had once said, *it is the total responsibility. Choice never comes into it.*

He fastened his coat.

'Go round the ship, Number One. They know what to expect, but just let them see you, eh?'

He reached the next door and knocked off the clip, bracing himself for that first freezing blast.

He could not explain it, to them or to anybody. But he was no longer afraid.

13

Face to Face

Another day. It did not seem possible. The wind had dropped, and the sea had rearranged itself into long undulating rollers, the swell sometimes so steep that *Java* appeared to be half-submerged until she lurched over the next obstacle. Hard going for any ship built for speed and agility, and for *Java* it was ten times worse. She was barely making good the expected eight knots. Her chief engineer must be at breaking point, Martineau thought, as he lifted his binoculars again.

At least you could see her, and you had the impression that if only the clouds would break there would be full daylight again. It was almost noon, after all. He watched the ice shimmering like jewels from *Java*'s rigging and halyards, spray freezing as it drifted back from the bows. The hull and superstructure were almost white, and there was ice on the sea, patches of it on or below the surface, occasionally breaking and turning over in the deeper troughs, more like frozen snow than anything dangerous.

Sometimes it parted across *Hakka*'s stem, and drifted abeam on either side. He let the glasses fall to his chest and wanted to rub his eyes; the lids felt as if they were sticking together.

One more day at the most. Surely a tug would arrive by then. He gripped his glasses and raised them yet again to watch more tiny figures which had suddenly appeared on *Java*'s forecastle, getting rid of the ice, clearing away the gun mountings, checking the boats and Carley floats. Just in case.

He heard Kidd clumping from the chart room to the bridge and then back again. He was a fine navigator, and one who never took anything for granted. At this pitiful speed he might be miles out already, but somehow he knew he was not. The youngster Wishart was with him, carrying his instruments or some extra chart. It was to be hoped he was learning something from all this.

Midshipman Seton handed a note to the duty boatswain's mate and swung round as the seaman asked him something.

'I just told you, man! Are you bloody deaf?' He seemed to realize that he had been overheard and hesitated as if about to apologize, but instead almost ran for the bridge.

Cracking up? It seemed unlikely. He was young, and had everything ahead of him. Promotion might mean getting away from this sea, he thought.

Fairfax might know what was wrong.

'*Aircraft!* Bearing Green one-one-oh! Angle of sight two-oh!'

It was pointless to ask why the lookout had seen it and the radar had missed it. The cloud, the nearness of ice, there were a dozen reasons.

'*Action stations!*'

He heard the alarms, muffled by watertight doors and sealed hatches, imagined the men rushing to their stations, some glancing back at their messes, wondering if it was the last time.

'Radar – Bridge!'

Kidd was there. 'Bridge!'

'Two aircraft, sir. Same bearing.'

Kidd grunted. *About time.* But he kept it to himself.

And there it was, low down over the water, suddenly real against the clouds and the wet mist.

Martineau watched it, holding it in the lenses until his jaw cracked with concentration.

Someone said, '*Java*'s seen it, sir.'

Driscoll's voice, metallic over the gunnery speaker.

'Junkers 88. Turning away.'

Martineau moved along the slippery gratings, never losing sight of the aircraft.

Moving with deceptive slowness, indifferent. So familiar to Martineau that he could watch it without surprise. The Germans' maid of all work, bomber, fighter if need be, a ground-attack aircraft, and used for reconnaissance as well. It had proved itself in every role, and with a maximum speed to match most conventional fighters it was always treated with respect. The second aircraft would be up there in the clouds.

It was turning again, moving right, probably trying to work out what the two destroyers were doing.

Martineau said, 'Tell Guns to open fire with X and Y guns. Not much chance of hitting him, but it'll show him we're awake down here!'

The four after guns fired almost immediately, the flashes painting some drift ice with flame as if they were being heated from below.

Kidd watched the patches of smoke as the shells exploded, the JU88 rocking its wings as if to signal its invisible companion. To him, it looked like a contemptuous gesture.

'Shoot!'

The guns banged out again, and the aircraft turned fully away, its twin engines making dirty smears across the clouds.

'Cease firing!'

They might return to their base or they could fly on and look for the rest of the group, or the convoy. They had range enough for either. Two more hours perhaps, and then darkness would close in. And tomorrow?

Fairfax's voice, turning away from the speaker, possibly to glance at the sky.

'Fall out action stations, sir?'

One of the lookouts muttered, 'Too right! Time for grub soon!'

Somebody else even laughed.

'Belay that, Number One.' He rubbed his eyes with his glove. What was the point? The two aircraft probably had their own orders. *Hakka*'s company were doing well, especially when you considered that most of them had served in the warmer climate of the Med before Fairfax had brought the ship home for repairs.

'Radar – Bridge! Ships bearing one-two-zero! Range one-double-oh!'

Martineau gripped the chair as the deck heeled slightly. Lovatt, the ex-schoolmaster, was on the ball.

Ten thousand yards, five miles. Like that U-Boat.

He heard Driscoll again. 'All guns, with semi-armour piercing, *load, load, load!*'

'Second ship on same bearing, sir!'

Martineau stared at the mist. *Java* was almost invisible in it. Hayworth was ready; his radar was working well too.

Martineau shut the other sounds from his mind. The click of breech blocks, the rattle of ammunition hoists, someone shouting orders to the secondary armament, probably to keep their heads down.

Two ships. Perhaps another would appear soon. Thirty-six knots, Fairfax had said. He made himself look over at *Java* again.

'Signal *Java*, Yeoman. *Take evading action when ready.*' He looked at the mist once more. '*Good luck.*'

Onslow lowered his lamp and said, 'From *Java*, sir. *Negative.*' He sounded unsure, but continued, '*We will never give in.*'

Lieutenant Arliss, who had donned a steel helmet, snapped, 'What the hell does he mean by that?'

Kidd did not look up from his table. '*Java*'s motto.'

Martineau thought the mist moved slightly as if taken by a sudden wind. Then he saw the first waterspouts burst from the sea, green like the water itself, followed almost instantly by the echo of gunfire.

Firing blind. Otherwise . . .

He said, 'Full ahead both engines! Starboard twenty!' To Arliss, somehow alienated by the steel helmet, he added, 'Have the signal ready. Note the time in the log.' He felt the ship quivering as the revolutions mounted. Did it matter? Who would ever read it?

Then he looked across at *Java*. She appeared to have increased speed, but it was an illusion caused by *Hakka*'s sudden, sharp change of course. *We will never give in.* Hayworth considered that two could disobey orders, and had said so in the only way he knew.

At one of the last meetings with Lucky Bradshaw, he had heard Hayworth say quite seriously that he would have quit the navy if he could not have been in destroyers, long before he had been given command of one. The air cringed and more great spouts of water burst through the mist. Closer now. He imagined that he could taste cordite in the spray.

Hayworth might be remembering it right now.

He leaned forward and said, 'Open fire, Guns!'

Then he peered at the compass, his mind like the edge of a knife.

'Midships! *Steady!*'

They seemed to be rushing headlong into something solid; the mist was probably the only protection left them at this stage.

Thirty-six knots. The Chief had once told him that *Hakka* had managed forty on her trials. But she had covered a few thousand miles since then.

He gripped the voicepipes and felt them shuddering, like heartbeats. *Flash. Flash.* The mist swirling again, brightly orange, the fall of shot unseen but felt like body blows.

He saw ice being shaken from the anchor cables and sent flying across the forecastle deck like broken glass. The jackstaff, where he had watched the flag lowered when they had left Scapa, was like a pointer, or Kidd's pencil on his chart. Into the mist at full speed: she would make a fine sight if there was anyone to see her.

He dashed the spray from his eyes but knew it was sweat, and when he looked up he saw them. The enemy.

'*Shoot!*'

Midshipman Seton slipped and almost fell as the ship turned suddenly and violently to port. He clutched a stanchion and saw solid water surging up and over the side, before receding just as quickly as the rudder went hard over again.

And all the time *Hakka*'s forward guns were firing, and during the last turn, the after four-point-sevens were brought to bear. Seton had felt the shells ripping past the ship, the guns trained as far round as they would bear, the noise making thought impossible.

He felt more explosions, and knew that they were enemy shells, near or far he could not tell. Gasping for breath, he threw himself into the break of the forecastle where one of the damage control parties was crouched down, already soaked in spray and barely able to cling to their tools and extinguishers. Spare hands, some of them stokers. One man, Leading Seaman Morris, he recognized.

'I was told to report to the first lieutenant!' He had to shout above the intermittent crash of gunfire and the din of racing machinery.

'Well, he ain't here!' Morris glared up at him, his eyes red from strain. 'Gone back to the T/S, most likely!'

Seton gathered his thoughts. He disliked Morris, who was said to be a bully, but careful to stay within the limits of discipline when he could. He could feel the man's contempt, even now, when the ship was under fire. No *sir*, for instance.

One of the stokers peered over his shoulder. ''Ow many of 'em, sir?'

'Two. So far.' Seton recalled the snap of orders, the instant response from the gunnery control. And through it, the Captain's voice, tense but controlled, handling the ship, finding the enemy.

How I wanted to be.

'Here we go again!' They clung to anything they could find, pressed against steel plating which was barely thick enough to stop a bullet. Seton felt the ship buck beneath him and realized that he was lying face down, his fingers like claws on the plated deck. No sound, more of a sensation, like being sucked under water.

He saw the great column of water hurl itself up and over the forecastle ladder, then falling across the hull like a cliff. Through and above it he heard small, sharper sounds, almost incidental to the surging water. He stared with disbelief at the big forward funnel, at the jagged splinter hole just below the half-leader's stripe. There was smoke seeping from it, and he rubbed his ear as he realized that the blast had made him deaf.

He felt a hand drag at his ankle. It was the stoker wearing a headset, his mouth like a black hole as he yelled, 'Main messdeck, sir! Badly damaged!' He screwed up his face and tried to listen again. ''Nother hit aft!'

Seton pulled himself to his feet. There was no one else, not even a petty officer.

He said thickly, 'Fire party, follow me!' He saw them staring at the heavy watertight door; there was smoke spurting around it like steam. 'I said *move it*!'

In those few seconds, all doubt and fear were gone. More like one more boring drill than the real thing.

They knocked off the clips and opened the door, staggering like drunks in a dockside bar as the ship heeled over this way and that.

There was a fire right enough, and as the foam and water were sprayed over the mess space Seton saw some rolled hammocks standing in their nettings charred and smouldering.

He had accompanied the O.O.D. on Rounds several times. The first lieutenant he especially remembered, remarking on one occasion, 'Remove your cap, Mid. It's their home, remember?'

It was hard to see it like that. Smashed tables and broken crockery, a nude pin-up still pinned defiantly to someone's locker, although that had been blasted apart. Worse still, he could see the water through one of the holes, surging past, the buckled plating bent inboard like wet cardboard, framing it. The nearness of it.

'That's done it, sir!' The tall stoker with an extinguisher peered slit-eyed through the smoke, his face blackened by it. 'Hope our mess is OK!'

Seton clung to a ladder and peered around. Every thought was a physical effort. He could even recall the instructor's voice, explaining patiently about the risk of fire breaking out through forced ventilation.

He said, 'Close the vents. Try and pack those holes with –' He stared at some scattered clothing. 'That'll do!'

Then they backed away, holding on to one another while the deck swayed over and then reared up again.

They wedged home the clips and Seton said, 'Tell T/S, messdeck fire is out. Request instructions.'

Another small party of men dashed into the forecastle, Sub-Lieutenant Barlow in the lead. He stared at the sealed door and then at Seton.

'You did it! Bloody good!' Then he seized his arm. 'What is it? Were you hit?' Over his shoulder, he said sharply, 'First aid party, chop chop!'

Seton wanted to clutch his groin, crush the pain, destroy it. But all he could say was, 'No! I'm *all right*! Leave it!'

They all threw themselves flat as more shells exploded, seemingly on either beam. A straddle?

Seton pulled himself to the side and pressed his forehead on to the freezing metal. He felt splinters cracking into the hull, or maybe higher up, and another terrible sound. Someone screaming on and on, scraping his brain. Until, just as abruptly, it stopped.

Barlow straightened up. 'Follow me! Mid, you can stay here.' He hesitated, not the competent officer but more like the schoolboy again. 'If you're sure, Alan?'

Seton managed to nod. The pain was leaving. Releasing him once more.

'Fine! We're doing fine here!'

The communications rating shouted, 'Help wanted aft, sir! Wardroom!'

Someone gasped, 'Share-an'-share alike, eh, lads!'

They ran aft, ducking as a shell burst beyond the drifting mist, or was it smoke? Seton could not be sure of anything. But he saw the flash, and swung round with shocked surprise as one of the party was hurled from his feet.

Seton dropped beside him and gripped his arm. So short. Was that all it took?

The man was probably a stoker; he did not recognize him. Only the face, so pale through the smoky grime, the eyes filling it.

And just two words. *'Help . . . me.'*

Someone dragged Seton away. 'Bought it, sir. Best leave him, or you'll be next!'

Seton paused only once, as the ship heaved over yet again, her forward guns firing so closely together that it sounded like one massive shot.

The dead man lay where they had left him, but as the deck went over his arm seemed to move, like a casual salute. In some ways it was the worst part.

The wardroom was being used as a refuge for the wounded. The doctor, Morrison, was in his shirtsleeves, some thread in his teeth, his gloved fingers bright with blood. Others lay or squatted where they could. Plonker Pryor was bandaging a man's hand, his expression totally absorbed.

Morrison glanced up and said, 'Shell hit the cooks' and stewards' mess.' He jerked his head. 'Through there. See if there are any more casualties.' Then he looked at the man he was treating and said, 'Well, *that* was a waste of time!' He lowered the man's shoulders to the deck and crawled over to the next one.

It was then that he realized that Seton had not moved. Even when another detonation shook the ship, he merely put out one hand to steady himself.

Morrison said, 'I gather your father is pretty big in the service. An admiral, no less!' He studied the man he was about to examine. 'He'll be damn proud of you after all this!'

Another explosion made him hold his breath, but above it he could hear men yelling; it could even be cheering. He shook his head. Impossible. Strange, too, about the midshipman. He could have sworn that he was laughing when he left the wardroom.

Martineau lowered his head as spray cascaded into the bridge. This time he could taste the explosive.

He stared at the gyro repeater. *Concentrate. Concentrate.*

Hakka had been hit twice, with several near misses, one of which had been only a few yards from the engine room.

The two enemy destroyers had separated after Driscoll had managed a straddle with the first salvo. They doubtless realized that *Java* was no real danger, that she was damaged in some way. Both ships fired again and again, while *Hakka* weaved back and forth, her jagged wake marked again and again by the enemy's fall of shot.

The range was down to three miles, even less, the visibility so bad that even when one of the German destroyers showed itself it was swallowed up almost as quickly.

He tore his eyes away and stared aft along his ship. Splinter holes and scars, the whaler blown to fragments in its davits, blood thinning in the drifting spray to mark where someone had been cut down.

It could not go on. Just one of those five-inch shells could alter the balance.

He gasped as the bridge shook as if to tear itself free of the ship. Over the side he could see the port Oerlikon pointing at the clouds. Its gunner, still strapped in his harness, was headless.

There was a lot of smoke, and he pulled himself to the screen as a voice croaked, 'Wheelhouse hit, sir!'

Then another voice. Somehow he knew it was Forward.

'Helm's not answering, sir.'

Martineau called, 'Switch to after emergency steering!' Fairfax would deal with it. He gritted his teeth. If he was still alive.

'A hit, sir!' Driscoll sounded totally absorbed. '*Direct hit!*'

It was taking too long. Martineau looked for Arliss, but he was sprawled by the bridge gate, a hole in the back of his helmet you could put your fist through. Kidd stared at him from the opposite side and gave what might have been a shrug.

'*Torpedoes running to port!*'

Martineau gripped the side, his body bunched up, like that other time. Waiting for the crash. He stared with disbelief as the torpedoes, which must have been at minimum setting, shot past and into the smoke. Three of them, perhaps four.

The explosion was dull, muffled, but it was followed by another which seemed to tear the mist and smoke apart.

Kidd could barely speak. '*Java*. She came to join anyway!'

Men were cheering. Wild. Scarcely able to believe what had happened.

'Starboard ten.'

'Wheelhouse, sir.' It was Forward. 'Helm's answering again. Ten of starboard wheel on!'

'What about the cox'n?'

Forward was heard to cough. 'Sorry, sir. The cox'n was wounded, sir. I've got young Wishart sitting on him to keep him still!'

Martineau looked at the sea as it raced past. As it had been doing since his first order.

'Half ahead together. Cease firing.' He raised his glasses to see the *Java* poking through the smoke: he watched her until his eyes smarted, and he had to look away. *We will never give in.*

He looked at the dead signals officer, and knew he would have to discover how many *Hakka* had lost.

There were no more shells from the enemy. The second destroyer had obviously thought it unwise to continue with the attack.

Martineau crossed the bridge as a lookout called, 'Lights in the water, starboard bow!'

'Slow ahead together. Tell the first lieutenant to lower scrambling nets.'

He leaned out over the screen to watch the dark shapes being swept past the ship, their little lifebelt lights marking both the living and those who had already given in.

Kidd said harshly, 'I'd leave the bastards right there!'

Martineau touched his arm, and felt him jump. 'Remember what you once said to young Seton, Pilot? Like looking at yourselves, wasn't it?'

A few responded, seizing the nets and heaving lines, unable yet to accept what was happening. Some held on, but only for a moment, their eyes already glassy as the cold killed their remaining strength.

And some were able to climb up unaided, where they took blankets and cigarettes without a word being exchanged.

Perhaps it was better never to see your enemy face to face. From the upper bridge, you really could not tell the difference.

As the way fell off the ship the motion became more pronounced and the sounds of repair and recovery intruded even into the shuttered wheelhouse.

The coxswain sat in one corner, his elbow propped on a locker as he tried to see and hear what was happening while Wishart finished fastening the bandage around his leg. A seaman lay on the opposite side, his face covered with a signal flag, his feet tapping to the movement of the deck, as if he was snatching a rest. The blood said otherwise.

Others crept in through the trapped smoke, to peer at the bright punctures in the steel plating before taking over from the dead and injured. Hammers were banging everywhere, and the Buffer's powerful voice could be heard above all of it, urging, threatening, encouraging. A seaman looked up and remarked, 'Gawd, 'e'd survive the bloody flood, that one!'

Bob Forward wiped his eyes with his sleeve, watching the compass, his whole body tensed like a spring. The crash of gunfire, the sound of water thundering inboard from the explosions had seemed endless. He looked at the wheelhouse clock. Less than half an hour. He had heard the cheering, even caught a brief glimpse of *Java* as she had shown herself through the murk and smoke, empty torpedo tubes still trained abeam. She had fired at extreme range, a full salvo. It had paid off.

He found that he was grinning, and had to contain it. He would not be able to stop.

He saw big Bill Spicer peering up at him, his teeth gritted against the pain. A small splinter of Krupp steel. Not fatal, but it must hurt like hell. And the ship was still answering well. When the steering had failed, he had thought it was all over. Steering from aft was no use in a battle. It took too long.

He glanced around the wheelhouse; the fans were at last clearing away the smoke. It looked worse than it was. The dockyard mateys would soon cover the holes and hammer out the dents. Paint would do the rest.

A seaman carrying a box marked with red crosses peered in, then stood stock-still when he saw the man with his face covered by a flag. The coxswain watched him, and said painfully, 'No use, Fuller. He's gone.'

The seaman nodded. It said it all.

Forward had known both of them; they belonged to the next mess. It was always rotten to lose a friend, someone who had shared everything or borrowed occasionally when things were a bit rough.

He looked over at Wishart. He had done a good job with the bandage, learned it in the Boy Scouts, he had explained. And nobody had laughed at him. Some of them could learn a lot from him, he thought.

Spicer said, 'You've done your trick, Forward. Time to stand down.'

Forward smiled. Not much wrong with him, either.

Lieutenant Kidd had arrived now, with a dark smudge on his cheek and flecks of broken paint in his beard. He looked at Wishart and said, 'Well done. I don't need you just yet.' He nodded to the coxswain. 'I'll get you moved aft where the doc can fix you up.'

'I'd rather stay here until . . .'

But Kidd did not seem to hear him. It must have been as bad as it had sounded up on the bridge.

A boatswain's mate asked, 'Where are we goin', sir?'

Kidd was looking at the dead seaman, his friend standing by the door, unable or unwilling to accept it.

He said, 'Back to Scapa. When we get the word. *Java* too.'

But he was thinking of Arliss, the signals expert. Why did death have to be so ugly?

It was dragging at his insides, his nerves, like claws. It was always the aftermath, and yet this seemed worse in some way.

He thought of the little hotel, her arms wrapped around him. It had made everything so different, so vulnerable, when before they would just have lined up the pints and drowned the madness and the hate.

He thought too of what Fairfax had said about getting a command. He reached out and touched the plot table. He could not help it. He did not know or care if the others were watching as he said quietly, 'You'll do me, my girl. That's how it's going to be.'

With half the ship's company once more at defence stations, the work of clearing up continued. But the guns were cleaned and the ready-use ammunition replenished. The dead were removed either from where they had been killed, or where they had lost the fight in the wardroom and sickbay. Eventually Fairfax, looking tired and strained, reported to the bridge. Nine men had been killed and thirteen wounded, three seriously. To the people who collected the statistics of the war at sea it might not sound too bad, out of a ship's company of a hundred and ninety. But in the crowded and confined world of a fighting destroyer it was a loss which was hard to brush aside. They were too close, too interdependent for that.

It affected every part of the ship, even the wardroom where Lieutenant Arliss had never really been accepted, nor had he appeared to want it.

Martineau listened without interruption, seeing it, sharing it. It would mean a refit, during which time the promised Bofors guns would be mounted. New faces too, so that the ones like Wishart would suddenly become the 'old hands'. For a time, anyway.

Java, the ship which had suddenly changed from being the bait, or the target, had changed the odds with her torpedoes. Only one had found its mark, but the mark had been vital. The destroyer had exploded, and at full speed she had gone straight down. And ten German sailors had lived to tell of it.

He said, 'They did well, Jamie.' He touched his arm. 'You especially.'

'W/T have a signal, sir.' That was Onslow, composed, unchanged by the battle or so it seemed.

'Haul it up.' Fairfax looked at his captain again. 'The dead, sir?'

'We'll take them home. It's the least we can do.'

The signal was curt and to the point. Decoded, it read, 'Hakka and Java will return to base. In company.'

Martineau had taken out the pipe and was delving into his coat for some tobacco.

Fairfax said, 'I'll pass the word, sir. Pilot can lay off the new course.'

'I'll speak to them, Jamie. Just give me a moment and then switch on for me.'

Fairfax turned away and stared at *Java*'s blurred outline.

He had seen the Captain filling the pipe he had given him. Like putting everything else behind him. And then he had realized that he was unable to do it; his hand, the one with the crooked scar on it, would not stop shaking. It had been like stealing a secret.

'Fire away, Jamie!'

Fairfax switched on the speaker, and saw men turning to peer up at the bridge. And it mattered.

He looked at Martineau and was surprised to see the pipe clenched in his teeth while he moved to the handset.

'This is the Captain.'

A solitary gull swooped down and around the radar lantern, very white against the dark backdrop of mist and spray. The spirit of some old Jack, or so the story claimed.

Martineau stared down, seeing the wounds, feeling them.

But all he said was, 'I am very proud of you!'

He switched off the speaker, but as *Hakka* turned once more towards the south, his words still seemed to hang in the air.

Like reaching out. Like trust.

Commodore Dudley Raikes folded his arms and stared across the room at the floor-to-ceiling map and at the cluster of coloured markers which were being moved by a Wren with her long rake.

Captain Tennant, the Chief of Staff, was with him, as well as the duty officer.

Tennant said, 'Sounds good. So far.'

Raikes smiled briefly. 'The convoy is right on schedule. Two air attacks, both driven off by *Dancer*'s fighters – one shot down. One merchantman damaged, but still able to proceed.' He nodded his sleek head. 'It's working. I just hope the Russkies are grateful!'

The duty officer said quietly, 'Two escorts sunk. No more information as yet, sir.'

Tennant watched the scene in the Operations Room, like a vast, complicated mime, silent beyond the glass window. He turned to Raikes, and tried not to feel envious of a man who could appear so neat and in control at three in the morning.

But he said, 'And *Hakka*'s back in Scapa tomorrow. She'll have to go for a dockyard job.'

Raikes shook his head. 'Not for long, I'll see to that. A good time to have her new armament fitted.'

'And what about Martineau? You can't ignore the fact that he disobeyed Captain (D)'s order to rejoin the group.'

'Well, the group was not required, was it? It might be for the return run from Russia, but that's another story. He was in charge. He chose to stand by *Java*. She would have been sunk otherwise. And they bagged a big Jerry destroyer in the process. Martineau'll get no knocks from me.' He added softly, 'Or anyone else, I'd suggest.'

'I shall tell the Boss.' He smiled. 'If he'll stop long enough to listen!'

Raikes pressed his fingers together. 'The Support Group system is working. We shall need more group commanders to make it improve still further.'

'Like Martineau?' He watched the Commodore curiously. He knew that Raikes disliked Captain Lucky Bradshaw. Something from the past? Something personal? He had heard that Raikes had once served under Bradshaw, until his sudden departure from the navy. Memories were long in the Royal Navy, and Raikes had his eye on something better and higher than commodore.

Raikes said suddenly, 'I'm going south shortly to meet some

important people, from Admiralty. It won't do us any harm at all, I would think.'

Tennant could see his mind moving on, the time ticking away.

Raikes said, 'Second Officer Roche reported back to duty yesterday.'

'But I thought she was still on sick leave, after that bombing – I mean, she got knocked about a bit.'

Raikes gave a thin smile. 'She insisted. She's got what it takes.' He patted his stomach. 'Guts.'

'I see.'

Raikes glanced at the telephones. He didn't *see* at all. But that was the Admiral's problem.

He said, 'I shall take her with me. Things will be quiet in the group until Bradshaw gets back. My staff will be busy working up the new flotilla.' He nodded, satisfied. 'Going well.'

Tennant had seen and spoken to the soft-voiced Canadian Wren officer several times. It was interesting. Raikes and a Wren? It had to be something else.

A telephone buzzed and Raikes snatched it up. 'Yes. Why the hell not? I shall tell them!' He slammed it down and said, '*Hakka* will be in Scapa tomorrow morning. Then she's returning here. A fleet tug is taking *Java* to the dockyard. There will have to be an inquiry. However . . .'

The Chief of Staff departed with the duty officer. It was half past three.

Raikes picked up another telephone and sat patiently, tapping one foot while he waited for an answer.

'Ah, Crawfie. Sorry to get you up. Flap on? Certainly not. Everything's in hand. Now, about Anna Roche . . .'

He looked across at the great map and its coloured markers, and smiled. Like a game of chess, he thought. The right moves counted, nothing else.

14

The Only Way

H.M.S. *Hakka*'s return to Liverpool was both dramatic and moving, and so different from her first arrival, when she had joined the Western Approaches Command. On this cold, clear forenoon while the destroyer manoeuvred slowly and carefully into her prescribed berth, even the old sweats and the hard men were affected by the stillness and the silence of the busy, overcrowded port.

It was Sunday, although that meant little to Liverpool, which had become the main artery of the Atlantic lifeline, but gantries were still, and derricks aboard a newly arrived freighter were motionless.

Here they were used to seeing battered ships, merchantmen and escorts alike, and yet in the eyes of the ship where Fairfax waited with the forecastle party, watching the narrowing arrowhead of choppy water which separated them from the land, he could sense the difference. He saw men leaving other ships as if to some invisible signal, ready to take *Hakka*'s first lines when they snaked ashore. No waving, none of the usual banter, more as if they were sharing some privilege. And the same jetty was crowded with blue figures, like that first time, although most of them were officially off duty. They, too, were unmoving, except here and there where a sailor's collar lifted to the cold breeze, or a white handkerchief was used to dab an eye, and not because of the keenness of the air.

Fairfax knew what she had looked like, how she still must look after her brief sojourn alongside the destroyers' depot ship *Tyne* at

Scapa. The ambulances waiting on the ramp, the injured being carried ashore on stretchers, the coxswain still protesting, in spite of his splinter wound. . . . The Captain had been down there to see them taken ashore. He had seen him reach out to take a man's hand, or stoop to speak to another too weak to move, and had watched him smile and hold the coxswain's clenched fist as if to assure him that *Hakka* would never return to active duty without him at the wheel.

And before that, when *Hakka* had stopped engines for the first time, on her way to Scapa, for three men they would not be taking home.

Fairfax had felt it then, perhaps more than ever. What it was costing Martineau. *Take the weight, Number One.* And he had left the bridge and had walked aft to where the makeshift burial party had been assembled.

Three men. The young Oerlikon gunner who had been beheaded, a stoker who had died of his wounds, and one of the Germans who had been rescued only to die of shock and exposure shortly afterwards.

Of the young seaman gunner Martineau had said, 'His family will have enough anguish without discovering how he died.'

Fairfax had noticed that he did not use a prayer book. Perhaps he had done it too many times. Three bodies, *two of ours, one of theirs.* For many the worst part had been the sudden stopping of engines. Like a missing heartbeat. Men on watch gripped their weapons more tightly, some peered out at the dark waters as if they expected to see periscopes on every hand. A few simply prayed.

The others they had brought home. They were laid out now, stitched in canvas and covered by flags, the blackened splinter holes and the broken remains of the whaler telling only a fragment of the story.

Hakka would be going into dock, however briefly, and her promised Bofors guns would also be fitted. Men who had lost their clothing and other gear would have to be re-equipped by Naval Stores, new men fitted into the watchbill and daily routine. Fairfax got no sympathy there. *It's Jimmy-the-One's job, anyway!* But he was going to miss big Bill Spicer until he pulled some strings to get him back to his ship.

He looked up at the bridge and saw Martineau silhouetted against an unusually clear sky. No bridge coat or duffle. The destroyer captain.

Fairfax said, 'Now!' His leading hand reached back and then hurled the heaving line across the oily water, and he smiled grimly as three sailors reached out to catch it.

The starboard screw was thrashing astern, and although he could not see it Fairfax imagined the other lines being flung from aft.

Next, the wires, while more men dragged the rope fenders to absorb the first shock of contact.

He felt the deck shudder, the screws motionless, and saw the shadow of the flag as it broke smartly from the jackstaff.

It was Slade, the baby-faced bunting tosser. He had grown up quickly, he thought.

The leading seaman muttered, 'Company, sir.'

He saw the cars moving slowly through the usual waterfront clutter, big camouflaged Humbers, fortunately none of them displaying an admiral's flag.

'Fall out, fo'c'stle party! Secure!'

He walked aft and was surprised at the sudden appearance of men wearing perfectly blancoed belts and gaiters. A miracle when you considered the state of their messdecks.

Ossie Pike, the Buffer, tossed him a formal salute. 'Escort for the prisoners.' He had seen the staff cars too. 'Must do it proper!' But even he could not manage his usual sparkle.

The admiral at Scapa had insisted that the Germans be brought to Liverpool. The Boss would wish to take part in the interrogation; it was something he did with U-Boat survivors, when there were any.

He saw men lining the guardrails of the other ships, watching in silence. Some of them found jobs to do when they saw the gold lace spilling out of the leading car.

Fairfax recognized Raikes, the Commodore, and another four-ringed captain, a clutch of other officers and some dockyard experts, all turning now to watch the ship finally moored alongside, the brow already being shackled into place. *What a time for a visit. Hakka* was a mess. It always fell at the first lieutenant's door. . . . He smiled suddenly, aware for the first time of the strain he had been under.

Hardly an unbroken bottle in the wardroom, either, except what they had managed to scrounge off *Tyne*.

He heard Martineau's feet on the bridge ladder and turned as he said, 'They must take us as they find us, Jamie!' Then he hesitated. 'I thought they said . . .'

Fairfax saw the girl getting out of the car, answering something one of the others had asked her, but looking directly at the ship. Up at the bridge where the holes were still stark against the paintwork, maybe remembering that time he had taken her up there, how she had touched the chair, and had spoken of the previous commanding officer.

From what he had heard, she was lucky to be alive after the bombing.

Martineau was looking at the corpses.

'She shouldn't see this, Number One.'

Fairfax answered simply, 'She wants to share it, sir.'

Their eyes met, then Martineau said, 'Man the side.'

They came up the brow in order of rank, Raikes responding to the trilling calls, his eyes hard as he glanced along the ship, at the dead, the assembled prisoners, and finally the crisp new ensign which Onslow had got from somewhere.

She came last, stepping lightly over the brass name plate, and saluting the flag as smartly, as easily as any Royal Marine.

But her eyes were on Martineau. She took his hand and whispered, 'I'm so glad. *So glad.*'

Raikes said, 'Couldn't keep her in hospital! Not like some I know!'

Everyone laughed politely.

Then Raikes said, 'The Admiral will want to see you, Graham. As soon as you've cleaned up.' His eyes took in the faded gold lace and tarnished cap badge, and the darn on one sleeve, without apparent emotion. The other visitors were moving closer. 'Two of the press bureau are with me. Do 'em good to see a real fighting ship.'

Lieutenant Driscoll saluted. 'Escort for the prisoners has arrived, sir.'

Raikes said to him, 'Your gun crews did well, I'm told,' and Driscoll's pale eyes shone with pleasure.

'Thank you, sir!'

'Quick march, there!' Ted Crabb, the chief gunner's mate, gestured to the Germans. 'Move yerselves!'

They walked to the brow, some carrying items of clothing, one a parcel which someone had given him. Authority, it seemed, sounded the same in any language.

One, a petty officer, his uniform still stiff with salt water and from being force-dried in *Hakka*'s boiler room, suddenly stopped dead, and looked quickly over the group on the quarterdeck. His eyes fastened on Martineau.

Before anyone could stop him he marched across the deck, and then halted, as if uncertain what had made him do it. Then he saluted, his hand to his cap, his eyes intense as he spoke, his voice surprisingly steady after his ordeal, and the destruction of his ship and most of her company.

Then he swung around and marched after the others. For a moment there was no sound, and then Martineau heard her say quietly, 'He thanks you. For stopping to pick them up.'

Martineau looked at her, seeing the pain and the emotion in her dark eyes. Everyone else seemed to fade into the distance; even the ship was unreal.

Raikes broke the silence.

'I said your German would come in handy!'

The Chief of Staff intervened. 'I have your orders, Graham. Devonport dockyard, the only place with a spare berth. Two or three weeks should do it. Plenty to do, new ratings, supplies, that sort of thing. All in hand. The Boss gave it priority.'

Martineau heard the waiting ambulances revving their engines. *Eleven burials. Relatives informed. Travel warrants arranged.*

He felt her hand on his sleeve. It might have been accidental, but he knew it was not.

She said, 'I must see you.'

He looked at her, barely able to accept that she at least was real.

'You held me together, Anna.'

217

'I could say the same about you.' Then she smiled, and it was like seeing a cloud clearing away. 'I'm so glad I was here to see you come in. Like that first time. It was *meant*.'

Raikes said airily, 'You chaps can take a look round, but no photographs.'

Martineau looked at the deck by the whaler's davits, but all the corpses had gone, and the flags had been put away.

He said, 'I have no right . . .'

She touched his arm again. 'You have every right!' Someone called her and she turned away.

Fairfax had heard the exchange, and was moved by it.

'When you have a moment, sir?' It was the Buffer.

'Now will do.' He straightened his cap, the first lieutenant again.

Surgeon Lieutenant Roderick Morrison said, 'Right, sir, that's me finished.'

Martineau picked up his shirt and after a slight hesitation pulled it over his head. Strange that his day cabin still looked unlived in. Only the sleeping cabin had been used, for one of the wounded who had been taken off the ship at Scapa.

The sickbay was undamaged, apart from jars and bottles shattered by the gunfire. He wondered if Morrison understood how much he hated hospitals, and anything which reminded him of them.

He said, 'How is it, Doc?' and was surprised by the edge in his voice. Morrison had examined his back, the wound which had healed so well. Or so they had thought at the time.

Morrison said, 'It was a bad one, deep but clean. Good surgery if I may say so, not like some of the knife-and-fork jobs I've seen lately. But . . .' He walked to the desk and touched it with his fingers. 'Under normal circumstances I'd say it was sensible to do nothing. Let it bide its time.' He turned, and his face was grave. 'But nobody in his right senses could have expected you to do what you have done since your discharge from hospital. A new command, a different assignment, to say nothing of working with people you did not know. It was asking far too much. Of anyone. Of you.'

218

Martineau faced the bulkhead mirror and slowly knotted his tie, if only to give himself time.

He said, 'It was painful, lower down, when we went to assist the tanker.' He tried to smile. 'I shouldn't have wasted your time.'

Morrison looked at the deckhead as calls trilled again and feet scampered along the upper deck. He could hear the murmur of machinery, the scrape of mooring wires, a man's sudden, uninhibited laugh. A good sound, he thought, for a ship which had been in the thick of it. A ship on the move again, so soon.

He said, 'While we're in Devonport, you could take some time to go over to Portsmouth. Shouldn't be too difficult.' He paused, feeling his way. 'With your rank, sir.'

Martineau watched him in the mirror. A round, homely face, more like a country vet than a doctor.

'Go on.'

'Actually, the naval hospital at Haslar. The P.M.O. is a friend of mine.' He saw Martineau's eyes fall on his two wavy stripes and added cheerfully, 'We met at school, sir.'

More voices from that other, impatient world. At any moment now Fairfax would be coming to make his report. The ship was ready to proceed. He thought of the high steel chair on the bridge, where he had first felt the pain.

Or was he making excuses?

Morrison watched the hesitation with professional interest. 'He's a nice chap, sir. It won't go around the fleet, I can promise that.'

Martineau reached for his jacket and winced as he pulled it across his back. It was strange how he thought about his father much more now than he had when he was alive. They had always got on well, but had never been close. Perhaps his father had resented seeing his son progressing in the service which had rejected him.

Of his first command he had once said, 'A great privilege, I thought. I soon learned that responsibility went far deeper.'

Martineau said, 'I'll think about it.' He guessed that Morrison had seen his discomfort. 'It may go away.'

He glanced at the opened letters on the desk and wondered if Morrison had seen the paper with the lawyers' names printed at the top. Alison, or rather her father, had fired the first shot. *The protection of reputations of all parties concerned. A more flexible view from the outset, and so avoid damage to future ambitions.* They had all the right words, he thought. It was a pity some of them could not have been in *Hakka* on that last run.

And the other letter, the one which Tonkyn had brought to him personally in this cabin at breakfast. His expression had been a mixture of curiosity and suspicion; he had probably had a sniff at the envelope to test it for perfume.

My dear Graham.

A very short note, written, he guessed, before she had left on some mission at which Raikes had hinted. She could not say how long it might be. She would write to him. Call him, if possible.

It was so good to see you.

She had signed it simply, *Yours, Anna.*

Perhaps Raikes saw his own promotion drawing nearer. The Admiral, the Boss as they called him, had made naval history by selecting a Wren officer as his flag lieutenant. A pretty one, too.

He said abruptly, 'Anyway,' and smiled, 'Roddy. I can't keep calling you "doctor", it makes you sound like an antique!'

Morrison hid his relief, something at which he had become quite good.

'I feel it these days!'

Martineau thought of the letter again. How could he involve her with the mess of his own life? He had not been hurt by the lawyers' careful wording, an echo of Alison or her father. Instead he had been angry, perhaps unreasonably so.

He looked at the clock. Fairfax was right on the dot as usual; a tap at the door, and here he was. No barriers, but a new understanding, friendship.

'Postman's ashore, sir, special sea dutymen closed up, ship ready to proceed.'

Martineau picked up his cap and studied the gold oak leaves around its peak. There had been another bill from Gieves, too.

'But not the cox'n, Jamie.' He felt the doctor watching and listening, hearing the casual use of his name. The man on the bridge few ever really got to know.

'Leading Seaman Forward is acting chief quartermaster. He's the best I've got.'

Martineau took down his binoculars and nodded. The senior quartermaster, the man whose face had been covered with a piece of signal bunting, had been buried with the others.

He said, 'We're not too likely to run into the *Tirpitz* between here and Plymouth, d'you think?'

They laughed and went out into the cold air.

The doctor closed his bag. He would go to the sickbay and check up on the few inmates. Real lead-swingers, a pleasant change after the pain and fear of the wounded he had treated on passage back to Scapa.

He thought of the savage wound on the captain's back. Fairfax would never know how close he had been to having *Hakka* as his own command.

Their departure from Liverpool was noisy compared to their arrival, horns and whistles drowning everything while the bobbing cranes and gantries, chugging tank engines and bustling tug boats made it seem almost incidental. Except to those who knew. Who always knew.

Martineau stood on the port side of the bridge, watching the grey city, the cathedral and the familiar Royal Liver building sliding away. Then he glanced down at the unmanned Oerlikon gun, and thought of the letter he had written to the seaman's parents. He had been nineteen, like so many in this ship.

Responsibility.

'Port ten. Midships. Steady.' That was Kidd, watching the markers, the buoys, and any moving traffic which might ignore the rules of the road.

Martineau saw him turn and stare astern, his features not so strained as before. There were cheers now from men working on a big ship with a deck cargo of fresh timber.

He heard Leading Signalman Findlay chuckle. 'Och, look at them, will you? Their patriotism measured by their pay packets!' But he waved to them nevertheless.

He leaned forward and saw the line of seamen on the forecastle, swaying slightly to the swell as *Hakka* broke through a tug's steep wash.

Responsibility.

Midshipman Seton was down there as well, beside Fairfax. Perhaps he had had a letter too, from his father. He looked very on edge; maybe Fairfax had noticed it.

He tried to think of Devonport, wondering if Raikes had succeeded in speeding up the repairs. There would be no leave, except for locals and compassionate cases, and most of the company would have to eat and sleep in the Royal Naval Barracks. They would hate that, with barrack stanchions in gaiters bawling their heads off and chasing them about.

And after that?

He saw a small coaster blowing out black smoke. Any convoy commodore would love that one.

It would be back to the North Atlantic again. The wolf packs and the bombers, and surface vessels if the weather improved. Like the one *Hakka* and *Java* had sunk . . . and the German who had thanked him for stopping to pick them up. A handful out of two hundred or so. But it mattered.

He saw her face again as she had translated for him, and thought of the letter in his inside pocket.

My dear Graham.

Someone swore as he caught his foot on a piece of bent steel, where shell splinters had cracked around this same bridge, and Lieutenant Arliss had been killed outright only a few feet away.

He eased his shoulder under his jacket, the pain like a reminder.

He saw Tonkyn coming up through the chart room carrying his bridge coat, looking neither right nor left, as usual.

The bridge messenger glanced up from a voicepipe.

'Permission to fall out fore an' aft, sir?'

Another youngster. His name was Buckley, ordinary seaman. Fairfax had told him about it. Buckley's mother had been killed in an air raid, another case for compassionate leave. When he had arrived home he had found his father consoling himself with another woman. A wound which even Morrison's friend could never heal.

He smiled. 'Carry on, Buckley.'

He saw the young seaman blink, surprised that the Captain should remember his name.

222

Responsibility.

James Fairfax stepped into the wardroom, carefully avoiding the shining paintwork and varnished fittings. His day-to-day uniform already bore several stains to mark the speed of the repairs after only two weeks in Devonport dockyard. The noise had been incessant, with hardly a space unoccupied or unused by dockyard mateys. Rivet guns and welding torches, hammers and drills; at times it had sounded worse than the action which had put *Hakka* in dock.

Commodore Raikes had obviously had the influence to get things moving. Fairfax had endured several visits to yards for repairs in the past. It usually took a ship months to recover, or so it seemed.

The wardroom carpet was new; the curtain which divided 'the eats from the seats', as Malt the Gunner (T) had put it, was also new. Some of the furniture was the same, patched and cleaned, but comfortingly familiar.

It was good to feel the ship moving slightly at her moorings. She was still connected to the dockyard by wires and power cables, pipes, and brows for hauling the heavier stores on board.

He had been right round *Hakka*, and she was alive again, although in the daylight you could still see the scars beneath the paint and the new plating, and the dents along the hull where shell fragments had made their mark.

Even the Chief was happy with his engines, although he was known for his mistrust of dockyards. *Screw it down or lock it up, or they'll pinch the stuff!*

The promised Bofors had been mounted, and trained seamen gunners had been drafted into the ship's watch and quarter bills. Driscoll was as pleased as punch with his new toys. They would be useful in convoy work; each had a crew of four, and could fire up to one hundred and twenty rounds a minute. Accurately, it was claimed.

Fairfax sat down and the pantry hatch opened instantly.

'Pink Plymouth, please.' He looked at the new pictures of the King and Queen on either side of the ship's crest. But nothing could wipe out the memory, not completely, not yet anyway. The wounded lying here waiting to be treated, the dead covered over, their blood staining the carpet; *Hakka* had seen it all before, and she had survived.

He glanced at the clock. That was new, too. The Captain had left the ship the previous day, probably worried sick about handing over to him at a time like this, although he had not shown it.

'You'll be all right, Jamie. I've left a number where I can be reached. Call me any time if you get worried.'

It was something to do with his back, and that was all Fairfax knew. He knew that the doctor had examined a wound Martineau had received when he had rammed the German cruiser; he had seen the pain in his eyes sometimes, after hours on the bridge, but had not understood the reason for it. Morrison was like a clam; he probably knew more about Martineau than any of them.

Day by day, the dockyard workers grew fewer, and more of *Hakka*'s own company were released from the R.N. Barracks nearby.

There had even been word that the coxswain would be rejoining the ship sooner than expected. He grinned to himself and sipped the gin. The team . . .

And then there was Midshipman Seton. He was obviously unwell, although he had denied it when Fairfax had questioned him. He had slipped up on a couple of his duties, and even the Buffer had remarked, 'Got somethin' on his mind, sir.' The doctor was ashore, and had mentioned casually that he was going to beg some extra gear from the hospital. Under the *Old Pals' Act*, he called it. When he returned he would see Seton and examine him.

There had been no mention of a replacement for Lieutenant Arliss, but that could mean anything. As a compensation Sub-Lieutenant Cavaye's promotion had come through, and he had put up his second ring. Fairfax thought privately that he would be more insufferable than ever now. Cavaye was O.O.D., and although it was very cold on deck Fairfax guessed he would not be wearing anything which might conceal his new status.

He heard Kidd's voice, telling Wishart to fetch something from the shed he used as a store at the side of the jetty.

He strode in, and paused to inhale the paint-filled air.

'God, it's like a Maltese brothel in here!' He signalled to the steward. 'Same as the first lieutenant, please.' He sat down heavily and stared at his scuffed seaboots.

'Be glad to get out of this dump, and that's the truth.' He seemed tense, and waited until the steward had put down the glass and returned to his hiding place. 'Back to Liverpool, d'you think?'

'Bound to. Regroup the rest of the troops, and then we'll be off again.'

Kidd did not seem to hear him. 'You see, I was wondering.' He stared at his glass; it was empty. Then he grinned through his beard, more shy than embarrassed, Fairfax thought afterwards. 'The fact is, Jamie, I'd like you to be my best man.'

Fairfax stared at him. 'You wily old bugger! I knew you were up to something!' He leaned over and seized his big hand. 'Well done, Roger! Sorry for her, though, whoever she is!'

Young Wishart heard their laughter as he straightened his cap and headed for the brow.

Lieutenant Cavaye snapped, 'And where do you think you're going, Wishart? Leaving the ship without permission is akin to desertion, didn't you know that?'

Wishart swung round.

'The navigating officer has sent me to collect a box from the store, sir.'

He was hurt and annoyed by Cavaye's unnecessary outburst, although others had told him it was the nearest he ever got to making a joke.

But all he could think of was his friend, Bob Forward. He had met him coming offshore, earlier than he would have expected in a place like Devonport. *Guz*, they all called it.

He had intended to ask him something about watch bills for his notebook. They had told him it would be useful to keep details of daily routine, for the time when he would be sent to *King Alfred* to train as an officer.

Forward had almost ignored him. 'I'm not your nurse, Ian. Stand on your own for a bit.'

Like Lieutenant Kidd, who had also been very distant since their fight with the German destroyer. And yet just now he had heard him laughing his head off with Jimmy-the-One.

He hurried on. It would be dark again soon. Too late to fall in with libertymen. He was almost out of money, anyway.

He found the door, but the padlock was already unfastened. He would probably get the blame for that too.

The windows were filthy but he saw the big packing case, the smaller one resting on the top, just as Kidd had described it.

He peered at it closely to be certain and then tensed, instinct telling him that he was not alone.

He turned and saw someone in the far corner. The battle must have got to him badly; he was as jumpy as a frightened cat.

It was Midshipman Seton, probably sent on the same mission. It would explain the padlock.

'Sorry, sir. I didn't realize . . .'

Seton turned slightly, the white patches on his jacket catching the last of the light.

Wishart wanted to move, to cry out, anything. But he could only stare. Midshipman Seton was still turning slowly, but even in this gloom he could see that his feet were off the ground.

Leading Seaman Bob Forward walked quickly along the jetty, breathing hard, still angry with himself, for being unprepared and for taking it out of Ian Wishart.

He had gone ashore with the other libertymen to find a telephone. In their house in Battersea they had never run to a phone of their own; not many did down that street. He usually telephoned the local dairy which was open all hours; his mother did part-time work there now since his dad had died. He wanted to pass on a message for her. It was her birthday tomorrow. It seemed too good a chance to miss.

He knew the milkman who had answered the phone. He explained that she had not been into work for a couple of days, then had covered the mouthpiece while a train had thundered past in the background. Clapham Junction, where the cups and saucers rattled every time an express went through. Locals never even noticed it after a while.

His friend had said, 'I don't know what's up, Bob, but the cops have been round to your house a few times.' He had lowered his voice. 'Not the Old Bill, neither, but the plainclothes mob this time, right?'

Forward had made some excuse and had hung up.

It was impossible. Or was it? They had released the one they thought had done it. Innocent, they said. He had felt strangely uneasy that he had not cared, one way or the other.

Probably blow over. He had covered his tracks. The railway warrant would prove that. Compassionate leave . . .

He tilted his cap; his forehead was wet with sweat despite the cold.

He saw Wishart standing in the doorway of a hut. There had been no need to give him a mouthful.

He stopped and said, 'What is it?' then he walked slowly towards him. 'Sorry I blew my top back there.' Wishart was staring at him, his face quite white. Forward tried again. ''Course I'll give you a hand with your notes. Don't want you to end up as another bloody Mister Cavaye, do we?'

Then he saw the figure in the corner of the hut, and managed to catch and hold Wishart as he fainted. Like that day in the sea together, when they had both nearly died.

'Bloody Christ!' He called to a passing sailor, 'Call *Hakka*'s quartermaster, will you, mate?'

The man nodded and ran off.

Forward lowered the youth to the ground and held him in his arms, the doorway shielded from his eyes.

I knew there was something wrong. He heard hurrying feet. It was Jimmy-the-One, thank God. Cavaye would have been too much.

'What is it?' Fairfax beckoned to the sentry at *Hakka*'s brow.

'He found Mister Seton, sir. He's done himself in. Poor sod.'

Fairfax glanced at him. Something should have rung a warning. Kidd had been complaining about Seton's manner, his failure to return when he had sent him for something from the hut.

Wishart opened his eyes, and for an instant they saw the terror returning.

Then he said, 'Sorry, sir. I didn't know what to do.'

Fairfax patted his arm. 'How could you?' He looked up as Kidd loomed above them. 'The Skipper will have to be told. See if you can raise the doctor. He's probably still in the hospital.'

227

They were all here, the Buffer, and two A.B.s with a stretcher, Pryor the P.O. sickberth attendant, and Cavaye.

Fairfax looked up at the bearded navigator and said, 'And *yes*, Roger, I'd like to be your best man. It's the best bloody thing I've heard this year!'

Pryor said, 'Better cut him down, sir.'

The Buffer strode into the hut. 'I'll do it. Lend a hand, Thomas.'

He had done it with a length of wire, and must have died slowly, his feet almost touching the floor. What must he have been thinking in those last agonizing moments? He might even have been able to save himself if he had so wanted.

One seaman picked up Seton's cap and laid it on the stretcher beneath his head. Covered with a blanket, it was carried out of the hut.

Fairfax followed, his own cap in his hand. There would be an inquiry. Maybe Seton had left a note, or some message for his father, the Admiral.

'Take him to the sickbay. I'll inform the captain of the dockyard.'

Pryor followed the stretcher along the deck, where men stood aside to let it pass.

He knew, or thought he knew, what had brought it about. Officers were not immune. It was a shame all the same; he had seemed a nice chap. He grimaced. For an officer . . .

Fairfax walked back into the wardroom. His drink was standing where he had left it, and Seton had died in that time. Still a stranger.

He thought of Martineau. He would be there by now. It could wait. He needed a break. *And we are going to need him.*

Kidd slumped down opposite him and said, 'Rotten thing to happen.'

Fairfax shook himself out of it. 'Tell me about this lady you're going to marry. And we'll have another drink to celebrate, on *my* chit.'

It was the only way.

And at the other end of the ship, on the lower messdeck, Forward opened his locker and took out a bottle half-filled with hoarded rum.

Opposite him on a bench seat Wishart sat gazing at him, his hands clasped together on the scrubbed table.

Forward poured two glasses, feeling the youth's eyes following every move. They might all be dead soon, or the war might go on for years and years. Nobody knew anything for certain any more.

He pushed a glass across the table and waited for Wishart to pick it up. Then he touched the glass with his own.

'Mates?' It was all he said.

And Wishart nodded, his eyes bright with shock or emotion, it was impossible to say.

'Mates!'

15

'Ours Not to Reason Why'

The camouflaged army lorry, a three-ton Bedford, shuddered to a halt, steam rising from its flat bonnet from the rain which had finally stopped shortly after leaving Southampton.

Graham Martineau turned to the driver, a corporal in the Royal Army Service Corps, and said, 'Thanks a lot. I'd still be waiting back in Southampton but for you.'

'You live round here, sir?'

He eased his shoulders away from the hard seat. He could imagine what Morrison's friend would say about it. The road was a minor one, used it seemed by a local tank detachment, and very much the worse for wear.

'Just down that road.'

'I'd take you to the door, sir, but my C.O.'s following somewhere in his jeep. You know how it is.'

'Same in the navy.' He climbed down and gestured to the tin of duty-free cigarettes he had left on the seat. 'Thanks again.'

The soldier grinned broadly and let in the clutch. There were three men sitting in the back. They were, the corporal had explained, Italian prisoners of war. Working on the land, helping the farmers who were always short of hands. They looked cheerful enough; no guards either. It was a different war.

He turned away and stared along the narrow lane. The village of Lyndhurst was on the main road, as they jokingly called it, and it was also busy with military vehicles. The house stood apart from the village, on its own piece of land. Now, looking around, he could barely believe it was the same place. All the signposts had been removed; even the old milestone which had stated *9 miles to Southampton* had been cemented over. Surely if the Germans had got this far they would know exactly where they were going, but, like the concrete pill-boxes disguised as newsstands and the tall poles erected in every field to prevent enemy gliders from landing, they were marks of defiance, a small nation standing on its own. Churchill's famous speech, *We will fight them on the beaches. . . . We will never surrender,* had been about all they had had in those first months to sustain them. Now the threat of enemy landings had receded, and the high command was talking openly of invading Europe. To most it was still a dream, a hope. The starker aspects of everyday life took precedence: food and clothing rationing, fuel shortages, and the constant risk of death and destruction from the air.

He had telephoned his mother to tell her of his impending arrival, but the transport officer had been unable to wangle him a driver for the last part of the journey. The cheerful soldier had provided the solution, glad of somebody to talk to, officer or not, and to discuss the other war beyond his own camp and his duties in the battalion.

It would be something to tell his friends while he was passing the duty-frees around at the local inn.

It was good to walk, to take time to think, to see and smell the countryside again, so near the sea, and yet to any stranger you could be buried in the New Forest.

He was aware of his own sense of guilt at being away from the ship, no matter how justified the reason. Fairfax could cope; *he did before I stepped aboard.* And it would only be for three days.

His mind returned to Morrison's friend at Haslar Hospital, on the Gosport side of Portsmouth Harbour. Another surgeon commander, but so different from the one he had encountered before. Like Roderick Morrison in some ways, he had looked vaguely out of place in uniform, even though he was a regular officer.

The examination had been thorough but informal, if that were possible in a naval hospital. But the sights and the sounds were the same, and the smells, and the fear.

There was, he explained, a weakness caused by the depth of the injury, and above all the lack of time given for recuperation.

Martineau had heard himself say, 'Then there's nothing more I can do.'

The surgeon had shrugged. 'Your command comes first. As a doctor I should dispute that, but I've seen enough in the last few years to make me hold my tongue.'

Martineau stepped around a huge puddle, and saw some cows peering at him over a farm gate. Despite the lack of exercise in all shipboard life, he was not breathless. Not yet.

He thought of a man he had come to know in hospital, a submariner who had been injured in an air attack. Of his surgeon he had said, 'The chap told me I was fit for duty, but that I would always have a limp. Said it was just one of those things. But I've always been a bit of a fighter, so I said sod that, I'm *not* going to limp!' And he didn't. He was, outwardly, perfectly normal again the last time they had met, a few days before his submarine was reported missing, presumed lost.

He squared his shoulders and quickened his pace, heedless of the mud that sucked at his shoes.

It was almost noon. Had it really taken that long to get from Portsmouth? A postgirl was riding towards him on her bicycle, and slowed down when she saw him.

'Welcome home, sir! Good to see you looking so well!' She rode on, the bike wobbling dangerously under its weight of mail. She probably delivered his letters to the house, and to all the others around here whose sons were away, in one uniform or another.

His mother had been upset on the telephone because her friend, a local vicar, was away at a funeral, otherwise he would have picked him up in his car. He did get a petrol ration, and to all accounts worked hard for it. His mother always spoke warmly of him, and Martineau had sometimes wondered if they had discussed marriage. They were both free; it might be the best thing for them. She had joked about it when he had last been here, but that was like her. She had said very little about Alison, for his sake rather than for hers, but he knew she had never felt there had been much between them.

232

He saw a plume of smoke rising over trees: that would be the little pub where his father had often dropped in for a drink. There and back, it had been about as far as he could manage towards the end.

How different this would be in the summer, the greens of every shade and texture, the deer, and the would-be artists trying to paint them. But he was thinking back again. There had been no uniforms then, filling the trains and the stations, the pubs and the streets. Just ordinary people.

He paused and looked to the south, towards Beaulieu and the sea. Where he had been taken out in a boat as a small boy. He smiled reminiscently. A few years later he had been at Dartmouth, no longer one of the ordinary people.

He eased his shoulders again. Nothing. He looked around. There was a stile just about here, or had been. He parted some overgrown bushes and saw it. With a bad list, as the Buffer would describe it.

But the same one. The rest of the path had gone, ploughed into an extended field. *Digging for Victory*.

He gripped the wet, slippery bar of the stile and stared hard at his hand. *Suppose* Hakka *goes north again?* He shook his head. *When she goes north again. Can I take it? With people trusting and relying on me, can I be sure?*

He looked up, more shocked than if he had spoken out loud.

On the other side of the hedge was a dog, a big black labrador, tongue lolling, the tail slowly and then more confidently beginning to wag in welcome.

'Ahab!' He held out his hand and saw the brief hesitation, the caution; the dog had been younger and much smaller when he had last seen him. 'Here, Ahab!'

The dog leaned against him and sniffed his shoes and legs. He was accepted.

'If only I had a camera! What a lovely picture you both make!'

He looked up and saw her in the lane; at first he thought he was imagining it. Out of the familiar uniform, dressed in a long tweed coat and heavy boots, her chestnut hair covered with a scarf, she was like somebody else.

She watched his face and then ran towards him, her eyes not

leaving his until she was pressed against him, her arms around his shoulders. As if it was the most natural thing in the world.

He said, 'I couldn't believe it!'

She leaned back while he held her, searching his face for something.

'I phoned your mother . . . you said I should. I had no idea you'd be here.' She seemed to shake herself, controlling the tears, but only just. 'Then you called from somewhere, and she said you'd take this path.'

He nodded, watching her, wanting the words, the right words. But all that came was, 'I always do.'

They turned and walked along the lane, her arm through his, her hair pressed against her face as more rain pattered down from the leafless trees.

She said, 'This is perfect.'

He glanced at her profile, the raindrops which looked like tears on her skin.

'You are very lovely.'

She laughed, like that other time, and held his arm more tightly, two fingers inside his glove.

'I'm just a nice, well brought-up Canadian girl.' Then she faced him. 'And I love you. And there's nothing either of us can do about that!'

He turned towards her and held her again. Then he removed his cap and kissed her very gently on the cheek, but she turned her mouth to greet his. It was a perfect moment, something stolen, and yet alive with an awareness which they had both known but tried to contain.

They walked on, the dog bounding ahead of them, barking excitedly.

She said quietly, 'You need me. I need you. Let's not fight it, shall we?'

And here was the house, exactly as he had always remembered it. He smiled at her. And now, so different.

Anna Roche stood beside the draining-board and dried the plates as they were handed to her. It was a big, homely kitchen, or must have been once, she thought. She glanced at her companion, touched by the genuine pleasure in her arrival. In her sixties, she supposed, with a striking face and intelligent eyes. It was strange to realize that there was more of Graham in her than in the several photos she had seen around the house of his late father. *Another naval officer*, was that it? But her eyes were exactly his, like the sea, blue-grey, thoughtful one moment, distant the next.

She dabbed some soap from her borrowed jersey. That, too, made her feel completely different. Her uniforms were all new; the rest had been destroyed in the nightmare bombing attack. She could still hear the scream of the bomb, her own rising to match it. The gentle hand stroking her face, but so cold when the rescue party had dug them out.

She tried not to listen to his voice in the adjoining room. Calling his ship, or contacting someone who would.

His mother had delayed telling him that *Hakka* had been ringing this number. She had been so excited about his unexpected visit that she had forgotten, she said. Anna had seen their eyes meet briefly. They had both known it was a lie.

She said, 'I so enjoyed the meal, Mrs Martineau.'

The other woman looked at her. 'Call me Joan, all my friends do. You are that, aren't you?'

Anna smiled. 'I want to be.'

'I do, too.' She put down some knives and seemed to listen for a moment to the voice in the other room. 'I get so worried about him. You never know, *really* know what they're going through. . . . Unlike you. You must be right in the thick of it.'

Anna dried the knives mechanically. In her mind's eye she could still see the ship, the pathetic bundles waiting to be landed for burial. His concern for her, when it should have been the other way round. And earlier when the news of the battle had started to filter through various channels, the casualties, including one officer killed in action. She had died several times until it had been clarified, and had been ashamed of her own gratitude that it had been a man she did not know who had been cut down.

She said, 'We all try to share it, Joan,' and saw the other woman's expression soften. 'But in the end it's still *out there*.' She

235

had already told her about the German petty officer who had offered his thanks. Joan Martineau had nodded, seeing it. 'It sounds just like him. His father, too.'

She said, 'Three days – can you stay that long too? You're more than welcome. I can arrange things . . .' She looked down as Anna put her damp hand on hers.

'A friend, Joan, remember? I wouldn't be the cause of gossip for anything.' She looked around the kitchen, the black dog dozing now on a much used blanket. 'Here, of all places. No matter what I feel for him.'

'Thank you for that. I don't blame you.'

Martineau walked into the kitchen and said, 'I have to go back. Tomorrow.' He knelt down to pat the dog, but she knew it was to conceal his feelings. 'I have no choice.'

His mother said, 'Is it something you can talk about, Graham?'

He looked up at her. 'One of my officers is dead. Committed suicide. Just a kid . . . I scarcely knew him.' Anna saw his fist clench, the scar on the skin stark in the soft light. 'I should have seen it.'

She said, 'You can't know everything, Graham,' and then, gently, 'Did I meet him?'

'Seton.' One word. Then he added, 'Midshipman.'

So that was it. An admiral's son. She had heard others mention him.

He said, 'I can stay the night.' He looked from one to the other. 'After that . . .' He did not finish it.

Anna said, 'I'll call Commodore Raikes. He can arrange transport for you.'

The dog yawned and then changed it to a growl.

Joan Martineau patted her hair, suddenly girlish. 'That'll be the Reverend. He's bringing some things for the W.V.S.'

She hurried away, Ahab padding after her.

Anna folded the tea towel and faced him again.

'I was right there in Southampton, and I had no idea you were passing through. No idea until I came here.' She brushed her eyes with her wrist. '*Right there*. We could have met. Been alone.'

He cupped her shoulders with his hands and held her. 'My

236

mother likes you very much. I can see that.' But he was thinking of her words. *Been alone.* 'Has Raikes been treating you all right, Anna?'

Even the use of her name made her reserve scatter. What would she have done? What might he have thought of her?

She said, 'He's a machine. Dedicated, and pitiless towards others who don't measure up.' She did not resist as he pulled her against him. Without the formal protection of the uniform she felt defenceless, something she had sworn she would never be again.

She could hear their voices in another room. The Reverend, Joan had called him. As if he had no other name.

She felt the hand against her spine, the other cupping her chin as he lowered his face to hers.

It was not just a kiss. It was like fire. She could hear pounding in her head, shutting out the voices, the danger of discovery like this, in his mother's house.

She responded, her tongue seeking his, her body pressed hard into him.

'They're in here, Reverend. You must meet them before you go to your service.'

Martineau slowly turned the girl in his arms, feeling the need of her, the passionate response which had burned through their carefully worded excuses.

She looked into his face, her dark eyes very steady.

'I love you, Graham.'

They both turned towards the door as the others entered. The Reverend, a man with shaggy white hair and a surprisingly young face, and his mother, her eyes seeing and recognizing all the signs which she had known, and had never forgotten.

'We'll go and listen to the wireless. The news will be on shortly.'

They followed, his fingers touching hers, his mind still reeling from the embrace.

She looked at him again, one hand to her breast, holding it there as if it was his hand and not her own.

Outside it was raining again, and for just this small moment the war seemed a very long way away.

Jenner, *Hakka*'s petty officer writer, laid a folder on Martineau's desk and observed politely, 'The last, sir.'

Martineau looked quickly over the neat columns of stores, most of which were replacing those lost in their fight with the German destroyers. He paused to massage his eyes. A lifetime ago. After all the rush and disorder of getting the repairs carried out and the ship refloated from the dock, there was almost a sense of anticlimax. Fairfax had done well, very well, and had been sincerely apologetic about telephoning him and ending his brief leave.

Seton's body had been removed from the hospital mortuary and taken to his home in Guildford. The storm which his father, the Admiral, had threatened to raise about *the lack of interest shown by his son's senior officers* had blown over.

Surgeon Lieutenant Morrison had reported, 'I got most of the flak, sir. I was told that I would be called to an official inquiry, at which Midshipman Seton's father would also be present, as was his right. I explained that I could only hazard a guess at his reason for taking his own life, as he left no written explanation. But I also said that I would have to give the full medical evidence, as I was the first to examine his body after his death. The presence of advanced gonorrhoea, though in no way fatal, would have to be mentioned.'

It had stopped right there, as Morrison must have planned, but Martineau could find little satisfaction in it. As a very young midshipman he had also known desperate loneliness at a time when he had most needed advice. He thought of Anna's quick defence, *You can't know everything.* But somebody should have known, most likely Seton's own father.

He watched the petty officer gathering up the papers. He missed nothing, and would make a good secretary, or even a flag lieutenant.

He heard the mutter of distant machinery, the Chief testing something. Even he seemed satisfied now that the last of the dockyard workers had departed. He had been reluctant to allow the most senior base engineer to inspect his department. *Don't want any deskbound plumber meddling with my things!*

The ship was ready again. Stored, ammunitioned and fuelled, with a full company, or it would be when Spicer the coxswain rejoined *Hakka*. A new sub-lieutenant had arrived, who looked even younger than Barlow. A round, innocent face: another wavy navy officer from *King Alfred*, but one who had the advantage of having taken an advanced radar/gunnery course. It was to be hoped Driscoll would see it that way.

There had been no replacement for Arliss, which might mean that more authority would be vested in the leader once they got to sea again.

Being confined to the dockyard made the news of the real war seem all the more impressive, but strangely distant. It was ridiculous after so short a time in the yard, but he sensed it even in the most casual remarks, or when used as an excuse for some misdemeanour across the defaulters' table, although there had been remarkably few of those.

In North Africa the Germans were in full retreat, and a proposed invasion of enemy-occupied territory was being openly considered. Among those who were in the know, he supposed that Raikes would see it as something already set down on a plan.

The Russians, too, were forcing the German armies back. After their bloodily fought battle at Stalingrad the impetus had swung in the other direction. It was good to hear, but to those concerned with supplying their distrustful ally it would mean more convoys. Tanks, aircraft, guns, everything.

One thing was certain. They were returning to Liverpool. The group would be reunited, except for the unfortunate *Java*, which had been kept in dock with a damaged shaft after losing a screw in that appalling weather.

It all came down to weather, time, and distance. The worst of the winter and the permanent darkness was over. Next month would see seven hours of daylight in every twenty-four. It would mean a longer route for every convoy, and heavier escorts in case German surface vessels ventured out again to sever the vital artery to the Russian forces.

Martineau did not need to be reminded. It was like yesterday.

He opened a drawer and took out the photograph.

They had spoken of it during those last precious minutes together. When there is never enough time, never the right words.

239

He had insisted that she not wait. 'Go when the car comes for me.'

That had been in Southampton again. Wanting to talk, to touch, to be alone, when it seemed that every sailor in the south of England was passing by, all intent on saluting him and getting the right response.

She had half-laughed, half-cried. 'They're jealous, that's all!'

The car had arrived; Raikes had been as good as his word, or maybe he saw his departure as a blessing.

She had said, 'That old photo? You've really still got it?'

'It's lovely, Anna. I'd never part with it.'

For an instant she had looked uncertain, reminded perhaps of the portrait's first recipient.

Then she had hugged him and they had kissed. Somewhere, amused servicemen had whistled and cheered. They had heard neither.

He looked at the portrait now. The eyes, the beginning of a smile. Like that first meeting.

He had turned to look back, and she had still been there, waving.

Liverpool: she would be there now. He thought of his mother, and what she had told him of their little chat in the kitchen. *A proper girl this time, Graham. Don't waste the chance.* It was rare for her to be so outspoken.

He got up and walked to a scuttle; the air was still very cold when he opened it. He could see the little hut where Seton had been found hanging. It would be good to get away from here. For all of them.

Especially for Kidd, who had told him about the special licence he was getting so he could marry the woman who had been part of his other life at sea with the old Roberts Line. Liverpool again . . . There must be something about the place.

Fairfax was to be best man, and he was touched that he had been invited also. The team.

He shivered and closed the scuttle. It was March. Where had the months gone? He picked up the portrait once more. *When we could have been together.*

Hakka slipped her moorings the next day and headed out into the Sound. Few watched her leave. Another warship, that was all.

But not to the men fallen in fore and aft, chinstays down in the brisk offshore breeze, collars flapping with the brand-new White Ensign. Onslow, the chief yeoman, had told them that it was bad luck to fly a flag which had been used for burials. Thinking of his son, perhaps.

And the men themselves, still a few who would be caught out, shocked even when they turned to seek a familiar face, a special mate, forgetting only for the moment that he was gone for ever.

On the upper bridge, the usual pattern of order and purpose had formed. Signalmen with their glasses trained on senior warships, ready to fend off some critical or sarcastic message. Kidd by the gyro compass, the youth Wishart by the ready-use chart table; he had proved that he could do far more than sharpen Pilot's pencils. And Leslie Tyler, the new subbie, his new cap carefully bashed out of shape to look like an old salt, enjoying every second of it.

And right aft by the depth charge rack, Malt the Gunner (T), squat and unmoving by his quarterdeck party, and his leading seaman, who had not been recommended for promotion. Malt remained alone in this crowded ship, which was how he liked it.

Others shared the moment in different ways. The elation of survival, coming to terms with the course ahead. Fear, and the ever-present dread of showing it to your friends when you needed them most.

And beneath his feet Martineau could picture the scene in the wheelhouse, where men had been cut down and Bill Spicer had fallen wounded. The coxswain had tried to stop them carrying him below, just as he had fought, argued, and pleaded not to be put ashore on their return to Scapa.

Forward, the new quartermaster, had held them together that day. Not for long, but in the ship's nerve centre it had been long enough, when the loss of a single soul could kill a ship.

And Wishart, who had showed his mettle, and later his humanity when he had found the dead midshipman.

He walked across the bridge to watch Plymouth breakwater sliding abeam. The swaying lines of men were gone, as were the wires and fenders; the Buffer's world of seamanship, chasing any-one who seemed too slow for his standards in a crack destroyer.

It would soon be time to test and fire the new Bofors gun, to settle down to watchkeeping and the necessary routine of running a ship of war.

But it could wait a moment longer.

Martineau gripped the screen and tasted the drifting spray on his lips, while the sea opened up on either bow to receive them. Some dents and patches covered with layers of dockyard paint, some new faces. *But the same ship.*

They were ready.

And so *Hakka* went back to war.

Captain Lucky Bradshaw stretched out his legs and leaned back in the only big chair in Martineau's cabin.

'Did my heart good to see you come puffing in this forenoon. Pity about *Java*, of course, but still . . .' His eyes followed Tonkyn's tall figure as he emerged from the pantry, the tray balanced expertly on his wrist. 'Pinkers! Just the job!'

Martineau took a glass from the tray, wondering how men like Bradshaw seemed able to drink any amount at any time, and still carry on with their duties.

'You know we had a pretty straight job to do. I'd been hoping for a spot of action. Thought for a time we were going to get it.' Bradshaw looked at his glass, and seemed surprised that it was empty. 'Which is why I sent you the recall. I expect you were fed up anyway playing wet-nurse to Hayworth's *Java*.' He showed his big teeth in a grin. 'Still, didn't do you any harm as it turned out. Your decision, I'd have done the same, and it's given you another feather in your bonnet, eh?' He roared with laughter and Tonkyn reappeared with another large pink gin.

Martineau had always thought that Bradshaw had been treated very badly when he had been dropped from the Navy List. So why the doubt, something like suspicion, at even a casual piece of banter like that? Was it because he had been absent on each occasion which had brought *Hakka* into the spotlight? The drifting tanker, the U-Boat, and then a fight with two German destroyers and another victory, with prisoners to prove it this time.

Bradshaw was the senior officer of the group, Captain (D); he had nothing to fear from anybody, unless he made a fool of himself or incurred the wrath of their admiral. What was it? Envy? The Victoria Cross did affect some people that way. It simply seemed so out of character.

Bradshaw settled more comfortably in the chair. 'You ought to put yourself about a bit, Graham. All work – you know what they say. That pretty young Two-Oh on the Commodore's staff, now, she's a real catch.'

Martineau said, 'Good at her job too, I'm told.' So that was it.

Bradshaw nodded. 'Take my wife, for instance. Doing her best to keep things running at home, not really interested in the naval side, never was, I suppose, looking back. Keep 'em separate, I say!'

'I think we're going to be pretty busy anyway, from all the signs I've seen.'

Bradshaw frowned, disappointed perhaps by the change of tack. 'The Russian convoys, you mean? I've already made my views quite clear to *our commodore*. Given the escorts, we can get the convoys through, all the way to Murmansk and back, no matter what the Russkies say about it. Fast escorts, *destroyers*, we can do it.' He rubbed his big hands together. 'And this year, who knows, we might be supporting an invasion, in the Med maybe, that'd be my choice. Better than the bloody Arctic!'

Tonkyn cleared his throat discreetly.

'The first lieutenant is here, sir.' The briefest glance at the other officer and then at the clock. It said it all.

'Have him come in. I should know what it's about.' He looked at Bradshaw. 'If that's all right with you, sir?'

Bradshaw studied his glass. 'Your ship, Graham.' He added for Tonkyn's benefit, 'Getting to be quite a *long* one.'

Tonkyn walked towards his little hatch, no doubt doing the accounts in his head. Fairfax stepped over the coaming, his cap beneath his arm. There were spots of rain on his uniform, but this was Liverpool.

'Sorry to barge in, sir, but there's a shore telephone call for you. We're connected again. Headquarters.' He did not look at Bradshaw. 'Probably want us to shift our berth.'

Bradshaw called over his shoulder, 'Tell 'em *I said no!*'

Outside the door Fairfax said quietly, 'It's a personal call, sir. I thought under the circumstances . . .'

Martineau followed him to the quartermaster's lobby.

'You thought right, Jamie.'

Her voice was very clear and soft in spite of the various rattles and clicks over the line.

'I had to call. We might be cut off, so please listen.'

'I was going to ring you.'

'*I know. I know.* We saw you come into port.' The line went dead as if they had been disconnected, but he guessed she had covered the phone with her hand.

Then she said, 'I'm going to be away for a few days. I didn't want it, but I have to go. I did so want to see you, you must know that. But I have no choice.'

'I can come and see you as soon as I'm free, Anna. At least we could talk for a while.'

He thought he could hear other voices and imagined her in some office in that maze of corridors, where the lights burned all day and all night. When she spoke again he had to press the instrument hard against his ear to catch each word.

'You won't be free.' She could barely continue. 'I just had to hear you again. Promise me, *promise* me you'll be careful. I love you, Graham.'

This time the line did go dead. Coincidence, a hint of 'careless talk', or maybe she had been unable to continue.

He put down the handset and stared at the quartermaster's duty-board to give his mind time to adjust, but her words remained with him. *You won't be free.* And she would know. It was like a cold hand closing tighter and tighter, until his heart seemed to stop beating.

He should have expected it, and been prepared; they all should. But it was different this time. Like a door being slammed in your face, when before there had been hope.

He heard Fairfax talking to someone outside the lobby and made another effort to control his despair.

And Lucky Bradshaw was waiting for him in the cabin. *How can I face it?*

Fairfax said, 'Signal just in, sir.' His eyes moved to the cabin door. 'Captain (D) doesn't know about it yet.'

Martineau took the signal flimsy, surprised that his hand was so steady.

It was from the Commander-in-Chief, and addressed to the Commodore, Special Support Groups, repeated all commanding officers in Bradshaw's flotilla. Leave was cancelled immediately. Ships would be at twenty-four hours' notice to move. Top security and censorship to be enforced.

He said quietly, 'A big one, Jamie.'

'Not altogether unexpected, sir.' He looked towards the ships moored nearby. 'Ours not to reason why, as somebody once said.'

But all Martineau could hear was her voice.

You won't be free.

16

Victims

The corvette, the navy's maid of all work, had been designed and built at the outbreak of war, and intended principally for coastal patrol work. In appearance it resembled the whale-catcher, and the minds which had begun a building programme of these tough, lively little ships had never contemplated the vast Western Ocean as their destiny. Now there were hundreds of them, the most hard-worked and best known escorts on the Atlantic convoy routes. With a company of less than sixty officers and men, they were nevertheless overcrowded, and any kind of sea made watchkeeping a strain on every one of them. Of the corvette it was said, *she would roll on wet grass*. Few would have contradicted this.

H.M.S. *Anthemis*, a Flower Class corvette, was typical of her breed. She had weathered three years of war, spent mostly in the Atlantic, the killing ground, as sailors called it. Hardly a foot of her stubby hull was without a dent or a scar, to mark some encounter at sea, taking off exhausted sailors from sinking merchantmen, or passing through another convoy without the benefit of lights or, in those early days, the magic of radar.

Despite the discomforts and the nerve-dragging demands of convoy work there were few men who requested a transfer, no matter what they had proclaimed when they had received their draft chits.

Officers too had this sense of belonging, a navy within a navy. The four officers, including the captain, shared the same wardroom, such as it was; there was nowhere to hide, to conceal fears and doubts, except when they were lucky enough to be in their bunks.

On this particular March day, the sea was a shifting pattern of grey, broken occasionally by the unending crest of an Arctic roller. Against this hostile and bleak panorama *Anthemis* looked shabby and untidy, her dazzle paint in need of several more coats, her hull pockmarked with rust. For her size she appeared to be high in the water, as well she might be after another long convoy haul, and now her fuel was low, her depth charge racks almost empty.

On her small bridge the commanding officer lifted his glasses yet again, his eyes sore from the hours, the days, and the endless strain. He was tired and, at this stage of the journey, very conscious of the clothes clinging to his body, unchanged and dirty, like another skin beneath his soiled duffle coat.

Around him, and forward of the bridge at the single four-inch gun, their only armament apart from a pom-pom, the men on watch were reminded of what they had all gone through. This trip, the ones before it, for ever.

In his mind he could see it on the chart, his ship somewhere to the east of Jan Mayen Island, steering south-west, making for Iceland. They would probably be ordered to Seydisfjord, now a naval anchorage, an inhospitable place but quite safe. And there, *sleep, sleep, sleep.*

His head lolled and he made himself walk to the opposite side, his heavy seaboots cold and damp despite the thick stockings of oiled wool which his wife had sent to him.

He was a lieutenant-commander, Royal Naval Reserve, a peacetime professional sailor, once of the Union Castle Line. He could still smile about that. The Capetown run, the ladies in their low-cut gowns, the parties, the familiar haunts ashore. It was hard to believe it had ever existed.

Anthemis did not compare with such great ships. But she was his, and that was the difference.

He thought now of the ships which had been returning from Russia, survivors from the last big convoy, or one of them. They had to be moved, otherwise they might be iced in during the bitter winter up there beyond the Arctic Circle. Some of the merchant-men looked so decrepit it was a wonder they had made it. But as usual there was the curse of every convoy, the straggler, in this case a big freighter which had been carrying aircraft and spare parts when she joined a convoy on passage for Murmansk. There had been a lot of ice about, and the freighter had suffered engine trouble, the convoy's commodore doubtless despairing as every signal was either ignored or misunderstood. But the old ship had made it that time. Several did not.

Anthemis and her chummy ship *Cranesbill* were sent to escort the straggler for this final part of the return journey.

He heard the monotonous ping of the Asdic, another part of daily life, and tried not to think of sleep. His ship was on the seventieth parallel, and probably already out of range of German aircraft based in Norway. Tomorrow, with any luck, they would be within of their own airborne protection from the airstrips in Iceland. He dug his gloved hands deeper into his pockets. And even before that, they might think fit to send other ships to take over the last stretch. He felt his unshaven skin catch against the towel wrapped around his neck. Eight knots was their speed. A corvette was no racer, but she could do better than that.

He walked to the rear of the bridge and moved his glasses carefully from quarter to quarter. A vast, empty sea with a thin strip of silver, like a taut wire to mark the division between sky and water. Nothing more. But *Cranesbill* was there somewhere, following astern of the hated straggler.

Anthemis had taken position in the lead, to sweep for any inquisitive U-Boat, although there had been no reports of any.

He thought of the nearly empty racks. Enough for three salvoes of depth charges, no more. As the coxswain had wryly commented, 'After that, we'll go for the bugger with a cutlass!'

They had used all the other charges on the last leg of the convoy. There had been no wreckage, no obvious signs of a kill. But it must have given the U-Boat's crew a good headache.

He moved to the radar repeater and wiped the salt from it with his sleeve.

The two ships were still on station: the little blip was *Cranesbill*, the blurred one was the freighter.

There had been some trouble with the radar. On the blink,

248

which was hardly surprising. They were due for a refit, had been for weeks.

'Radar – Bridge?'

'Captain.'

'I'm having break-up with the reception, sir. It's just that –' He heard him gasp. 'Another ship, sir, at zero-five-zero! I'm sure of it!'

The corvette's captain was not a young man; he had been at sea all his life, since he was a cadet. But he had the mind and the resilience of one.

'Action stations!' He ignored the clamour of the alarm, and the way men were jerking out of the chilled torpor of watchkeeping, staring at him. As if he had gone mad.

He wiped the repeater again. It was all blurred now.

'Ship at action stations, sir.' It was his first lieutenant. 'Might be another escort, sir.'

'At that range? Too big, Number One.' He stared at the sea. 'Too big.'

He wiped his binoculars again with some tissue. The radar must be at fault.

He called, 'What range?'

'Five miles, maybe more, sir.'

He glanced at the sky. Still too bright. Another hour of daylight.

The air quivered, a heavy thunder, far away. He was just in time to see the reflection of a glare, as if above the clouds rather than beneath them.

'Signal, plain language, from *Cranesbill*. *Under attack by cruiser, request . . .'*

The yeoman said, 'End of R/T message, sir.'

The Captain nodded. 'Tell the Chief. Revolutions for full speed.' He tugged his cap over his eyes. 'Hard a-starboard.' He stared at the swinging compass, his mind quite clear.

Cranesbill had no chance. They would die today. But they would not be left to die alone.

More explosions thundered against the ship, the glare of the bursting shells making the clouds writhe and change shape. It was the straggler's turn now. In ballast, she would sink like a stone.

'Signal, sir?'

'No time for code, Number One. Make to Admiralty, *Immediate. Am engaging enemy warship.* They'll have our approximate position, so *get it off*!'

He heard the roar of shells, the explosion engulfing the whole ship, the columns of water bursting higher than the ragged ensign itself.

They were too slow to run, too weak to fight, and nobody would ever know what really happened.

The next salvo hit the corvette, blasting away the four-inch gun and its crew, severing one of the anchor cables like a knife through a carrot.

The Captain made to seize the compass for support but his boot had caught in something. *It was all wrong.* His face was pressing against ice-cold metal, and he knew he was lying on the bridge deck. He reached down to free his boot, but there was no boot, nor was there any leg.

Something slid past him, a seaman's glove, but it still contained a hand, so why was it moving?

The ship began to turn turtle even as another salvo ripped into her bowels and changed her into a hell of fire and steam.

And then there was only darkness.

The other warship continued to fire, but there was nobody to care.

Commodore Dudley Raikes stood by his window staring down into the main operations room. He held a telephone pressed to his ear, and reached out with his free hand to snatch a signal folder as Anna put it down.

'Where is it? Show me.'

She put her finger on the signal, but was looking beyond him at the constant activity below. Like a giant fish tank, she thought. All movement, but because of the special window and with the speakers switched off, completely silent. It had been like this since the brief, desperate signal from the corvette *Anthemis*. She saw Raikes's secretary's reflection behind her, with more information for his superior. In the adjoining room the teleprinters were going all out, Wrens and sailors hurrying from department to depart-ment. The chain of command. She was tired, her throat like dust, but nothing normal seemed to matter any more.

She looked at the big map, where two Wrens were moving another cluster of markers while a lieutenant called instructions from the floor.

Raikes had sent her on a mission to the Signals Distribution Office and she had not been here to see *Hakka* and the others head out from their moorings. Perhaps it had been deliberate on his part. Those same ships would be in Scapa Flow by now, or soon would be. She looked at the clock. About now, according to the last signals.

She was haunted by the two corvettes and the freighter which had been destroyed, wiped away, like the names of ships written in chalk on the casualty boards in the room below. Nothing left . . .

Raikes's telephone came to life, and she heard him snap, 'Well, get on to the R.A.F. *yourself*! What are you, a halfwit?' He slammed it down and looked at her for the first time.

'It's on. The big convoy is going through, no matter what! Thirty-seven ships!'

Nobby said quietly, 'Captain Bradshaw has just reported that his ships are in Scapa, sir, taking on more fuel.' He glanced at the girl and smiled thinly. 'I'll lay odds that *Java*'s skipper is none too happy about being in dock at a time like this.'

Raikes was scanning another signal but said sharply, 'He'll be a bloody sight *less* happy when I've finished with him!'

A telegraphist peered in from the adjoining room and said, 'Chief of Staff coming, sir.'

'Good.' Raikes pushed his hand across his hair. 'Now we shall see.'

Anna touched her inside pocket and felt the letter press against her shirt. It had been awaiting her return. She could not imagine how he had found time to write it with so much to do.

She had gone over it a million times. How she had clung to him at the house in the New Forest. Unable to stop herself. Not wanting to.

My dearest Anna. She had cried when she had read it the first time. But afterwards she had been able to read it with joy, and in a way it had given her strength. Perhaps it had done so for him too.

Captain Tennant strode into the room and looked through the window, as if he hated what he saw.

'We're all set. Iceland Command are prepared, and our escorts will be ready to take over the convoy exactly on schedule.' He was ticking it off in his mind, searching for flaws. 'There will be an escort carrier with the convoy, and a cruiser squadron is expected to cover both possibilities should the enemy have a go. The Commander-in-Chief Home Fleet is sending the cruiser *Durham* to join Bradshaw's group. It's about all we can do.'

Raikes regarded him calmly. 'May I ask, what does the Admiral think about it?'

Tennant shrugged, but smiled his thanks as a small Wren handed him a cup of tea.

'You know his views. He was firmly against another big convoy. Firstly, large convoys are more likely to be split up by bad weather or damage, small groups scattered over a wide area, which present the enemy with a better chance of dividing our support vessels and using their surface forces to good effect. Quite apart from the fact that it makes smaller groups more liable to detection by U-Boats. But he was overruled. The First Lord as well as the prime minister wants an all-out effort this time. If the Russians are to follow up their recent successes on land, they need every damn thing we can give them.'

Raikes was unconvinced. 'I agree with the Admiral.'

She watched them, and remembered what Crawfie had told her about Raikes's admiration for the Admiral. Seeing his own future, perhaps?

Like the trips she had made with him to Plymouth and Southampton, and to a top-secret staff meeting in Manchester. She had caught the glances when they had seen her with him. *His assistant.* Raikes never explained, not in her presence in any case. He never shared his thoughts with anyone.

What was he thinking now, for instance? Did he see all those little counters and flags as real ships, flesh and blood? Or could he separate one from the other?

Raikes said suddenly, 'I'm going down to the Met Office.

252

Coming?' He saw Nobby and asked almost softly, 'Is there *something* you wish to add?'

Nobby grinned. He was used to every mood.

'Full security in force, sir. We had some last-minute request from the Provost people, in connection with the civil police, I understand. Something about records of travel warrants issued in special cases, for one of *Hakka*'s ratings.'

Raikes exploded. 'In God's name, Nobby! I hope you told the silly buggers to jump off! Security indeed!' He snatched up his cap.

It was then that she noticed that, for the first time she could recall, his hair was over his collar, and he needed a shave. It made him seem quite human.

He said sharply, 'Come along, Anna, lot to do, you can powder your nose later!'

She saw Nobby smile. It was catching.

Another door opened and the noise flooded in, overwhelming, suffocating. Like her first day back from the hospital. She had wondered then if she would be able to go through with it. Like being buried alive.

But she could do it without flinching. Almost. She looked at boards and scribbled names but she saw only *Hakka*, and the scarred hand on hers.

Raikes was talking to the senior Met officer, and they were looking at a chart. Iceland, the Denmark Strait, the Norwegian coast, all the way up to North Cape. How could men stand it, day after day?

There was another figure now, very tall, with a single, thin stripe on his sleeve. Mr Holmes, the Admiral's signal boatswain, with the weathered face of someone who had stood on more ships' bridges *than most sailors have had hot dinners*, as Nobby had once said.

He had even been a boy signalman at Jutland, aboard the flagship *Iron Duke*. The Boss certainly knew how to choose his team.

He had a pad in his fist but did not bother to consult it.

He said, 'R.A.F. report just in, sir. Two German cruisers were reported in Bodø, bad weather prevented any useful reconnaissance.

253

Until today. They've both slipped out.' He observed Raikes impassively. 'No intelligence information as yet.'

Raikes clenched his fist. 'I wonder what their lordships will have to say about *that*?' Then, just as quickly, he was calm again. 'Going north, is my guess. They came from the Baltic originally. Narvik, Tromsø, or up to *Scharnhorst*'s old lair, Altenfjord, right at Russia's back door!'

Captain Tennant had quietly joined them, and acknowledged the tall signal boatswain as he departed.

'If we had more time . . .'

Raikes touched Anna's elbow. 'I'll buy you a drink.' He glanced at the Chief of Staff. 'Time? It just ran out.'

Martineau stood alone in his day cabin, aware of the shipboard noises above and around him without truly listening. They had taken on extra fuel, although they had used very little on the fast passage from Liverpool. But even a small amount could make that difference, the margin of endurance. There was still a tang of fuel in the air, although they had returned to their allotted moorings nearly an hour ago.

He wiped the glass scuttle with his sleeve and stared across the busy anchorage. It was unusual to see Scapa bathed in sunlight, which through the toughened glass gave an illusion of warmth.

Lying apart from the destroyers was the cruiser *Durham*. A fine-looking ship by any standards, powerful too, with twelve six-inch guns in four turrets, as well as torpedoes and smaller weapons. In addition she carried three aircraft which were launched from a catapult athwartships, invaluable for the work she was required to perform.

It was as if some superhuman power had taken over from the minds of mere men, rolling everything before it, as if nothing would or could divert the chain of events. The great convoy was already moving to its assembly point; reinforcements like the cruiser *Durham* had been transferred from their normal duties at virtually no notice. It was no longer a case of how, but when. Tomorrow, *Hakka* and her consorts would leave Scapa, with *Durham* in close company.

Thirty-seven ships of vital war materials: he had skimmed

through the lists at the conference aboard *Zouave* this morning. There would be time later to study the cargo details, to memorize the names of the ships and where each one would be in the convoy.

He swung away from the scuttle and looked at the signal pad on his desk. A huge operation. He felt his jaw tighten. But the smaller pattern of events could not be forgotten.

He had heard the motor boat returning alongside. Sub-Lieutenant John Barlow had been sent ashore to collect some charts from the base while *Hakka* had been taking on fuel. Now he was back. The schoolboy in a man's guise, like so many. Too many.

Fairfax had offered to break the ice. Martineau had heard his own curt reply.

'My responsibility, Number One. It goes with the job.'

Tonkyn had made himself scarce. But he was never far away.

There was a tap at the door and Sub-Lieutenant Barlow peered in at him. He had removed his cap, so that he looked younger than ever. But he had done well, better than many he had known who were much senior.

He said, 'Come in. Shut the door.'

It was all there. Anxiety, curiosity, nervousness because he expected a bottle for something.

'Sit down, if you like.' He stared at the signal pad, hating it. He should be used to it. But it mattered, and he was not.

'I've some bad news, Sub.'

Barlow swallowed hard and seemed to straighten his back. In a very level voice, he said, 'It's my father, sir?' He gazed at the ship's crest on the bulkhead, his eyes distant. 'He's had a weak heart for a long time now.'

Martineau said, 'I'm afraid not.' He walked over to him and gripped his arm. 'There was an air raid. Two nights ago. The house was destroyed.' He gripped the arm more tightly, wanting to help, to share it, when he knew he could not. 'Nobody survived.'

The young sub-lieutenant turned and looked at him, his face frozen with disbelief.

'My sister, too?'

He said, 'It was a direct hit. They couldn't have known anything.'

He felt sickened by those words. They always said that. *Of course they knew.* Like Anna, when she had heard the bomb's terrible scream.

Barlow did not resist when he pushed him into a chair. 'Two nights ago, sir?' The disbelief was still there. 'I was going to try and phone them, to find out if Dad was any better.' He shook his head. 'And poor Jane . . .'

'Is there anyone?'

Barlow said, 'My brother. He's a doctor, at the local hospital. He'll know what to do.'

Martineau moved away. He had sensed the bitterness. Something else hidden behind the schoolboy's face.

He said, 'We are under orders, Sub, but that you know. Otherwise I'd send you on compassionate leave this instant.'

Barlow was looking at him again, but was almost too blind to see him.

He murmured, 'I want to stay, sir. With the ship. With you. I'm a part of it here!'

Martineau heard a slight movement from the pantry.

'Would you care for a drink, Sub? Just the two of us. While you get your bearings.'

He shook his head. 'I'll be all right, sir.'

But two glasses had appeared through the hatch nonetheless.

Martineau handed one to Barlow and said, 'Just for a minute or two.'

He sipped the drink; it could have been anything. 'I'm glad you said that, John. We're going on a hard run this time.' He watched his words breaking through the pain, the loss. People he did not even know, and yet they were right here in the cabin, all three of them. He added quietly, '*Hakka*'s going to need the best we can give her.'

Barlow drank the neat Scotch without even spluttering. Then he stood up, and visibly braced himself.

'Thank you, sir.' It was all he said. It was everything.

Martineau sat for a while looking at the closed door. So many things required his attention, and there were people waiting to see him.

In all respects ready for sea. It must be fixed in every captain's mind. He thought of the secret report Bradshaw had shown him concerning the two missing corvettes, and that brave fragment of a signal. An epitaph.

Two cruisers were on the move. In his mind he saw the big operations room at Liverpool. She would be there, would know about the German cruisers which had been in Bodø. He confronted it, as young Barlow was facing his own anguish.

It was too important to allow personal doubts to intervene. It always was, now, and the one after this, and so on.

Fairfax opened the door.

'Go all right, sir?'

Martineau looked at him. 'It was hell, Jamie. Bloody hell.'

Then he walked to the ship's crest and touched it. As she had his medal ribbon when they had first met.

'But he's determined to stay aboard. I'm glad. He's good at his work.'

Fairfax relaxed very slightly. It was not the reason at all. It was because he cared about Barlow, *about all of us*.

He said, 'I thought you should know, sir, that Bill Spicer, our stubborn coxswain, has reported back for duty. Cursing like Long John Silver, and half awash with neaters, which for once I chose to ignore, *and* he's got a proper discharge certificate from the sawbones. I don't know how he did it, but it will make *my* life a lot easier!'

Tonkyn, stooped behind his hatch, listened gravely, and heard them laugh together.

He glanced at the whisky bottle. Still quite a lot left. He smiled. *Fair shares for all, I say*. He took out a clean glass.

In *Hakka*'s Number Nine Mess, starboard side, forward, the occupants were sitting around the table, waiting for the midday meal. When it was piped it was always, 'D'you hear there? Hands to dinner!' And there was always the rejoinder from the messdecks, 'And the officers to *lunch*!' Like most jokes on the lower deck, they were always word-perfect and never stale.

The mess was looking more like its original self again. New pin-ups adorned the dockyard paintwork, and neatly lashed hammocks packed the nettings which had been blasted into splinters.

Wishart sat on a bench, jammed between two other seamen, while Forward was in his usual place beside the mess locker.

Wishart had written another letter to his parents, and with luck it would go ashore tonight. He hated the idea of somebody reading and censoring his letters, and wondered if that was why Bob Forward never wrote to the girl he had seen in the photograph. He even kept that hidden. Maybe it was over, or maybe she was somebody else's girl? Like now, it was never easy to guess what Forward was thinking. The dark, deepset eyes gave nothing away, except for rare flashes, like the time he had caught him when he had almost collapsed after finding Seton's corpse. *Watching him from a corner.* Wishart shivered. And times when, without making a show of it, he had stood up for him when sneering remarks had become insulting or hostile. That never happened now, thanks to Bob Forward. It was said that he would become chief quartermaster because of his proficiency during the battle. The coxswain was back; they had all heard the din in the chief and petty officers' mess. Jimmy-the-One had been up there with them. No secrets in a destroyer. He glanced around. In *Hakka.*

Like the subbie, Barlow. His mother, father and young sister had been killed in an air raid somewhere in London. They all knew, but nobody would mention it. It was like that here.

And now they were going on a really big convoy operation. To Russia. Nobody had said so, yet everybody knew. What would the censor say if he had put that in the letter?

Up on deck the rum was being issued to the senior hands of messes. Down here they were all waiting expectantly. Lieutenant, as he was now, Cavaye was O.O.D. and would be supervising the issue as if it was coming out of his own pocket.

Wishart wondered if he would ever be able to wear that uniform, and be the part. It was all so different. He could smell the rum now. That was enough to go to your head. Someone might offer him sippers, but he hoped not; he knew his own limits. Like the time Bob Forward had brought him down here and had plied him with some of his own hoarded supply. When he had

258

apologized, or as near as he ever could, for not being interested in his studies.

He looked at him now, a man alone, despite the bodies crammed around the table, and the other messes nearby. He was using a needle and palm to put the finishing touches to a belt he had made to carry his knife and marlin spike, the mark of a real seaman.

It was hard to imagine anything which would hang on his mind, but something was. If only he could do something, to make up for all the other times when the withdrawn Forward had helped him.

Forward was well aware of his scrutiny but concentrated on the needle, the careful stitching on the leather.

Under orders. In many ways he was glad. Although that would stop or prevent nothing if it was true about the cops. But how could it be? Nobody knew, and his travel warrant had been wrongly dated. He was covered. For one day at least.

What made a girl like her into a bloody tom? Sleeping with anybody and everybody, letting them do what they liked with her, to her. It was wrong, although he knew that many were not so squeamish. In Alexandria he had seen the soldiers shuffling along in queues outside a brothel, some reading magazines while they waited, the whole thing supervised by hard-faced redcaps. *Next, please?* Sick, dangerous too, as the snotty, Seton, had found out the hard way. And his father was an admiral. He frowned. Serve him right.

But suppose . . . It had to be faced, like any danger. *You think it out.* When splinters had ripped through the wheelhouse and men had fallen dead or twisting in agony, blood everywhere, and the coxswain bellowing like a bloody bull on heat, he had stayed calm. It was the only way.

If the cops had really wanted to make trouble he would have heard by now. He had been at enough parades to watch some sailor weighed off for punishment, his skipper reading the Articles of War as if he was Nelson or somebody. There had been no delays when he had laid into the coward, and had dipped his hook because of it. No delays at all.

This was a top secret job. Even if every man-jack in the Andrew seemed to know about it. Outside inquiries would be unwelcome.

259

He looked down at the new medal ribbon on his jumper. A hero as well.

But if . . . He could run, desert. Plenty did. He paused, the needle poised like a dart down at the local his dad had used.

They knew nothing.

A pair of legs appeared on the ladder and the odour of rum filled the messdeck.

'About bloody time, Hookey!'

'When you pour, no thumbs in the measure, right?'

Forward relaxed and looked over at his young friend, for that he was. And for some strange reason, it mattered.

Outside a tug pounded abeam, the wash making the destroyer's graceful hull rise and dip to the moorings.

As if *Hakka*, too, needed to leave.

Lieutenant Roger Kidd shrugged his shoulders deeper into his heavy bridge coat and stared at the craggy, timeless panorama of the Orkney Islands. The group had left at first light, south through the boom-gate at Hoxa Sound and then west and north along the coast of Hoy. It was strange to be in one company again, he thought, with the cruiser *Durham* showing off her lines as she turned slightly in the watery sunlight.

Directly abeam was the oldest landmark, the tall pinnacle of rock called the Old Man of Hoy. Why was it there? How had it survived when the rest of the island had been eroded by wind and sea?

He looked round and saw the new subbie, Leslie Tyler, lowering his eye to the gyro compass to take a fix on the lonely pinnacle, as thousands of other sea officers had done before him.

Seemed pleasant enough, keen and well versed in radar. That was as far as it went. Kidd knew he was being unfair, just as he knew the reason why. On the bridge this morning, with all the bustle of getting under way again, lights blinking, orders and counter-orders from the shore and the cruiser, and Bradshaw's intention to do much as he pleased in his own group apparent, Kidd had gone to the chart table and had been surprised when he had bumped into Tyler. He had been expecting to see Seton. He shook himself. *Getting past it.* Seton was dead, kaput.

That was the real trouble. He had spoken impatiently, unfairly, to Seton the day he had killed himself. God alone knew, he must have been at the end of his tether, desperate, but he had not bothered to ask or listen. And he had sent Wishart after him. That, too, had been nagging him.

He stared at the passing landscape until his eyes watered. Once clear of the land, Marwick Head, where Lord Kitchener had met his death when the cruiser *Hampshire* had hit a mine in the Great War, the group would reform, with *Durham* in the centre, the leader and *Hakka* positioned on either bow, the others following in line astern. It might put some heart into the poor merchant seamen who would be relying on them in this big convoy. Kidd had sailed in larger convoys, but had had an ocean to move in. There was always a chance in the Western Ocean that you might get through undetected, unseen by the periscope's eye. Not much, but a chance.

On this run there was only one route, one destination, all within reach of enemy ships and submarines for much of the way. Aircraft, too.

He had not been able to see Evie when they had been in Liverpool. Officers' conference, intelligence reports to consider, hazards to navigation. There had simply been no time. Not even for the Skipper. He looked over at the empty, upright steel chair. Especially the Skipper.

But he had managed to speak to her on the telephone, conscious the whole time of others waiting to use it, their tempers and patience measured against their rank and status.

She had tried to console him. To reassure him, and to remind him of the one, special time they had shared.

In his mind he had seen the little hotel in Birkenhead. It was no Ritz, but it was always busy when the ships were in, and it was hers.

She was too pretty to pass unnoticed. There would be others who would soon be after her. Her, and the hotel.

They probably say that about me!

'I'll wait, Roger. I shall always wait for you.' He had heard the hesitation. 'Do take care, dearest Roger, I want you back. In my

261

arms.' She had been unable to go on. He knew he had not been much better.

He had told Fairfax about it, and he had listened, and had said, 'You get that special licence, and I'll get my sword out of hock for the occasion!' But Liverpool was a long way astern now.

Evie would hear about the two corvettes; they always announced losses on the news eventually. Bloody ghouls. Kidd had known the skipper of *Cranesbill*, an ex-first officer in a tanker. They must have taken on a bloody cruiser from the sound of it. Hopeless. Like trying to stop a charging bull elephant with a peashooter.

He moved across the bridge and raised his glasses to study *Durham*. Plenty of firepower, with raked funnels to give the impression of speed. Not that she needed it. She could manage thirty-two knots with no trouble at all.

But compared to a destroyer she was big. Big, and a liability if things went wrong.

He ground his teeth together. *Stop thinking of disaster. You know the score. Or should, by now.*

Lights flashed in the hazy glare, and flags soared up the cruiser's yards.

Onslow said, 'Preparative, sir.'

Kidd came out of it. 'Stand by to alter course. Acknowledge, Yeo.'

He stared at the island. Back to sea again. No reminders.

Leading Signalman Findlay said quietly, 'Captain's coming up, sir.'

Kidd nodded. *Get a grip on yourself.*

'Warn the wheelhouse.' He saw Tyler looking at him, his face a picture of innocence.

'Can I take over, sir?'

Kidd felt the spray in his beard. Somehow it helped.

He said, 'Stand by, Sub. Course to steer is . . .'

Martineau walked across the bridge and glanced at the cruiser as Onslow called, '*Execute!*'

Martineau smiled. 'Carry on, Mr Tyler. Take the con.'

He gripped the back of the chair and waited while Tyler gave his orders precisely and clearly to the voicepipe. Just a few degrees, and he heard the response from the wheelhouse even from here. A few degrees, but to Sub-Lieutenant Tyler it was doubtless like the breadth of an ocean.

He felt the pipe in his pocket and recalled what Fairfax had told him about the delay in Kidd's marriage arrangements. He would be thinking of it now, as the land dipped away. And young Barlow down aft with the depth charges, with no home to come back to. And Seton who had died because of his secret, and Arliss who had fallen just here, another stranger.

And all the others who had become a part of memory.

He climbed into the chair and heard somebody hammering shackles into place. The forecast was not bad, but that meant nothing up here.

He saw his reflection in the salt-smeared screen and thought of Anna. The girl with rain in her hair, walking with the dog named Ahab.

Like a dream.

'Port watch at defence stations, sir.'

'Very good.'

It was beyond their control now. They were all victims.

17

'Flag 4!'

Five days after leaving Scapa Flow, Lucky Bradshaw's support group and the cruiser *Durham* were steering north-east, some two hundred miles west of the Lofoten Islands. A gale which had been forecast to follow them in from the North Atlantic changed direction, and left in its wake long, unbroken banks of glassy rollers, rank after rank which lifted the ships almost playfully before fading into the distance. At times a roller would create such a trough that even the cruiser appeared to be sinking, with only her bridge and upperworks visible.

The sky was clearer for longer periods, the air intensely cold, so that even the briefest contact between bare skin and metal fittings offered a real chance of frostbite.

Men stood on watch, taking the motion with straddled legs, or braced in gun mountings, their breath freezing into scarves and balaclava helmets, while others peered through their binoculars, faces completely hidden by the special fur-lined Arctic clothing.

Martineau sat in his bridge chair with a thick scarf wound around his throat and mouth, the ends wedged into his duffle coat. Like most sailors he disliked having his head covered when he was on watch, and contented himself with his cap, on which the oak leaves were already tarnished beyond recognition.

Signals were rare, brief and, of necessity, vague.

The convoy's sailing day had been delayed by that same gale, and so the group should rendezvous with the covering escort a day earlier than originally planned. Martineau shifted his buttocks on the chair. They felt numb. He heard Onslow, the chief yeoman, speaking with two of his signalmen. No slip-ups; be ready for anything. *Durham* had already made some witty signals when the veteran destroyer *Harlech* had lost station on her.

In a rare show of anger Onslow had snapped, 'It's all right for them big ship wallahs – dry decks and a place to swing a hammock! I'll bet they bake fresh bread every day, too!'

'Aircraft! Green four-five, angle of sight three-five!'

The nearest gun muzzles swung on to the bearing, as if the movement was automatic and not controlled by stiff, freezing fingers.

Someone managed a cheer. 'Stringbag!'

A bright green flare drifted lazily towards the dull, heaving water, but all eyes were on the Swordfish torpedo bomber, the familiar 'Stringbag'. Not unlike the biplanes of the Great War, and with a personality all their own: pilots who flew them swore they would never change. Slow, with open, windswept cockpits, it was impossible to imagine how the crew felt in this weather. Even now, as the aircraft dipped and tilted its wings, *Hakka* plunged her nose into another roller, the spray bursting up through the hawsepipes, more like steam than water. The deck up there would be like glass.

It was Fairfax's watch, and he said, 'Bang on time, sir.'

Martineau nodded, and winced as the scarf scraped his neck like broken wire. The escort carrier *Dancer* was with the convoy escort. In this kind of sea those little makeshift carriers could rise and fall thirty feet or more; he had seen aircraft trying to land in those conditions, the deck rising like a wall, or falling like a giant slide at the very moment of approach. Usually they made it. Some did not.

He stared abeam and watched the Swordfish turn away and skim over the cruiser's mastheads.

He had pictured the giant operation in his mind. The convoy, thirty-seven ships packed to the deck beams with weapons and supplies, with more stowed and lashed outside in the weather, the escorts, small and large, ranging from sloops and corvettes to fleet destroyers like *Hakka* and her consorts.

They had seen and been seen by the bigger aircraft based in

Iceland, Liberators, Catalinas, all drawn together like Kidd's pencilled lines on a chart. There was a cruiser squadron at sea also, just in case *Scharnhorst* took this opportunity to leave the security of Altenfjord, the last lap of the convoy's route before North Cape and the Kola Inlet.

But now, at this moment, here on the edge of nowhere, they had the sea to themselves. They had broken formation twice to investigate possible U-Boat contacts, but they had proved worthless. They all had to be investigated, exactly as if it was a genuine threat of attack, phase by phase, by men so drained by the sea and the cold that the possibility of failure was always a lurking fear.

Lookouts shifted around, a quick grin here, a thump on the back with a fur-lined glove there, a new voice up the pipe from the wheelhouse as the helmsman stepped down for a break. Hot, sweet tea, or gut-clinging pusser's ki, a touch of rum in it if you could pull some strings. Sandwiches as thick as boards, corned beef or spam, tinned sausages, 'snorkers', and layers of mustard; you could even forget that the bread was already five days old. No wonder Onslow hated the *big ship wallahs*.

Martineau rarely left the bridge, and despite the constant movement, the routine which carried all of them with the ship, he had found himself able to doze in this chair, his body pressing this way and that, until some sudden, unexpected sound intruded to drag him back to reality.

Once he dreamed of Anna, walking with her, perhaps reliving that one moment of freedom in the New Forest.

He had thought of the letter he had written to her. So many things he had wanted to say, to share. What would she think about it now that they were separated again? He stared at the spray as it drifted so slowly aft from the raked stem, to spatter across the glass screen and there transform itself into diamonds of ice. *This hated ocean.* He shook himself, and saw Slade, the baby-faced signalman, turn to look at him. Two red-rimmed eyes peering out of a shapeless hood. What would his family think if they could see him right now?

Or Tyler, the new subbie, who was helping Kidd with the charts. If he lived through this he would not need to act like a true veteran. He would be one.

'Time to alter course, sir.'

'Very good.' He stifled a yawn. 'Watch *Durham*, Number One. We don't want to annoy Father!'

Fairfax grinned and bent over the voicepipe, poised as Onslow and his team watched the cruiser's yards.

The signal flags made the only touches of colour against the grey and the black-sided troughs, he thought.

'Starboard ten. Midships. Steady. Steer zero-six-zero.'

Martineau shifted in the chair. It was so damned uncomfortable. He acknowledged it. *It was not the chair*. He wondered if the doctor had spoken with his friend at Haslar hospital.

Someone said, 'Wow, where'd you get that fancy pencil from, Bunts?'

The baby-faced Slade replied, 'Mister Seton gave it to me. It's a good one, too.'

Martineau turned away. So even Seton was here, in this sea of ghosts; he had not left the ship after all.

That evening they made contact with the convoy, although only the radar and the blink of signal lamps gave any hint of its size, and the enormous area of water such an armada required.

Could a convoy like this one change the course of the war? The Russians thought it would; the Admiralty did not question it.

He imagined Lucky Bradshaw on the opposite wing of the group in *Zouave*, waiting for a chance to prove or distinguish himself, or was it a need to even some old score, with Commodore Raikes, for instance?

He heard Kidd's heavy seaboots clumping across the deck, and the edge in his voice.

'Look at that bloody sight, Number One! Miles and miles of bugger-all, and all those ships out there somewhere! After this lot's over I'm going to swallow the anchor for good!'

One hour later the first torpedo exploded astern of the convoy.

There was no longer room for doubt. Or hope.

The convoy's first casualty was the fleet minesweeper *Sesame*. She had been acting as Tailend Charlie, some three miles astern of the main body of ships, to render assistance, round up stragglers, and as a last resort pick up survivors.

She had been zigzagging at the time when a single torpedo had exploded amidships, flooding both engine and boiler rooms and rendering her helpless: a lone U-Boat trying to stalk the convoy, perhaps to determine the strength of its escort and the speed and course at that given time, so that a signal could be sent to Group North. Probably one of a full salvo fired at extreme range to avoid detection; they might never know.

Sesame began to break up almost immediately, and although the forward half remained afloat for an hour, by the time an armed trawler arrived to take off her company it was already too late for most of them. Out of eighty officers and men only five were rescued, one being her commanding officer.

The next day was the last time they could rely on land-based aircraft. The little escort carrier *Dancer*, with her own guardians, four fleet destroyers, was their floating airfield for the long haul to the Kola Inlet.

Aboard *Hakka*, the size of the convoy became apparent with the coming of an indefinite daylight: four long columns of ships, with a big cargo-liner, *Genoa Star*, wearing the commodore's flag.

Martineau took time to study the nearest ships as the group hastened past to take up station ahead and to the north-west of the convoy, between Jan Mayen and Bear Islands where several attacks had been launched in the past. Within range of German aircraft as well as the Norwegian naval bases, it seemed the likeliest choice for an all-out attack.

The sea was calmer now, with a hint of ice in the bitter air. On watch there was no time to brood. With the group zigzagging or fanning out to investigate an uncertain echo or blur on the radar, any lack of vigilance could leave the ship open for a collision. The cruiser *Durham* exercised her main armament of twelve six-inch guns, the four turrets moving smoothly as one, her captain making quite sure that there was no possibility of something icing up, common enough up here despite the anti-freeze and the grease.

It was halfway through the forenoon watch, the sea stretching away to an invisible horizon, fragments of ice still adrift to jar against the ships as they surged amongst it.

Dancer flew off two aircraft, the snarl of engines making the air cringe. There was a smell of some kind from the galley funnel, and the Buffer had chosen the moment to take a working party to check the boats in their davits, the Carley floats and scrambling nets, a twice-daily precaution. It was not unknown for rafts and life-saving gear to be frozen solid when they were needed.

Martineau was standing by the voicepipes, holding the rack and bending his legs to restore the circulation. It was on the far side of the convoy, out of sight in the haze and wet mists, that the torpedoes exploded. A big freighter directly astern of the Commodore's ship began to fall out of line, smoke bursting from a well deck as if it was under pressure.

The U-Boat had either worked around the leaders during the night, or more likely was one of a line of patrols lying in wait.

Signals flew back and forth, and escort vessels on the starboard wing of the outer column speeded to intercept the target.

Depth charges hurled columns of water into the air, the explosions pounding against *Hakka*'s flank as if she was in the thick of it.

Martineau walked to the side of the bridge and trained his glasses on the stricken freighter. She was showing a list, but not much, not enough to reveal the terrible damage torpedoes could inflict on an overloaded ship. He and many others here today, on this godforsaken ocean, had seen it before. It made it no easier.

The big ship was stopped now, and falling out of line, the other vessels altering course slightly to avoid collision, politely it seemed, as if it was the way to behave. *Keep going. Don't stop. Don't look back.* Yes, it was old enough.

Armed trawlers were hurrying through the columns, the undertaker's men, as they were known, but all attention was on the sudden flurry of activity on the far side: more depth charges, and then, unexpectedly, the crash and crackle of gunfire.

Kidd said flatly, 'They've hit the bastard. He must be blowing his tanks.'

But his eyes were on the freighter, passing the last ships in the columns now, the list more pronounced, small fragments spilling through and over her side. Only through binoculars could you see that they were armoured cars and tanks, like toys at this distance, going down to litter another seabed.

'*U-Boat on the surface, sir!*'

More gunfire, and now the staccato rattle of machine-guns. The real war: no quarter, no giving time to surrender.

There was a muffled rumble. Down amongst his racing machinery Trevor Morgan would feel it, even if he could hear nothing. He would know. A ship's boilers exploding, a ship dying.

'U-Boat destroyed, sir!'

Once they would have cheered, Martineau thought. But not any more. He raised his glasses again, but the sea astern was empty, except for two armed trawlers and what looked like ash circling lazily around them.

And the convoy sailed on.

Anna Roche looked at herself in the mirror and touched the shadows beneath her eyes with her fingers.

She had dressed with care, remembering that Crawfie had said how important it was, although she had not fully understood the significance at the time. She was learning fast. Like this morning when the alarm clock had gone off, right beside her pillow. She had sat bolt upright in the bed, her mind reeling, until second by second she had set her reactions in order.

In her new quarters she had a room to herself. That had taken some getting used to, and it was still not gone from her thoughts. Caryl with her outrageous jokes and stories she had always sworn were true, until she had been unable to contain her amusement. Nearly always short of money. She had asked to borrow a quid that night, when the bomb had screamed down to bury them.

The new quarters were in a small group of offices once owned by a Japanese shipping company, and commandeered for the duration. For ever, more likely, she thought. And there was constant hot water here, tons of it.

She had set the alarm early so that she could have a shower without somebody switching it off, or the supply suddenly running ice-cold. The Japs obviously took such things very seriously.

A clean shirt and collar, her bag, all she might need.

And just for a moment in the bathroom, which she had never had to share because the other girl was a watchkeeper at the signal station, she had stood quite naked, had looked at herself, like now, as if someone else was with her. She had twisted round to look at her bare shoulders; there was still bruising, but it was going. Crawfie had said acidly, 'Not bad for someone who had a house fall on her!' She would never forget her kindness.

She had thought of the photograph Graham had kept, the one with bared shoulders taken when she had been a student at the University of Toronto. Her mother had described it as *rather daring*.

She touched each corner of her mouth and smiled. What would her mother think now?

She looked around the room, remembering the days and hours since the ships had left Liverpool. Regular reports and signals, intelligence, supposition, guesswork. She worked hard, glad of it, driving herself until there were moments like this, when she could test her endurance. Her love.

She checked her bag, although the letter was not there but in her inside pocket. She read it often, and always heard his voice, sensitive, introspective. Not at all like the man described in the newspapers, the holder of the Victoria Cross. One of the elite, the few.

In his letter it was even more intense. How he had described their walk with the dog, their touch, their parting.

Throwing sticks for the dog. Was that too much to ask for a man who had already given so much? And his words, written, but she could hear them.

I want to sit with you. To lie with you. To stay with you.

She sighed and picked up her hat. It still felt very new.

Another glance around. Lights off. Taps tightly closed. *Don't you know there's a war on?*

She was glad she had set the alarm, and that she had taken care over her appearance.

How he would want to see me.

And it was not yet four in the morning.

It was only a short walk to the headquarters bunker and Derby House, shorter still if she took the direct route. Perhaps one day . . . But she could not yet bring herself to pass the place where they had been buried together, where Caryl had died.

There were always people about, or so it seemed in this sailors' city. A lot of servicemen going on or off duty, the Jolly Jacks on

271

shore leave for the night. Searching for the adventure and enticement which in truth rarely showed itself.

She could ignore the wolf-whistles now; there was no point in looking for a culprit anyway. Just as she could ignore the military policeman sitting astride his motor cycle, one boot on the pavement, occasionally twisting his grip to warm the engine. She knew what he was doing, what he was waiting for. The line of camouflaged ambulances would be parked up a street somewhere, awaiting his signal to move.

Going to the docks, like the day she had seen them arrive to pick up *Hakka*'s dead.

And it happened nearly every day.

Up the steps and through the gloom, her shoes ringing on the bare floor. A torch to check her identity card, even though it was the same patrolman as yesterday, and the day before.

Someone always remarked on the weather; it seemed very British. Just as people always greeted each other with 'good morning', even if it was afternoon. And the way they queued. For everything. Cigarettes, pet food, soap, or simply to discover what was on the other end of the queue. It was as much a part of the war as those patient ambulances, the bombing, and the young midshipman who had killed himself, and had unknowingly destroyed their only chance of being together.

She braced herself for the harsh lights. Always the glare. Without a watch you would not know if it was day or night outside.

There were a lot of people around, even at this hour, and for the first time she felt the fear, running through her body like ice in the blood. Messengers hurried past her, not seeing her; telephones rang for mere seconds before being snatched up.

She slipped her hand inside her jacket, around her breast, to his carefully folded letter.

I am here, darling. We are together now.

Nobby was waiting in the main office, and she saw Raikes at his window, looking down at the great silent tank, so full of purpose and movement.

He turned and saw her, nodded, almost smiled.

272

'Good timing, Anna. Long day today, though there's nothing we can do. Except pray.'

She made herself walk to the desk where she kept her files of top secret signals, the measure of Raikes's trust in her.

Raikes watched her, while Nobby signed something brought in by a messenger.

'Convoy's been attacked. It's all there on the table.' He saw her press one hand on the polished wood, each finger extended. Nice skin, which would brown very easily in any sort of sunshine.

'Just had reports from R.A.F. Intelligence. Two enemy cruisers have been reported at sea. On the move. Their lordships were convinced that *Scharnhorst* would make the first sortie. I think I was, too.'

A telephone buzzed impatiently but he ignored it.

'One of the cruisers is the *Dortmund*. We've had trouble with her before.'

She raised her eyes slowly. 'I know, sir. And the other one is *Lübeck*.'

Nobby said, 'How could you know that?'

But in her mind's eye she saw the tall chair on its open bridge. She answered softly, 'He *always* knew.'

'Action stations! Action stations!'

The insane scream of alarm bells, the thud of watertight doors and hatches. Something you always expected, and yet were never prepared for. The men off watch, some trying to sleep and others afraid to, ran without conscious thought, snatching protective clothing, glancing around for a particular friend, or back at their empty messes as if for the last time. Ian Wishart was up each ladder as if he had always done it, fastening his duffle coat, his mind empty of all but the need to *get there*, no matter what.

He caught glimpses of other hurrying figures, strangers in their fur-lined coats, faces intent, each to his own station. Gun crews, and damage control parties, spare hands, cooks and stewards making their various ways aft to assist the medical section, and the doctor with his array of instruments.

And beyond them all, the sea, dark and menacing, broken here and there by pale fangs of leaping breakers, the aftermath of a gale which had risen the previous night and caused havoc amongst the convoy. No collisions, but three of the ships had lost contact with the main columns, in a maddening game of follow-my-leader which had taken the hard-worked escorts a whole day to round up.

One of the other fleet destroyers, the *Levant*, which had been with the carrier's escort, had developed serious gyro compass failure, and the Commodore had reluctantly ordered her to make her own way back to Iceland. The fact that *Levant* was one of the navy's latest and largest destroyers did nothing for morale.

Wishart hurried past the Oerlikon guns and pushed into the sealed wheelhouse. The steel shutters were clamped down, and the only lights came from the compass and plot table. They were all here, as if he was the only one who had been away. Big Bill Spicer on the wheel, feet slightly apart, hands loosely on the spokes, or so they appeared, the lower part of his face very red in the compass glow. A messenger, boatswain's mate, telegraphsmen, and Bob Forward, who gave him a curt nod as he took his position by the table.

Spicer said across his broad shoulder, 'Enemy ships reported to the east of us.' Matter-of-fact, like someone remarking on the weather.

Wishart listened to the steady beat of engines: about half-speed, everything quivering slightly, the ship now fully awake. It had been dark outside; apart from the wave crests there was nothing. And yet it was about eleven in the forenoon. He adjusted his mind automatically. *Six bells.*

He heard thuds overhead, the officers on the bridge, the signalmen and lookouts. He frowned with concentration. And the Captain. He had called Wishart over. He tried to think more clearly. That was yesterday, after a sharp alteration of course for some reason, and a rapid exchange of signals between Captain (D) and the cruiser *Durham*. Ships zigzagging, the *Levant* rolling in a heavy sea, her gyro and all that it entailed out of action, and yet the Captain had found time to speak to him. Like that moment in the sickbay, after his rescue from the sea.

'After this convoy, Wishart, you will be leaving *Hakka*. I expect you're surprised. But the signal came through. You'll be getting drafted to *King Alfred*.' He had been called away to deal with another signal from Captain (D) in *Zouave*. Wishart had been stunned, and he still could not grasp it. All he had dared to hope for. What he had planned to write to his parents in Surbiton when, *if*, he was finally recommended for the officers' training course. In the blink of an eye, and it had meant nothing. Nothing at all.

He glanced at the deckhead, dripping with condensation from the heated pipes, and the swaying bodies packed into this metal box. The Captain was up there now, waiting to act. Enemy ships. What did it mean? Again he tried to think. He knew from the charts that the route to Murmansk had been prepared long in advance. A cruiser squadron was on the move, and the convoy itself had a full escort and the carrier. One of *Dancer*'s aircraft must have sighted the enemy. There were no reports from the radar.

And there was the group. *Us.* He looked around the wheelhouse, watching Spicer's hands moving the spokes this way and that, his big frame seeming to rise and fall with the ship while the rest of them remained motionless, like cut-outs.

In his heart he knew they would be called to fight. Not the group, not the escort carrier, but *us.*

Once, he had heard his father discussing his war with one of his friends, a neighbour, who had been with him at the Menin Gate. Wishart was not supposed to hear, but it had been after an Armistice service, and the two men were still wearing their medals and poppies.

His father had said, 'We stopped asking how. We only asked when.'

Wishart looked at his companions, men he had come to know. Good, bad, tough, or 'all for it', as he had heard Forward say of some of the hotheads. Here they *meant* something, and he knew that they had helped to change him in some way. Not discipline or training, and loyalty did not even describe it.

'Wheelhouse?'

Spicer said something into the bell-mouthed tube and then jerked his head.

'Up on the bridge, Wishart! Pilot wants you, so chop, chop with it!'

Wishart felt the ice inside him. Like seeing Seton's eyes watching him that day.

He made for the screened door, his fingers dragging at the clip.

Then he heard Forward's voice, close, personal, casual. 'Watch it, Wings. Keep your nut down. You still owe me that drink, remember?'

Wishart did not remember, but it made all the difference. With something like a sob he seized the ladder and was up it before he realized what Forward had meant.

The light was stronger, the clouds ragged and low-lying, moving fast across the masthead and radar aerials, spray lifting occasionally over the maindeck and the crouching shapes of the torpedo tubes.

He saw the Captain with Cavaye and the new officer, Tyler; Kidd must be in the chart room. Lookouts and signalmen stood out more clearly against the dark sea, and it seemed strangely quiet up here, so that the rattling of signal halyards and bridge fittings intruded above the muted throb of engines.

And there was *Durham*, on the port beam again as if she had never moved. Powerful, like the ships in the photos in the magazines he had read at school. Invincible.

Cavaye snapped unnecessarily, 'Wait here, Wishart. The navigating officer has a job for you.' Wishart did not see the Captain's eyes, nor would he have recognized irritation for that brief second.

Instead he heard the chief yeoman say, 'Now there's a sight, Paul! I never thought I'd see that again in my service!'

The youngster, Slade, peered up at his chief and then at the *Durham*. She had hoisted her battle ensigns, huge and white against the drab backdrop, their crosses like blood. For an instant he had thought that the yeoman of signals had mistaken him for somebody else. He was not to know that Paul had been the name of his dead son.

The air quivered, like the time with the German destroyers, when they had been hit. But deeper, louder.

The Captain was on his feet, his scarf gone from his neck, one hand gripping the voicepipes as he watched the sea directly ahead.

It was then that Wishart realized there was no sign of the

convoy. It had altered course, disappeared while he had been below, off watch. He had seen the chart, the rough plot, and knew from which bearing the enemy would appear. *That, he knew.* He had learned more than he would have believed possible since he had first stepped aboard *Hakka*.

No ship could move that fast. So it was reasonable to believe that there was nothing between the convoy and its escorts but the group, a cruiser and six destroyers. He licked his dry lips. *Us.*

They were altering course again, and he heard the Captain pass his orders, it seemed unhurriedly, down to the wheelhouse.

Huge flashes lit up the clouds, and what seemed an age later came the crash and roar of explosions.

Kidd was here now, breathing heavily, his eyes everywhere until he saw his yeoman.

'Keep with me, Wishart.' He turned sharply as more explosions shattered the air. He said, 'Not us, then.'

Wishart heard the Captain say, 'Yet.'

'Signal, sir. Increase speed as ordered.'

'Full ahead together.' A pause. 'Yes, Swain. It is.'

A great flash reached down from where the horizon lay hidden in mist or haze, followed by a single explosion and then a rising ball of orange and scarlet flame. Solid, terrible; you could imagine you could feel the heat even from miles away.

Durham had increased speed, her bow wave rising like a huge frothing moustache as she ploughed into the choppy water, her four turrets all moving in unison, the guns at their various angles, seeking a target.

Onslow called, 'From *Leader*, sir. *Remain on station.*'

Martineau strode across the bridge, dragging out his binoculars. *Zouave* was already signalling to her own little column.

He turned away, one gloved fist beating the cold steel until the pain steadied him. *Too soon. Too soon. Think, man!* He pictured Lucky Bradshaw, the old destroyer hand. This was his big chance.

The young signalman, Slade, asked, 'What signal was that, Yeo?'

Onslow glanced down at him.

'Flag Four, boy.'

Attack with torpedoes.

'Radar – Bridge!'

Martineau waited, but could not prevent himself from turning again to watch as *Zouave*'s raked bows cut across the cruiser's wake and headed to re-form her brood.

'Three ships at zero-nine-zero.' The rest was drowned by the roar of gunfire.

No waiting this time, although everyone was consciously counting the seconds. A cliff of broken water was rising, as if every shell had plunged down to explode in a single line. You could feel it, like running aground, punching every plate and rivet.

Martineau looked at Cavaye. 'Go forrard to A and B guns, will you? Tell Guns what I said.' He looked at the cruiser, sensing the moment. *'Now!'*

Durham's forward turrets were motionless, only two of the six guns still moving. The flashes were as one, the explosions loud and sharp enough to scrape at a man's brain like a scalpel.

Martineau lowered his glasses and covered them with his coat. Two cruisers and possibly one smaller, a destroyer. Maybe the sister of the ship they had fought alongside *Java*.

Help would be on its way. But until then . . . He winced as more flashes tore the clouds apart.

And the convoy sailed on.

18

Victors

Martineau listened to the ceaseless chatter of information, ranges and bearings, alterations of course, and the fall of shot from the enemy salvoes. Driscoll, never the most patient of officers, sounded strained to the limit, no doubt sharing the sense of helplessness, impotence, as *Hakka* and her two consorts, *Jester* and the old-timer *Harlech* maintained their common station on the cruiser. The two German ships were bows-on to *Durham*, at a range of about six miles. It enabled their gunnery officers to maintain a rapid fire with all their forward weapons, bracketing the zigzagging *Durham* again and again.

He made himself turn to watch *Zouave* leading the two other destroyers of the group. Despite the noise and the danger, the scream of shells and the stench of gunsmoke, he was moved, gripped by the sight of the two Tribals, *Zouave* and *Inuit*, with the big K Class, *Kangaroo*, going at full speed, their bow waves rolling away on either beam while they moved in echelon to begin their torpedo attack. It was all that might make the enemy alter course to avoid the possibility of a hit. And the moment they turned to present a smaller target, *Durham* would get her chance, and be able to bring her unused after turrets to bear.

He saw more shellbursts hurling waterspouts beyond and beside the cruiser. Even *Durham* was dwarfed by them. Martineau gritted his teeth. A straddle. Any second now . . .

'Enemy ships turning, sir!'

Martineau did not even look towards *Durham*. Her captain would be watching, waiting to hit back. His ship had already taken a lot of punishment, punctured plating, fires below the bridge only just being brought under control.

He watched the destroyers, *Zouave* hurling up spray as she swung towards the enemy. Martineau did the sum in his head. *Kangaroo* mounted ten torpedo tubes, the Tribals only four each. But only one hit would even the score.

He swung round as Kidd exclaimed, '*Durham*'s hit one of them!'

A flash, puncturing the rolling bank of smoke and wet haze, but the explosion was massive.

'Both cruisers are still turning, sir!'

Martineau gripped the side of his chair and felt the hull tilt over as more explosions thundered against the keel.

Two cruisers. What had gone wrong with the intelligence services? Someone should have known that such a convoy as this would rouse every trick in the game. *Durham* fired again, and more explosions echoed across the surging bow waves, and the wash from *Zouave*'s racing screws.

The leader was turning again. Martineau paused to wipe the lenses of his binoculars, mere seconds, but it was long enough. Too long for *Zouave*. A salvo must have ploughed through and over her; he could see the shells exploding far abeam, splinters ripping from the sea like feathers.

Bradshaw was still trying to hold his ship on course, but Martineau knew by the falling wash that she had been badly damaged.

'She's fired her tin fish!'

Martineau gripped the chair to steady himself, willing the other captain to disengage and leave it to the others. Perhaps Lucky Bradshaw was already dead. Somehow he knew he was not. He watched, sickened, as a shell exploded just below *Zouave*'s forward funnel, a sharp flash, like a winking light as the armour-piercing shell smashed down into her lower deck and exploded. *Zouave* was stopping. No, she had stopped. But there were no more shells, and Martineau realized that the larger of the two enemy cruisers must have taken one of *Zouave*'s torpedoes, the sound lost in the loud explosions nearby.

Durham had been hit again, and her B turret was jammed, the guns pointing at the clouds, smoke spouting from the deck below.

Inuit was pressing home her attack, but she was hit repeatedly before she could work past the drifting leader.

Martineau moved to the voicepipes, pain shooting through his legs as if they were fighting every action. He saw the faces nearest to him, and the others in memory, who would not stay hidden.

He said, 'Make to *Durham*. *I am engaging*. Repeat to *Jester* and *Harlech*.'

He wanted to swallow, to cling to something that would give him faith. There was nothing. He had lost a glove somewhere, and as he steadied himself once more against the motion, the rise and dip of *Hakka*'s bows, he saw the scar on his hand. The place where she had touched, and had held him.

He said, 'Repeat – *Flag 4*!' He was surprised it was so easily done. 'Stand by. Increase to full revolutions!' He stared at the gyro until his eyes throbbed with concentration.

'Starboard twenty!' He watched the stem and bull ring swinging across the sea's angry face. Smoke everywhere, flotsam too. And something long and black, shapeless, with the sea rolling across it. It was *Inuit*'s keel, held aloft a while longer by air still trapped in her shattered hull. She must have capsized at full speed; he saw a hole in her plates big enough to drive a bus through. There were men too. Not many, only a few, faces leaping into focus as his lenses passed over them. Some reaching out, others already dead from the cold, but a few still able to grasp that *Hakka*, one of their own, was hurtling towards them. Martineau allowed the glasses to fall to his chest.

'Ease to five! Midships!' He raised his glasses again, level with the compass, the dying ship and the men cut to pieces by *Hakka*'s whirling screws mercifully hidden.

Zouave was still afloat; there was no sign of *Kangaroo*. He knew that *Durham* was firing again, but with longer gaps between salvoes, and only one turret at a time.

The convoy would be able to hear this last fight, and perhaps would know what it had cost them.

He said, 'Tell *Harlech* to make smoke. The wind might help. Until the next turn at least.' He did not need to see it. He knew they were doing what he required. He was their captain. They had nothing left but trust now. *Harlech* would be trying to lay a smoke-screen, and *Jester*, *Java*'s sister ship, would be working around to take up position for the attack. He thought of the old house in the New Forest, the girl in his arms, while his mother and her Reverend were preparing to listen to the B.B.C. news.

The Secretary of the Admiralty regrets to announce the loss of H.M.S. . . . He pressed his forehead against the frozen metal. *And Anna would know before anyone.*

He looked up, suddenly angry, sickened by the inevitability, the waste. *And there was the enemy.* Even without the glasses he would have known her. How could he forget? So many times he had seen her in his wakening moments, heard the grinding scream of tearing steel and felt the terrible destruction when he had rammed the cruiser.

Because of tradition, duty, a matter of honour? All, and none of them. Because of Alison and his own stupidity, when he had known that Mike Loring, his friend, had not been the first one to be tempted?

He said, 'Tell Number One to stand by. Local control if all else fails.' *When I am killed.* 'I want the depth charge party to follow orders.' He thought he could taste the foul odour of *Harlech*'s smokescreen; it was moving past the ship now, keeping pace.

The depth-charges would be seen and heard by the enemy. With luck they might think it was a faulty fall of shot, or that some U-Boat commander was mad enough to interfere between the committed juggernauts.

Water rose silently beside the bridge, and seemed to fall incredibly slowly. As his hearing returned Martineau measured the force of the explosion. *Too near.*

'Depth charges, *now!*'

It was a stupid ruse. He looked at Kidd and grinned. Insane, but it was all they had. He could hear the voicepipes reporting damage, splinters, nothing fatal. The muffled roar of the depth charges was matched almost immediately by more shellbursts from the invisible foe. They had shifted their sights slightly. Driscoll might still get a chance to use his precious guns. And Cavaye too, down there now with the forward weapons; to him it must feel like rushing headlong towards the enemy with nothing to sustain him. And young Tyler on the opposite side, with Wishart near him, a broken pencil between his fingers. He must have snapped it without noticing. He heard more gunfire. *Kangaroo*, he thought, having a go now.

More shells screamed overhead, *Durham*'s or the enemy's it was impossible to tell. Like tearing canvas, and then the sharp, savage bangs. More splinters. A voice called, 'From T/S, sir! *Standing by*!'

Only four torpedo tubes. Perhaps, after all, the designers had been wrong. Even *Harlech* mounted ten.

He saw them all in his mind. Malt the Gunner (T) and his chief torpedo gunner's mate, Harry Glover, would be ready by now. They would only get one chance.

He felt the plating jerk against his hip, knew that the ship had been hit.

To the voicepipe he said, 'All right, Swain?'

And Spicer's calm reply. 'Right as ninepence, sir!'

The bow wave was still folding away from the stem like something solid. They were going in. *Going in.*

Down aft, Sub-Lieutenant Barlow heard the tinny rattle of the bell and saw his depth charge party jerk their lanyards, saw the charges roll from the stern and lift away on either beam before dropping to add their noise and disturbance to the madness. *Hakka* was going at full speed now, her stern digging so deeply into the churned wash that it seemed she was submerging. As the charges exploded, decoys this time, Barlow shook his fist, his mind full of hate, and the memories of his parents and his sister.

'That's the lot, sir!' The leading seaman stared at him with sudden disbelief, and even as Barlow skidded to help him he fell.

For a few moments more Barlow tried to hold him, to cushion him from the wildly vibrating deck. There was blood everywhere.

'I'll get help!' He was shaking, shocked and furious that he could not remember the man's name. He repeated, 'I'll get help!'

'Don't go!' He stared up at the young officer, and thought he saw Barlow nod, understanding at last that there *was* no help. He could even ignore the spray and the freezing cold; it helped to numb the pain which had frightened him at first.

Barlow clung to him, able to ignore the clash of splinters against and into the hull, like the one which had cut down this dying man.

Kidd saw it from the bridge, and when Barlow got up and stood quite still, his body angled to the deck while he looked down at the dead man, he thought it was the most moving thing he had ever seen.

Someone was yelling like a maniac, 'A hit! *Kangaroo* got the bastard!' The echo of the explosion still hung in the air like thunder across the hills. The larger German cruiser, which someone had identified as the *Dortmund*, had been hit twice, and was in a bad way.

Martineau heard and saw most of it. The rest was stamped in memory. A quick change of helm, Spicer down there with his own little team, the wheelhouse shuttered and bolted, with only a voice coming down to guide them. Or to destroy them.

The wind seemed to be changing but he knew it was *Hakka*'s alteration of course. The smoke was pulling away, dragged aside by the wind like some great obscene curtain.

Slowly and deliberately he lifted his binoculars again. It seemed suddenly much clearer, although he knew in his heart that the light was no better or worse than before. What did he feel? Despair, anger, disappointment, because he had given in to the folly of hoping?

Anna, I love you so.

But his voice said, '*Stand by to engage! Start the attack!*'

And he heard Kidd say hoarsely, 'That's *Lübeck*, right enough!'

Martineau watched the sudden sparkle of flashes, the cruiser's blurred outline already shortening as she prepared to take avoiding action while she kept up rapid fire with her secondary armament.

Onslow said, '*Durham*'s losing way, sir. But she's still firing!'

The youth Wishart swung round and stared at the Captain, unable to believe what he had heard. As if he had been reading his own thoughts when he had stampeded with the others at the first scream of the alarm bells.

Martineau said, 'It's us, Yeo. Something we have to do. Why we're here.' He looked at each of them in turn. '*Together*'.

Lieutenant Eric Driscoll sat squarely on his steel chair in *Hakka*'s gunnery control position, his ears and eyes taking in every sound and movement around him. As always on these occasions, he was very conscious of the wires of communications which connected him to each link of this, his own world.

He could picture them all clearly in his mind, as the ship shook and swooped beneath his armoured pod, the gun crews fore and aft, barrels swinging obediently to the unending stream of instructions, bearing, range, course and speed, while down below decks in the Transmitting Station the control team would keep the information moving. Radar, rangefinders, down to the human element, the lookout with his binoculars.

But everything related to Driscoll, the gunnery officer. Even his hands were moving, as if independent of the man himself. An adjustment here, a switch there, a terse acknowledgement to one of his two ratings who were jammed in the pod behind him, his eyes and ears.

He felt his heart pounding steadily against his ribs, but accepted it. It was not fear, or doubt, it was genuine excitement, which never left him at times like these. Mounted directly in front of him were the massive stereoscopic binoculars, the final touch, like a sniper's hairline sight, or the tip of a lance in some bygone cavalry charge.

And he knew he looked the part. His fair hair was neatly cut, his headphones at a slight angle so that he could hear the vital information, and still be able to listen to the outside noises, the creak and rattle of steel, the surge of water against the hull. Driscoll wore his immaculate white scarf tucked into his jacket. He knew they talked about that, too. Imagined that some girl had given it to him, when in fact he had bought it himself.

A bit flash, they thought. But it did not bother him. They noticed him, they remembered him, and more to the point they obeyed him.

He was twenty-five years old, and for reasons he scarcely remembered he had always wanted to be in the navy, an officer, of course. But his parents had been against it, and his naval training had been confined to lectures and drills with a unit of the supplementary reserve. And always, always, gunnery had been his consuming interest. When war had broken out, and even before that as a reservist, he had been accepted for the real thing. Eventually at the gunnery school at Whale Island he had managed to win the respect of even the most sceptical instructors. *An R.N.V.R. officer, a gunnery expert?* It had been hard for them to accept.

He had seen all kinds of action since he had been sent to *Hakka*. Exchanging fire with shore batteries along the North African coast, fighting off E-Boats, as well as aircraft in a dozen different situations.

He knew he was not popular, either with his gunnery ratings or for that matter in the wardroom. He was pleased about that. He hated weakness more than anything. And in an officer, wanting to be liked, popular, was something of a crime in his view.

Like *Hakka*'s previous captain, for instance. Everything for effect, shallow behind the good looks and bonhomie. Fairfax Driscoll respected, and was surprised that he had not seen through their lord and master.

And that day when *Hakka* had been raked by German aircraft, he had known that his gunnery team had been blameless. And the captain had paid for it.

He pressed one earphone to his head, if only to shut out the rapid-fire stream of orders to the torpedo tubes.

They were going in now. He could feel the urgent thrust of the screws, imagine the tubes being trained into position for firing. An expensive and overrated form of attack, except perhaps for submarines which had the stealth to get away with it.

'*Now*, sir!'

Driscoll pressed his forehead on the rubber pad and made a slight adjustment. Again, he could feel the excitement taking over. Like seeing the flags go up to announce the first direct hit at target practice under training. Or watching a Junkers spiralling down in flames when moments earlier it had been diving like a hawk over the ship.

Ship and aircraft recognition, 'Ours and Theirs' as they described it at Whaley, had always been one of his strongest points. He concentrated every fibre of his being as he stared through his sights, one elbow taking the strain as the ship swayed over violently. He thought he heard the measured thuds as the torpedoes leaped from their tubes. To perform this *Hakka* had made a sharp turn to port, the four pairs of four-point-seven guns moving in unison to compensate for it. As he had trained them to do, again and again until they loathed his guts.

He watched the other ships slide into view, although it was the destroyer's swift turn which made it look so fast. Just like the silhouettes and the aerial photos. Her guns all trained on the same bearing, her grey hull and superstructure dominating everything, filling the sights.

He pressed his switch. *'Shoot!'*

He felt the instant recoil of *Hakka*'s guns, their first challenge to 'the Captain's cruiser', as *Lübeck* was nicknamed by the older hands.

The Captain would be watching right now. His own guns, hitting back. He was a true professional; he would not forget when the time came.

He covered his ears again. As one instructor had said wryly, 'You never hear the one with your name on it, so why bother about the others?'

Driscoll never had time to know the truth. He did not hear the shells which blasted his control top and radar to fragments, and ploughed into the W/T office before exploding.

He might have heard a brief scream. But it was his own.

Martineau peered around the bridge, barely able to breathe in the smoke and the stench of charred paint and explosives.

'Starboard fifteen!' He felt the hull sway upright again and heard Spicer shout, 'Starboard fifteen, sir!'

'All right, Swain?' He had to know. With the helm gone . . .

Spicer fought down a fit of coughing. 'Few dents, sir. We're all on our feet!'

Voicepipes were beginning to recover, and he heard Kidd calling to someone to fetch help. For a few seconds more he stared around the bridge. A signalman lay in one corner, head pillowed as if asleep, although he was bathed in blood. The youngster Slade was twisting a signal flag around his own leg, his eyes squinting with pain and determination.

Onslow was on his feet again, taking charge, and he saw Wishart getting up very slowly, looking around as if unable to believe he had survived.

Kidd saw him and yelled, 'Wheelhouse! Get a couple of hands to assist in the W/T office!'

Martineau said, 'Give me your glasses, Sub!' His own had been torn from his neck by the blast. But Tyler, the brand-new subbie, stayed where he was in a corner by the table, as if he was searching for a chart. As Martineau dragged the binoculars from beneath his body he saw the splinter hole in his back. Death must have been instantaneous.

He made himself listen to the reports. *Hakka* had been badly hit, but the engine and boiler rooms were intact, giving their best, the pumps adding to the strain.

He heard the roar of an exploding torpedo, and saw a jagged column of smoke lift above the chaos. He was in time to see *Jester* turning away, her tubes empty, and every gun which would bear spitting fire at the cruiser.

The Buffer was here, cut and bloody, with some of his men at his back.

Kidd asked, 'W/T?'

The Buffer shook his head. 'Like a butcher's shop down there. They all bought it!'

Martineau gripped the chair and waited, counting seconds. One cruiser, the *Dortmund*, had vanished, crept away, too damaged to continue, and the third ship had not even joined the action.

There was only *Lübeck*. Still firing, still moving, but her high stem already lower in the water.

He heard someone screaming and saw Plonker Pryor with his red cross bag hurrying across the scarred deck to deal with it.

He passed another order to the wheelhouse and watched the gyro compass responding. There was even a splinter scar beside that, inches from where he had been standing.

'Gunnery control is knocked out, sir!'

Martineau had already seen that. Nobody could have survived in there.

He said, 'I'd like the first lieutenant up here.' He hesitated. Fighting it. 'Is Number One all right?'

288

Kidd forced a grin through his beard. It made him look worse. 'Aye, sir. Just as well. We're going to a wedding, remember?'

Wishart heard them laugh and somehow it steadied him. For a moment he had thought . . .

He gasped as he saw the crater left by the shell, the armour plate folded back like a pusser's cocoa tin. And blood, not red but almost black, as if their lives had been seared out of them. The petty officer telegraphist named Rooke, the one with the pointed terrier's face, who had been celebrating his promotion when they had left Scapa, and others he had come to know. Gone, just like that.

He heard the first lieutenant's voice, on his way to the bridge. Even he found time to speak with someone amidst the debris and the smell of death.

'You all right, Stripey? Good man! You're too ugly to die!'

How can he? Will I ever be able to act for others when all hell is breaking loose around me?

And then all he could think was, *I am leaving this ship.*

In the wheelhouse, with smoke still trapped and eddying around the knocked-out and useless air ducts, Leading Torpedo Operator Bob Forward held on to the revolution counter for support while the ship altered course for what seemed like the millionth time.

He watched Bill Spicer, shoulders as rigid as ever, the big, awkward-looking hands as gentle with the wheel as when the first shots had been fired. His wounded leg must be giving him a hard time, but he scarcely showed it. Always in charge. His own man.

Like those few moments just before the action stations gongs had changed them into weapons again, when they had both been outside this wheelhouse, each knowing the signs. That action was inevitable.

Spicer had said, quite openly, 'I should tell you, Bob, I heard something. When I was checking out of hospital.' He had glanced at the deadlights, soon to be slammed shut, wondering perhaps if he had already gone too far.

But he had continued, 'There was a Jaunty rabbiting on about his work with the Provost boys and the civil police. Your name came up.'

Forward had felt everything stop dead around him. Like closing a door. The Jaunty, a master-at-arms, was hated by all sailors except the Crushers in his own regulating branch.

'There's a warrant being got for you. After what we've survived together, I thought it was the least I could do.'

Then the alarm bells had intervened. Forward stared at the expensive watch Wishart's parents had sent him. For saving their kid.

The whole action had lasted less than an hour. *Inuit* gone, *Zouave* as good as, and God alone knew how many killed. Because of a convoy. Because someone at the top said it should be that way.

He heard shouting and Spicer said, 'Open up, lads!'

Together they stared through the scarred and smeared glass, at the long, grey shape, silent in the heaving, bitter water. Three miles away? No more, surely.

Somebody murmured, 'The bugger's sinking!' But there were no cheers. Then he saw Wishart, his face like chalk as he made his way through the wheelhouse.

'Just a minute!' It was quite easy, once you had made up your mind. Dying was nothing.

He pulled him to one side; everyone else was either looking at the Jerry, or watching their instruments.

He gripped his shoulder. God, he *was* only a kid underneath the ill-fitting jumper.

'I've got something for you.' He held out a package and when Wishart took it he said sharply, 'Not now. Later. I want your word on it. In case something else happens.' He shook him, almost gently. *'Mates*, remember?'

A messenger called, 'Pilot wants you up top!' He too looked wild-eyed, not yet able to accept that he was still alive.

Forward held up his hand to show the watch. 'Fair exchange, eh, Wings?'

It was done.

Fairfax lowered his glasses and said to Martineau, 'She's going, sir.'

Martineau laid Tyler's binoculars on the chair. Ten killed,

fifteen or more wounded. Bad enough, especially when added to those in the other ships.

Then he made himself look at the sinking *Lübeck*. Her forecastle deck was now almost awash, ant-like figures lowering boats and rafts, facing the inevitable. The W/T office was destroyed, but his small sea cabin was intact. Her photograph would be there to remind him. Perhaps to restore him.

How do I feel? Everyone will think I have the answer. Why is that? After *Firebrand*, and all that had followed. A sense of victory, or one of revenge? Triumph or tragedy?

They had done what was expected of them, more than expected. The convoy was safe. There would be others, many others. He ran his bare hand along the wet steel, feeling it, sharing the pain.

'But not for you, my girl. Not for a while, anyway.'

Fairfax listened and watched, feeling the ship, their ship, rising to the challenge like this man whom he had come to admire, and care for so much.

He saw young Wishart joining Kidd by the chart table, his eyes averted from the stain where Tyler had died. And when he stared aft along the littered deck he saw the empty tubes, still pointing towards the enemy they had helped to destroy.

Some would go to other ships, and many would be ashore for some time to come.

He saw Tonkyn, the chief steward, picking his way towards the bridge, carrying something covered by a spotless napkin, his passage bringing a few grins from the exhausted victors.

And another figure going in the opposite direction. Forward, who had made up his mind, and had given his medal, the only thing apart from the watch he had left to value, to his young 'winger' Wishart.

They would all remember *Hakka*.

Martineau said, 'Here comes the cavalry, Jamie!' Two of *Dancer*'s Seafires roared low overhead, dipping their wings in salute, when they had probably expected to find only the enemy left afloat.

Wishart watched and shared all of it. He knew the package

291

contained Bob's medal. Just as he somehow realized he would never see him again.

The other ships were moving closer ready to take station as ordered. On the new leader.

Martineau found himself holding his breath as *Lübeck* began to slide under the drifting debris. There was much to do. Dead to be buried. He saw Tonkyn by the bridge ladder, watching him, then nodding as if satisfied in spite of the carnage he had witnessed.

A signal would have to be made through *Jester*. And then she would know, and *Hakka*'s little marker would not be taken down from the Operations wall map.

But first . . . 'Take over, Jamie.' He touched his arm lightly. 'I'm going round the ship.'

Fairfax saluted as he left the bridge without knowing he had done it. When he looked again, *Lübeck* had gone.

Is Anything Impossible?